Praise for Karen Karbo

Karen Karbo is a very funny writer – from near slapstick to wry wit. Amazing.

THE NEW YORK TIMES

The Diamond Lane

· A *New York Times* Notable Book

A flawless, page-turning story ... this is a tale to treasure.

PUBLISHERS WEEKLY

A wonderfully comic novel about savvy Hollywood outsiders trying to get in ... not only is the plot ingenious, but the writing remains deft all the way through.

THE NEW YORK TIMES

It is a testament to Karbo's skill at high comedy that the ending of this book – a funeral rather than a wedding – leaves you smiling.

THE NEW YORKER

This astringent, humorous novel tackles two subjects ripe for satire: the Hollywood movie industry and marriage – both notoriously fickle institutions requiring blind hope to sustain life.

THE LOS ANGELES TIMES

This kind of novel is a devil to pull off ... and Ms. Karbo has done her job brilliantly.

THE NEW YORK TIMES BOOK REVIEW

Julia Child Rules:
Lessons on Savoring Life

I want to make wallpaper out of this original and beautiful book just so I can have Karbo's unparalleled wit and wisdom always on hand.

CHERYL STRAYED, author of *Wild*

[A]nyone with even the slightest interest in cooking and pop culture may find it hard to resist this series of epigrammatic guidelines for living large, especially when they come from a master at doing just that.

THE LOS ANGELES TIMES

Karbo's Kick Ass books follow a unique structural blend of biography and advice-giving. When you read *Julia Child Rules*, you not only learn more about Julia's fascinating life, you come away feeling as though you can be a little bit like Julia too.

GLAMOUR

A lighthearted trek through a food icon's life, studded with satisfying tips for modern living.

KIRKUS REVIEWS

This intriguing book is about how Julia Child became an icon, and Karbo attributes Child's success to her unique view on life. Here, through a fun and engaging set of rules, Karbo instructs readers on how they can follow Julia's example and find true joy in life, too.

FOREWORD REVIEWS

Karbo's joyful take on the ebullient, self-described "California hayseed" will charm readers new to the twists and turns of Child's life, as well as devoted fans.

PUBLISHERS WEEKLY

Julia Child Rules is a blast.

HEADBUTLER

Out of all the other Julia Child literature that's out there, Karbo succeeds in pointing out something that should be, but isn't always, obvious to us: the way Julia lived life with abandon, first and foremost, was by not allowing her age or place in life to dictate her career.

THE BRAISER

You won't get any gushing food description here. In its place you'll find humor, a little heartbreak, and a lot of wit and grit to inspire your own inner Julia.

THE OREGONIAN

How Georgia Became O'Keeffe:
Lessons on the Art of Living

"Georgia was a proto slacker," writes Karbo. "There were days and weeks when she would read, spend hours tramping around outside, write letters, sew, and play dominoes. ... But when Georgia worked, she worked her ass off."

O MAGAZINE

Simply a revelation.

ELISSA SCHAPPELL, *Vanity Fair*

Karen Karbo's fresh and revealing take on the epic life of Georgia O'Keeffe is both effortlessly entertaining and profoundly inspirational.

SHEILA WELLER, author of *Girls Like Us: Carole King, Joni Mitchell, Carly Simon*

[I]ntimate, joyful, and absolutely fun biography ...

JULIE METZ, author of the *New York Times* bestseller *Perfection*

I want to give this book to every young woman I know who's setting out on her own in the world – not to mention the rest of us ...

MEGHAN DAUM, author of *Life Would Be Perfect If I Lived In That House*

How perfect that a writer as thoughtful, original, and hilarious as Karen Karbo takes on as a subject as talented, passionate, and fearless Georgia O'Keeffe. The result is a fresh, funny, highly personalized take on "the nation's greatest woman artist," a meticulously researched, page-turning romp through the life of a painter whose days were as bold and unique as her art.

CATHI HANAUER, author of *Sweet Ruin* and editor of *The Bitch in the House*

This intimate, quirky, and sassy essay makes its iconic subject into an accessible, relevant figure with whom readers can identify.

PUBLISHER'S WEEKLY

[T]old with great wit and hilarity throughout. While O'Keeffe is already revered by millions of women and aspiring artists everywhere, Karbo's original, wry analysis is bound to enrich her status even further.

SHELF AWARENESS

The Gospel According to Coco Chanel: Life Lessons From the World's Most Elegant Woman

Karbo delivers a mini-biography, with perceptive and amusing commentary ... The fashion is merely fascinating, a means to an end. The life lessons? For a woman trying to find a safe haven in America, this book delivers more wisdom – and wit – per page than Dr. Phil will dispense in a lifetime.

HEADBUTLER

Reading Karbo is like listening to a dear friend talk about the legendary designer over brunch. This is a fun, insightful look at the genius behind the little black dress.

THE LOS ANGELES TIMES

Anyone with a good sense of humor should hugely enjoy, or should I say *enjoie*, Karen Karbo's funny and stylish take on Coco Chanel. Like a little black dress, this handy life guide will take you from day into evening. K.K. on C.C.: *oui, oui!*

HENRY ALFORD, author of *How to Live: A Search for Wisdom from Old People (While They are Still on This Earth)*

Wise, witty, and refreshingly colloquial, *The Gospel According to Coco Chanel* is an enchanting tour through the complex, often controversial life of fashion icon Chanel. Filled with relevant life lessons for the modern woman, this book is Karbo at her irrepressible best.

HILARY BLACK, author of *The Secret Currency of Love: The Unabashed Truth About Women, Money, and Relationships*

How to Hepburn: Lessons On Living From Kate The Great

Karbo presents all this heterodox advice with great humor, but there's a point she's making to sister Gen-Xers: Hepburn broke all the rules women were supposed to follow and still had a fabulous life.

PUBLISHERS WEEKLY

These days, women in Hollywood and everywhere else are following [Hepburn's] fiercely independent lead – and *Redbook* contributing editor Karen Karbo is no exception. Her sassy new book, *How to Hepburn: Lessons on Living from Kate the Great* explains what we can learn from the iconic leading lady, who makes most of today's heavy-hitting celebrities look pretty lightweight.

REDBOOK

Karen Karbo's *How to Hepburn: Lessons on Living from Kate the Great* strides magnificently before our eyes, much as Hepburn did onscreen. Perhaps because Karbo's mother turned to Hepburn and not Jackie Kennedy as her 1960s household saint, Karbo goes for honesty over hagiography – and still finds much for us to emulate. And Karbo has the same appetite for a good sentence that Hepburn had for life.

MORE

Karen Karbo manages to come up with some offbeat gems in her witty new book, *How to Hepburn*.

USA TODAY

… Captures Hollywood mores and largely succeeds as an homage to "Miss Hepburn."

NEW YORK TIMES BOOK REVIEW

In an interesting blend of self-help book and star biography, novelist Karen Karbo seeks to extract lessons from the life of Katherine Hepburn. *How to Hepburn: Lessons on Living from Kate the Great* is a fun and spunky take on the life of the star.

CHRISTIAN SCIENCE MONITOR

An exuberant celebration of a great original.

THE PHILADELPHIA INQUIRER

… A delightful, insightful little guide.

SEATTLE POST-INTELLIGENCER

…smart, witty and profound in a low-key way – everything you'd expect in a book by Karbo.

THE OREGONIAN

The Stuff of Life

· A *New York Times* Notable Book
· *People Magazine* Critics' Choice
· Books for a Better Life Award finalist
· Winner of the Oregon Book Award for Creative Non-fiction

With generous honesty, Karbo describes nuanced moments of nearly excruciating tenderness, embarrassment, frustration, and love, balanced with passages of often side-splitting humor. A compulsively readable memoir about family and the writing life.

BOOKLIST

Karen Karbo is nothing if not funny, so you'll forgive her – no, you'll thank her – for not turning her chain-smoking father's death from lung cancer into a *Lifetime* movie weepfest. Instead, this bittersweet book honestly shows death to be what it is: a part of life, with all its annoyances, inequities, miseries and joys.

PEOPLE

Karbo's willingness to portray the tough business of grief and mortality in all its unmanageableness and confusion makes *The Stuff of Life* a book you want to keep reading, and laughing with, to the end.

THE SEATTLE TIMES

…The book works beautifully on many levels. A lively, insightful and astonishingly unsentimental read, it's intensely funny in places.

THE WASHINGTON POST

Motherhood Made A Man Out of Me

· A *New York Times* Notable Book

Motherhood Made a Man Out of Me should be clutched to the "corn-silo-sized" breasts of every new mother.

THE NEW YORK TIMES

Brilliant! The righteous, thoroughly American Karen Karbo delivers a swift kick in the kegels to those sappy *What to Expect When You're Expecting* moms in her funny and appallingly honest novel *Motherhood Made a Man Out of Me*.

VANITY FAIR

Trespassers Welcome Here

· A *New York Times* Notable Book of the Year
· A *Village Voice* Top Ten Book of the Year

The Russians have come – and they're fascinating. Karbo's first novel, about Soviet émigrés in L.A., has passionate characters colliding in love, jealousy, politics, and the ongoing cold war between the sexes. An extraordinary debut that combines compassion with raucous comedy.

THE NEW YORK TIMES

r

Copyright ©2014
Karen Karbo

All rights reserved. No part
of this book may be repro-
duced in any form or by any
electronic or mechanical
means, including informa-
tion storage-and-retrieval
systems, without prior permission in writing from the
Publisher, except for brief
quotations embodied in
critical articles and reviews.

"Paperback Writer" by John
Lennon and Paul McCartney
©1966 Northern Songs Ltd.
All rights for the U.S.,
Canada and Mexico Con-
trolled and administered
by EMI Blackwood Music
Inc. under license from
ATV Music (MACLEN) All
Rights Reserved. Inter-
national Copyright Secured.
Used by Permission.

Library of Congress
Cataloging-in-Publication Data

Karbo, Karen
The diamond lane / Karen Karbo.
pages cm
ISBN 978-0-9893604-4-9

1. Man-woman relationships-
   Fiction.
2. Motion picture industry-Fiction.
3. Hollywood (Los Angeles,
   Calif.)-Fiction.

I. Title.

PS3561.A584D5 2014
813'.54-DC23
2013044757

Hawthorne Books
& Literary Arts

9   2201 Northeast 23rd Avenue
8   3rd Floor
7   Portland, Oregon 97212
6   hawthornebooks.com
5   *Form*:
4   Adam McIsaac/Sibley House
3
2   Printed in China
1   Set in Paperback

Originally published in
1991 by G.P. Putnam's Sons,
New York

First Hawthorne Edition,
2014

Dedicated to my dad, Richard Karbo,
and the memory of my mom, Joan Karbo
A toast and a wink to my fine editor, Stacy Creamer

ALSO BY KAREN KARBO

Non-fiction
Julia Child Rules: Lessons on Savoring Life
How Georgia Became O'Keeffe: Lessons on the Art of Living
The Gospel According to Coco Chanel: Life Lessons
        from the World's Most Elegant Woman
How to Hepburn: Lessons on Living from Kate the Great
The Stuff of Life: A Daughter's Memoir
Generation Ex: Tales from the Second Wives Club
My Foot is Too Big for the Glass Slipper (with Gabrielle Reece)
Big Girl in the Middle (with Gabrielle Reece)

Fiction
Motherhood Made a Man Out of Me
Trespassers Welcome Here

For Young Adults
Minerva Clark Gets a Clue
Minerva Clark Goes to the Dogs
Minerva Clark Gives Up the Ghost

The
Diamond
Lane

A Novel
Karen Karbo

r❧ Hawthorne Rediscovery
FROM HAWTHORNE BOOKS & LITERARY ARTS
Portland, Oregon | MMXIV

Introduction
Jane Smiley

EARLY IN *THE DIAMOND LANE*, KAREN KARBO ARRIVES at her subject (as opposed to her plot). Mimi FitzHenry, in her mid-thirties, works at a production company, where she reads scripts for a (small) living. Her sister, Mouse, is calling her collect from Africa, and she has to justify taking the call to her boss. She staves him off by telling him that her mother, Shirl, was hit in the head by a falling ceiling fan and needs surgery. Her boss says, "'Where'd it happen?'

"'Gateau on Melrose.'

"'Good God, I ate there a couple weeks ago.' Solly seemed both baffled and repulsed. He had never heard such a thing. Wasn't bad luck and misery and brain surgery and estranged sisters the stuff of TV miniseries? How tasteless to drag them into real life.'"

But this is Hollywood, where real life and miniseries are only distinguishable by who is getting paid and how much. No one is more aware of this than Mimi, who embraces it, or Mouse, a year younger, who rejects it. How and why Mimi and Mouse are who they are and what will become of them when Mouse returns after sixteen years is the subject of Karbo's novel, which is hilarious, dark, playful, edgy, ephemeral, and enduring all at the same time.

The Diamond Lane is Karbo's second novel, first published in 1991, two years after *Trespassers Welcome Here*, a novel about Soviet emigres to L.A. Karbo was thirty-three years old. There is

never a moment in The Diamond Lane where Karbo doesn't
know just what she is talking about – the movie business, how to
drive across town, what it is like in Africa, how to put together
an absurdly expensive wedding, what love feels like, what doubt
feels like, what bulimia feels like, what despair and sibling
rivalry feel like. Of course, Mimi and Mouse have lovers. Mouse
brings her English boyfriend, Tony, home with her, her collaborator in her current project, a documentary about an African
tribal wedding. Mimi has a clandestine relationship with Ralph,
a married man, who is teaching the class she is taking in "How
to Write a Blockbuster." Ralph has never written a blockbuster,
but he has plenty of students. And then there is Ivan.

Karbo doles out measures of information with exquisite
literary timing, weaving each new outrage (according to Mouse)
or prize (according to Mimi) into her sour-sweet but always
funny discourse. The reader comes to trust her completely – to
wait patiently for the mystery to be solved because there will be
so many sharp insights along the way. One of my favorites comes
when Mouse is observing a friend of Mimi's reading scripts.
Karbo writes, "Each one took about ten minutes. She read the
first ten pages, the middle ten, the last ten. If she liked those
thirty, she'd go back and read the first twenty, the middle twenty,
and the last twenty. If she liked those sixty, she'd go back and
read the first thirty, the middle thirty, the last thirty, which
generally amounted to the entire script." Carole, the enviable
reader, would rather go to nursing school.

Karbo has a wonderful gift for populating her novel with
amusing and revealing minor characters. There is Lisa, the
sound editor: "She worked sixteen to eighteen hours a day syncing up footsteps, thwoking tennis balls, high school boys playing the edge of their desks with number 2 pencils, rat-a-tat- a-tat-
a-tat-a-tat-a-tat-a-tat. Every rat, every tat had to be there, and
had to be in sync. Then, in the mix, the producer covered all of
them with a song from the soundtrack album. It would have been
a wonder if she wasn't addicted to Lithium." One of my favorites

is Shirl's sister, Auntie Barb, who lives in Boring, Oregon, where she cultivates her sense of superiority. "Your eyeballs are drifting all over the place," said Auntie Barb. "Everyone here does that. They pretend they're listening but all the while they're looking around for somebody more interesting. In Oregon people look you in the eye."

When *The Diamond Lane* first came out, it was admired for its edgy style and hailed, for good reason, as "a deft, tragicomic social satire – of Los Angeles and the movie biz in particular and modern mores in general – noteworthy for the complexity of its characters, crisp prose, and loopy comic style." (*Library Journal*) The *New York Times* loved it – declaring it one of the best novels of 1991: "A wonderfully comic novel about savvy Hollywood outsiders trying to get in—and to juggle their disastrous but funny love lives." In the twenty-two years since publication, things have changed – or not. Filmmakers do not, perhaps, lug around the miles of celluloid and the burdensome cameras and sound recorders that they once did. Mobile phones ring all the time now, and perhaps Solly can reach his target-connections in New York more readily that he could then (perhaps not), but the convoluted relationships between art and commerce, truth and fiction, love and rivalry, wit and sadness that Karbo explores in *The Diamond Lane* have not changed. This novel still feels knowing and audacious and up-to-the-minute.

Preface

THIS NOVEL, MY SECOND, WAS FIRST PUBLISHED TWENTY-two years ago. You would think enough time has passed that I might be able to look back at the experience with nostalgia and fondness, to see with the clarity afforded by time what I was trying to accomplish and how I've grown as a writer. You would think.

But for reasons that remain an utter mystery to me, I'm unable to do any of these things. It's a well-known fact that people can't tickle themselves, and that's how this kind of literary self-reflection strikes me.

Rereading *The Diamond Lane*, my primary feeling isn't expansive and mellow but akin to the alarm a high-strung horse feels when an unexpected plastic bag skitters across his path: In my lifetime there was a smoking section on airplanes? Owning a car FAX was once the height of high tech?

The 1987 Oliver Stone film *Wall Street*, whose reverberations could still be heard as I sat down to begin writing *The Diamond Lane* two years later, spawned a disappointing, mildly embarrassing sequel in 2010. The best scene from the latter film offered one great visual joke: when Gordon Gecko (Michael Douglas) is released from prison, he collects his personal effects, including his big brick cell phone. That's how long he'd been in the joint. Paging through this novel, I feel not unlike Gecko on the day he picked up that phone and tried to call out on it. Videotapes? Walkmans? Answering machines?

And yet, perhaps not surprisingly, the basics of human nature, the timeless desire of women over thirty to wed, and the odds that most people will never break into Hollywood haven't changed one bit. VCRs may be a thing of the past, but competitive sisters, the fear of growing old alone, and taking pointless meetings in which nothing happens are right this minute.

In terms of how I've grown as a writer ... it's possible I've shrunk. Especially when it comes to putting my butt in the chair until the allotted daily word count (1,000, then as now) has been squeezed out like the final nub of toothpaste from a cheapskate's crumpled tube.

I wrote the novel over the course of thirteen months, working from 9:00 a.m. to 2:00 p.m. five days a week. My desk was an adjustable Art Deco drafting table with cast iron base that I'd inherited from my father, an industrial designer and engineer, and my favorite method of procrastination consisted of reading the style section in the morning paper. Sometimes I really went crazy and called a friend before I sat down to write. The leviathan distractions for those of us who make our livings sitting at desks of e-mail and the Internet were then glimmers in the far-sighted eyes of a handful of brainy geeks.

What I can speak to were my intentions in writing this book, which I do remember clearly. My first novel, *Trespassers Welcome Here*, had been purchased by Stacy Creamer at G. P. Putnam's Sons in 1988; a few weeks after she bought it, I asked her what I was supposed to do now.

"Just write your next book," she said. "That's your job."

There was no expectation that I would spend the next year mounting a one-woman, four-figure publicity and marketing campaign, including but not limited to jazzy new website complete with giveaway contest and podcasts, tedious Facebook author's page, completely irrelevant yet somehow absolutely necessary Twitter presence, *Goodreads* whatever.

I was the writer, and my job was to write.

It really was a simpler time. And a much better time to be a serious writer.

So I set about writing a new novel, per Stacy's instructions. All I knew was that I wanted it to be different from *Trespassers*, a collection of linked stories, each chapter told from the point of view of a different character. I'd stumbled upon the structure of that book by accident. I'd written the first story for a fiction writing class, and the instructor, Joyce Thompson, made an off-hand remark that she liked the characters in the story so much she could imagine each of them having their own story. After having spent the decade before writing screenplays (eight; rights still available) that were optioned once in a while but otherwise went nowhere, I was an expert at taking the off-hand notes of strangers. So when Joyce said each character could have their own story, I sat down and wrote them.

I wanted *The Diamond Lane* to be a big novel stuffed with lots of characters and ideas, the opposite of *Trespassers*, which relied on brevity and voice. I was a big believer, and still am, in the power of emotional autobiography, which means not telling true tales, necessarily, but inventing stories that tap into true, powerful, and usually conflicting emotions. Those emotions – my emotions in this case – animate the characters and power the action.

As I was writing my thousand words a day over those thirteen months, I often felt a little strapped, like I was trying to make the best meal I could out of only the ingredients I already had on hand. Into the giant pot of the plot went my love/hate relationship with my home town of L.A. (into which I indiscriminately tossed suburban Whittier, where I grew up); the incomparable joy I experienced learning to make movies in film school; the culture shock I experienced returning to L.A. from a trip to Africa in college; the enduring questions I had, and still have, about the institution of marriage; and the deep frustration I felt at trying (and failing) to make it in Hollywood. That it came out funny, as the reviews all noted, is a function of temperament, not of intent.

Most poignant for me in rereading the book is revisiting the ceiling fan accident that befalls Shirl, the mother of Mouse and Mimi, the precipitating incident that sets the plot in motion. Like Shirl, my own mother had had brain surgery. Hers was not the result of a darkly comical accident but of a malignant brain tumor. *The Diamond Lane* includes the fantasy that my mother recovered from her surgery and went on to boss me around and annoy me into my thirties and beyond. Instead, she died. I was seventeen, and it was the loss of my life.

The novel represents my first (admittedly immature) effort at putting characters on the page whose catastrophes come close to echoing those of our family's. It would be many years before I could approach it again, and I still don't think I've done justice to my mother's life, sudden decline, and death.

When *The Diamond Lane* published in May 1991, I remember being ecstatic and somewhat taken aback with the positive reception: the *New York Times* thought to give it a full page review, complete with short interview and author photo, and later named it one of their notable books of the year.

That spring, fittingly, I was working on a movie, walking foley on Gus Van Sant's *My Own Private Idaho*, a gig I'd landed through my then-husband, who was the supervising sound editor. (Foley is a post-production chore, performed on a foley stage, where the walker "covers" every natural human sound – mostly footsteps – that appears in the film; the foley track is then used to either replace muffled sounds on the original recording or augment existing sounds.) I "was" Keanu Reeves, or at least his footsteps and squeaky leather jacket.

During the production I got to know Laurie Parker, the film's producer. She took an interest in the novel and eventually optioned it for a feature film. Predictably, there was a lot of enthusiasm, but nothing ever came of it.

Perhaps the most amusing, gratifying part of having written

The Diamond Lane, seeing it published, and now, decades later, reissued in this beautiful Hawthorne Books edition, is witnessing the degree to which it was far ahead of its time. The central conceit of the book, far-fetched and satirical in the early 1990s, foretold the future. As of 2014, there are dozens of "reality" wedding shows, among them TLC's hit *Say Yes to the Dress*, in which an hour-long episode revolves around the drama of a woman shopping for her wedding dress. The show has enjoyed an eight-season run, and also spawned a gaggle of spin-offs (*Say Yes to the Dress: Atlanta*; *Say Yes to the Dress: Bridesmaids*; *Bridal School*; *Something Borrowed, Something New*.) Every show focuses on the tempest in a teapot that is the modern first world wedding.

You gotta laugh.

KAREN KARBO
Portland, 2014

Love is an ocean of emotions, entirely surrounded by expenses.
LORD DEWAR

THE DIAMOND LANE

1.

FREAK ACCIDENTS RAN IN THE FAMILY. WHAT ELSE WAS Mimi to think? First Fitzy, now Shirl. What happened to lingering diseases? What happened to people dying in their sleep at eighty-five? The world was as reliable as patio furniture in a hurricane. It was so awful it made her laugh. The day after it happened she called in sick. She was convinced if she went to work, on the twenty-first floor of a building on Sunset Boulevard, the FitzHenry luck would bring on an earthquake. Mimi and Mouse were ten and nine when their father, Fitzy, was run over by a dolly. Fitzy had been crossing the street at the bottom of a freeway ramp, on his way to get new keys made for the front door of Fitzy's, his bar. A truck waiting to merge at the top of the ramp was towing the dolly, which was not properly hooked onto the trailer. The safety chain was taped together with hundred-mile-an-hour-tape, the silver duct tape that lazy truck drivers used to patch everything from wobbly rearview mirrors to broken radiator hoses.

Fitzy stooped down to pick up an earring in the crosswalk. The truck jerked, snapping the tape. The dolly hurtled down the ramp. Fitzy leaped out of the way, only to trip and crack his head on the curb. He was thirty-four, dead on arrival.

It was a Thursday. By the next Tuesday he was in the ground. They found the earring when they pried open his fist at the coroner's office. It was an 18k gold clip-on knot. Seven different women called up to claim it when the description ran in the paper. Shirl, Mimi and Mouse's mother, was comforted by the fact that at least he stooped for the genuine article, not gold-plated.

Mimi recounted this to her fellow drudge, Alyssia, who was answering Solly's line while Mimi tried to track down Mouse in Nairobi. Alyssia was a Yale graduate with curly brown hair, squinty eyes, and lips so full Mimi wondered if she'd gone in for silicone injections. Alyssia was only twenty. She made Mimi feel too old to be doing this job.

Calling Africa was not cheap. Mimi vowed that after Mouse came home, if she came home – Mouse hadn't come home for her wedding, why should she come home for this? – she would get Mouse to reimburse her. Her phone bill was already two months past due.

Mimi tried the BBC office, then Mouse's place in Nairobi. They had never heard of either Mouse FitzHenry or Frances FitzHenry at the BBC. Mimi was sure that was where Mouse worked. Who else made documentaries in Africa? At the house some African girl with a fluty voice answered the phone and told her to call Zaire. *Zah-ear.* She felt stupid. All this time she had thought the word rhymed with *hair.* Where in *Zah-ear?* Mimi asked. The girl on the other end of the line didn't know.

At the American Express office, in one of the two or three places in Zaire where they had American Express offices, Mimi left this message: Mouse FitzHenry, phone home. Zaire was apparently the type of place where you could leave messages like that. The lady Mimi talked to in Kisangani said, "I tell her you called," as if the country was a house and Mouse was just out walking the dog. Wasn't Zaire the size of India or something?

Then, the next morning, a modern-day miracle: Mouse returned her call.

But she called at the worst possible time, nine o'clock in the morning. Mimi placed calls to New York every morning at nine-thirty in hopes of reaching New York film people before they bolted out the door to "do" lunch.

Her boss, Solly, needed New York. He needed Mimi to get

New York for him. He hovered over her while she dialed. He chomped on a chocolate croissant fresh from Gourmet-on-Wheels. He dribbled crumbs. She did her best to ignore them.

When Mimi heard the Gourmet-on-Wheels vendor rattling through the front door of the office, she locked herself in the bathroom and chewed sugarless gum so as not to be tempted.

Mimi tried never to touch the stuff. Any eating she did, she did in private, as if she wouldn't gain weight as long as there were no witnesses, And since she also enjoyed an active social life, she was thin. Thin enough, but not as thin as she could be. She was not anorexic, but would love to figure out how to be for about two weeks a month. She liked to wear bright-colored cotton-knit miniskirts, which showed off a concave abdomen stretching between the bony parentheses of her hips.

Solly, on the other hand, was the Goodyear blimp incarnate. He kept his own appointment book, the better to schedule double-header breakfast meetings, triple-header lunch meetings, without anyone knowing it. But Mimi knew about it. All the drudges in the office knew about it. Solly weighed in at about two-eighty. Mimi saw it one day when she was sending off some life insurance forms.

Sometimes, when Solly infuriated her, when he accused her of being stupid, negligent, unappreciative of the importance of talking to New York at nine-thirty in the morning, she went to the Xerox room and found another drudge who had in some way been driven over the edge. Behind his back they sang: "Fatman! Do-do-do-do-do-do-do-do, do-do-do-do-do-do-do-do, Fatman!" to the tune of the old *Batman* theme song.

The flakes from Solly's croissant trickled onto Mimi's shoulders as she put in calls to ICM, CAA, CBS, NBC, and a couple of ritzy farmhouses in Connecticut where clients were holed up, working on screenplays.

"Solly Stein calling for Jonathan Wild. He's in a meeting? Could you leave word?"

"Solly Stein calling for J. J. McIntosh. When is he expected back from lunch? Could you please leave word?"

"Solly Stein calling for Hillary Madison-Edelman. Is she reachable in St. Bart's? Fine. Just leave word."

In desperation, Solly chewed faster and faster. Mimi could hear his molars clacking together inside his mouth. He swallowed a lump of croissant the size of an egg. Glunk. "Get me Lore Director at Orion, no, no Marty, get me Marty Schepsi, no, Christ, Marty's in Geneva, what time is it in Geneva? Did you send that thing out to what's his name?" He wadded up the plastic wrap the croissant came in, then between tubby thumbs and fat forefingers frantically pinched it into a teeny ball. "What about Rocky Martini?"

The phone rang. Mimi sighed. Saved!

Solly had already deposited the tiny wadded-up Saran Wrap ball at her elbow and was poised in the doorway of his office.

"Who is it?" he hissed, before the receiver had reached her ear. "Is it Wild? I need Wild."

Mimi felt the blood pounding in her throat. She waved him to shut up. Through the earpiece, the telephone equivalent of a snowstorm. Then, "ALLO! COLLECT PERSON-TO-PER-SON FROM FRANCES FITHENRY!"

Shit, she thought. It's Mouse. Solly's going to have my head. And collect? She has to call *collect*?

"Who *is* it, for the love of Christ?"

"It's long distance."

Rubbing his fat dry hands together, Solly bounded into his office and hurled himself into his big black leather chair. The sound the chair made was the same as if it'd just been hit by a wrecking ball. Suddenly, he came on the line. "Mazel tov!"

"Solly, it's personal."

"Who is this?" he bellowed.

"It's Mimi, Solly. It's a personal phone call. I've got to take it."

Then, from through the snowstorm, a third voice. Under the static the voice was thin and faint. "Mimi? *crrrrrrrrr* Mouse!"

"Solly," said Mimi, "get off the phone. It's my sister in Nairobi."

"*Crrr*llo?" yelled Mouse. "Mimi?"

"Mouse! It's Mimi!"

"*Crrrrrrrrr* Kissing Gani," yelled Mouse.

"Kissing *who*?" said Mimi.

Solly banged the phone down in Mimi's ear.

"What's going on?" said Mouse. Even through the snow she sounded uneasy and a little suspicious.

"It's Mom!" yelled Mimi. Hearing herself say "Mom," the tears she'd been swallowing all morning filled her throat. "She has a, there's been an accident. They're doing surgery this morning, drilling some hole in her head."

"*Crrrrrrrrr* God," said the other end of the line. "Middle *crrrrrr crrrrrr* marriage."

"You are?" Mimi yelled. "You must be thrilled. I remember how I felt when – "

" – *crrrrrrr* now."

"I need Rocky Martini." It was Solly. Mimi could smell his chocolate breath on her neck. He stood behind her, loudly fondling the change in his pockets.

"Just a second," Mimi said to Solly. Then into the snowstorm, "It's a hematoma thing she's got. It's bad. They're drilling a hole in her head. You got to come home!"

"I need Miłosz Benik," said Solly, pouting. "I need Rocky Martini."

Mimi thought she heard Mouse say okay, then the hollow far-off roar of nothing. She hung up. She hadn't talked to Mouse in over five years. And here was Shirl having, having, brain surgery. Mimi thought if she was older – she was thirty-six, practically an adult – it wouldn't be so awful. Everyone has to go sometime. But death was the easy part. If you're dead, you're dead. It's the in-between. It's the decline part, the part between bouncing around rosy-checked healthy and some guy with cold hands dragging the sheet over your face. Not that she knew one whit about decline. But she worried she was about to find out.

She worried that Shirl wouldn't be able to do her crossword puzzles anymore. That her hands would shake so much she wouldn't be able to do her découpage. Would her hair grow back? Would she have to wear a bad wig? Mimi gingerly wiped her eyes with her ring fingers, so as not to smear her mascara or tug the extra-sensitive skin under the eyes. She felt better, glad to know that even under the most excruciating circumstances she was not one to let her looks go.

Solly glared. "If you're done–"

"My mom is dying, okay?" She wasn't technically, but she was in intensive care. Mimi stood up so fast she knocked her steno chair over. She loathed that chair. It was a slave chair. The assistants to the agents at least had chairs with arms. The agents, of course, had massive leather-upholstered thrones. Whose butt was supposed to fit on her chair, anyway?

"She was hit by a ceiling fan, okay? She's in intensive care. My sister lives in Africa, okay? We haven't talked in a jillion years. I had to talk to her. Have you ever tried to talk to Africa? It's not like calling stupid New York. So get off my fucking back for a minute all right? All right?"

"Mimi, Mimi. I. I. A ceiling fan?"

"It hit the side of her head by her right eye. She got a skull fracture and now there's, I don't know, blood leaking or something, they've got to drill a hole. They're shaving her head. What if she's a vegetable?"

"Where'd it happen?"

"Gateau on Melrose."

"Good God, I ate there a couple weeks ago." Solly seemed both baffled and repulsed. He had never heard such a thing. Wasn't bad luck and misery and brain surgery and estranged sisters the stuff of TV miniseries? How tasteless to drag them into real life.

He ran his hands over his balding head. There were a couple of dime-size dark-brown blotches on it. Watch your karma, Mr. Pre-Cancerous Condition, Mimi said silently to the blotches. It could happen to you. Anything can happen to anybody.

"I knew you were miserable, but I didn't think anything was wrong," he said.

"God, Solly." Brilliant. He should give up the film business and be a brain surgeon instead. Oh, she thought, oh, a brain surgeon. Everything suddenly seemed unfairly ironic, which was troubling. Mimi didn't believe in irony. She felt it was more a literary convention. She put it in the same category as *deus ex machina*. The tears started up again. She felt them tip over the edge of her eyes. Fuck the mascara. She resigned herself to being a mess.

"Everyone in the business is miserable," said Alyssia. "It's all relative."

"She's having surgery right this minute," Mimi sobbed.

"What can I do? What can I do?" asked Solly.

"It's just so awful," said Mimi. "I'm sorry."

"Take some time off. Please. Take all the time you need."

Mimi wiped her nose with the back of her hand. She stared at the framed poster over her typewriter, taking deep breaths, trying to calm herself. The poster was from a terrible movie directed by one of Solly's clients, one which Solly would defend to his death. He refused to let anyone, including himself, think that he'd made an obscene commission on a movie that should have been put out of its misery when it was still just an idea. And here he was, now, offering her time off. People were wrong when they said people in the film business had no morals.

"All the time I need?" asked Mimi.

"Well, a long lunch why don't you? But be back by three. I gotta talk to New York today. And Rocky – "

" – in a minute."

"Fine, fine." Solly looked at his plastic diving watch. He tapped the face nervously with his fingertips. He owned the requisite gold Rolex but was afraid to wear it for fear it'd get dinged up, wet, or stolen.

Mimi took deep breaths. Alyssia came over and rubbed her back between her shoulder blades. Mimi suddenly felt good and calm, but kept on with the deep breathing. Steeped in misery though she was – it was *awful*, she wasn't saying she *liked* the idea of her mother getting cracked on the head with a ceiling fan – she did enjoy being someone who had something in her life which warranted deep breaths. Deep breaths were the domain of mothers in labor, actors, athletes, mystics. People at the center of Drama.

"Maybe Alyssia has some Kleenex, or, or something." Solly waved in her direction and wandered back to his office, pulling on his lower lip. "Jesus," he said. "Half the places in town have ceiling fans. Alyssia, get me Rocky Martini. Please."

2.

THREE MESSAGES AWAITED MOUSE FITZHENRY IN Kisangani: one from the Office of Native Affairs in Kinshasa, for whom she and Tony Cheatham were producing the Zairian wedding film; one from Camisha, the girl in Nairobi who was taking care of their house while they were away; one that read, simply, "Mowz FitHenry fone home." The prefix was familiar. Either her mother or her sister had called. Besides Tony they were the only two who used her nickname.

Mouse and Tony had just spent three weeks in the Ituri forest shooting a BabWani wedding ceremony, part of *Marriage Under Mobutu: Tribal Wedding Customs in Contemporary Zaire.* From there it had been two days on foot through the forest to the Catholic mission near Nia Nia, then three days from the mission by Land Rover down the rutted road to Kisangani, where they had just checked into the Hotel Superbe, a five-star hotel featuring greasy sheets, a sagging, infested mattress, and one bare bulb. Luxurious, compared to the stinky plastic tent they were used to.

They shared a shower of cold brown water, their first in nearly a month, went to American Express to pick up mail and messages, then went to the post office. It was the only place in town to make a long-distance call, requiring a written request to the operator, the necessary *matabeesh*, the bribe money, and a Jobian amount of patience. Sometimes it took forty-five minutes, sometimes four hours.

They sat on a long wooden bench and waited. They sat, sweated, and slapped flies. Despite the shower, a thin sheen of mud coated their skin. Breathing was like sucking air through a washcloth. But Mouse was grateful for the discomfort, her exhaustion. It prevented her worrying too deeply about the phone call from home. It could not have been easy to find her. Surely the news was not good.

"Perhaps they're just coming for a visit. Popping over from Egypt or something," Tony tried to reassure her.

"My mother refuses to drive on the freeway. I kind of doubt she's in Egypt."

"One never knows." Tony sat scribbling in a notebook bowed from traveling in his back pocket, making notes on a screenplay he was writing in his spare time. He pinched the end of his sunburnt nose, glanced over at Mouse. *She had a mop of thick dark hair, small regular features, glass-green eyes, an unexpectedly dimpled chin.* No, too specific. Vince Parchman, the Peace Corps volunteer from whom he had taken a filmic writing seminar in Nairobi the year before, had said description should be written so any actor could play the role. Height, hair color, and the like were too limiting. *A hundred pounds of trouble.* Better. *She was an iron fist in a velvet glove.* An iron fist in an iron glove was actually the case, he thought. A cute iron glove. *An iron fist in an extremely appealing iron glove.* Yeccch. He flipped the notebook closed and slid it back in his pocket.

Vince had inoculated Maasai babies in Ngong during the week, and taught filmic writing on Tuesday nights in a quiet corner of a local bar, You'll Regret It. In addition to the usual restless expatriates, he had had a few Maasai and Kikuyu. The best script in the class had been a corning-of-age piece written by a Maasai teenager.

"Where do you think Gideon is these days? You know, the kid with that terrific circumcision script. From filmic writing."

"You didn't hear? He's president of Warner Brothers."

"Har, har, har."

A gang of children with big bellies and the cottony yellow-tipped hair of the malnourished stood in a half circle around Mouse and Tony, watching. Flies buzzed in the corners of their eyes, clustered around their nostrils. A man in a limp skullcap napped against the wall by the front door. His job was to whip the children with a bamboo switch if they so much as extended one thin grubby palm.

Mouse fumbled around in her bag, extracting a bottle of pearly pink nail polish. The tiny silver ball inside clicked as she shook it. She spread her brown hand on her knee, slapped a coat of polish on her nails. Somewhere she'd picked up a fungus that had turned them greenish black. To her lasting irritation there was no cure, only cover-up.

The boldest child spread his hand next to hers. She painted his nails, as well as the nails of anyone else brave enough to approach. The children solemnly spread their hands, one by one, as though the spreading of their fingers, the resting of their hands on her kneecap was part of the ritual. She felt Tony's eyes on her.

"Now don't go putting this in your bloody screenplay," she said, smiling, twisting the bottle shut.

"Sorry, poppet, going to be the opening scene. A lyrical moment 'tween a girl and her nail polish."

"I'll sue."

"On what grounds?"

"Emotional stress caused by the revelation of all my beauty secrets."

"Is that a threat?"

"A promise, *bwana*."

Mouse was opposed to fiction of any kind. She was against many things that documentarians did all the time to get the damn thing shot and over with. She was against going back and filming reaction shots. She was against staging events, against editing a sequence dramatically and passing it off as reality, against scripting people's lines. She was a purist. Tony teased her about it all the time.

It made her job and her life difficult. For example, the recent BabWani wedding shoot. An hour before the wedding, the bride had backed out.

Marie-Claire was only twelve years old. She'd sat huddled against the mud wall of her mother's hut, her skinny legs pulled up to her chest, her chin thrust between kneecaps as bony as elbows. Everything was wrong. First her hair. Then her face. In truth, the groom.

"Ayyyyyy-ayyyyyy-ayyyyy ... " Terese, the bride's mother, moaned. She stood over her daughter, slapping her shoulder with the backs of her wrinkled fingers. Get with it! the slap said. You should feel lucky anyone wants a skinny girl like you!

Marie-Claire said the groom was a drunk and a glutton. She said it was well known in the village that he was cruel to his other wives. He beat them silly. He poked their buttocks with the sharp quills of porcupines, which he was supposed to sell, but would instead drag into the forest and eat all by himself.

All this was told to the translator, Ovumi Obrumba, who turned and translated it into English for Mouse and Tony.

As a single woman who thought marriage was dicey under the most ideal circumstances, Mouse couldn't blame Marie-Claire for not wanting to spend the rest of her life yoked to some palm wine-guzzling sadist twice her age; however, as a documentary film producer who had spent the better part of a year trying to get this shoot off the ground, Mouse wanted to strangle her.

"So the wedding's off?" asked Mouse, instantly regretting her words. It hadn't come to that yet. Perhaps this was just part of the BabWani wedding experience. Perhaps all BabWani girls went through this. She didn't want to give anyone any ideas. "What's going on?" she amended.

"The man not good," sniffed Ovumi. "He have pygmie wives also." The BabWani, who shared the Ituri forest with the Bambuti pygmies, thought the pygmies were stupid and odd. They had pygmie jokes like Americans had Polack jokes.

"We don't want to interfere, but we need to know. We're leaving tomorrow, tell her. *Nous partirons demain.* So if the wedding's *off…* "

Mouse tried not to think of the money they'd spent just to get this far, but she couldn't keep herself from the cash register in her mind. It was huge, an ominous old-fashioned cash register, the kind which exists in the mind of every documentary film producer.

Travel expenses. *Ca-ching!* Food. *Ca-ching!* Ovumi, who received a salary and expenses. *Ca-ching!* The BabWani guide, Tanisa, who'd brought them through the forest from the Catholic mission. *Ca-ching!* In addition to the cigarettes and clock-radio, Tanisa was receiving a daily wage out of petty cash. *Ca-ching!* The *matabeesh*, to secure a reliable Land Rover from the Office des Routes, the highway department, to get to the Catholic mission. *Ca-ching!* The film stock. *Ca-ching!* The audio tape. *Ca-ching!* A new magazine for the camera. *Ca-ching!*

Ca-ching! Ca-ching! Ca-ching!

Thousands of dollars, hundreds of days, dozens of arguments. Mouse saw the production flash in front of her eyes. She told herself: Get a grip. It can still work out. Never forget that hardship filmmaking is your specialty.

Mouse and Tony, who was rolling sound, and Ovumi, the interpreter, stood in a circle around the stubborn bride and her keening mother. Between them, on the floor, at Marie-Claire's feet, stood an avocado-green enamel fondue pot, bottom scorched, handle missing. The fondue pot held a handful of maroon powder, which the bride was supposed to apply to her upper face and scalp. It was made from the dried blood and hair of the groom. The powder was sacred. The fondue pot had been culled from the rubbish at the mission, obviously brought to Father Vanderboom, the Catholic missionary, from some cuisine-savvy American trader. Mouse stared down at the pot, trying to collect her thoughts.

Terese's hut was low-ceilinged and dank. It had the cock-eyed look of a structure that had barely survived an earthquake. The mud walls all leaned in one direction, like handwriting. The thatched roof stopped several inches short of the top of one wall, admitting a shaft of green forest light. The BabWani were not known for their architectural prowess.

What they were known for, among anthropologists, among the government officials in the Office of Native Affairs in Kinshasa who'd commissioned *Marriage Under Mobutu*, was their unusual wedding ceremony. Despite the persistent influence of the Church and the kitchen-utensil-toting Westerners who were lunatic enough to venture this far into the forest, it had remained unchanged since Mary and Joseph of Nazareth had tied the knot centuries before.

"What Mouse is trying to get at," said Tony, "is whether it's off or off off."

"Off?" said Ovumi. "Off off?" He sounded like someone at a cocktail party doing an imitation of a barking dog.

"You know, whether it's officially off, or the bride's just saying she can't go through with it, when in fact it's only a case of cold feet."

Ovumi, confused, stared down at Marie-Claire's wide dusty toes.

"You see, Ovumi, we're in rather desperate straits here," said Tony.

"It's important to show the world how her people live," said Mouse. "Tell her we've got a Bantu ceremony and a Pitishi ceremony.

"Certainly she wants the BabWani represented among their countrymen," said Tony.

Female giggles. Mouse and Tony turned to see a gang of old women peeking in the doorway. All morning they had been pounding manioc for the wedding feast. They wore dull cotton wraparound skirts. A few wore T-shirts. The university of this or that, the ubiquitous Harvard and UCLA.

Mouse looked up at Tony, imagining how he looked to them, imagining what they saw or heard to make them laugh. Beyond, of course, the obvious hilarity of being white.

The BabWani, like the pygmies, were small people. Discreet. Mouse could move around them with ease. But Tony seemed extraordinary, as colorful as a parrot. An orange-spotted giant with red skin and orange hair. Eyes a color only a few of them had ever seen, a blue that didn't exist in their green and brown world, but only in pictures of a thing called an ocean, which Father Vanderboom had hanging on the wall at the mission.

White women found Tony extraordinary, too. Mouse had watched them eye him in Nairobi. Embassy wives, giggling Peace Corps girls, the stray, mooning professional researcher, all bowled over by his strawberry-blond curls, six-foot-plus frame, imperious nose, and Oxbridge accent.

"...tell her it's *imperative* that we film this ceremony–" Tony smiled. Even in the greenish gloom, Mouse could tell it was sardonic. He shook his head. "–Christ. This is no good."

"Wedding *dead*," said Ovumi impatiently. Ovumi had had it with this women's business. Besides Tony, who didn't count, he was the only man around for miles. Following the BabWani tradition, the groom had been spirited away by the men of the village for a few days of drinking and hunting. After the ceremony, which only the women attended, the men would return, and the groom would join his new wife.

Ovumi had been forced on Mouse and Tony by the Office of Native Affairs. Some Byzantine initiative having to do with getting tribal men in the cities back to work. They had no idea where he picked up his English. He was a dandy. They called him Ovumi Wilde. He had two identical changes of clothes. Brown flared slacks, black plastic ankle boots, white dress shirt, and gold cuff links. He sported a thin black eyepatch held on to his head with a sanitary-napkin belt. Mouse admired his ingenuity. Another example of the African ability to make absolutely anything do.

Ovumi fiddled with the cuff links of one sleeve, then the other, like an impresario.

"Did they say that, or is it your interpretation?" asked Tony.

Ovumi shrugged. "Wedding dead."

"It's just marital jitters," said Tony, bailing water on the *Titanic*. "Quite typical. Tell her. Tell her she'll get used to him. It'll all come right in the end. She's just gone off her head a bit. It's all the excitement."

"Let it go," sighed Mouse, picking up the camera, which had been resting against her shins. "The guy's a wife beater anyway."

"I don't know," said Tony. "A few pokes in the bum with a porcupine quill doesn't sound like wife beating to me. All brides go through this anyway. It's a universal thing. Like smiling."

"All brides do not go through this," said Mouse.

"So says noted marriage expert Mouse FitzHenry."

"Let it go," said Mouse through clenched teeth.

In the past four years Tony had proposed marriage twice. Twice Mouse had refused him. It worried her that he kept asking. She thought marriage was something a couple resorted to only after they'd run out of other things to do.

MOUSE SAT ON a dead rubber tree and stewed. At her feet ran a tributary of the Congo, whose sunlit banks were choked with deep-red poinsettia blooms and white lilies.

It was five-thirty. In half an hour the abrupt equatorial night would drop on them like a theater curtain. There would be no chance of filming anything now, even supposing Marie-Claire suddenly changed her mind. Then tomorrow they would leave. Two days overland to the mission. Three days from the mission down the rutted road by Land Rover to Kisangani. A day by air to Nairobi. An apologetic phone call to the Office of Native Affairs in Kinshasa. The wedding was off. Nobody's fault.

Mouse felt by turns exhausted, angry, doomed, deprived. A familiar feeling. *Documentarius interruptus.*

Thousands of dollars, hundreds of days, dozens of arguments. She was hot and sticky. She could smell herself. The river looked inviting. But sixteen years in Africa, and a doc she'd done for the World Health Organization on bilharzia, had taught her a sweet brook like this one was teaming with invisible organisms, evil micro-water polo players, treading water with their cilia, waiting for an unsuspecting human to happen by so that they might launch their offensive. So that they might bite her, shit on her, lay their invisible evil eggs upon her, sprint up her most private orifices, where they would snack on her vital organs. She would remain oblivious until, one week or twenty years later, she would die from a horrific, disfiguring, lingering, utterly incurable disease.

But wasn't she a taker of ridiculous risks? Wasn't this what she excelled at? What she got paid for? She'd already had malaria, amoebic dysentery, the green fingernail fungus.

"I'm going for a swim," she said, standing. So I die, she thought. We could film it. Do a thing on the young(ish) documentary filmmaker who risked getting a gruesome tropical disease for Her Art. The problem was, if she went swimming, that wasn't exactly in the line of duty. She wasn't swimming in infested waters in order to get the shot of a lifetime, for example. She paused.

For the past week, while they'd been in Ibonga waiting for Marie-Claire's wedding – strategizing on how they would cover it, planning lighting, following Marie-Claire around with an empty magazine, pretending they were filming, so that she might get used to the camera – they had lived in a tent by the river. When they didn't join the BabWani for manioc bread and bananas and monkey, they cooked food in freeze-dried packets on a butane camp stove.

"I'm going swimming," she repeated. "Don't stop me. Here I go."

Tony sat on an overturned kerosene can by the tent,

hunched over his notebook, writing on his infernal screenplay. He wouldn't tell her the subject. She suspected it was some cop thing. Several months before, one of their friends in Nairobi had gotten *Beverly Hills Cop* through the diplomatic pouch. Tony and the friend recited lines back and forth from the movie until Mouse threatened to move out. Even their night watchman, a cinephilic Kikuyu with his own VCR, rolled his eyes when he saw Tony launch into his Eddie Murphy impersonation.

"Nn-hn," he said. He scratched along the page, nodding and smiling at the notebook balanced on his knees, as though it was telling him a great joke to which he already knew the punch line.

"Any ideas what we're going to do?" said Mouse. She sat down next to him on a piece of tarp. She watched while two dung beetles rolled a piece of goat dung into the bush. She thought they looked like a small pair of animated black patent leather shoes.

Tony sometimes annoyed her. The same kind of even temperament that made him a good co-producer made him a lousy partner in misery. "Two weeks the rainy season starts. We won't be able to get back here until next spring. We need this ceremony. I didn't realize it until it looked like it wasn't going to happen. The Bantu and the Pitishi are so similar. We really needed this one for balance. And the camera loved Marie-Claire. She would have been great. All that great red makeup."

"*C'est le documentaire.*" He sung it to the tune of "*C'est la guerre.*" "I don't suppose you'd consider staging something."

"We could get them to go through the ceremony for the camera. It's completely ethical. Even if Marie-Claire isn't getting married this time, she will eventually, and this is what her wedding will be like, when she does."

"Try explaining that. We want you to go through it, but it doesn't mean anything. It's not real. You aren't really married. These things are sacred, Tony. More sacred than a film they've halfheartedly agreed to participate in."

"'Fraid we're sunk, then. How did Ovumi phrase it? Wedding off?"

"Dead," said Mouse. "Wedding dead."

Tony wrote it in his notebook.

"Don't go losing any sleep over this."

Tony looked up. He put the cap on his pen and closed his notebook. "I'm terribly frustrated, Mouse, just like you." He pinched his blond eyebrows together in what he hoped was sincerity. From the inside the expression felt dangerously close to scowling.

He was lying. Or not lying. He wouldn't say it was lying. It was a matter of degree. He cared. Yes. Of course. It was just, face it, the films meant more to her than they did to him, they always had. He wanted them to be *good*. Yes. Of course. But if they weren't good or if, as in this situation, unexpected and uncontrollable events conspired against the production, it was no skin off his soul. It was simply part of his African Experience. After London Film School his father, a retired officer in the British Foreign Service, had pulled strings to get him on at the BBC in Nairobi. Grip, assistant editor, location sound man. Without too much effort he'd worked his way up, and finally out, finding a niche as a co-producer and sometimes director of less prestigious documentaries made by penny-pinching foreign governments, universities, corporations that either wouldn't or couldn't attract the attention of the much-hallowed BBC, the much-envied *National Geographic*. This rankled Mouse. She said it made her feel like the tray under the toaster that captured all the crumbs.

"We should have seen this coming and lined up another wedding in another village," said Mouse.

It was nearly dark. The night shift of sounds in the canopy relieved the day shift. Caws and screeches segued into singing chirps and buzzing. Tony laid his hand, Pope-like, on the top of Mouse's head. He slowly stroked her thick hair. He wished he had an answer, something to cheer her up. He hated to see her so blue. And that crack about noted marriage expert. That was brilliant.

Somewhere a tree hyrax screamed. It sounded like someone being murdered in an overwrought horror film.

"God," he said, "that noise."

"Oh," she said, "I thought that was you."

He pulled her hair. She reached up and pinched his wrist.

"We could shoot the wedding *not* happening," said Tony, only half sure of what he meant.

"Yes," said Mouse. "Yes. Like Herzog. The volcano thing. What was it called? He goes to shoot the volcano erupting, but it never does. He shoots the steam seeping out of the cracks. He shoots the old guy – remember that old villager? – who refuses to leave. But never the volcano. This is *great*." She leaped to her feet. "We could get up early and interview Terese, Marie-Claire. Talk to the villagers. And how about the groom? Does he even *know*?"

"– it's the last minute and the bride's uncertain. The groom has fled – we don't have to say that's part of the wedding ceremony do we? We do, I know, I know, it was just a thought – anyway he's rather a jerk. She's been going along with it all this time to please her family –"

"Of course! I'm sure that's a common thing among the BabWani. It happens all the time in western culture. People live their entire lives to please their mothers."

"Can't imagine you'd know much about that. Tramping about Africa with a man you're not married to, exposing yourself to AIDS and malaria and God knows what else."

"You forgot political uprisings and possible hostage situations. Maybe we can get the groom just as he's finding out. He comes back from his outing with the other guys, expecting his bride to be there waiting for him –"

"That'll spice it up a bit."

"This is *great*," Mouse yelped.

"Sorry I snapped at you earlier. That marriage expert business."

"That's okay. This is great. This'll make the film even better." Mouse stood in front of Tony, playfully bouncing her knees against his, slapping at mosquitoes.

"I love you," said Tony.

"You are so brilliant," said Mouse. "You know what it's like?"

"What?"

"This! Our lives! You know that saying about you can only be happy when you realize that the object of life is not happiness? What it should be is, doing docs you can only be happy when you realize the object of documentary filmmaking is not happiness. We wanted this to be easy. Straightforward. But that's the whole point of doing films like this, isn't it? I mean if it was just talking heads, just boring professorial types yakking in their book-lined studies what would be the point?"

He ran his freckled hands up the side of her legs and under her T-shirt. "Let's think." He rested his forehead against her stomach.

" ... IT WENT BEAUTIFULLY," said Mouse. The call had finally come through from the Office of Native Affairs.

Next to the bench there were two cubicles equipped with old black rotary-dial telephones. The telephones sat on a low, narrow shelf. There were no stools, so you were forced to choose one of two tortuous positions: squatting or standing bent over like a swimmer preparing to spring from the starting block. Mouse preferred the latter.

Tony slouched on the bench, cleaned his fingernails with the nailfile on his Swiss Army Knife, listening to wisps of the conversation.

" ... rethink the African view of marriage. It's not all it's cracked up to be. Marie-Claire wanted something more for herself..."

Mouse talked as though Marie-Claire was setting about to

become Zaire's answer to Betty Friedan when all the stupid girl really wanted was to hitch her wagon to someone less repulsive.

"...we've come up with ideas for other projects, particularly, I was thinking, the dilemma of the tribal teenager..."

He finished with his nails, closed up the knife and, on impulse, offered it to the circle of children. One of them pounced on it, and the rest pounced on him. Their shrieks awoke the snoozing sentry, who chased them off. Mouse had given him that knife, on his thirty-fifth birthday.

"They were very pleased," said Mouse, rejoining him on the bench. She threw her arms over her head and stretched noisily.

"I gave my Swiss Army Knife away to those kids," he said.

"Great," she said, patting his knee.

"You gave that knife to me for my birthday. Have you forgotten?"

"I know."

"Christ, you're a hard nut." That was it. *She was a hard nut in an iron glove.* He reached into his back pocket for his notebook.

"Me? You're the one who gave the knife away."

"Mowz FitHenry? Mowz FitHenry?" The operator yelled from behind the counter. "Number one."

"Here it is." Mouse took a deep breath before returning to the cubicle. "Hello?"

"Solly, get off the phone! It's my sister in Nairobi!"

"Hello? Mimi? I can hardly hear you. It's Mouse."

"Mouse! It's Mimi!"

"I'm in Kisangani."

"Kissing who?" said Mimi.

"What's going on?" said Mouse. "I can hardly hear –"

"It's Mom!" yelled Mimi. "She has a, there's been an accident. They're doing surgery this morning, drilling some hole in her head."

"Oh God. Is she, will she be all right? We're in the middle of this film on tribal marriage customs, and I –"

"You are? You must be thrilled. I remember how I felt –"

" – it's really hard for me to come home now. How serious is it?"

"It's a hematoma thing she's got. They're drilling a hole in her head. You got to come home, Mouse. It's bad."

3.

SOLLY HAD A MEETING AT COLUMBIA AT FIVE, SO MIMI snuck out early, hoping to get over to the hospital before traffic started. Alyssia said she'd cover the phones. If Solly called in for messages she'd say Mimi was in the bathroom. If he called in twice, she'd say Mimi had cramps. This always worked. Men like Solly never knew what to say when confronted with a gynecological excuse.

Anymore, there was traffic from early morning until late at night. Morning rush hour began at six and went until ten, when Early Lunch rush hour took over. Evening rush hour began at three, half an hour after Late Lunch rush hour ended. This went both for freeways and for popular side streets. The diamond lane, the car pool lane on the freeway, didn't help. Single drivers whizzed up the diamond lane all the time and never got caught.

Normally Mimi didn't mind the traffic. It gave her a chance to listen to National Public Radio. It was the only time she paid attention to what was going on in important places in the world to which she had no desire to travel: Israel, Libya, Pakistan.

She bumper-to-bumpered over Laurel Canyon. It was late September, still light outside. The sky was red at the bottom, yellow at the top. Sad sooty twilight. A sticky breeze blew in from Santa Monica. On the radio was a story about a couple who recently got married. The groom was in a minor plane crash on his way to his wedding in Florida. When he finally arrived he found out the wedding had to be postponed; the church had been wiped out by a recent hurricane. What were the odds of this happening? What were the odds of a father dying at the bottom of an on-ramp, run over by a two-ton converter gear, a mother permanently brain damaged from getting bonked on the head with a ceiling fan? Big, those were the odds. And how come it never worked the other way around? How come you didn't win the lotto in the morning, meet the man of your dreams that night?

Mimi was anxious to get to the hospital, anxious to see Shirl. Anxious to get it over with. She wished Mouse was home. Mouse would arrive just in time to help out with the boxes of candy, toss out the flowers sent to the hospital.

Dr. Klingston, the neurologist, said Shirl should be out of surgery by seven o'clock. He said it was a standard procedure. As if getting a hole drilled in your head could ever be standard procedure. She idly wondered if she couldn't accidentally drive off the edge of the narrow canyon road, nothing fatal. Just something where she'd be fed by tubes for a couple of weeks, lose a little weight. Then Shirl would be forced to recover and come to visit her.

Mimi turned off the AC and rolled down the window. She had read that air conditioning uses up gas. She ticked off her monthly expenses, a habit she had when she was driving, the awake equivalent of counting sheep. Rent, Hair Care, Gas, Food. Hair Care included cut, color, and perm. Rent she shared with a roommate. Food she tried not to waste money on. There was no way to get around Gas. Outside it smelled of eucalyptus and exhaust fumes and going back to school. Except there was no school to go back to. Except How to Write a Blockbuster at Valley College, but that didn't really count.

Crawling through Laurel Canyon at this time of day reminded Mimi of the time Shirl took her and Mouse to see the Beatles at the Hollywood Bowl. Shirl hated to drive. She had never driven on a freeway in her life. She never drove faster than thirty-five miles an hour. She never parallel parked. If the choice was between parallel parking and not going to the grocery store, the dry cleaners, the craft shop, she gave up and went home. But she had driven Mimi and Mouse to see the Beatles. Over the hill, she drove them, through the Cahuenga pass. In traffic. In the dark. That was the kind of sacrifice Mimi hoped to be able to one day make for her daughters. *If* she had daughters, *if* she had children. Not that she was interested in getting married. Although she wouldn't mind having a boyfriend who wasn't. Married, that is.

It had been nineteen sixty-eight or –nine. Along with pierced ears, Shirley thought the Beatles were barbaric, except "Norwegian Wood," and any other song that could be successfully translated into Muzak. She got dressed up in a black and white op-art dress and dangling red plastic earrings she'd found at Pic 'n Save. She had her hair frosted.

It was close, the Hollywood Bowl, just over the hill, but it seemed like such a trek to them, then. The Cahuenga Pass, Laurel Canyon: it was all wilderness in nineteen sixty-eight or –nine. There were no streetlights. In the summer there were scorpions and coyotes. People who were hippies before there were hippies lived there. They lived in shacks, with steep twisty narrow driveways. Now you couldn't touch a place there for less than a million.

Mouse and Mimi were thirteen and fourteen then. Shirl justified spoiling them with this because they had no father. It was a cold night, a freezing night. Their seats were in the next-to-the-last row, All they could make out onstage were four bouncing, clothespin-thin figures with hair. All they could hear were other girls their own age shrieking and crying. They didn't care. They shrieked and cried, too. It kept them warm. Shirley sat in her op-art dress with her hands clamped around her prickly elbows. Shirley had very dry skin. "You'll remember this one day and thank me," she promised, her teeth chattering between light-pink lips. When Paul McCartney sang what they thought was "Yesterday," even she had cried.

Mimi rested her forearms on the steering wheel and sighed. It was happening already. She knew how it went from when Fitzy died. Everything and anything remotely related to Shirl would now remind her of how it was before the Accident. She would be unable to look at a jar of Cheez Whiz, Shirl's favorite snack, without being racked with sadness. She would be unable to drive through Laurel Canyon or any of the passes. They would all remind her of Shirl and the Beatles.

SITTING IN A hospital waiting room waiting for word of someone you love, someone whose head was just drilled into, someone who's been beaned with a ceiling fan.

It was seven-fifteen.

Mimi sat in a loveseat, her chin hovering inches above her knees. The waiting room was done in sea blues and lavender. Two loveseats and a square glass coffee table, *National Geographics* like thin fallen dominoes. Fiber wall-hangings and a framed poster of a tan, non-brain damaged couple strolling on a luscious beach. It was a nice waiting room. It reminded Mimi of the inside of an airplane.

At seven-thirty she hauled herself out of the loveseat and approached the nurse at the desk. The nurse had thick wrists and a crooked part, a wide white river bisecting the brown crown of her big head. The nurse would not look up. She was making out wedding shower invitations in a tight, hostile hand. Mimi asked the crooked part when she could see her mother.

"Mrs. FitzHenry is out of surgery and resting comfortably. Dr. Klingston will be with you when he can."

"When will she be able to go home, do you know?" Mimi asked. She wanted to get the nurse to look up, so she could see if her eyes were filled with the special type of pity reserved for the relatives of the terminally ill, as opposed to just the temporarily hospitalized.

"Dr. Klingston will discuss that with you," she said.

Mimi sank back into the loveseat.

If she's out of surgery and resting comfortably, what's the surgeon doing? Trading war stories with the boys by the water cooler? She tried to think what it was they did after surgery on television. Washed up, traded witty dialogue with the female love interest, also the scrub nurse. Unless the relatives of the patient were important to the plot, they were characterized as pitiful but superfluous.

She stared up at the television, bracketed to the ceiling. It was bigger and nicer than the one she had at home. It was turned to a cable station. She imagined they tried to stay away from the news and hospital shows. On the screen just then was a cheap game show that looked as though it was filmed in someone's garage. There were two categories from which the contestants could choose their questions: Women Who Love Younger Men and Antibiotics. The contestants all had shiny faces.

A man came and sat across from Mimi on the edge of the other loveseat. Out of her peripheral vision he looked okay. He looked good. A little too beach boy for her taste, but you never knew. You had to give people a chance. His hairline was only slightly receding. He wore a striped polo shirt, and had a bright-blue coil of what looked like rock-climbing rope slung over his knee. The important thing was that he looked over twenty-five, straight, and *not* in the film business. She crunched up her stiff blond curls.

They both watched the game show.

"Streptomycin," he said.

Mimi wondered what his tragedy was. Maybe his wife fell off the side of a mountain.

"Barbra Streisand," said Mimi.

Their eyes met across the *U.S. News & World Report*s.

"Are you Mimi FitzHenry?" he asked.

No, better if he's divorced.

"How do you know?" she asked lightly. She glanced over at the nurse with the crooked part, only half visible from behind the counter. She could hear the pen scratching fiercely. Maybe he'd spotted her and asked the nurse her name.

"What do you do?" he asked.

She liked a man who was direct. "Have you heard of Talent and Artists? I work with Solly Stein. We represent directors and writers. What do you do?" she asked, trying to make it sound provocative.

"I'm Dr. Klingston."

"Oh, hi! Hello!" Her face boiled with embarrassment. "I'm Mimi, Shirl's daughter. How, how – " She had only talked to him on the telephone. She slammed her knees together, arched her back, and struggled up from the loveseat. She shook his hand.

" – there was a fracture, as we suspected. Not much we can do for that. Got her on Dilantin, a seizure preventive. There was also a small epidural clot, which we evacuated. As far as the subdural goes, we'll have to wait. They generally don't manifest themselves for a month or so after the trauma."

"She's not, uh, dying?"

"She'll be fine. Though there might be some memory loss, perhaps a slight personality change."

"Personality change? We're not talking *Sybil* here are we?"

The electronic doors swept open, admitting a man in suede shorts, plaid shirt, and hiking boots. He wore a red and white bandanna around his neck and a few shiny carabiners dangling from a belt loop. It was an Outfit. He bounded up to Dr. Klingston. "Hiya, Gary. Ready to bag some peaks?"

"Be with you in a minute, Todd."

"Super. Gals are in the car." Todd stared up at the television.

"How changed will she be?" Mimi noticed that Dr. Klingston's mustache disguised the fact he had no lips. She didn't trust a man with no lips. He glanced up at the television set. There were two new categories: Great Dictators and Reptiles. She wished they could talk in private. "Will she be able to do her découpage? Where you get a picture and, well, she likes to burn the edges, but you don't have to, and then – "

"Giant salamander," said Todd.

"Sure, sure. There may be some giddiness, headaches. We'll have to keep an eye out. Some big exec from one of the movie studios was in here six months ago. Brain tumor size of a tangerine. Took half of his frontal lobe, he was doing a movie a month later."

"That Mack Stoner?" asked Todd. "Got a deal with Mack Stoner is why I ask."

MIMI FOUND SHIRL with a turban of snowy gauze wrapped tightly around her skull, eavesdropping on her neighbor. Her cheek was covered with a square of gauze. After the fan had struck her head it glanced off the side of the table, sending her just poured cup of scalding coffee into the air, splashing her cheek as she fell off her chair and onto her wrist. Her cheek was burned, her wrist broken.

She was sitting up, her head cocked toward the plastic curtain drawn between the beds. Shirl was a famous eavesdropper. In restaurants, ladies' rooms, and beauty salons, and now, Mimi saw with relief, hospital rooms. The cheap curtain provided the illusion of privacy. The people on the other side were foreign. They were talking loudly about suppositories.

Mimi had not expected her mother to be sitting up. She thought there'd be tubes, high-tech monitors, sunken cheeks, and black eyes. Instead here was her mother as she might appear sitting at the kitchen table, wearing a white version of the orange turban she normally wore the day before her weekly hair appointment. The orange turban had coins on it. Even Shirl had a sense of how silly it was. She wore it only inside the house.

"Mom!" said Mimi. "God, you look really terrific. I just saw the doctor –"

Shirl's faded brown eyes slid toward the curtain. "The wife of the caviar czar of the Valley," she whispered. "He, the husband, imports for all the stars. He had a polyp in his nose."

"Oh right. We have a bunch of clients who buy from him."

"I forget you're always mingling with the stars," Shirl said. She rolled her eyes and shrugged her shoulders, which caused her to wince.

"How are you feeling?"

"Don't ask me that. You don't ask a girl who's just had brain surgery that. Sore. My wrist hurts more than my head. It was divine intervention. I was about to go off program, don't you know? I'd ordered those white chocolate dumplings in strawberry soup."

"What program?"

"Weight Watchers." She tugged at the roll around her waist through the blanket. "I hate it."

"You look all right. You look like you never had surgery," said Mimi.

"I'm dying," said Shirl.

"You are not dying. He said you're doing terrific."

"He's good looking, the surgeon."

"He was sort of coming on to me. I mean, here I was trying to find out how you were and he was giving me the eye."

"When Mimi sets her cap for a fella, look out," said Shirl.

"Please be quiet!" came a foreign voice from the other side of the shower curtain. "Sick peoples here."

Shirl patted the side of her head gently. "It itches like hell. I've got the nubs already. At least this solves what to do with my hair. You know I'm against coloring it, even though on you girls it looks fine." Even though Mouse had been gone for almost sixteen years, Shirley still said, "you girls." "That's a nice blond on you."

"Thanks."

The thought crossed Mimi's mind that maybe her mother was dying. That the lipless, rock-climbing Dr. Klingston was lying, or humoring her. Now that she'd adjusted to the hospital bed and turban, Mimi saw that her mother didn't look exactly herself. She was bloated, her olive skin flushed. There were webs of broken capillaries on her nose, and crêpey pouches under her eyes, which Mimi had never noticed before. The whites of her eyes were too glittery. Opalescent. Drugs, thought Mimi. Morphine or something.

It bothered Mimi that Shirl had been so unlucky. Accidents happened to people who attracted them. Hadn't Fitzy been depressed for months before he died? Hadn't business been down? Shirl had thought so. Shirl had confided to her little girls that their father was a magnet for misfortune. She had proof. Appliances that broke. Get-rich-quick schemes that only got them poorer quicker. An accident waiting to happen, that was Fitzy. Hapless and melancholy, his middle names. She should have known better than to marry a cleft-chinned black Irishman, Shirl always said. She laughed when she said it, but it was true.

Shirl was the opposite. She said everything she thought and thought everything she believed in was beyond reproach. She was untroubled and stalwart as a Maine woodsman, a true exotic to her friends, all beautiful, ambivalent Southern Californian matrons.

People set their clocks by Shirley FitzHenry. She lived in the same bungalow on Cantaloupe Avenue in Sherman Oaks for thirty-eight years. She had been watching the soap opera *As the World Turns* for twenty. Every year since the Korean War Shirl had her New Year's Day party and sent out Groundhog Day cards. Every year she bought illegal fireworks in Tijuana for the Fourth of July, and put away all her white clothes the day after Labor Day. Year in, year out, she got smashed at her own dinner parties and waltzed with herself around the swimming pool, singing either "Yellow Bird" or "*Ave Maria.*"

Mimi hated the idea that the universe was perhaps paying her back for her incaution. That her mother should have been peering over her shoulder all this time instead of blithely telling off the timid Jehovah's Witnesses who came to the door and eating butter instead of margarine.

Shirl lay back on the pillows and closed her eyes. Mimi stared at her crinkled bluish eyelids. She was afraid of the silence. Hematomas formed themselves in silence, never when you were yukking it up.

"I talked to Mouse," she said.

"My little world traveler. Does she still have that disease? You know, that fungus that makes her fingernails turn green?"

"She's coming home," said Mimi. "I thought she'd want to see –"

"She's coming home? Not because of *me*."

"What do you think? Of course because of you. There she is running all around bum-fuck Egypt Africa while you're here – "

"Shhh, they may be Egyptian over there," she said without opening her eyes. She rolled her head toward the curtain.

"I thought you said it was the wife of the caviar king."

"Czar, caviar czar."

"I thought you'd want to see her. It was pretty easy to track her down. You know, I call long distance all over the world for Solly. She's in Zah-ear. She got married."

Shirley's eyes flew open. She sat straight up and said loudly, "Married? Mouse married?"

"Or maybe she's getting married. The connection wasn't too good."

Shirl stared. "My baby. I thought all this time she was into that Women's Lib."

"She'll probably want a big wedding. There's really no other way to do it. I mean, my wedding could have gone bigger, but then I got married in the days when people didn't really get married. I was sort of a trailblazer. You know me. If I was doing it today I'd have a sit-down, four hundred guests, the whole bit. I'd have more bridesmaids."

"Your wedding was lovely."

They never talked about the divorce.

MOUSE AND HER husband, boyfriend, fiancé, whatever, were flying in the same night as Bibliothèques, the third Tuesday of the month. Mimi debated. Should she cancel or not?

Bibliothèques was Mimi's book group. Someone had suggested the name at their first meeting and it stuck. They thought it meant book-lover, then one of the members assistant-edited on a film shot in France and found out it meant *library*. They had been thinking of biblio*philes*. There were ten of them, all film people, aspiring actresses, aspiring directors, and like that. Mimi was proud to be the only hyphenate, an actress-writer.

They read one difficult book a month, then met to discuss it. It had to be a book they wouldn't read on their own. This was not a problem, since most of them only read and wrote coverage. Coverage was a one-page synopsis of a screenplay. This month was Mimi's pick, *Lust for Life*. The meeting was held at the duplex she shared with Carole, which was why she was hesitant to cancel. The duplex was in West Hollywood, a great place for the price. Two big bedrooms, wood floors, high ceilings, no glitter in the stucco. The only drawback was the noise. All night, every night, disco music thumped and brayed up in the gay bars on Santa Monica Boulevard, a few blocks away. There was also the Special Police Task Force to Prevent Mimi FitzHenry From Ever Having a Good Night's Sleep. At three o'clock every morning the police helicopter patrolled the alley behind the apartment. The *whopp-whopp-whopp* of the blades and the jillion-watt searchlight sweeping through her bedroom sent her hurtling from a deep sleep into an adrenaline overdose in a matter of seconds. No wonder she was a high-strung, stressed-out basket case.

She knew it was selfish to put her book group above the arrival of Mouse, but she did have to think of herself sometimes. Who'd kept an eye on Shirl all these years while Mouse had been living it up in Nairobi? Who called all over Zah-ear? It wasn't like Mouse went out of her way for the family. Mouse had gone – supposedly for a semester – to Tunisia, on a study-abroad program through UCLA, then never came home. Who shipped her stuff over to her? Who tried to explain it to Shirl, who was still a mess nine years after Fitzy's death and couldn't understand why her baby, her Mouse, had left them?

Not that Mimi had the foggiest idea. *Africa?* Come on. In her book that was like suicide without the commitment. Why not just the Peace Corps? Two years, good stories, great pictures. Mouse could have gotten on in one of those –ibia countries, teaching the natives how to use video cameras. But no, she had to live there.

Mimi asked her boyfriend, Ralph, what he thought. Did he think she should she cancel and pick up Mouse and her fiancé at the airport?

Ralph told her she was a patsy. He said that people were too enslaved to their families. He asked her why she should rearrange her entire life around a sister she hadn't received a genuine in-an-envelope-letter – postcards didn't count – from in sixteen years. A sister who wouldn't come to her wedding, even after she'd offered to pay her airfare. Ralph said, hypothetically, if you put one hundred strangers in a room, the six people you'd like the least would all turn out to be members of your own family.

What finally clinched it was that Mimi felt more guilty about *Lust for Life*. It had been her pick, and had turned out to be seven-hundred-something pages long.

Also, she had already cleaned the apartment.

Ralph arrived first, already whipped up and mad at the world. When he was in that state, which he was quite often, he looked like an angry baby. He had a downy bald head fringed with wispy oatmeal-colored hair, creamy skin, a simple oval face, and a mashed nose. He had full cheeks that got very flushed when he drank and not much of a chin. Mimi liked him because he made her laugh and knew the power of an unexpected flower arrangement delivered to her office in the middle of the afternoon.

He pushed past her, dumped his briefcase in the green butterfly chair by the door, hauled out a roll of photocopies of an article in *Vanity Fair* called "They're New, They're Hot, They're Young!" about new film directors under twenty-five. Ralph obsessively searched for bad news to confirm his worst thoughts. Then he photocopied whatever he'd found and passed it out to prove how crazy the business was, as though anyone had any doubt.

"These clowns were just getting their drivers' licenses when Lennon was shot. How can they direct anything? What do they know? Would you please explain it to me. I can understand how you'd keep giving movies to jerks who'd already made you some money, but what's the appeal of *these* guys?"

"It's another mystery of the universe," said Mimi, punching his shoulder. He was wearing her favorite shirt, the pink and green Hawaiian rayon. It had that campfire smell of brushfires burning in the hills, the sad end-of-summer smell.

Coming up the steps behind him was his almost ex-wife, Elaine. Her expensive leather-soled shoes sounded like sandpaper on the plaster stairs. Elaine hardly ever came to Bibliothéques because she was always out of town on business, selling car FAX machines to corporate raiders. She also always seemed to have read whatever book they'd picked for the month. She had her master's degree in Comparative Literature. She was a snob. "You're so lucky," she'd say, "reading *Death on the Installment Plan* for the first time."

Even though Ralph and Elaine were officially separated, Mimi and Ralph kept a lid on it when Elaine was around. It was too weird and cozy, otherwise, too sort of Appalachian. Mimi could never bring herself to put an arm around Ralph or steal a kiss with his not-yet-ex looking on. She wasn't sure Elaine even knew about them.

"I thought she was at a sales conf–" Mimi whispered to Ralph.

"–she's back earl–"

"–Elaine! Hiya!" said Mimi.

"What's he yammering about now?" Elaine appeared at the

door. She had long, bowed legs, waist-length hair the color and texture of dried twigs. "Have you ever heard anyone complain like this? I hope he isn't like this in class." Ralph was the instructor of How to Write a Blockbuster at Valley College, the class through which they had met.

"That's a great skirt," said Mimi. "I tried on a skirt like that at the Gap but it was too big. I mean the waist was too big. I'm into minis, but not, like thigh-high. It was one thing when we were sixteen. Even though I'm thinner than I was then. Some people have knees only God should see. Not that I'm one. Not that I believe in God. I mean, I believe in an *energy* – "

" – hi Elaine," said Carole, appearing from the hallway. Behind her, Sniffy Voyeur, Mimi's dog, swayed into the room. He was a big black and blond mutt, a remnant from her marriage. He trotted up to Elaine and stuck his long nose into her crotch.

"This dog is so needy," said Elaine, batting Sniffy away.

"Just don't tell me these guys are getting their chance because it's the appeal of the unknown," said Ralph. "I'm unknown. I'm as fucking unknown as you can get."

Ralph was desperate. Desperation clung to his clothes like the smell of the brushfires. It hung in his blue-gray eyes. He had been trying to get the same movie, *Girls on Gaza*, a musical comedy about the Palestinian situation, off the ground for over twelve years.

He had done all the right things, to no avail. He went to the right parties. Made the right contacts. Wrote treatments, screenplays, teleplays. Studied classic films. Read criticism, read theory: Eisenstein and Kuleshov. Made two short films, which he funded by letting his car insurance lapse. Entered them in festivals. Applied for grants. Snuck into workshops conducted by famous directors, by infamous studio executives and agents. Re-snuck into the same workshops the following year to meet the new famous directors conducting it, the new infamous studio executives and agents. He approached the famous and the infamous, thrust *Girls on Gaza* at them, tolerating their glazed expressions, their hardly hidden sneers. *Oh God, not another screenplay!*

But Ralph persevered. Invited them for coffee. Made thin jokes about picking their brains. Picked their brains. They told him Work Hard, Hard Work. They reminded him that Sylvester Stallone wrote fifteen scripts before he came up with Rocky.

Ralph said, "I've written sixteen."

Mimi felt sorry for him. Sure, she was a drudge by day, too, but at least she'd done that thing with Bob Hope. She'd done something. In addition, she rationalized, while she was Solly's secretary, she was not his slave.

Ralph had been with the same producer, Keddy Webb, for eight years. During that time Keddy had landed two Academy Awards, and the only change in Ralph's life was the new word-processing program Keddy bought to help Ralph catalogue his wine collection. Keddy made Ralph pick up his dry cleaning and drive an hour across town during the lunchtime rush hour in the rain to pick up sushi from Keddy's favorite restaurant. Keddy wouldn't even let Ralph do coverage. *Anyone* could do coverage. Some of Solly's producer clients had beautiful, hot-eyed Iranian assistants they'd hired because they liked the accent answering the telephone. These women, if they could read, read only Farsi, and *they* did coverage.

Mimi begged Ralph to quit, but he stayed on because Keddy held out the same old limp carrot that was dangling in front of the bent-out-of-shape nose of every drudge in town: Keddy promised to get Ralph a Deal.

And maybe someday he will, thought Mimi, begging Ralph to chill out and have a beer. Who knew? Mouse was getting married. Shirl got bopped on the head with a ceiling fan and *lived*. Something good might as well happen to Ralph.

After everyone arrived and sat down, Mimi brought out a tray of *haute* cheese and crackers. The cheese, which was runny and French, and smelled like a high school gym after a boys' basketball game, was expensive for Mimi at $14.95 a pound. She had spent far more than she should have, considering her finances.

Carole got the drinks, flavored seltzer water and imported beers. The evening was smog-sticky and warm. It was October and there was no sign of anything resembling fall. Leaves dropped miserably off the trees like shriveled scabs. The front page of the *Los Angeles Times* kept running pictures of grandmothers in shorts fanning themselves in grocery store checkout lines with Halloween cards they were buying for their grandchildren who lived in less relentless climates.

Outside, a burst of Santa Ana wind blew the fronds of a palm tree into a telephone wire, sending off hot blue sparks and a sizzling *zitz*.

John Sather sat cross-legged on the floor, reading Ralph's photocopy. To Mimi, he looked like the quintessential Greenwich Villager. He wore his straight brown hair combed straight back, kept his jaw in five o'clock shadow. He chain-smoked and listened to jazz. No one else Mimi knew listened to anything other than what they played in aerobics or on the car radio.

"Not more about People in Film," Sather said, folding the article into a paper airplane.

"Would you please explain it to me?" said Ralph.

"As opposed to Film People," said Darryl D'Ambrosia. Darryl was built like a wrestler, all bulging veins and muscles and fierce black hair. Testosterone gone mad.

"Ho ho," said Sather. "People in Film and Film People, completely different animals."

"People in Film actually *make* movies. They actually *touch* celluloid –" said Darryl.

" – projectionists don't count – " said Sather.

"People in Film, on their income tax forms? No more than two words to describe what they do. Film Director. Screenwriter. Film Editor," said Darryl.

"But Film People always have a lengthy explanation. 'I'm a waiter and do some reading for Fox on the side, but I'm working on this development deal for a two-hour miniiseries –'" said Sather.

"– TV doesn't count, this is only features – "

"– right, right – "

"You know you're a Film Person if you avoid someone at a party who's going to ask you what you do."

"You see them coming and you run the other way."

"Film People live in a state of perpetual humiliation. People in Film live in a state of perpetual self-congratulation."

"Film People have been reduced – "

"– much to their chagrin – "

"– *much* to their chagrin, to making a career of trying to be a Person in Film!"

"People in Film send their children to Ivy League schools but can be reached at home in the middle of the afternoon," said Ralph. "Film People can also be reached at home in the middle of the afternoon, but it's because they're unemployed."

"By jove, I think he's got it," said Sather.

"You guys," said Mimi, irritated.

She hated it when Sather and Darryl talked in code, like a clique of thirteen-year-old girls. She thought it was rude for them to leave everyone else out. Darryl and Sather and Ralph all shared a house in the Hollywood Hills. Ralph was the only one who had ever been married. They had a pool table in their living room instead of furniture. In the family room they had seventeen thousand dollars' worth of stereo and video equipment and two straight-backed chairs with plastic upholstery, the style popular in the lobby of the Salvation Army. One of them did the cooking, one vacuumed, one scrubbed the bathrooms. Mimi and Carole were forever trying to set Darryl and Sather up, but the women were never thin enough, never mysterious enough, never successful enough, or else too thin, too mysterious, and too successful.

"But it gets tricky," said Sather, "it gets tricky. Are you a

Person in Film if you're below-the-line talent but don't have any higher aspirations?"

"Take Lisa," said Ralph.

"Please don't," said Lisa. She twisted open the top of her beer with the bottom of her T-shirt. Lisa was a sound editor and Lithium addict. She had shoulder-length red hair and had made pleated linen shorts and French filterless cigarettes her trademark.

"Lisa is a Person in Film not only because she actually touches celluloid. She also doesn't aspire to anything great. Not that cutting sound is not great, don't get me wrong, Lisa." Ralph smiled, revealing a gleaming set of expensive teeth. Like so many others in the business, he had made it a point to have the right teeth.

"How many Hollywood schmucks does it take to screw in a light bulb, Ralph?" said Lisa.

"We've pissed her off," said Ralph.

"No," said Lisa, leaning forward on the wicker ottoman, pointing her bottle at Ralph. "*You* piss me off."

"I'll get back to you," said Sather. "That's the punch line, 'I'll get back to you.' Did you hear about the Polish actress who fucked a screenwriter to get ahead?"

"That's an old one," said Marty Phillips. Marty had heard every movie joke in town. He washed hair at a famous Beverly Hills salon. On the side, he had a tidy business selling locks of the stars' hair he swept up off the floor. He sold a baggie full of Cher's hair for $400. His screenplays always had hair images in them.

"Any chance we can have one meeting where we don't discuss the business?" asked Carole.

"Yeah, like maybe we'll even get around to talking about the *book*," said Lisa, pulling her ragged copy of *Lust for Life* out of her shoulder bag.

"PMSed-out tonight?" said Sather. He and Lisa had once been an item.

"I'm about ready to slit my throat, all right? I cut one more car wreck and I don't know what."

People pitied Lisa but envied her paycheck. She made more money sound-editing than any three people Mimi knew put together. But sound editors were the least respected people in town. It was unglamorous, unsexy, boring brute labor. Lisa had once thought of directing or writing or even editing picture. But she hadn't known what she'd wanted, really, so when she got offered a sound-cutting job she took it. She hated it. But sound-cutting was like drug dealing. You did it a few times because you needed a job and you got paid a fortune. You started getting used to the money and couldn't bring yourself to quit. There were always sound-cutting jobs around because anyone who had the discipline to take less money to do something else, did. Lisa bought a new car every other year, and had an apartment in Brentwood. She worked sixteen to eighteen hours a day syncing up footsteps, *thwok*ing tennis balls, high school boys playing the edge of their desks with number 2 pencils, rat-a-tat-a-tat-a-tat-a-tat-a-tat-a-tat. Every *rat*, every *tat* had to be there, and had to be in sync. Then, in the mix, the producer covered all of them with a song from the soundtrack album. It would have been a wonder if she wasn't addicted to Lithium.

Mimi admired Lisa anyway. She was one of those women who felt no compulsion to be nice. Mimi felt that was her main problem: she was too nice.

"Film People go from being young and idealistic to old and jaded with no appreciable change in their résumé or level of experience," said Ralph. He liked this game.

"Why don't you just get out of film then, Ralph," shot Lisa. "Jesus Christ."

"I was just kidding," said Ralph.

"The film industry is relieved," said Darryl.

"Fuck you," said Ralph.

"You guys!" said Mimi. Everyone was in a bad mood.

No one had really read the book. It was too sweltering all

week. Luke, who was a runner at Paramount, said no one was even reading coverage, it was so hot. Also, there was the World Series, even though the Dodgers weren't in it. And the new fall releases were out, so everyone was going to screenings. Mimi always read the book, heat wave or not. It was a point of pride with her. She sighed, rustled her blond bangs with her fingers.

"You know what's different about us and van Gogh?" said Ralph. "At least he could practice his craft. At least he could paint. He had that kernel of satisfaction. We can't even do that. I'm a producer but I've never produced, and I can't practice producing unless someone gives me a million dollars."

Everyone agreed.

"We're the new underclass," said Luke. "Perpetual aspirants. Middle-class hopefuls who never make it, yet refuse to give up."

Mimi was suddenly worried. What if Mouse walked in the door and everyone was slouching around with long faces complaining about how they were nobodies? They were supposed to be having a literary discussion. She had made such a deal of telegraming Mouse. *Can't be at airport. Book group. Important meeting. Unable to cancel.* She made it out to be one step below a summit meeting between the superpowers.

"We're not middle class," she said. "We're *artists*."

"Heh-heh-heh." Luke's laugh was the vocal equivalent of a sneer.

She would have done better picking up Mouse at the airport.

4.

IT WAS FIVE HOURS FROM NAIROBI TO CAIRO; FOUR and a half from Cairo to Paris; eight from Paris to New York; five more after that to L.A.

Nairobi to Cairo was a Boeing 737. A bus with wings. A flying, hollowed-out metal hot dog. Mouse and Tony were packed together, rubbing thighs. It was irritating, not erotic. Mouse loathed jet liners. She trusted only bush pilots in prop planes, grizzled, pidgin English-speaking men who could negotiate mountains half-drunk in the dark. Ten minutes after takeoff she was already homesick for every last one of them.

She spent the flight with her nose plastered against the dingy oval window, keeping the plane in the air. If she looked away for too long a wing might snap off, an engine plunge into the Nile.

This was what happened when you looked away. She had looked away. She had moved away. She never wrote or called.

Mouse and Tony had flown together only twice before. He was also a nervous flier. Mouse couldn't help wondering why he always resisted the short painless flights around East Africa in conjunction with their films – he would drive, he would take the train, he would argue that the interview, the shot, the location wasn't really necessary – but was delighted at the prospect of flying five hours to Cairo, four and a half to Paris, eight to New York, and five to Los Angeles.

During the first few stunned hours after Mimi's phone call,

sweating over mugs of warm beer in a crowded bar in Kisangani, Mouse begged Tony to stay in Nairobi. She would go home, see how things were. He would continue to work on *Marriage Under Mobutu*. She would call for him, or she would come back.

Tony was a talker, an aisle-sitting, martini-drinking talker. His way of coping was to pretend he wasn't on a plane at all. Mouse found this to be somewhat cowardly. She was in favor of execution without a blindfold. She was a believer in staring at highway wrecks, revolting pictures in medical books, your own arm as blood is being extracted for a sample.

Tony chattered away about anything. About the evils of the Trilateral Commission. About who was the most talented Beatle. About the ten movies he would take with him if he was stuck in a submarine for a year. *Klute*, he said to the back of Mouse's head, as she stared out the window at the yellow-washed sky, *Sunday Bloody Sunday*.

This is just one more way in which we are incompatible, Mouse thought. She tried to think of the other ways but couldn't. Her thinking was fuzzy. She blamed it on the altitude. On dinner, which was a thin piece of beige meat, a triangle of sweaty cheese, two stale rolls which she planned on using as floats, one under each arm, in the much-touted unlikely event of a water landing.

Cairo to Paris. A DC-something-or-other, obscenely huge. Mouse and Tony wedged together in the middle section. Mouse thought that without access to a window it was quite possible that she would die, not in a crash, but of not having a window. Tony was able to sleep sitting up, and did. Mouse couldn't, and didn't even try.

The prospect of going home roused The Pink Fiend, who lived inside Mouse and whose sole function was to torment her. In Mouse's mind she sat somewhere just under her sternum, her chubby white hands folded, swinging her feet. She was no modern little girl. She had long beribboned sausage curls, ankle socks trimmed with stiff lace, petticoats. She was impervious to both criticism and psychotherapy, as hardy as a cockroach. Mouse was not sure whether The Pink Fiend was in fact her girlhood self or just a brutish enforcer of feminine values that lurked in the gene pool, like the evil microorganisms living in African rivers, and was passed on, quite invisibly, from mother to daughter.

The Pink Fiend made herself invisible for long periods of time, when Mouse was filled with her usual confidence and sense of purpose. Like the good girl she was, The Pink Fiend sat quietly and listened, fingering her silky, beribboned curls. Mouse would forget she was there – the first mistake – or she would think finally, *finally* she was rid of her. Then Mouse blessed her years in Africa for toughening her up. She imagined that somehow The Pink Fiend had been baked out by the blistering heat, jounced out during a horrendous ride over a potholed road in a shock absorber-less Land Rover, driven out in the face of Mouse's not unremarkable achievements: eight films in eight years; a credit card based on her earnings as a documentary film producer.

But The Pink Fiend never left her chair, there under Mouse's sternum. She swung her feet. And waited.

She waited for the recurrence of self-doubt, which always seemed to have something to do with one of their docs. Was the idea workable? Was it fundable? Was it of remote interest to anyone anywhere?

The last screening Mouse and Tony had at the British Consulate before leaving Nairobi for Los Angeles drew eleven people; a few yawning aides from the Consulate, the rest self-deluding students from the University of Nairobi, interested in knowing how they too could make documentaries. Amidst the humiliating smatter of applause, The Pink Fiend cleared her throat. Mouse, depressed at the familiar sound, prepared for the onslaught. What did you honestly expect, Mouse? Who in his right mind would pay to see a film on a nun who runs a leper colony in Uganda? What normal woman would produce a film on a leper colony? What normal woman would produce a film? No normal woman. No good woman. No good girl. And any woman who is not a good girl gets exactly what she deserves. You know this. All things considered, Mouse, you should he thankful you didn't contract a nice case of leprosy yourself.

The Pink Fiend was naturally delighted by Mimi's phone call, the unhappy news that Shirl FitzHenry, who had been crushed by Mouse's move to Africa, had been bonked on the head with a ceiling fan.

The mother whom Mouse rarely wrote.

The mother who loved Mouse More Than Life Itself.

And what about Mimi? The sister whose wedding Mouse spurned. The sister who loved Mouse At Least As Much As Life Itself.

As Mouse crouched in the telephone cubicle in the post office in Kisangani, bellowing across two continents and one ocean, she felt The Pink Fiend unlace her fat fingers and rub her sweet moist hands together.

Oh boy. Oh boy oh boy.

The Pink Fiend left Mouse alone while she packed and made travel arrangements – *a good woman is a good organizer,* The Pink Fiend admitted; *at least you've got that going for you* – and shipped books, film prints, videotapes ahead to the address Mimi gave her in West Hollywood and threw a hasty party for their few friends and carted their few sticks of furniture to the house Camisha, their housekeeper, shared with her family. Now, however, she had no sympathy.

The plane was filled with caramel-colored men in dusty, ill-made suits. Tony found out, chatting with a Somalian sitting next to him, that many of them were attending Muslim World Day in Paris. The Somalian didn't eat the plastic food distributed by the flight attendant but tucked it into his carry-on bag.

Mouse tried to read but found it as impossible as sleep. Instead, she took a datebook from her purse and counted time. In forty-eight hours she would be in Los Angeles. In a month, provided her mother had recuperated, she'd be back in Nairobi, spotting the sound track for *Marriage Under Mobutu*. With luck, and a few twenty-hour days, they'd be able to finish it and have the print in Kinshasa within two weeks. She closed the date-book and tucked it back in her shoulder bag. The counting used up five minutes.

She glanced over at Tony, who was reading a thick book with a garish cover, given him by his buddy Vince Parchman, before Vince left for the States the year before. Tony had been so busy writing his screenplay that he was just getting around to reading it now. He laughed out loud and kept saying, "I say, you *must* read this. It's a stitch."

The Somalian, thinking Tony was speaking to him, said, "I shall."

For dessert, there was some viscous taupe-colored glop sandwiched between two slabs of sugar-coated cardboard. Apparently it was pear cobbler.

Tony cut it into fours with the side of his plastic fork and slurped it down without looking away from his book. "Try some, poppet, this isn't quite as dreadful as it looks."

Mouse suspected that Tony was utterly free of demons and fiends. She was irritated, then jealous.

There was a night spent somewhere. Either Paris or New York. Anyway, it was by the airport. Mouse could not get over so many English speakers in one place. So many pasty faces. It was disconcerting, like picking up a rock and discovering a colony of albino insects.

The room was overheated, Mouse couldn't sleep. The sheets were slippery and untucked themselves every time she rolled over. Tony fell asleep while she was still in the bathroom inspecting a row of pimples along her jawline. She hadn't had pimples in ten years. She wondered if Mimi had pimples.

Their room was across from the housekeeper's supply closet. The housekeepers began work very early, much earlier than the rooms were ready to clean. They sat on a bench outside the closet and talked about their lives, which sounded bleak, but they laughed more than anyone Mouse had ever heard. They were Haitian or Jamaican and had loud, lilting voices. Mouse recorded their conversation, slipping the microphone of her portable tape recorder just under the door. She squatted next to the recorder, her head on her arms, tired, dehydrated, disoriented.

New York to Los Angeles. A Stretch Overwater 727. It bothered her that they were using this plane but not flying over any water. Everyone on board was white. Next to them, Tony looked ruddy and exotic, handsome with his curly, reddish-blond hair, his outrageous freckles, and big crooked nose. She had managed to snag a few hours of sleep and was glad, this morning, that he was with her. She felt this sudden surge of love because they booked too late to get seats together.

Tony had an aisle seat in row 5, next to a genial, balding set designer.

Mouse had a window seat in row 23, in the smoking section, among a gang of noisy teenage girls: the Manhattan Beach High School Women's Volleyball Team.

Mouse tossed her duffel bag into the overhead compartment, crawled over the knees of an extraordinary-looking fifteen-year-old with nutmeg-colored hair. She said nothing but excuse me.

Back among Angelenos, Mouse was suddenly shy.

Bending to the advice of The Pink Fiend, Mouse had spent her last Kenyan shillings at the most expensive women's store in Nairobi, buying a presentable travel outfit. This was before she received Mimi's telegram. *Can't be at airport. Bok group. Unable to cancl.*

Mouse wore the outfit anyway. White cotton blouse, tweed blazer, brown A-line skirt. Pantyhose. She had not worn a pair of pantyhose since she graduated from high school.

There were twenty or so girl volleyball players. They were returning from a tournament in Syracuse, where they had won second place.

Their shimmering hair and ferocious good health were merely the accoutrements of youth. They chain-smoked, knocked back gin and 7-Ups as fast as the flight attendant could deliver them, crushed into the rest room two at a time for a toot of cocaine. They called each other by their last names, discussed in the same loud voices volleyball, bladder infections, past bad dates.

Mouse felt as though she was a prisoner in an airborne locker room. She tugged self-consciously at her short dark hair, cut by Camisha at the kitchen table. She felt stuffy, stodgy, utterly out of it. She felt like Margaret Thatcher, minus the prestige, money, and power.

The seat belt sign pinged off. She could relax a bit, now that she'd gotten them safely off the ground. She took off her blazer and jammed it between her and the girl with the nutmeg-colored hair. She tried to read her book, a history of the British Documentary. The type was tiny and hard to read through the smoky soup engulfing the rear of the plane.

She pressed her nose against the window. What, she wondered, remembering Mimi's telegram, was a bok group? *Can't be at airport. Bok group. Unable to cancl.* It sounded like something to do with Eastern religion. Whatever it was, it was bound to be the height of fashion. From the time they were small Mimi had doggedly followed trends like a fogbound ship fixated on the beam of some far-off lighthouse.

She's your sister. She loves you so much, The Pink Fiend purred. You are so judgmental.

The two girls behind Mouse began arguing over the best ways to make yourself throw up. One favored mustard and hot water, the other her index finger. Mouse felt like turning around and telling them that all they needed was a pink fiend hounding them day and night.

"Blowin' chow is blowin' chow," said one of them.

"Yeah, but why make yourself sick? Mustard is disgusting."

"All I gotta do is think about you sucking off Zack O'Keefe

and I want to throw up," the girl sitting next to Mouse bellowed back over her headrest.

"Fuck you, Matson."

Mouse cut a glance at the sullen, smoking Matson. She was over six feet tall, with that silky nutmeg-colored hair, tied in a loose lopsided knot on top of her head. No one in Mouse's high school had ever looked like this. Matson's bone structure was the kind that inspired black and white photographers, but her clothes had Mouse baffled. From the waist down she was dressed for scuba diving, from the waist up for yard work. She wore tight black rubber pants that accentuated every curve and cleft on her fully developed body, and a short Manhattan Beach High T-shirt which afforded a view of her rippling brown midriff. Mouse had no idea the female body could ripple there. A number of small, dirty, once brightly colored woven bracelets were tied around her bony forearm. Her nails were bitten down to the quick.

"Fuck *you*," Matson laughed without turning around.

"Pardon?" It was the flight attendant, bending toward them, a dinner tray swaddled in plastic in each hand.

"I meant fuck *her*," Matson said to the attendant, gesturing blandly in the direction of the girl sitting behind her.

Cruelly, the dessert was the same pear glop encased in sugar-coated cardboard. Mouse had a brief image of crates of this cardboard cobbler being lowered from a freighter by crane, then rushed to the airlines of the world. Tears leaped to her eyes. As a thing that existed in the universe she found this pro-foundly depressing. The plane hit an air pocket and dropped a few dozen feet, leaving Mouse's stomach on the ceiling, wedged in between the concealed oxygen masks. She was so tired. She resolved that when she got to Los Angeles, *if* she got to Los Angeles, she would go straight to the hospital to see her mother, skipping Mimi and the bok group.

Matson unwrapped her meal and stuffed the plastic in the pocket on the back of the seat in front of her. She pinched up a bit of salad in her fingers, shoved it on her fork, then steered it into her mouth, wiping her fingers on the first thing they came into contact with: Mouse's blazer, jammed between them. Orange salad dressing dribbled down her chin. Mouse watched, transfixed. This was certainly worth a trip to the dry cleaners.

"Hey, Katalski, got a smoke?" Matson yelled behind her.

Out of the corner of her eye Mouse saw a white slip of something wavering between her seat and the window. She glanced over to see a bunch of brown fingers lacquered with magenta nail polish waving a long cigarette by her ear. "Hey, lady, pass this over, would ya?"

Mouse passed the cigarette to Matson. She was dying to see how this girl tackled her peas.

"Whatcha reading?" asked Matson, by way of saying thank you. She picked up a sirloin tip dripping in partially congealed gravy. Shoved it onto her fork. Steered the fork into her mouth. Wiped her gravy-stained fingers on the blazer.

"The History of British Documentary."

"Oh."

Matson picked up the peas one by one, stacking them three to a tine, very meticulous. Into her mouth. Fingers to the jacket. Mouse wondered what she'd do when she discovered it wasn't her own jacket she'd been using as a napkin. Mouse wondered if maybe there wasn't a documentary somewhere here. Here was this ravishing middle-class American beauty with the table manners of a girl raised by wolves. For the first time since the phone call, Mouse felt hopeful.

Matson glanced over at Mouse. She started chewing with her mouth closed. She finished her meal, wiped her mouth with her braceleted wrist, then wiped her wrist on the jacket. She lit up her cigarette, tipped her head back and blew circles.

"That's my blazer," said Mouse.

"You want it?" She picked it up and held it toward Mouse. Her blue eyes were empty of embarrassment. Enlisting whatever was at hand, including the clothing of strangers, in the service of personal hygiene, was simply a habit with her. Suddenly Mouse felt quite elated. She was traveling to a foreign country after all, something she was very good at.

Mouse hated using the bathroom on airplanes. For one thing, it took her away from her window. For another, she expected to flush and see clouds. She made Tony stand outside, in case she was sucked out. She mentally forgave him for his shortcomings because he willingly stood guard without making fun of her. He talked to her through the door, telling her about the genial set designer. He really was a good man.

Before they returned to their seats they stood by the emergency exit. They took turns peering through the window.

According to the pilot they were forty-five minutes away from landing, but outside, below, there was Los Angeles, winking in the twilight. A strip of orange sky sat on the western horizon, where the sun had recently set. The channel islands were purple humps in the gray Pacific.

"I'd like to go right to the hospital," she said.

"I should think your sister would be expecting us."

"I have no idea how she is, my mother. I would really like to see her. Then we can go to Mimi's."

They crossed a knot of freeways, coiled around and under each other like a mass of snakes. Mouse recognized, or thought she recognized, this particular interchange, downtown, next to USC, where she took her first, and only, filmmaking class. She recognized a brick tower which used to play a record of tolling bells on the hour and a monolithic parking structure. The plane banked. She grabbed Tony's arm, worried, suddenly, that she would slip through the emergency exit and land back in that class of sixteen years ago, like some time-traveling movie character.

5.

MOUSE AND TONY SPED NORTH ON THE 405 FREEWAY, through the Sepulveda Pass to Encino. After the sopping heat of Nairobi, the Los Angeles night seemed cold and dry. They had tried to rent a car, but it turned out to be impossible, due to a lack of official documents – driver's license, car insurance – and account numbers which would reveal them to be, honest, upstanding adults.

Mouse stared out the window, silently munching her bottom lip. Tony felt sorry for her. He had never seen her so crinkled with worry. Brain surgery was such odious business. Even if her mother survived, the very fact she'd undergone something so excruciating was bound to change things. To think otherwise was like cracking an egg, redepositing the contents back in the shell, taping it back together and imagining it was still the same egg. The thought sent a chill zipping up his spine. Still, he couldn't help feeling a bit grateful – hell, extremely grateful – that Mrs. FitzHenry's misfortune had afforded him the chance to get out of Africa. He reached over and covered Mouse's hand with his own.

Even though it was nearly nine o'clock, traffic was heavy. The cabbie, a large scowling Latino, drove seventy miles an hour, six inches from the bumper of the car ahead of him. In any other circumstance this might have been alarming, but everyone else drove this way, too, so it seemed quite safe.

The freeway was elevated, affording Tony a view for a half-dozen blocks in either direction. He was astonished how clean the streets were, how empty. They were so wide and black, lit with strange acidic orange streetlamps. Low clouds bounced the orange light back onto the roofs of modest apartment buildings, small stucco bungalows, L-shaped malls that bracketed every corner of every block on every main street.

The back windows of the apartments and bungalows faced the freeway. What Tony glimpsed through them was not glitzy, glittery, or wild, as he had expected. Vince Parchman had lived in L.A. before joining the Peace Corps and had bags of stories about sex-starved women with tits that rivaled Kilimanjaro, bowls of drugs set out with the canapes at round-the-clock parties, guru-worshiping Hollywood producers with cocaine encrusted nostrils, all of whom were functionally illiterate. Tony was mildly alarmed, looking through these windows, to see people doing dishes, watching television, reading the newspaper.

In fact, Los Angeles seemed a little plain, merely a backdrop for the huge colorful billboards that shot up into the sky. About the worst you could say about the place, he concluded, after they had chugged over the pass–through stark blue hills, marred only by a few half-occupied housing developments–was that it was rather unimaginative. It reminded him of the backgrounds in cheap cartoons, where the cat chases the mouse past the same tree, the same house over and over again: minimall Mexican restaurant Xerox copies tanning salon liquor store. Minimall Mexican restaurant Xerox copies tanning salon liquor store. Minimall Mexican restaurant Xerox copies tanning salon…

And in each minimall, the same shops, all geared in some way to the upkeep of feminine beauty–hair salon, weight reduction, weight training–or the renting of videotapes. There seemed to be a preponderance of shops that recycled the same four words: Happy Nails, Friendly Nails, Friendly Rosy Nails, Rosy Happy Nails. The cabbie, who turned out to be Korean, snorted that these were fingernail salons all run by scheming

Vietnamese. Tony looked over at Mouse and thought she could stand a session at all of these places, save the tanning salon.

"Vince said once a woman in front of him in a queue at the grocery store invited him to her place up the coast somewhere, Santa Cruz, I believe. Her 'place,' it seemed, was a nudist colony of some sort. John Denver was there, serenading the nudists. His guitar rather artfully placed over–"

"–oh Tony, really," said Mouse. She was not in the mood to hear Vince Parchman's clichéd observations and anecdotes about life in L.A. Up to the age of nineteen she had lived here her entire life. Without exception it had been dull dull dull.

She leaned her head against the back of the greasy plastic seat and closed her eyes. The insides of her lids felt like emery boards. She had no idea what she felt or what she thought. She did know that she craved a shower and a bed.

"I'm sorry I'm cranky," she said. "It's just, you used this as an excuse to get out of Nairobi, didn't you? Be honest."

"I did," he said. "No one can leave Nairobi without an excuse. They ask you at customs. 'What is your excuse for leaving Kenya, *bwana*? It had better be good, *bwana*.'" He snaked his long, freckled arm along the back of the seat around her bony shoulder.

"Just do me a favor and don't look like a kid in a candy store, all right?"

"Far be it from me."

AT THE HOSPITAL Mouse spoke to a young nurse with white-blond hair and heavily mascaraed eyelashes. Mouse was gradually getting used to all these beige-faced blonds of the First World. The nurse was tall and strapping, and wore a diving watch.

"I'm looking for Shirley FitzHenry." Mouse glanced down at her hand on the counter and saw a thread of African dirt embedded under each nail. She knew she looked like hell. Greasy hair, mossy teeth, BO that would warrant a head turn even in the most odoriferous corner of Kenya. Cleanliness, Mouse realized, was not next to godliness, but affluence. The surfer nurse smelled like flowers, the hospital like mouthwash. You could count the germs in this place on one hand. Surgery could safely be performed on the floor of the waiting room.

"You must be Mouse," said the surfer nurse. "Your mom's in 456. Congrats."

"Thanks," said Mouse, confused. For what? Getting here in one piece? Maybe it was some new California colloquialism.

The nurse shrugged. "Sure."

Mouse found Shirl propped up in bed snoozing through a news show. The other bed was empty and freshly made up. Her first impression was of the godawful white bandage. She thought her mother resembled the peg-legged piccolo player in the famous painting depicting the American Revolution. *How can you think that at a time like this!* The Pink Fiend scolded. Mouse chewed on her sunburned lips.

On her mother's lap were stacked two or three slick magazines, thick as telephone directories. Her head hung to one side, her thin lips loose, shiny with saliva. Her skin was sallow, and the dastardly duo of Age and Sun had left their usual calling cards: wrinkles, lines, and spots. It was not the woman Mouse remembered. It was not the Olive.

Tears flooded Mouse's weary eyes, the side effect of an old memory being freed from its cage. *That's more like it*, sniffed The Fiend. *Show a little womanly sentimentality.*

When Mouse was very young, someone in Shirl's women's club had described Shirl as having olive skin. Mouse thought the lady meant her mother, who was short and oval-shaped, with a smallish head and small feet, and twenty extra pounds that had found a happy home around her waist, *looked* like an olive. Mouse read up on olives in *The Golden Book of Fruits and Vegetables* and thought that she and her mother – for Mouse took after Shirl's side of the family, as the taller, fairer Mimi took after Fitzy's side – had been grown on gnarly trees in Italy and imported to the United States. It was not the stork who delivered them but the teamsters.

Mouse laughed out loud at the memory.

Shirl's eyes cracked open. She slowly rolled her head upright. "The wife of the caviar czar is gone," she intoned in a flat voice, like a member from an underground movement delivering a dangerous message in code.

"Who?" Mouse's voice was dry. It occurred to her that perhaps she should have talked to Mimi before she came. What was the prognosis? How much damage had the falling ceiling fan done? Her mother had survived the surgery, but what if she was now in some complicated neurological way totally bonkers? She should talk to a doctor is what she should do. She backed toward the door, hoping to escape before her mother recognized her. "I'm sorry," said Mouse, "I must have the wrong room."

"Is that you, Mousie Mouse?" Shirl lifted her head off the pillow, fumbling for her glasses on the metal tray next to her bed. The bandage half-covered her ears, leaving only the red buds of her lobes exposed. She shoved them on anyway. They had large frames and plastic turquoise rims. Her little round nose bore the brunt of balancing them before her eyes.

"Mom! It's you!" Mouse stumbled forward. Too eagerly she leaned to kiss her mother's cheek. She knocked the glasses off her face and onto the linoleum, one earpiece snagged in the stainless steel bedpan tucked half under the bed. "Bloody Christ." Mouse knelt to retrieve the glasses.

"Why, Mousie Mouse."

"Mouse, Mom, Mouse." She gritted her teeth, wiped the dripping earpiece on her skirt and handed the glasses back to her mother.

Shirl pursed her lips. She returned them pointedly to the metal tray.

"Sorry," said Mouse. *Clumsy! Vulgar! Boorish!* "I'm just… I'm so… It's good to see you." She wrung her sunburned hands.

"This boy is British, then?" said Shirl.

This boy? Mouse wondered. Could her mother really be that disoriented? She decided it was best to ignore the stray remark. "Mom, how are you? How did the surgery go? I came straight from the airport. I haven't slept in about forty hours. That's why I look such a mess."

"Grubby. Your middle name."

"I thought it was more important to see how you were."

Shirl sighed, as if the decision Mouse had made was, as always, the wrong one. "I'm dying." Her head lolled away from Mouse. She stared at the wall for a few seconds, then became interested in a news story on how modern technology has changed the world of artificial limbs.

"How long?" whispered Mouse.

"What?" said Shirl. "I had the nurse pick these up for you." She patted the magazines on her lap.

"Thank you," said Mouse. "Thank you." She sniffed back tears. It was important to be like a rock. The low drone of the jet engines still hummed in her ears. Her bead throbbed.

"Is he British?"

"Who?" croaked Mouse. She had come all the way home for this. Somehow she'd thought if she'd made the effort, spent the money, rushed back without a decent night's sleep or a shower...

"Is he British?"

"I don't know who you mean, Mom."

"Your fiancé."

"Ralph?" her mother suggested.

"Who?" Mouse felt as if she'd landed in a bad production of a Harold Pinter play.

"No, that's somebody else. Somebody Mimi knows." Shirl sighed with effort. "I'll think of it."

Mouse took her mother's hand and held it. She rested her forehead against the side of the cool, clean bed.

"Tom?" said her mother. "Toby?"

Mouse quivered with shame. Her shoulders shivered and

shook. The globe-trotting, family-deserting, tough-as-nails, hardship documentary filmmaker was unable to control herself while her brave little mother, who was afraid of snails on the sidewalk and driving on the freeway, of shopping after dark (rape and vivisection while walking to the car parked, inevitably, at the end of the lot), of public restrooms (loitering heroin-shooting lesbians hiding in the stalls), of eating shellfish (food poisoning), whitefish (choking), of the possibility of her daughters having boyfriends (sex and pregnancy) or not having boyfriends (no sex and social humiliation), was the picture of calm and strength in the face of death.

"Now now now," said Shirl, "it's only natural. I cried too. Just promise me one thing."

"Anything."

"You will wear white."

"To the, to the –" She couldn't bring herself to say funeral.

"And it will be done at a proper church."

At that moment the surfer nurse glided in, a tiny paper cup balanced on her palm. She poured Shirl a glass of water from a carafe on her bedside table. "How we doing here?" she chirped.

"My daughter just returned from, where is it you were?"

"Kenya," said Mouse.

"She doesn't normally look like an Amway saleswoman. Where did you get that jacket?"

Mouse combed though her hair with her fingers. The lighting in the hospital room made everything shine with a greenish tinge. Her stomach churned and boiled in the heroic task of digesting three days' worth of airplane food. Her bones felt like overcooked noodles. She had to sit down, lie down, something.

She settled for something, which was to doze for a minute or two standing up. Her eyes remained open. An obsequious, guilt-ridden smile hung on her lips.

"…the date," the nurse was saying.

"Maybe sometime in the spring. Although that's up to the bride and groom. It's certainly none of my business. April is nice."

Shirl and the nurse both turned to look at Mouse. "It is," she said. She had nothing against April. She had missed something. Who was getting married? Mimi, no doubt. Probably to her best friend's boyfriend.

"Well?" said Shirl.

Mouse looked blank. She was starting to suspect that in her absence the English language had changed.

"You haven't discussed it, I take it," said Shirl.

"I haven't even seen her. I told you, I came right here."

"Her?"

"Mimi."

"Your Maid of Honor!" said Shirl. "Of course you need to check her schedule. She has been one busy girl since you've been hiding out in, where was it? She's a big talent agent now, some show biz thing, and she's writing a book. She's really made something of herself. And you should see all her fellas! Well, you know, she's always attracted them."

"Maid of Honor?" said Mouse. "*My* Maid of Honor?"

"You are having a maid of honor," said Shirl. "You promised."

Suddenly Mouse laughed. She had a deep hooting laugh that sounded like an owl being strangled. "Hoog-hoog-hoog-hoog..."

"I hope you're not taking this lightly. It does not bode well for the marriage, taking a wedding lightly."

"Uh-huhuggg-hugggg-hoog-hoog-hoog-hoog."

"Honestly, Mousie Mouse."

The nurse, anxious to avoid the crossfire of what she could see was developing into a mother-daughter skirmish, scampered out of the room, promising Shirl the doctor would check in later.

"I'm sorry," said Mouse.

"I hope the groom is more stable than you are."

"What groom? You sure you're not thinking of Mimi?"

"You're not getting married?" Tears welled up in her mother's eyes, then coursed down her crêpey cheeks. She dropped her bandaged head onto her chest and held it in both hands, as though it was a fragile, overripe melon. "Fitzy. I think of Fitzy–"

"–Mom, please–"

"–just a day or two before he died we were talking about your wedding."

I was nine years old, Mouse wanted to say, how could you be talking about my wedding? She patted her mother's hand.

"He was such a good, gentle person, Fitzy. I'm not just saying that because he's dead. People get revised after they die, their personalities, but he was always a gentle, honest man. Uncouth, but honest."

"He was," said Mouse.

"How can you remember?"

"I do," said Mouse. She blotted the tears from her own eyes with her knuckles.

"Be careful of that skin under your eyes. Remind me to give you some cream before you go. I have a sample of some of that Estée Lauder Mimi gave me. It's for women my age, but you look like you could use it. Did you put anything on your skin when you were in…"

"…Kenya."

"I know where you were!" she suddenly yelled. "Don't treat me like… I have trouble remembering. I was in that Gateau on Melrose, you know, no, you wouldn't. I ordered and the girl came with the coffee and suddenly I've got a tube coming out of my nose and a damned IV and my wrist–" She lifted up her cast, then dropped it back in her lap. "When's the date? All I ask is it's after my hair has grown back."

"Of course, Mom, of course."

MOUSE STOLE A glance at Tony as they stood shivering on the sidewalk in front of the hospital, waiting for yet another cab to come and take them to Mimi's apartment. He was bouncing up and down on the balls of his feet, like some fair-haired, broken-nosed Maasai warming up for a tribal dance.

She was dead set against allowing a sense of guilt about leaving her mother and sister to live in Africa or about her mother's recent brush with death to change her mind about marriage. Anyway, even if she wasn't dead set against marriage, she was dead set against marrying Tony. She loved him, she supposed, but he was basically Not Her Type. *It would make your mother so happy*, said The Pink Fiend.

He was attractive, intelligent. All right. But he was too tall and rangy. He laughed very loud at things that were only marginally funny. He had large, loose joints, and was forever dislocating fingers, even elbows. He was lazy, congenial, uncritical. He was the dancing-on-a-sinking-ship type, whereas she was inclined to discover why the ship was sinking and see if it could be remedied. Give me a brooding Latin, she thought, a hairy, compact, cross-eyed Arab. Give me someone more dangerous, less decent. Tony was that–decent, and an awfully good companion into the bargain.

She could always call the thing off. Get engaged, then, if she absolutely could not bring herself to go through with it…

It was eleven o'clock. Hardly the time to broach the subject. They'd been waiting in front of the hospital for fifty minutes. They were freezing. They were jet-lagged and constipated, depressed and cranky. A cold wind blew in off the desert, rustling through a windbreak of eucalyptus trees growing in a vacant lot next door.

All she had to do was mention the conversation she'd had with her mother. Tony would do the rest. Although this was hardly his style. Standing in front of the Good Samaritan of the Valley, duffel bags leaning against their shins, surrounded by a ragtag assortment of camera gear and an impossibly heavy light kit which they had not sent ahead, for fear it would disappear into the black hole of international shipping.

Tony was a devotee of the hackneyed flourish. He would require flowers, champagne, proper music. This would hardly do. It was the opposite of a memorable romantic moment. It was one of those horrendous bits of transitory time which, mercifully, our memories generally refuse to have anything to do with. Mouse had to go to the bathroom but was afraid if she scurried back inside the cab would arrive and refuse to wait. She pressed her thighs together and tried to conjure up images of the drought in Sudan.

No. This was definitely not the time.

"Do you still want to get married?" she asked.

"Pardon?" He was daydreaming about the Lakers. He'd read an article about them in the in-flight magazine on the airplane and was wondering how one went about getting season tickets.

"I think we should get married. If you still want to."

"Eow Gawd! M' girl's gone off 'er bean." He did a silly cockney accent at serious moments that drove her crazy.

"Do you have to do that?"

"What happened to marriage as a prison without walls?" He dropped the accent. "A method of self-sabotage synonymous with stagnation? You quoted someone. Auden, perhaps? No, Voltaire. 'Marriage is the only adventure open to the cowardly.' Am I missing any of your major points?"

These were the reasons she had refused him before, and he had not forgotten. His ego had taken a drubbing. The first time he had proposed was on the balcony of their hotel during a vacation in the Kenyan seaside town of Malindi. He went to a great deal of trouble to get an ocean view and a bottle of decent wine sent up. Thereafter he'd popped the question when he was drunk and feeling disgusted with himself and looking for an argument.

Even though Mouse insisted she loved him, he didn't believe her. He didn't believe that any normal woman in love could resist marriage, even if it wasn't in her own best interest. Which left two disturbing options: either Mouse wasn't normal or she wasn't in love.

"You can't just say yes or no, can you?"

"Considering our history, I certainly think I'm entitled to whip you a hefty rasher of shit."

"You mean considering the number of Peace Corps girls and embassy wives you passed up in the interest of fidelity."

"I didn't pass up so many."

Mouse looked into his face, just to double-check that he was teasing. "So all that graffiti I read about you on the ladies' room walls of East Africa was true."

"Quite. Give you a demonstration on our honeymoon."

"Our honeymoon." Mouse tried not to cringe at the thought.

6.

NINE O'CLOCK CAME AND NO MOUSE. TEN O'CLOCK. TEN-
thirty. Mimi was beginning to worry. What if their plane had
crashed? What if they'd been taken hostage? If it would happen
to anyone it would happen to a FitzHenry. If the plane was
simply delayed and Mouse had not called, she would be pissed.

The Bibliothèques struggled to discuss the book for an
hour, then gave up. Elaine left, off to Dallas the next morning for
a car-FAX-machine convention. Luke and Marty begged off too.
The rest of the women migrated to the kitchen to slouch against
the counter, finish the wine, complain about men and the business. The men turned on the World Series, forgetting everything.
Then Mouse and Tony arrived.

Mimi thought Mouse looked terrible. She'd expected
someone tan and fit in a safari suit with big shoulder pads and a
cinched waist, not this broom with teeth.

"Mouse! You look great. You still look nineteen." Her eyes
looked great, anyway, light as green glass next to her sunfried
skin. And that weirdly sexy cleft chin. Mimi suddenly understood
a law of beauty: all you needed was one exotic feature. Mouse
had two, the eyes and the chin. Everything else about her was
plain and parched. She had the look of someone who'd been
camping out for the last sixteen years. She was wearing some
Mom Outfit even Shirl wouldn't be seen in. A-line skirt, pumps,
a blouse. A brown-and-beige blazer with food stains on it.
Mouse was still a dolt when it came to normal girl stuff, which

only made Mimi happier to see her. Who said travel changed you? Mousie Mouse hadn't changed a bit. Mimi tried to imagine her in a wedding dress and couldn't.

"Sorry we're late, we went right to the hospital. Mom seems to be doing okay."

"She's fine *now*. It's the aftereffects you got to worry about."

Mouse put down her duffel bag and camera. They hugged. Mimi could feel Mouse's bones through the back of her blazer. Bird bones. She was too thin. Mimi felt proud of herself for thinking *someone* was too thin. That proved she did not have an eating disorder. Mimi felt that if she wanted to she could pick Mouse up with one hand and wave her over her head. "You're so skinny. You really do look great."

"You do too. You're a blond."

"I have a great haircutter guy now!" cried Mimi, releasing Mouse to wildly scrunch her stiff blond curls. "I used to go to this woman who was great until she permed me. I looked like I'd been electrocuted. My new guy cuts my hair on the front lawn of his house. Sometimes the neighbors come and watch. It's cheaper at his house than at the salon. I'll have to give you his name." Over Mouse's shoulder Mimi peeked at the future husband-boyfriend-fiancé. He stood to one side politely, a suitcase dangling at the end of each long, freckled arm.

Mimi was an expert on men, especially the kind like Ralph who grew on you. Men whose weak chins you could ignore because they had nice eyes. Men whose funny jokes could be loved instead of a good bone structure. Men who were plain old nice, who had a couple of okay features which always seemed more than okay when there was no one else. Ugly men whose power or wealth made up for everything. Men you needed to know to find attractive.

This guy was none of these men. He was the type whose careless glance made you feel as if you were standing on your head while riding an express elevator to the top floor of a building during an earthquake.

At the sound of the doorbell Lisa and Carole had drifted back into the living room, curious about Mimi's little sister, and about what type of man was to he found roaming around East Africa. Now she noticed them discreetly rearranging themselves, leaning at more alluring angles against the doorjambs. Mouse had lucked out. Unless, of course, Tony turned out to be a serial killer or an aspiring director. Mimi wasn't sure which would be worse.

"Where should I deposit these?" he asked.

"You're English!" Mimi cried.

Tony turned round as though Mimi was talking to someone behind him. "So he is."

"Let me show you where to put your junk." Mimi led Mouse and Tony back to her bedroom at the end of the hail. "I can't believe you made it here in one piece. I was really starting to worry. It's such a long trip. I know how long a flight can be, just from when I flew to Miami for that Bob Hope thing."

"You did a film with Bob Hope?" asked Tony.

"A credit card commercial. It aired nationally. Maybe you saw it? I was the one in the red bikini with the hot-dog buns."

"First time I've been to the States, I'm afraid," said Tony.

"Maybe you saw it in Kenya. Do they even have TV in Kenya? I'll clean out a shelf for you in the medicine cabinet. And the closet. I have towels and stuff, sheets, I can get that later, I guess. It's just so good to see you!"

Mouse put her bag down in the corner by Mimi's bureau. She looked around the room. Mimi had obviously spent her energy and money on the living room. The carpet was brown and threadbare. There was a double-bed box spring on the floor, a faded blue comforter covered with dog hair tossed over it, an unfinished dresser clotted with junk: jewelry, mail, a Diet Pepsi can, blow dryer, diaphragm case, an oak-framed mirror with two curling postcards tucked into the frame. The postcards were from Mouse. Two postcards in sixteen years.

"It's nice to be home," said Mouse.

"Ugh, wait'll you're here awhile. You'll hate L.A. as much as everyone else," said Mimi.

A burst of clapping and hollering rolled down the hall. GOGOGOGO, ohhhh.

"What's happening?" Mimi trotted back out to the living room. "What happened?" She stood behind Ralph, massaged his shoulders.

"Thompson – " began Ralph, leaning away from her hands.

" – COME ON, YOU PUTZ!"

"Who's playing?" asked Tony. Ralph made room for him on the green wicker settee.

"Reds and the A's. Top of the seventh."

The men stared at the set in communal silence, a circle of snakes held rapt by the charmer.

Mimi said, "I love baseball," and returned to the kitchen.

Mouse stood behind the settee, staring in the direction of the set but seeing nothing. She wondered whether she was really here or still on the plane imagining herself here. What time was it? What day?

No one asked her to sit down. She marveled at how Tony had plugged right into this gang of guys like a reliable travel appliance. A beer appeared in his hand. During the commercials he regaled them with tales of Africa. He exaggerated, making the stories seem more exotic than they were, transforming them from interesting personal experiences into uproarious party chat.

Mouse fumbled for her pack of cigarettes in the pocket of her blazer. She lit up, glanced around the room. Was it just her, or did everyone in Mimi's *bok* group seem only slightly older than the Manhattan Beach Women's Volleyball Team? Mimi in particular looked frantically teenage, her grass clippings-colored hair frozen in a permanent state of tousle, her thin lips outlined in light pink lipstick. It made Mouse nervous and shy.

"Can I bum a cigarette?" asked the jittery redhead standing next to Mouse. Lisa, she thought her name was.

Mouse passed her the pack. "They're Kenyan."

"Mimi says you're getting married," said Lisa.

"Boy, word travels fast," said Mouse. Shirl must have telephoned Mimi the minute she and Tony left the hospital.

"I doubt I'll ever get married. I'm thirty-four. I want to have at least two children but the odds of that are shit. I *want* my life to be narrow and uninteresting, stuck at home with the kids, baking cookies. I *want* to be bored out of my skull. I'm bored out of my skull now anyway. I'm a sound editor," she added as if that explained everything.

Click-click-click, toenails on the hardwood floor. Sniffy Voyeur emerged from the hallway, swayed over to Mouse, where he stuck his graying muzzle in her crotch. She tipped his face up to look at him. He had opaque brown eyes, rimmed in black.

"You're no spring chicken, are you, buddy?" She rubbed the top of his head with her knuckles. He leaned against her, grinning with his pitted yellow teeth.

"I know this might seem weird since we just met, but why should I pretend this isn't on my mind all the time? What I'm wondering is, does Tony have any brothers? I could go to Nairobi. I've wanted to do a safari anyway. There's a group in town for singles that make over seventy-five thousand a year. We do hikes, picnics, roller-skating. I've put personal ads in all the papers. It's not like I haven't exhausted the market."

"The market?"

"You have to take a consumer approach."

"I'm sure you'll find someone," said Mouse. What else do you say to a desperate woman breathing smoke into your ear?

"Everyone getting married says that."

"Maybe you shouldn't try so hard. Just let it go."

"I tried that, it doesn't work. I say, 'Okay, it doesn't matter, I'll just be in the moment and meet who I meet.' I know I'm just bullshitting myself. Pretending you're not trying and not trying are two completely different things. I even became a Buddhist for a while. You know that Buddhist saying, 'If you don't have a good time doing the dishes, nothing will make you happy'?

I tried to be happy doing the dishes. All I got was depressed over not having a china pattern. It doesn't even have to be love. I'd settle for kind of a warm feeling."

"Tony's an only child. But I think he does have some cousins – "

"Mouse! What are you doing out there!" Mimi yelled from the kitchen. "Come keep me company while I put away the food."

Mouse and Lisa obediently left the baseball game for the kitchen. Sniffy Voyeur stuck to Mouse's side.

"Sniffy Voyeur likes you," said Mimi. She stood at the sink, flamingolike, the sole of one bare, pink-toenailed foot propped against the opposite knee.

"You named a dog Sniffy Voyeur?"

"Ivan named him. We got him when we were first married."

"HOW IS IVAN?" said Mouse. Her voice sounded too perky. She slid into the chair across the kitchen table from Mimi's room-mate, Carole. A stack of screenplays in bright colored covers sat at Carole's elbow. Unlike Mimi and the others, Carole was not sleek and chipper. She was heavy and quiet. She had short pur-plish red hair and a parade of diamond studs marching up the lobe of one ear. Mouse sensed a kindred soul.

"He's a complete crackpot. Try some of this Saint André stuff." Mimi brought Mouse a pale yellow slab from the refrig-erator, a silver butter knife that had obviously taken a few spins in the garbage disposal, a box of fancy English water crackers. "This stuff costs a fortune but I'm a real cheese person. I have really refined taste."

"Ivan always was different," said Mouse, slicing a bit of cheese.

"Different! He's way beyond different," said Mimi. "I never see him anymore anyway. I don't like to have regrets, but that is sure one."

"Who's Ivan," said Lisa.

"You know Ivan," said Mimi. "Ivan, my ex."

Nausea rose to meet the Saint André descending Mouse's throat. She struggled to swallow.

Mimi pulled on her big blue rubber gloves and lined up all the dirty glasses on the kitchen counter, squirting dishwashing soap in each one, assembly-line fashion. A bottle of soap like that would clean dishes for an entire village for a year. Mouse was about to say something but stopped. She would be accused of being too serious, too critical, oversensitive.

The breeze blowing through the kitchen window smelled of some familiar autumn night flower Mouse couldn't identify. Lisa and Mimi talked about what they wanted to name their children, should they have children. Lisa pointed out that Mimi was closer to having children than she was, because Mimi at least had a boyfriend, even if he was married.

"He's *separated*," said Mimi.

"That's worse than being married," said Lisa.

Mimi said even if Ralph was single she wasn't sure she'd marry him. This was a lie but she liked the way it sounded. She said she thought being married to Ralph was probably like being married to Kafka. Lisa said Kafka was better than nobody. A long conversation followed in which Mimi and Lisa thought of awful, famous men no one could pay them enough to be married to.

Mouse lost interest. She petted Sniffy, ate cracker after cracker smeared with the rich, pale cheese. She was suddenly ravenous for something that had not been microwaved. From the living room there was the occasional crack of the bat, followed by hoots and shouts. She could not recognize Tony's voice.

Carole was reading screenplays and participating in the conversation at the same time. Mouse watched her read six scripts. Each one took about ten minutes. She read the first ten pages, the middle ten, the last ten. If she liked those thirty, she'd go back and read the first twenty, the middle twenty, and the last twenty. If she liked those sixty, she'd go back and read the first thirty, the middle thirty, the last thirty, which generally amounted to the entire script. Mouse was fascinated.

"What are those for?" asked Mouse.

"Gotta have notes on them tomorrow morning." Carole yawned.

"Carole reads for Allyn Meyer," said Mimi.

"In Nairobi Tony read for a blind coffee farmer one night a week. They were reading – "

Mimi hooted. "Not *that* kind of reading. She does coverage. Allyn is a VP at Columbia."

"I want to go to nursing school," said Carole.

"Isn't she wild?" asked Mimi. "Her Dad's in the business and she wants to go to nursing school. I love big strong independent women like that."

"Do your one-second script analysis," said Lisa.

"The characters aren't developed enough. You could cut the opening scenes. The idea is a good one, but it drags in the second act. It falls down in the end after a promising start. I enjoyed the humor throughout. You could have played up the love story. It needs more of a motor, also a hook and a spin. I just didn't spark to it. I'd love to see the next draft."

Mouse looked at Carole blankly.

"You can say a variation on that about every script," said Carole.

"Mouse does documentary," said Mimi, by way of explaining why her sister didn't get it. "Which reminds me. I was thinking. Mouse, you should try to get some screenings of your stuff. I mean Africa, some people might find it boring, but someplace like the LAFI should be interested."

"Doesn't Dale Rooks work there?" asked Lisa.

"He's over at TriStar now," said Mimi.

"I went out with Dale a couple times. Get this. He said he had a mental block against women with red pubic hair."

Mouse laughed.

"They'll use any excuse, I'm telling you," said Lisa.

"What I was saying," said Mimi, "is Solly could probably make some calls. But you got to know, even if the LAFI or some place agreed to show them, documentaries are no draw in this city. People can barely stand to watch them on television, why would they pay money to see them? Anyway, I'll ask Solly, but don't get your hopes up. I'm in features, which is completely different than documentaries."

"Did he say what color was acceptable?" said Mouse.

"I mean look at the Oscars. During Best Documentary just about the whole audience sneaks out for a smoke. You know the people you see when the camera pans the auditorium?"

"The thing is, *he's* a redhead. His whole body's covered with red hair."

"Maybe I should talk to him. You know Tony…" Mouse nodded her head toward the living room.

Lisa screeched. Her cheeks bulged with white wine.

"You probably think they're big Hollywood types, the people in the audience. They're not. They're unemployed actors. They rent gowns and tuxes and the Academy pays them to sit in the empty seats so it doesn't look like everybody's beat cheeks to the lobby at the mention of the word documentary."

"*Genug*, Mimi – Jesus," said Carole.

"I'm just saying, I'd love to help."

Meanwhile, in the living room, the Reds had left the A's in the dust, eight to three at the top of the ninth, and Tony had passed exhaustion hours ago. He was deep in the region of serious sleep deprivation, where you begin to think, "Sleep! An over-rated concept! I could go on like this for days!"

Why sleep when he was finally in Los Angeles? Why sleep when he could watch American baseball on a good box with some really terrific chaps? Why sleep when the girls were giggling in the kitchen, the beer colder and better than any he'd had since his last trip to Hong Kong to visit his parents?

He was stupefied by his good fortune. Sather, Darryl, Ralph all worked in the film business. Ralph was right-hand man to an

Academy Award-winning Scot, Keddy Webb, and taught a writing class to boot. He wondered if perhaps they knew someone called Vince Parchman.

"There's a V. J. Parchman," said Ralph. "Got a deal over at Columbia."

"Probably him," said Darryl. "This guy's an Africa nut. He's got blowguns in his office."

"Vince was something of a collector. It's impossible though, isn't it? It's like these African blokes you'd meet. They'd have one relative in Britain, they'd never know what city. They'd ask, 'You know my uncle Thomas? Tall black man?' Disappointed as hell when you couldn't help him."

"Keddy'd know," said Ralph through a belch. "I think this V. J. was in the Peace Corps."

MOUSE COULDN'T SLEEP for thinking about Ivan – not the whole bad business with Mimi and their marriage, but before.

She and Tony were sleeping on the living room floor. Mimi had tugged a dusty futon from her bedroom closet and dragged it to its current spot, wedged between the dining room table and the back of the green wicker settee.

It was odd and unfair, Mouse thought, lying next to a gently snoring Tony, that your fondest memories were comprised of inconsequential images, smells, and tastes you never noticed while the memory was in the making. The Watergate hearings, the smell of formaldehyde, the cheap brand of chocolate sandwich cookies Shirl had always had on hand, the mournful love songs overplayed on the radio all that summer. It all reminded her of Ivan.

Once, in Nairobi, she had argued long into the night with Vince Parchman about whether Richard Nixon was evil or just shady. That night she dreamed an aching dream of Ivan. She was the age she was now, but he was still eighteen.

It was 1973. Mouse was taking her first and only filmmaking

class, Beginning Super 8mm, at USC. She had just graduated from Citrus High School and was entering UCLA in the fall.

At that time USC was still ashamed of its Cinema Department. It was several years before *Star Wars* would make them realize that movies could be wholesome, harmless, and a license to print money. At that time, in 1973, the only people interested in something as abstruse as film school were East Coast transplants from left-wing colleges who aspired to be a Bergman, a Godard, a DeSica. Intellectuals, obsessives, and probable communists, or oddballs like Ivan Esparza, wanted to make documentaries. The department was tiny, as cramped as a slum. It was housed – thankfully – at the edge of campus in a rat-infested clutter of green clapboard outbuildings which had been used as stables during World War II.

There were people there, then, who took documentaries seriously, instead of as a setup for a joke.

Because the Cinema Department was so small, and this particular section of Beginning Super 8mm was for nonmajors, the class was shunted to an air-conditionless classroom across campus in the science building, next to the biology lab. The class spent four hours three mornings a week dissecting one another's films, while the students next door dissected frogs and brown grasshoppers the size of model airplanes.

Ivan was from the questionable side of the tracks in a questionable suburb, El Monte or Pico Rivera, a gritty, flat place known for light industry and carbon monoxide. To this day, even though Mouse had committed so much of Ivan to memory, she could not remember where, exactly, he was from. He had an unusual look. Even eighteen-year-old Mouse, who was not people-smart, much less boy-smart, knew that. He was Mexican and Czech, a honey-colored dark blond, with dark blue eyes, broad lips, a flat Indian nose. He was thickset, with heavily muscled shoulders and a slim waist. He had been the star welterweight on his wrestling team in high school, which didn't prevent Mouse being his partner in Beginning Super 8mm, though it did, at first, give her cause to wonder whether or not she should kiss him.

At Citrus High, where Mouse and Mimi had gone, wrestlers were the lowest of the low. They were always pale and sweaty. It was assumed they wrestled only because they had a peculiar need to tug on a classmate's crotch in front of an audience. They were more unpopular than the Drill Team or the jerks who played the bagpipes in the Citrus Highlander pipe band.

Not that Mouse had been popular, but Shirl had taught both her daughters the value of upward-mobility. Mimi did not disappoint. She'd made cheerleading finals – she was hope-lessly uncoordinated; Mouse had secretly thought it was a miracle she'd even made it that far – and was on the homecoming court two years in a row.

Mouse, on the other hand, was on par with the wrestlers. She was the Girl A-V Nerd. The A-V Nerds were in charge of the audiovisual equipment. They lugged around slide carousels and threaded movie projectors, oversaw the sound systems at pep rallies. They were generally all knockkneed boys with acne and respiratory problems, except Mouse. Even though she was small, she hauled forty-pound 16mm film projectors down the halls, ignoring the bruises they inflicted as they banged against her scrawny brown shins. She took her job seriously. Once, in Mrs. Peabody's World History class, rather than allow a faulty projector to chew up a piece of film, she stuck her finger inside the gate to pull it out. In her haste and dedication she didn't think to turn off the machine and it chewed off her fingertip.

When Ivan Esparza appeared on the scene, ex-crotch-grab-bing welterweight or no, Shirl had loved him. More, Mouse suspected, because he was a Boy, any Boy, than because he was Ivan, with his velvet voice and rollercoaster moods.

Shirl's great fear in life was not that Mimi would be an unwed mother but that Mouse would die a virgin. She gave Mouse books like *How to Get a Teenage Boy and What to Do with Him Once You Get Him*. She took her to Dr. Roy, her gynecologist, where Mouse was fitted for a diaphragm. She bought Mouse Maybelline Blooming Colors Eye Shadow. Frustrated when none of these more subtle tactics worked, she exhorted Mouse to be more like Mimi.

"Use your eyes more," Shirl had said.

It was the spring before Ivan. Mouse was skimming dead slivers of eucalyptus bark from the surface of the Lagoon, the FitzHenrys' *faux*-mountain lake swimming pool. It was a wide, irregular oval trimmed with flat rocks: black, slate gray, ocher, brick. The shallow end was shaded by trees, and it had a real waterfall, which Fitzy, when he was alive, had turned on every morning, whether or not anyone was home.

Shirl sat at the patio table drinking a beer, streaking through a crossword puzzle.

Mouse was silent. She plucked bits of bark from the wire mesh of the skimmer. She didn't understand. She *did* use her eyes. Hadn't Mr. Larue, track coach and English teacher, commented that even though Mouse's spelling was atrocious, she never missed a detail? Wasn't she only one of five members in the Citrus High Bird Watching Club? Didn't she always find the everyday objects hidden in the jungle illustration in the *Highlights* magazine in the dentist's office? If anything, she overused her eyes. What was Shirl talking about?

What she was talking about was eye contact. "Flutter your eyelashes, for God's sake," said Shirl. "Find a boy you like, isn't there any boy you like? Once you've got his attention look down, act demure. Can't you act demure? I can't believe I have to explain these things to you. You knew where babies came from when you were four and a half, and I have to explain about using your eyes. Jesus, Mary, and Joseph."

Babies are biology, Mouse wanted to say. This other business is goofy.

But Shirl's Mousie Mouse was nothing if not obedient. She did, in fact, have a painful crush on Kent Charpentier, row monitor in French IV and water polo champion. He sat in front of her. The sight of the back of his square head of shiny, blond-green hair made her feel as if she was suffocating. In class the next day when he turned to pass a quiz back to her, she stared at him, alternately fluttering her eyes – maybe she was rolling them, she couldn't quite get the hang of it – and looking down. Finally, unnerved, Kent raised his hand and said, *"Madame Robertson, C'est Mouse. Elle a un epileptic fit, je pense."*

Shirl gave up. Her youngest was simply an ignoramus in the ways of men. Femme fatality was not in her blood.

Then, literally out of nowhere – in Shirl's opinion, a summer school class called Beginning Super 8mm was about as nowhere as you could get – there was a boy. Ivan Esparza. Half communist, so she could forgive the other half. (Shirl liked the communists, her name for everyone east of the Iron Curtain, better than the lazy Mexicans, who never cut the lawn short enough.) And he was polite. He called on the telephone. Mouse! It's for you! He called at all hours. Tying up the line. Arranging meetings. Meals. Outings. It was a boy! A boy for Mouse!

Ivan came to the house almost every day. Parking in the driveway in his blue Camaro, radio blasting, as it should when you're young and have lots of hearing still to ruin. Leaving suntan oil-stained towels in a heap by the swimming pool on a blistering smog-swollen July afternoon. Sprawling in the den in Fitzy's old Barcalounger – Mouse in a neat cross-legged sit on the floor, Shirl on the couch – an iced tea balanced on his knee, watching Haldeman and Ehrlichman grin, fume, and lie. Shirl religiously left the room during commercial breaks to fetch her favorite dry-as-dust bakery-outlet sandwich cookies, hoping, upon her return, to find her Mouse in mid-makeout with her new boyfriend. Unfortunately, often as not she returned to find them talking camera angles.

Mimi, who was between men that summer (at nineteen she had already made the switch from *boys* or *guys*) and living miserably at home to save money, told Shirl that Ivan was just Mouse's classmate and friend. Shirl refused to believe it.

"No boy pays this much attention to a friend," sputtered Shirl.

There were other disquieting signs, however, that Shirl preferred to ignore.

When Mouse talked to Ivan on the phone she didn't lie sprawled on her bed weaving the phone cord in and out of her toes, as Mimi did, wheedling, whispering, and giggling. Instead, she sat at the kitchen table, elbows parked on a yellow legal pad, debating the latest installment of the Watergate hearings or their class film projects. She didn't demand privacy or new clothes. Shirl never caught her watching herself walk as she passed a mirror or plate glass window. She didn't attempt to even up her tan – she sported a half dozen different tan lines from three different bathing suits. She didn't pine, moon, or blush when Shirl and Mimi teased her.

One Saturday, while Shirl was out shopping for a new washer and dryer, Mouse was out by the Lagoon, storyboarding a scene for her and Ivan's third class project. Every team in Beginning Super 8mm was required to make four five-minute Super 8 films, the last two with sound. Mouse was directing and shooting this one. It was about a girl who invites her mother and sister over to a barbecue and poisons them by roasting their hot dogs over the grill with oleander branches. Ivan was rolling sound and editing. His sisters had been cast as Shirl and Mimi. The Pink Fiend, already flourishing in Mouse's adolescent psyche, had prevented Mouse from asking Shirl and Mimi to play themselves.

Mouse paced from the diving board to the waterfall, her index finger laid along the cleft of her chin in thought. She was wondering whether one of them should fall off the patio chair and into the pool for her death scene. Too hard to control. Then again, Mouse thought, if one of them cracked her head open she could turn it into a documentary on poolside safety.

"Mom thinks you and Ivan are Doing It," said Mimi, who

was sporadically weeding the lawn (her job; Mouse took care of the pool) in between stabs at topless sunbathing.

"Doing what?"

"I told Mom it was a just-friends type of deal. You know how she is, always snoopy about our boyfriends."

Mouse continued to pace, stopping occasionally to scribble in her notebook. She knew, as she had known for years, that it was very simple to have a conversation with Mimi without ever saying a word, In fact, Mimi preferred it that way.

And where Ivan was concerned ... Ivan! ... just silently saying his name made her internal organs sizzle.

Yes, she loved Ivan. But it was terrifying, not fun, like Shirl and Mimi had promised. In the course of one slim day she'd want to strangle him, kiss him until she choked, forget she ever knew him, sleep at the end of his bed curled up like a dog for the rest of her life. And deep down she knew that however it turned out, the thought of him would be with her forever. He might go away, but his memory wouldn't. It would be like a glob of accidentally swallowed bubble gum that would stick to her ribs until ants carted it away while trekking through her coffin-encased remains.

There had been no dates, no flowers, none of the regular do-si-do that led to sex, then disillusionment. It should have been that way. It would have been easier. Instead, Mouse and Ivan's feelings were akin to those which soldiers who'd shared the same trench had for one another. There was respect, camaraderie, the sense that each had seen the other at his best and worst.

In this case, the trench was Beginning Super 8mm. When Ivan and Mouse hardly knew one another they were showing up at each other's doorsteps at 5:00 a.m. for a sunrise shoot; turning Mouse's bedroom into a set, once using her underwear for a prop; doing the coffee-No Doz two-step to stay awake while editing or completing the sound track.

"I mean, Ivan is really a fox. Man, those eyes! But he's too intense. A bean James Dean. Hey, that rhymes!" Mimi stood, chucking three clumps of weeds over the fence into the Rosenthals' yard next door. She wiped at her grass-imprinted knees, slunk over to the chaise where she arranged herself languorously. She untied her bikini top, rubbed her breasts with baby oil. She eased herself down, then laid a quarter on each flat rosy nipple, a trick she had learned to prevent sunburn her first year at Cal State Northridge.

"He is not a bean," said Mouse.

"I know," said Mimi.

"Then why'd you say it, if you knew?"

"You are so fucking sensitive. Maybe you're sleeping with him. Men are only after one thing anyway, that's what Mom says."

Mouse was intrigued. "What thing?" She thought it was probably money.

"You *know*," said Mimi. "At least all the men I know want it from me"

No, it couldn't be money.

"Money?" said Mouse.

"Sex, dummy! You are such a retard. Smart about the dumb things and dumb about the smart things, that's what Mom says."

Mouse had gone back to blocking out her scene, thinking Mimi must have it confused. Sex was the thing Shirl wanted for her, not Ivan. Ivan wanted someone to go with him to Italian neo-realist movies on Saturday afternoons. Now, trying to get comfortable on the lumpy futon, Mouse's lips curled up at the thought of her eighteen-year-old self struggling with what it was that all men were after. She still wasn't sure she knew. Sex scratched the itch of instinct, but certainly men were more complex than that.

Tony rolled toward her, crept his long arm under her neck. "You're not still bloody awake, are you?"

"What do all men want?" Mouse whispered.

"What?"

"What do all men want?"
"A three-picture deal, I should think."

7.

ONE DAY WHILE MOUSE AND MIMI WERE RUNNING ER-
rands, Mouse decided she wanted to drive by the on-ramp
where Fitzy was killed. It was smoggy and overcast, the sky like
cold dishwater whose bubbles had gone flat. She bought a
plastic tube of carnations from a boy selling them on the median.
She wanted red, but all he had was blue. She wanted to leave
them on the curb, at the exact spot where Fitzy's head had struck
the pavement.

Mimi argued for the middle of the ramp. The middle of the
ramp symbolized, in Mimi's opinion, the entire event. She said
Mouse was too stuck on the specific. Mouse said she was the one
who bought the flowers. Mimi said it was a silly idea anyway.
They should just go to the grave, or to Fitzy's. Shirl had recently
sold it to Abde, a knockout Persian with big brown eyes like
Sniffy Voyeur's. Mimi said they should go before he started serving kabobs and souvlaki along with the Guinness.

Mimi turned right onto the ramp and stopped.

"You could have pulled *over*," said Mouse.

"Just do it already," said Mimi. The line of cars behind them
was a block long, growing longer by the minute.

Mouse hurried across the ramp. Where there should have
been sidewalk was a strip of dirt, rock hard, an intimation
of what Los Angeles would have been like without the miracle
of irrigation. She knelt by the curb, partially overgrown with
parched blond weeds. She couldn't help but scour it for old

bloodstains and clues. Even though she was having trouble
remembering what Fitzy looked like, she still sometimes wondered about his last thoughts. How long did he suffer? What
if he hadn't picked up the earring? It had been twenty-six years.
The curb, as mute now as it was twenty-six hours after the
accident, twenty-six minutes, wasn't saying. Still, she had to look.

Horns blared behind Mimi's Datsun. "Move it, bitch!"
a man in a hairnet hollered over his ear-splitting sound system.
Mouse could feel waves of music pounding against her back
as she laid the plastic tube among the snarl of weeds and litter.

Back in the car, they zipped up the diamond lane, passing
the line of disgruntled drivers waiting to merge.

"I love having you home. I finally get to be a car pool."

Mimi had taken a mental-health day off from work. There
was not enough time on weekends to write her blockbuster,
clean the apartment, read the book for Bibliothèques, and get all
her errands done. Plus, even though Mouse had been back over
a month, that night Mimi was cooking her a welcome-home
dinner.

It was no secret that in L.A. you could make a career out
of running errands. What would take twenty minutes in an average town took an hour and a half here. Today Mimi and Mouse
had spent two hours and a quarter-tank of gas in search of a can
of Solo Poppy Seed Filling for Mimi's famous lemon poppyseed
cake.

She didn't mind, though. In the car, driving, she and
Mouse had a chance to catch up. There were times when they
didn't even turn on the radio. It was good, talking in the car,
especially in traffic. You were like people stuck in a cabin during
a snowstorm with no books, no TV or jigsaw puzzles or games.
You had to talk, there was no way around it. It was cozy.

During the week Mimi hadn't seen much of Mouse, who
was busy trying to set up screenings for her documentaries.

When Mimi worked, Mouse took the bus. No one in L.A.
took the bus if they could help it. The poor, the blind, the

foreign took the bus. The demented took the bus. Mouse took
the bus. She liked it. It was cheap, and you got an all-important
glimpse of how the average man lived. Tony, on the other hand,
happily borrowed Mimi's car. He dropped her at Talent and Artists in the morning, then picked her up at night. Tony had bought
a Walkman. He had discovered the Venice Beach Boardwalk. He
had made friends with Mimi's boyfriend, Ralph.

If Mouse's destination was within five miles, she walked, a
plastic 7-Up bottle retrieved from Mimi's garbage full of tap
water, half a sandwich wrapped in a recycled swatch of crinkled
aluminum foil stowed on her back in a knapsack. She claimed
that true knowledge of a place could be gained only through the
soles of one's feet. Twice in one day she was stopped by the
police. What, they wanted to know, was she doing? Walking, she
said. They remained suspicious.

Mimi was suspicious, too. She was beginning to realize that
half a lifetime spent making documentaries in Africa had
turned Mouse eccentric. She wondered – sometimes to herself,
sometimes aloud to Carole or one of the drudges at work – what
Tony saw in her. Besides, of course, the dreary obvious: small
hips, big boobs. Those light eyes and cleft chin. That aloofness.
She seemed to take Tony for granted and he loved it.

Mouse was not really interested in L.A., to Mimi's lasting
irritation. Lepers and cannibals her sister was hot for, but
point out a good health club or the salon with the cleanest tanning beds and her eyes glazed over. Mouse needed to relearn
Los Angeles for one reason and for one reason only: so she could
find her way to some film society at a sleepy junior college in
Glendale, or the Kenyan consulate located somewhere on Wil-
shire Boulevard, or the struggling theater that showed only
art films in Los Feliz, the Society for the Preservation of African
Customs in America somewhere in Inglewood, the Southern
Californian Animists League on Cahuenga – which smartypants
Mouse, despite her smattering of French and Swahili and a
number of tribal dialects, kept mispronouncing *Ca-hew-ga*

instead of *Ca-wheng-a* – any and all places, however obscure, which would be interested in giving her a screening. She'd spent hours spread out on the living room floor, assembling packets of videotapes, still photographs, résumés, clippings from reviews, days on the un-airconditioned bus, going to the copy shop, the photo developers, the film lab.

Despite the knowledge she had gained through the soles of her feet, Mouse kept getting lost. With the exception of the film lab, which was in a graffiti-covered warehouse on a boiling, treeless street in Hollywood, everything else she needed was in a minimall. They all looked alike to her. Once she passed the copy shop where she'd left her clippings and résumés, then demanded to see the manager at a similar-looking shop one block down, certain they'd lost her order.

Finally, after she'd assembled the packets, made the correct-sized videotape for the people allegedly interested in screening the films, ridden the bus for an hour and a half to deliver the material in person, they always said no.

Once, by the time she had taken the bus back to Mimi's apartment, there was already a message on the answering machine.

Sorry, the voice told her, but there was really no interest in Africa, unless it was South Africa, or a rock group putting on a concert to send wheat to people who were starving. Did Mouse and Tony have anything like that?

The best, the voice continued, would be a full-blown concert featuring many rock stars for South African famine relief. The best would be anything with lots of images of bony black children, tin cups dangling from their clawlike hands, or exploited black diamond miners intercut with images of fat white Afrikaaners in madras slacks lawn bowling, over which was laid an anthemlike rock hymn. Anything like that? Anything at all?

People are starving in Mozambique, said Mouse, returning the call. They're starving in Rwanda.

But no one's heard of Mozambique, the voice countered.

And who was Wanda? Hopefully no relation of Winnie Mandela, because the market for Winnie Mandela had most certainly dried up. Now, Ethiopia. Ethiopia was a possibility. Mouse said no. They had no starving Ethiopians, no rock stars. Nothing like that.

After this particular rejection, when she went back to retrieve her material, she realized, looking through the plastic window of the tape, the guy hadn't bothered to rewind it, and that he'd watched only two minutes' worth.

Sometimes, as she was leaving the film institute, the university, or junior college, they felt sorry for her. Here was this painfully suntanned, painfully earnest woman, dressed in raggedy flares (Flares! Mimi could not believe her eyes. They had been Mouse's favorite pants in *high school*), hauling around an African laundry basket-like purse that smelled of camel, a raft of impossible-sounding documentaries on her résumé.

Documentaries on tropical diseases, singing bats and African killer bees, tiny little-known tribes whose ancestral homes were at the bottom of narrow caves, the tops of remote mountains, expatriate hot-air-balloon enthusiasts who practiced their sport high over the Sahara, Berber rockclimbing clubs that scaled the chilling peaks of the high Atlas in sandals and *djellabas*. Documentaries which, when you happened to catch them on some obscure cable channel at an ungodly hour, you thought, "This stuff is incredible, but *where in God's name was the camera?*"

She prompted a mixture of pity and admiration, so they would ask to keep the tape, to hold on to it just a little bit longer, in case they got any good ideas as to someone else who might be interested in showing it. They would keep the tape, which would disappear into the universe of their cluttered desks and credenzas, and Mouse would never hear from them again, leaving her frustrated but determined.

Mimi found all of this maddening. Mouse was getting married in six months – pressed by Shirl, they'd finally set the date, May 11 – and she was obsessed not with the wedding, like any normal woman, but with some dumb movies about Africa. Exercise in Futility City if you asked Mimi, though Mouse never did, even though she was the only one in the family plugged into the film business.

"Let's plan your wedding," said Mimi.

"A judge, me and Tony, rice," said Mouse. She and Tony had not actually discussed it. Their decision in front of the hospital had been enough, had kept her from being a liar. She figured eventually they'd decide where, and how, inching forward like timid bathers facing a cold ocean. They'd move slowly, get used to it. She half wished everyone would just sort of forget about it. "I talked to the LAFI yesterday, did I tell you? They turned us down. They did a series of docs on Africa a couple years ago. Apparently it's like leap year."

"You're kidding, right?"

"Imagine a theatrical exhibitor saying, 'Oh, sorry, Warner Brothers, we booked a violent cop movie last month, we're not interested.'"

"No one gets married by a judge anymore. You want to go for elegance, and a priest is much more elegant than a judge. You only get married once, or once for the first time, anyway. You think you just want to get it over with, but you don't."

"Maybe we can get the Pope."

"You slough it off. That's what I did too. Just a wedding, no big deal. But as it gets closer you'll realize you want the cake and the dress and the whole megillah. You'll want everything to be perfect. It's only natural. It's normal."

Mouse reached over, punched on the radio. It was an oldies station playing an Ivan song, a girl singer with a deep rich voice moaning about faithless love. Mouse wondered how hurt she would be if she jumped out of the car. They were only going forty-five.

"I'll help you. I've got fabulous taste. I mean that's what people tell me. I did my own wedding. You didn't get to see it, it was really lovely. I should really be a production manager instead of an actress-writer. Maybe we could do a medieval theme, which is what I had. Or no, mine was more Victorian. We could get old-fashioned flowers in blues and pinks, lilies and stuff, snapdragons. I had the most gorgeous snaps! The ushers could wear morning coats. We could have a string quartet. We could even rent some little girls to be flower girls, people do that now. There aren't enough kids around anymore."

Mouse sighed. She had thought she'd organize a wedding in the same way she'd organize a shoot. Budget it, break it down, see where she could save money by getting services or locations donated (a ceremony on the beach, for example, would cost nothing; she could buy bulbs and grow the few flowers she wanted herself), make the necessary phone calls, have the necessary meetings. Working a few hours in the morning each day, she estimated it would take a week. Rent flower girls! An image of acres of shiny girls in white patent leather shoes parked in rows, surrounded by a Cyclone fence, like used cars, came to Mouse's mind. It was ludicrous.

"– a wedding weekend," Mimi was saying, "you have the ceremony on a Sunday, the day before have a brunch for your friends who've come from out of town and who aren't in the wedding party. If you have it around a holiday that's always fun. You can have a theme then, like an Easter Egg hunt if it's around Easter. Or a Dickens Christmas. You can get snow brought down from Big Bear. Then the rehearsal dinner. I had a really nice one at –"

Jet lag. Culture shock. The hum of the wheels on the grooved asphalt. The drippy crooning of the girl singer. The hollow crash of the empty diet soda cans on the floor of the back seat every time Mimi slammed on the brakes or accelerated. Mimi's eternal yattering. Mouse slid into a waking nightmare of the future. She saw herself, days or weeks later, washing her face before bed, Mimi leaning in the doorway yammering about the pros and cons of having gold-lined envelopes for the invitations. She saw herself waking up on a cool winter morning, and there is Mimi, at the foot of the futon, saying lilies and tulips are *de rigueur*, that anyone who has anything else in her bouquet is a hopeless boob. She is walking alone in the evening – something she loved to do – and Mimi is on her heels, proffering advice about the cake, the veil, the ring. She is trying to read and Mimi pulls the book from her hands, what about the silver pattern! The china pattern! The crystal!

"– save one bottle of champagne and drink it on your first anniversary. That's what I would have done if I'd have had a first anniversary," Mimi laughed.

A tiny Mimi stood on each of Mouse's shoulders, angel and devil both, yapping in her ears: For *my* honeymoon, on *my* cake, in *my* ceremony, at *my* reception, with *my* dress, from *my* wedding party, by *my* maid of honor, since *I've* been through it once already, Mousie Mousie Mouse!

And never a mention of Mimi's groom. Never.

Mouse rolled down the sleeves of her thin gingham blouse and buttoned the cuffs with shaky fingers. For some reason the air conditioning was on. Fury burned in her throat. Her puckered sunburned lips stretched into a painful smile. "We'd like to keep it small."

"If it's a *time* thing, if you don't want to hassle with it, you should use a wedding consultant. My friend Nita does great work. She'll probably give you a deal because you're my sister. I would have brought it up before but I didn't think you'd be into it. Wedding consultants are the in-thing these days, and you're so…well. You're the girl who thought a prom dress was an unnecessary expense."

"That pink one you and Mom liked at Bullock's could have clothed and fed India for a year."

"You wanted to wear my old one, remember? With the spaghetti straps? You used those words, 'unnecessary expense.' I remember. You probably should have worn it, too, it really was meant for someone with less of a waist. Nita can do anything. Or else, well, I don't have tons of time, what with my job and my writing and acting and stuff –"

"I'll call your friend tomorrow," said Mouse.

THEY EVENTUALLY FOUND the poppyseed filling at Rancher Bob's market. The overstuffed grocery stores of America still made Mouse's head swim; she read a magazine in the car while Mimi ran in.

Mimi found two dented, dusty cans at the back of a shelf, lurking behind some Italian cooking chocolate. Her sense of victory momentarily tempered her bad mood. She hated that Mouse would not take her advice. Mouse thought she knew everything, when, in fact, it was she, Mimi, who knew everything, at least about planning weddings.

The blood boomed in her eyes as she rammed her cart through the aisles, crowded with hip young neo-fifties wives and their petulant children. She remembered when Rancher Bob's had sold natural food in bulk straight from the box it was shipped in, reminding Mimi fondly of her hippie days. But Rancher Bob's had become chic. There was valet parking now. Charge accounts. Catering. An entire aisle dedicated to Condiments from the Seven Continents. The wives of overpaid, undertalented television executives, insensitive to the fact that some single, childless shopper on a time schedule might actually want to pass, clogged the aisles, babbling about good pediatricians and preprep school day care. Mimi loathed the entire scene. Even though she had recently dared to take out a loan for a tiny eye tuck – office procedure, low risk, guaranteed to lob off ten years – she still had her principles.

I'm a hard-as-nails working girl, she thought, jauntily tossing a roll of cheap paper towels into her cart. An actress-writer struggling to make ends meet, generous even though I've got nothing, sadly in love with a married, misunderstood genius. Mouse should make a movie about *me*.

As she dropped a bag of pistachios into the cart she caught a glance of the price on the cans of poppyseed filling. Three dollars and thirty-five cents!

She scrunched her hair angrily. She couldn't afford it. She could go ask Mouse – forget it, Mouse already thought she was a flake. She was not above floating a check, but Rancher Bob's had recently installed a system whereby, at the checkout counter, the checker slid your bank card into a small box resembling a time clock next to the cash register, which provided a digital reading of your checking account balance. To her knowledge her balance was currently somewhere in the high single figure. She could put back everything but the poppyseed filling, or…

Her purse yawned innocently in the kiddie seat of the shopping cart. The cans would fit snugly between her makeup bag and her Week-at-a-Glance.

No. She did not do that anymore. Lifting a Jimi Hendrix album at thirteen was one thing. It was rebellious, daring. Lifting poppyseed filling at thirty-six was neurotic and desperate. Mouse would never do anything so base. Mouse didn't even make poppyseed lemon cake. It did smack a bit of Shirl and Tupperware, Mimi reflected as she dutifully retraced her steps. Suddenly she was infused with a sense of purpose.

This would be her last lemon poppyseed cake, her last married boyfriend, her last dumb job, her last day of vomiting. Back went the pistachios, the jicama, the Ethiopian Swiss Water-Processed Decaf. As she trundled up to the checkout counter she dug for her checkbook, feeling proud, adult, in control.

She would definitely rethink her thing with Ralph. He was married, and egotistical, and not even very attractive. There was Someone out there for her. She would go back to her yoga class. She would call Bob Hope and see if he had anything going. She would eat more tofu.

Then, she looked down at her checkbook. The austere white pad of deposit slips stared back at her. No checks! She had forgotten to put more in, and, it turned out, she had no cash.

She yanked her cart out of line, tears flooding her eyes.

" – AND THEN –you're not gonna believe this, Mom!" yelped
Mimi, bouncing on the edge of her chair.

It was nearly midnight. Mouse and Tony, Mimi and Shirl
sat in the living room of the house on Cantaloupe Avenue having
coffee and Mimi's famous lemon poppyseed cake. Auntie Barb,
Shirl's sister, an antisocial clean freak from Boring, Oregon,
who had come to take care of Shirl after the accident, was mop-
ping the kitchen floor. All the windows were wide open in support of Shirl's stubborn belief that Southern California weather
was temperate and subtropical all year long. The night was
sopping with fog. Between bites, Mouse's teeth chattered.

" –the unbelievable thing is our Mousie Mouse getting
married. We're so pleased." Shirl dimpled at Tony, perched on
the other end of the sofa. He raised his blond eyebrows in
acknowledgment, his ruddy cheeks full of cake.

The white helmet of bandages Shirl had worn in the
hospital had since been removed. Because Tony, i.e., a Man, had
come to dinner, she'd gotten dolled up. She wore rouge, and
an aqua blue turban, a get-well present from Mimi. Normally she
went without, wandering around the house scratching at the
rusty eye of a scab, getting her nubby scalp sunburned sitting by
the pool reading her decorating books and bridal magazines.

This new lack of vanity worried Mimi and Mouse. Also, the
glazed doughnuts. All her life Shirl had been a starch person.
She lived for pasta and bread. They had never had desserts growing up. Shirl didn't know the first thing about making chocolate
chip cookies, except from the prefab logs of dough from the
grocery store. Then, the accident, and suddenly she was transformed into a sugarholic. Glazed doughnuts for lunch, cookies
for dinner. Sometimes Auntie Barb caught her in the kitchen in
the middle of the night licking tablespoons of canned chocolate
frosting and peanut butter mixed together. Dr. Klingston had
warned them there might be a personality change, due to the
damage to the temporal lobe. Mouse thought it was more likely
that during the operation Dr. Klingston accidentally nicked the

all-important wad of gray matter that governed her mother's sense of taste. Shirl gobbled down her fourth piece of poppyseed cake as though it were her first, poppyseeds dotting the corners of her mouth.

"Two seconds after he says he's not going to report me, he asks if I want to go get a cup of coffee!" said Mimi.

"He asked you out?" said Shirl. "He didn't ask you out. Now wait, honey, you go too fast. This boy who caught you *shoplifting*, this box boy –"

"– assistant manager, Mom. He's an actor anyway –"

"When that Mimi sets her cap for a fella, look out!"

"I can't believe you shoplifted," said Mouse.

"It was really a riot," said Mimi. "It was just this one time, anyway. I forgot my checks –"

"– uh-huh. First poppyseed paste, next convenience stores," said Mouse.

"– filling, poppyseed *filling* –"

"Now I'm confused. I thought you said this boy worked at Rancher Bob's –"

"– he *does* work there, Mom."

"He's the assistant manager," said Mouse.

"But he's really, you know, an actor."

"Like twenty-seven thousand other people in Los Angeles," said Mouse.

"More than that," said Mimi. "He just does the Rancher Bob thing to pay the rent. Like I work for Solly."

"What did you say his name was?" asked Shirl.

"Cliff Lyonswood. He's been on a bunch of soaps."

"On *As the World Turns*," said Mouse.

"Not that dumb show," said Mimi, "*Days of Our Lives*. Anyway, he said those cans of filling were ancient, so I was saving him having to take them off the shelf."

"Very comforting. I survive sixteen years in Africa only to die of ptomaine in L. A."

"Cliff Lyonswood." Shirl tasted the name. "That sounds

made-up. Bad policy to go out with someone with a made-up name."

"They're not going out," said Mouse.

"I just said he asked me out," said Mimi. "He's not my type."

"That never stopped you before," said Shirl.

Mouse froze for a split instant, her fork between her lips. Ivan hadn't been Mimi's type either. Mimi's gaze clicked from Tony and Shirl, to her mug of lukewarm coffee.

"Well, anyway," said Mimi lamely.

Mouse fell silent. She licked her ring finger, then poked up the leftover poppyseeds on her plate.

All evening Mimi had been as twittery as she'd been at sixteen, her messy-on-purpose hair flung up at a more gravity-defying angle than usual. She wore a limp black tank top, blue jeans tight enough to bruise her kidneys, scuffed red cowboy boots. She scuttled around Shirl's newly remodeled kitchen, constructing elaborate dishes with exotic ingredients that required every bowl and appliance in the place, worked up a sweat, drank too much wine, told windy anecdotes for the benefit of Shirl and Tony, sitting cozily at the kitchen table watching her. They didn't eat until ten o'clock. By then Mouse was so hungry that black and white pinwheels twirled on the insides of her eyelids every time she blinked.

" – really a pill, this client, Janice. She kept calling for Solly, and I mean calling!" Mimi gestured in the air with a whisk festooned with egg whites. "I mean six and seven times a day she'd call. Solly was waiting to hear on her deal from Fox and he had nothing to say to her. So I kept asking him if he wanted to take the call and he said, 'Tell her I'm in a meeting, tell her I'm at lunch.' All these excuses. And I tell her, and she starts getting pissed at me. She says, 'I know he's there, Mimi.' She accuses me of not giving him his messages. Finally, one morning, Janice calls, and I don't even ask Solly if he wants to take it, because I know he hasn't heard from Fox, so I say, 'He's at lunch.' Only problem is, it's ten o'clock in the morning. Janice goes, 'I can't believe this.

Put Solly on the phone right now,' and I go, 'He doesn't want to talk to you, Janice,' and she goes, 'Mimi, who did you fuck to get this job,' and I go – it just pops out of my mouth, I don't even know what I'm saying – 'I fucked you, Janice.'"

"Margaret FitzHenry," said Shirl, pursing her lips to keep from smiling. Tony hucked and hawed politely. A beat of silence while Mimi folded the egg whites into her soufflé, waiting for them to ask her what happened next.

Mouse had anticipated an interminable evening of strained pleasantries, forgetting that wasn't how it worked on Cantaloupe Avenue. Instead, Shirl had ushered Tony straight to the kitchen, where she complimented him on his lankiness, then plied him with a plate of deviled eggs she'd made up especially for him. Fitzy, her late husband and Mouse's father, had *loved* deviled eggs, she'd said. Especially with paprika. Shirl hoped he wasn't scared off by paprika.

She grilled Tony about his background and about his and Mouse's life in Africa. It did not escape Mouse that until tonight Shirl demonstrated no interest in Africa whatsoever. Tony, one long leg slung over the other, fingers laced over his lap, guzzled steady refills of gin and tonics, courtesy of Auntie Barb. He looked as if he already had a regular place at the dinner table, his own toothbrush hanging in the bathroom.

Mouse, exhausted from running errands all day, leaned in the doorway, clutching her brown elbows, smiling and nodding politely, as per instructions from The Pink Fiend. *They love you so much.*

"We were working for rival production companies –" began Tony, on the saga of how he and Mouse fell in love.

" – s'cuse me, I've got to go put on the love theme from *Romeo and Juliet*," said Mouse. Tony wasn't really going to start on *that!* She darted out of the kitchen with the ready excuse that she had to go to the bathroom.

"That's right, run off, just like you ran off to Africa!" called Shirl, lassoing her back into the room.

"I didn't run off to Africa."

"Go, go. God forbid we should keep you from doing whatever it is you need to do."

"I was going to the bathroom." Mouse hung in the doorway.

"She thinks I exaggerate," said Tony. "The story embarrasses her."

"She's blushing," said Mimi. "Isn't that sweet?"

"Well, don't keep us in suspense," said Shirl, pushing the plate of deviled eggs under his nose, her eyes glinting beneath the aqua turban. "Sit, Mousie, sit. You make me nervous."

Obediently, and against her better judgment, Mouse sat.

"About four years ago, my Uncle Nigel was producing nature shows for the BBC in Nairobi."

"*Pro*-ducing, I love that. Just like on that *Mantelpiece Theater*–"

"*Master*piece, Mom," said Mimi.

"–go on, go on–"

"I'd been bumming round Africa, when Uncle Ni offered me a position on a documentary they were shooting in southern Kenya, around Maasai Mara, the Game Reserve, as a sound recordist."

"It's really a gorgeous place. Solly has a client who wrote a script about going on safari there."

"Mimi, shush."

"The film had as its subject elephant poaching – you know, killing elephants illegally for their tusks. The first day out we were set to interview some poachers at their hideout in the bush. They were ex-soldiers armed with assault weapons. They would just as soon shoot you dead as have a chat. In order to interview them Uncle Ni had to bribe them, then promise not to disclose their whereabouts, et cetera, et cetera. Quite an elaborate arrangement. In any event, we got out there, and a minute or so into the interview they decided they'd had quite enough of us. They forced the cameraman to turn off the camera – this was at gunpoint – but they'd somehow forgotten about me, the sound recordist. I allowed the tape to roll –"

"– honey, you could have been killed!"

"– I nearly was."

"You were not," said Mouse.

"See, she thinks I exaggerate."

"You do exaggerate."

"Don't let's have a lovers' quarrel now," said Shirl.

"One of the poachers spotted me. He ripped the Nagra, the tape recorder, from my shoulder, bashed me in the face with the butt of his gun. I was in bad shape, bleeding, a broken nose, God knows what else. It so happened that in a neighboring village there was another crew, a West German crew, shooting a television documentary on the very same subject. The crew hauled me into the village with the intention of radioing the flying doctor, but there wasn't time. I had lost consciousness and a frightful amount of blood. The West Germans were heading out to shoot some second unit business when one of the women on the crew – your daughter – saw us. She'd had first-aid training, and with the help of a lunch box full of Band-Aids, one still isn't sure how she managed it, she patched me up.

"Even though one of my eyes was nearly swollen shut, I liked what I saw. She sat there with me for several hours – even though it meant holding up the West German crew – making sure the bleeding had stopped and I didn't develop a fever. It would have been to her advantage to leave me for the flying doctors. We were making a film on the same subject, Losing the sound recordist would have held up the BBC production indefinitely."

"Isn't that nice. I always worry about my girls. They didn't have a father, you know. I worry about their moral fibers. This just goes to show."

"The next day I was feeling much better, and could not get Mouse out of my head."

"Here comes the sexy part," said Mimi.

"I'm getting there –"

" – so there really is a sexy part? This can't be a story about my sister." Mimi smiled at Tony from behind her glass of wine.

"I was angry with myself for not finding out her last name or where she lived, nothing. So I told Uncle Ni I needed to see her to see about getting some painkillers and he let me go. He was quite proud of my heroic feat. They'd recovered the Nagra and the tape, which showed up those bastards for what they were. It was quite good stuff. Anyway, the bit about the painkillers? An absolute lie. She'd given me more than I would ever need.

"When I arrived back at the village, I was told by a production assistant who had stayed behind that a skeleton crew – just Mouse, the director, and a soundman – were out filming some elephant herds. I was surprised she was shooting. I had imagined she was a production assistant or the fish 'n' trinkets girl – the person who goes into a village ahead of the production crew and smooths the way, giving them fish or fabric or mirrors, whatever they want or need, so the crew can come in and do their work with no local interference. But Mouse was a cameraman! I worried if that wasn't dangerous – considering what I'd just been through – and the production assistant, whose name was Flora, a big ruddy Irish girl, said it was suicide. Flora was in awe of Mouse. She said she was fearless. No fear of heights, no claustrophobia, and absolutely no fear for her personal safety. Not only that, all her footage was always in focus.

"Finally, late that night, the crew arrived back at the village. Flora and I had been waiting in a local bar for hours. I'll never forget that place. The proprietor, afraid the wooden tables would be devoured by ants, had put pie tins full of gasoline under the table legs. Mouse came in and ordered a beer. She was quite knackered, and filthy, but still I could smell some of her perfume. Anyway, I was quite drunk, and could tell Mouse wondered what in the hell I was doing there. I made up a silly lie. I said that before we had left Nairobi we had forgotten to recharge the batteries for our camera, and did she have any she could spare?

She didn't believe me. The venerable BBC botching something so basic? But she gave me all the batteries she could, at the risk of needing them in the future. They had two more weeks out in the bush."

"So it was love at first sight. On her part, too, I mean. I always worried that Mousie had a kind of cold streak."

"That's nice, Mom," said Mimi. "Calling Mouse frigid."

"We're all family here. Can't I speak honestly in front of my own family? Tony should know these things."

"Indeed –" Tony looked confused.

"See what you started?" Mouse stood and lurched out of the room. Behind her she heard Mimi say, "Just ignore her. She always overreacts."

Mouse sat down on the diving board and lit a cigarette. While the rest of the house had been remodeled, the lagoon was exactly as Mouse remembered it. The colored lights were on; the waterfall burbled for the benefit of no one.

Even though it was teeth-chattering chilly out here, it was better than listening to Tony recast the story of their courtship into a Norse saga. The more gin and tonics he had, the more heroic the elements became. He was near death! She had the gift of healing and nursed him back to health! In point of fact, he had a broken nose which she plugged with gauze and a black eye whose swelling shrunk under an ordinary ice cube. She had not given him all the batteries she had (she was starry-eyed, but not that starry-eyed). She was not romantic, nor was she frigid. She lay down on the diving board and closed her eyes. The sliding glass door to the kitchen was open.

"Meanwhile, back in Nairobi," Tony continued, "Uncle Ni's favorite cameraman had thrown out his back playing cricket. Uncle Ni was a good person to know. He had bags of connections in the London film community, and since I wasn't planning on staying in Africa forever anyway, I told him about Mouse. He'd actually heard of her before. She had a reputation for being able to take care of gear under the most horrendous conditions, also, her size allowed her into small spaces where a man just wouldn't fit. I told him I would be talking to her soon. It gave me an excuse to call her and invite her for a drink. I told myself if it turned out she was involved with another man, or married, I would turn the evening into a business meeting.

"We met at an Indian restaurant for dinner and I was quite sort of *taken* with her. But when the meal came to an end I found myself – I still am not sure why I did this – telling her about Uncle Ni and the camera position with the BBC. The evening went thud. Much later I would find out that she was as interested in me as I was in her but then believed that I had only invited her out to recruit her for my uncle. She did not like staff jobs, preferring to freelance, but she took the job with Ni out of spite.

"At this point I should say that Uncle Ni is a good-looking chap. Sort of your typical outdoorsy colonialist, graying temples, nice tan. My father's little brother, then about forty-five. A man women liked.

"So Mouse goes to work for him, and I'm not rolling sound anymore. I've been promoted to associate producer and we're in pre-production on *Charles Rydall: Man of Kima*. Rydall was a little-known police superintendent of Nairobi round the turn of the century whose great claim to fame was being eaten by a lion while sitting in his compartment on a train making a stop at the tiny village of Kima. It was a dog of a project, but the BBC was doing some series on historical Nairobi and somehow this fit in.

"In any event, Nigel falls for Mouse. He hires her, then he falls for her. I don't know what's going on and I can't very well ask. Mouse is impossible to read. I think, I'm not sure what I'm thinking. Uncle Ni says he wants to marry her, so I ask her out for a drink, using the pretense of the production schedule. I say I'd like her input. No one ever asks for the camera operator's input, but she agrees to meet me."

"So Mouse had two marriage proposals?" asked Shirl.

"I'm getting to that."

"I can't believe she never wrote to tell us. Two marriage proposals."

"She was probably totally wigged out. I had three guys who wanted to marry me once. It was really thrilling, but kinda nerve-racking."

"What three boys wanted to marry you?" asked Shirl.

"It was a long time ago. I can't remember. One was that guy who came to get the possum that drowned in the pool. From the animal control place."

"Anyway," Tony continued, "we meet for a drink at The New Stanley Hotel. It's a touristy spot, but an easy spot. Mouse is early, and waits for me outside where she is witness to something quite strange. There are quite a few beggars who work The New Stanley. She's got her eye on one man in particular, a chap with a rather powerful upper body who gets around on a skateboard. He's all torso, the legs of his jeans folded up under the stubs of his thighs to cushion them. Mouse watches while he reaches into a woman's bag and steals not her wallet but her *journal*. Mouse is fascinated, and as shy as she is with me–I don't know it's shyness up until that point, I think she's merely indulging me as her fiancé-to-be's nephew–she strikes up a conversation with the pickpocket who's, quite ironically, also called Stanley. He steals tourists' journals so he can discover what their lives are like. Then he travels back to his village, near the Ethiopian border, where he is considered a wise man and a mystic, and he tells his tribe the white man's secrets.

"At that moment I arrived, and Mouse and I went inside. She told me about Stanley. We tried to imagine how he got into this racket, how he supported himself, what stories he told, and how his village reacted to them. We never got to the production schedule. We both knew without saying it that he would make an incredible documentary. We sat there an hour before we realized no one had come to take our order. We were intoxicated anyway. The idea of working together was ... " Tony took a sip of his gin and tonic.

"Go on," cried Shirl.

"It's rather embarrassing," he said, "my future mother-in-law."

"She can take it," said Mimi.

"We got a room upstairs."

"Mousie Mousie Mouse!" Mimi shook her head in mock wonder.

"At The New Stanley. We both had houses in town, perfectly big empty houses that were less than fifteen minutes away. It was quite mad –"

"– romantic," said Shirl. "We're all adults here, right?"

"It was. Well. We quit the BBC. We never worked on *Charles Rydall: Man of Kima*, though I'm told it didn't turn out as bad as it sounded. Uncle Ni was furious, but a good sport. Frankly, I think he was more upset at losing Mouse as a camera operator. We pooled all our resources and made *The New Stanley*. Mouse had been saving most of her salary for just something like this. I had been saving, well, mostly because I had nothing to spend it on. No wife or family. So, *The New Stanley*. So much can go wrong making any movie, but a documentary in Africa…weather, language, health, tribal disputes, you name it. We had none of it. Stanley was a brick, his people, an offshoot of the Turkana, were quite patient and polite. Everything went right – with the production, with Mouse and me.

"Finally, though, after we were done shooting, back in Nairobi to begin post-production, it became apparent that we would not be able to finish unless one of us got a grant or a job. We were living off plantains and rice. I was still underweight due to a bout of dysentery, and Mouse was becoming anemic. We needed to do something. I didn't want her to live like that. It was sad. We knew, somehow, it was the end of something. We blew the rest of our wad on a long weekend in Malindi. Mouse gave me this ring, see? It's carved ebony.

"Uncle Ni heard about our dilemma. We had all this terrific footage shot and nowhere to post it. He offered to donate post-production services, and told us there were jobs on his next show if we wanted them. Even though Mouse had reassured me a thousand times that she had only dated Ni because she had nothing else to do, and in fact looked on him as an uncle, just as I did, I was still hesitant. I loved Ni, but I did not trust him. Mouse begged me. We needed the money. We said yes to Ni, then, it turned out, there was only one job, an assistant editor position. For Mouse.

"She worked long hours. She was never home. Even though Ni had given us the use of the BBC post-production facility, she was always too busy to work on *The New Stanley*. I felt somehow banished, deserted. Then, after moping about for weeks on end, I got offered a job on a French production shooting in Rwanda. An update on the mountain gorillas for French television, I heard about it through Flora, remember Flora? The production assistant on the West German elephant-poaching film. Mouse was a little too anxious for me to take it, so I did. To punish her. She says now she just wanted me to do whatever it was I had to do to be happy, but I thought she was trying to get rid of me.

"I was in Rwanda for three months. Not a peep from Mouse for the first three weeks. Up there in the fog, in the forest, with the gorillas. It was difficult and boring. I was sure she had taken up with Uncle Ni. I had the entire scenario in my head. I suppose this is all a way of justifying –"

" – you had an affair with Flora," said Mimi.

" – with Dominique, the director."

"That dummy. If I was going out with you I'd never let you out of my sight," said Mimi.

"I was miserable," said Tony.

"She could have…what do they do over there? Send signals with drums?" said Shirl.

"Called American Express. Or, we had a FAX machine at the production office."

"She deserved it, then," said Shirl. "She made her bed."

"I'm not proud of it, but there it is. Dominique was very… persistent."

"And there you were up there in the fog, in the forest, with the gorillas," said Mimi. "I'd have done the same thing."

"The weeks passed, still nothing from Mouse. I was convinced she was seeing Uncle Ni. It turned out she hadn't contacted me because word had gotten back to Nairobi about me and Dominique. Then I heard that Uncle Ni had proposed and she had accepted him. I thought I would go off my bean. I got sick. An abscessed liver, a result of the medicine I'd been taking for the blasted dysentery. Fever, horrid cramps. Dominique got a local doctor up from Butare. He gave me something, to this day I'm not certain what exactly, which provoked a toxic reaction. The cramps got worse, the fever higher. I was dead sure I was going to die, and before I did, I wanted to see Mouse, Uncle Ni or no Uncle Ni. At that time Flora was heading back to Nairobi. I asked her if she would go to Mouse and tell her the situation. I gave her the carved ebony ring Mouse had given me, and asked her to give it to Mouse as proof that this was true.

"I began to recover. Still, nothing from Mouse. Then, one day, at the production office, I saw a FAX had come over the wire, ripped in two, tossed in the garbage can. Dominique had intercepted it and thrown it out. It was from Mouse, saying she was coming."

"And did she?"

"She did."

"And you've been together ever since," said Mimi.

"Indeed. When we returned to Nairobi she moved in with me."

"And to think we thought she didn't have a romantic bone in her body," said Shirl.

Tony drained his drink, stood and stretched, dissatisfied with his performance. He'd made it sound as though all he and Mouse ever did in the way of a date was meet for drinks. Then again, he didn't want it to seem as though they'd just hopped into bed like a couple of characters in a Kingsley Amis novel, although they had.

Mimi checked on dinner. Shirl wandered into the other room to see where Auntie Barb had disappeared to. Tony found Mouse lying on the diving board, blowing smoke rings into the night.

"'Eow, poppet, takin' a bit a the evenin' air, are we?" Tony knelt by the side of the pool, twirled a finger in the water. "It's bloody freezing. Vince said you could swim all year long here."

"Vince obviously doesn't know what he's talking about."

"Your mother and sister loved the story."

"They also love those phone company commercials where babies are held up to gurgle into the receiver for Gram and Gramps."

"We're not having another row about this."

"I just don't like our personal life being turned into a David Lean epic."

"You would be bloody lucky if Lean wanted to do it." You're bloody lucky Ralph and V. J. Parchman have taken an interest in it, he wanted to say.

Several days before, Ralph had rung him up. He'd done some calling around and found out that V.J. Parchman was in fact Tony's Peace Corps friend Vince. Also, and more importantly, V.J. had a deal at Columbia and was actively looking for a true-life story set in Africa. Tony and Ralph met for drinks, and Tony told him the same story he had just told Mimi and Shirl. It was, in fact, the basis for *Love Among the Gorillas*, the screenplay he had begun in Vince's filmic writing seminar in the quiet corner of the bar in Nairobi the year before.

Ralph went berserk. He adored the concept. It was a three-hankie weepie. It was a thousand theaters at Christmas. Every other movie love story paled in comparison. With Tony's permission he called V.J.'s office and briefly pitched it over the phone. The assistant pitched it even more briefly to V.J., who was interested enough to set up a meeting. Could I, Ralph asked reverently, read the script? Tony dropped it off at his office on Wednesday afternoon at three o'clock. By the time he got back to the apartment there was a message on the machine. Ralph loved it. He would love it to be his directorial debut. He had a good relationship with V. J., or at least with his assistant, and he was sure this was something V. J. would really spark to. Tony had not told Mouse.

"Lucky? What do you mean? This is our life, not *entertainment*."

"It's the wedding that's gotten you so on edge." Tony sat down next to her on the diving board.

"Why am I the only one it's gotten on edge? You're involved in this too, you know."

"Yes, but as the groom, my job is merely to get myself to the church on time, whereas –"

"– whereas I'm responsible for everything else. Great."

"Are you saying you don't want to get married?"

Mouse looked through a wobbly, dissipating smoke ring at Mimi, Shirl, and Auntie Barb in the kitchen. They seemed to be engaged in careful debate over the appropriate salt and pepper shakers. "No."

"Good." He took a drag off her cigarette and gave her the smoke back in a kiss.

The end of his screenplay ended not with Mouse coming to him in Rwanda but with their wedding on the mountain, in the fog, among the gorillas.

8.

NITA KATZ'S OFFICE WAS IN AN OLDER BUILDING IN Beverly Hills, the kind that used to house third-rate detective agencies in *film noir* from the nineteen-forties. It was on the sixth floor, between two mediums, each of whom was allegedly possessed by the spirit of one of the original Warner Brothers.

"How do they both stay in business?" asked Mouse. She perched uncomfortably on the edge of Nita's mooshy mauve sofa. Nita handed her a cup of coffee in a big white cup balanced on a steering wheel-sized saucer. Mimi stuck to an Evian. Sometimes even the bubbles in a Perrier brought on a binge.

"One channels Jack, the other channels Sam," said Nita. "You should see the studio executives in and out of there. All day long. Fiancé of a client of mine has been to both. Jack always counsels making the picture but keeping the cost down. Sam says don't make the picture unless you can get somebody big box office."

"How are they in life or death situations?" asked Mouse.

"Those *are* life or death situations," said Mimi. "She just got back from Africa."

"Really? Safari?"

"She *lived* there," said Mimi. "That's why she needs you. I told her you were a genius."

Mouse had to hold the cup and saucer with two hands. They were special *café au lait* cups imported from Italy, Nita said. Used to drinking everything from goat's milk to vodka from the odd jar or tin camp cup, Mouse was stunned by the size. They held enough coffee and milk to float a tanker.

In fact, everything in the office, from the coffee cups to the eight-by-eight-foot lithograph of Nita's eerily poreless face – executed by, Mouse presumed, some well-known artist – hanging behind her big black laminate desk, to Nita herself, red corkscrew curls, a wonderful Roman nose, was oversized and gleaming. Mouse felt as though she had gone through a shrinking machine.

But Mouse liked Nita. She had a soft, Southern accent-tinged voice. She didn't tell Mouse what Mouse was supposed to want, would wind up wanting, or would regret she didn't have. She listened. She took discreet notes in a black snakeskin notebook.

"What kind of name is Mouse?"

"It's Frances, really. Mouse was a nickname growing up."

"Just like I'm Mimi. Our real names are Margaret and Frances. Yucky, huh?"

"When Mimi said her sister Mouse I thought it was Mowz or something. Something Arab."

"Nothing so exotic. Mouse, like it sounds, M-O-U-S-E. Frances, Fran, that's not such a great name. There was a girl in high school, Fran Martinotti – she's probably your cousin – anyway, she had a huge mole on her eyelid. So Frances, no. Mouse is good professionally, too."

"It is?" said Nita. "In what sense?" She scribbled a few notes. On what, Mouse could not imagine.

Mouse was nervous. That morning she had tried on everything in her suitcase, wondering what the bride-to-be wore to one of these appointments. She settled on the Uniform of the Adult Western Woman: the oatmeal tweed blazer, khaki twill skirt, and brown pumps she'd bought in Nairobi. She saw now she could have stuck to her jeans. Mimi had warned her. Nita wore ballet tights, flats, an old linty black sweatshirt turned inside-out. She sat sideways in her chair, her legs slung over one arm.

Mouse's stomach sputtered and gurgled, making the kind of sounds rarely found outside a high school chemistry lab. "I don't know if Mimi told you," she continued, too late to disguise them. "I make documentaries. That is, I try to. In Nairobi I found myself specializing in hardship films, documentaries that because of their location or subject are more difficult than usual to make. For example, I did a film on stalagmites. I shot for ten days in a cave a mile and half long, the width of a phone booth."

"Oooghh." Nita shook her wide elegant shoulders.

"You know what they said in third grade about prepositions: anywhere a mouse can go. I'm like a preposition in that sense. Or that's how I bill myself."

"Anywhere a mouse can go?" said Nita doubtfully.

"Under, over, in, on, by–" said Mimi.

"–with," contributed Nita.

"With, yes, with is a preposition."

Nita stared at Mouse blankly, her thin silver pen poised above her notebook.

"Now I'm getting married," said Mouse. "I figure I can shoot in a cave the width of a phone booth, I can get married, right?"

Nita pointed at Mouse with the end of her silver pencil. She tapped the air in front of her pale face with it. "You," she said, "are a smart woman. What I call a Thinking Bride."

"That's what I thought *I* was," Mimi sputtered into her water glass.

"You want the most and the best for your money. You don't have time to waste."

"The Thinking Bride," laughed Mouse. "Now there's an oxymoron. Not that I don't want to get married. I do want to get married. It's just, I want something…"

"Perfect."

"Perfect," Mouse echoed. "The adjective on everyone's lips."

Nita petted the glossy red nails of first one hand, then the other. Mouse watched, mesmerized. The nails were wide and shiny. They looked like the hoods of ten tiny foreign sports cars.

Mouse raised her cup with two hands and sipped her *café au lait*. Suddenly she said, "I tell people I'm getting married, and they're all so *happy* for me. Even people who've never met Tony and hardly even know me."

"They're jealous you have someone to work the VCR and they don't," said Mimi.

"As a rule, the people whom you think are the most happy for you are those whom are the least happily married."

Mouse couldn't help noticing that even though Nita seemed intelligent, she did have trouble distinguishing between that puckish grammatical duo, who and whom.

"You know," said Mouse, "things have changed since I've been gone. I left in the early seventies and marriage was out. Out, out, out. Everyone thought of it as a prison without wails, being strapped to the same person. It made sense. Even though I was pretty young, it made sense. Why would you want to enslave yourself for life? Now I come back. I come home, and women – Mimi's friends, women I meet around – are frantic. Dying to tie the knot with anyone who's remotely eligible. Falling all over themselves to become their *mothers*, which is what I always thought we never wanted to be," Mouse blurted out. Her knees were shaking beneath the giant saucer resting on her lap.

"We're all finding out it's easier to be our mothers than ourselves."

"Are you your mother?" asked Mouse. "You're not your mother, surely."

"I was my mother. I was a first grade teacher and clipped coupons in Rochester. Who could stand it? I left Gary and moved to L.A."

"I was Shirl, Mouse," Mimi said. "You weren't here while I was married. I made tuna casserole and scrubbed the bathroom tile once a week."

"And now what are you?" Mouse asked Nita. "Happy?"

"I'm happy," said Mimi.

"Lonely, mostly." Nita laughed. The chair she was sitting on was taller than the mooshy mauve sofa. Mouse glimpsed the pink roof of her mouth; her teeth were fillingless, bone-china white. Even the back ones. "Used to be, everyone wanted to be free. Now everyone wants to be trapped. But at least they can do it in *style*, right?"

The phone rang, a modern melodic purr. Nita slid off her chair and went to her desk. "...no, no darlin'...they're going to *airlift* the crystal in...uh-huh, as in an *airplane*...six hundred thirty, wine and water...you decided on the orchids? The Fijian ones are the perfect shade, but they do wilt, I can still FAX that florist in Sumatra...I know darlin', I know...it is important... overnight service...right..."

"Isn't she great?" asked Mimi.

Nita hung up. "One of my clients. She's getting married in Death Valley."

"In the desert?" asked Mouse.

"They met on a camping trip. They wanted to get married on the site of their first kiss. Everyone wants something special. I had a couple last year who did it on a float in the Rose Festival Parade. But let's get on with what *you* want, shall we?"

"Something small," said Mouse.

"They don't have much money," said Mimi. "I told her you were a whiz with a small budget."

"Okay." Nita wrote in her notebook. "What, two hundred?"

"Oh no," said Mouse. "No, no, no. More like twelve."

"Twelve hundred?"

"Twelve *people*," said Mouse, feeling her cheeks go hot. Quickly, she outlined her ideas, which she had been formulating without knowing it. Beach wedding. Few close friends. Non-denominational minister. No bridesmaids, save Mimi, who would buy her own dress. As for Mouse, she could either sew her own or pick up something at a used-clothing store. Tony had a few nice suits. "Flowers are optional. So is rice. So is the ring."

"They just want something basic," said Mimi.

"The reception will be potluck," sighed Nita, holding her mechanical pencil up like a syringe, slowly rolling in the lead.

"Yes," said Mouse.

"Potato salad. Pork 'n' beans."

"We were thinking more along the lines of london broil. A buffet."

Nita closed her notebook and stood up. With one hand she relieved Mouse of her cup and saucer. "It sounds like you don't need me," said Nita.

"But I do!" said Mouse. "To organize everything."

"Sounds like you've got everything under control. The brides I generally work with aren't like you. They don't know whether they want to run away to Las Vegas or have a sit-down dinner at the Bel Air Hotel. They don't know whether they want to wear their grandmother's dress or plunk down fifteen grand for something new."

"Fifteen *grand*?"

"Six hundred for flowers. That's just for the bride's bouquet."

"Fifteen thousand dollars for a dress?"

"Not just any dress," said Nita. "One you'll wear for three hours, then put on once every ten years to see if you've gained weight."

"I see." Mouse pulled herself up from the couch, her chest leading, dignified. But hauling her bag up on her shoulder she upended it. A few videotapes bounced out.

"Ideally, I need thirty thousand dollars to create something truly wonderful," Nita said.

Nita stooped down to pick up a tape. She read the label on the side. "*Elephant Men: Elephantiasis in the Sub-Sahara.* Sounds fabulous. Best of luck in your new life and let me know how it goes."

Nita uncurled her long white fingers and shook Mouse's hand, opening the door at the same time.

Outside, walking to the car, Mimi said, "That Nita is really a bitch."

"I understand," said Mouse. "I'm small potatoes."

"It wasn't *that*. Did you see the way she looked at your outfit? That's a nice blazer. I mean, it's not, like *in*, but still. It's classic. You know, your style. And the way she said 'sounds fabulous.' What a snot. Just because it's a documentary. I got a half hour before I have to be back, want to grab a bite?"

"No. I think I'd just like to walk."

"Want me to drop you anywhere? 'Mowz,' she thought your name was Mowz, 'something exotic'! Anyone could tell by looking at you you're just plain old whitebread American. You sure I can't drop you? I can take you back to the apartment. Don't let this get you down. We'll plan a great wedding. After I get home we'll go get some of those bridal books. Fuck her is what I say."

THE EMPTY WHITE sidewalks of Beverly Hills in the rich afternoon light. Mouse walked. She had left Los Angeles when people still used words like "far-out" with a straight face. She left Los Angeles when people, when they got married, got married on the beach and had potluck receptions. They had weddings that were the most like not having a wedding without not having a wedding.

She stumbled down the street in her tight brown pumps, the mesh of her pantyhose embedded in the backs of her thighs from sitting on the edge of that infernal designer sofa. Impulsively, she ducked into a doorway. In one brisk move she reached up under her skirt and rolled down her pantyhose, She stepped out of her shoes. She wasn't the least embarrassed. She may as well have been changing her clothes on some unknown, unnamed beach in Africa. There was no one around. Most of the cars that slid by had tinted windows. Even if they could see her, she couldn't see them, so what did she care?

She walked on, looking back once. In the shadow of the doorway the withered hose drooped over the shoes, looking as though a wicked witch had melted. She dragged her old Moroccan sandals out of her bag and put them on. She strode down the sidewalk, the sandals slapping out her anger on the hot, clean pavement. She passed her bus stop and kept going.

Fifteen thousand dollars for a dress! Six hundred dollars for flowers! In Afghanistan the average annual income was one hundred and twenty dollars. A Ugandan civil servant made the equivalent of ten dollars a month. SLAP! SLAP! SLAP! went her sandals, statistics rocketing around her head. She was supposed to spend the annual income of 125 average Afghanis on a dress that has the lifespan of a mayfly? She was supposed to fly in orchids from Tahiti, or whatever that Death Valley-bride person was doing? It was insane. And if she didn't succumb to the insanity?

Mimi. Ho, ho, Mimi! It would confirm her worst and most cherished suspicions. She would think Mouse was a freak. A loser. Deficient in the basic ways of girliness, ignorant in the ways of the world.

Oh sure, thought Mouse, the World. The world is a piece of cake. Over, under, on and by, anywhere a mouse can go, Mouse could go. It was this other business that gave her fits.

And Tony. How would Tony take it? That was a tough one. Men always seemed to gripe about the amount of time, energy, and money women put into weddings, then became misty-eyed and faint of heart when they saw you walking down the aisle wearing the down payment of your first house. Tony, who thought he'd found himself a wise and levelheaded woman, would be profoundly disappointed if she said, "Yo babe, let's just forget about it and live together."

And Shirl. Oh, Shirl.

"Who invented marriage anyway?" Mouse asked the empty Beverly Hills sidewalk. It wasn't that she was against it, but look, just for a minute, at who invented it! Human beings. The same species who kept insisting there was an organizing principle to the universe! The species that suspected new cars were the root of human happiness! Didn't Mouse know this from experience? Was there one *Zairois* who, despite his hunger, would not feel more blessed if the barge that slid into Kinshasa once a month from upriver delivered not the bags of manioc, the slats of smoked fish he'd been expecting, but a Toyota Tercel with air conditioning?

And this was the species that applauded your decision to marry! It lent its support by reminding you that Your Wedding Was the Most Important Day of Your Life. That You Only Do This Once. That You Only Have One Time to Get It Right. That if you didn't have engraved matchbooks, a private heart-shaped hot tub in your honeymoon suite YOU'D REGRET IT FOR THE REST OF YOUR LIFE. This was what you were fed from the moment you announced your wedding. And it was layered on top of something which, if you were a sensitive woman, a thinking woman, was even tougher to swallow: you were expected to spend the rest of your life with your date to this event! A man who, the instant you decided to marry him – like magic the scales fell from your eyes! – you realized had a paunch like your father's, a hair-line like the Pope's, a view of women and the family like the Pope's, a nasty habit of gargling in Dolby Stereo morning and night, or any other number of revolting behaviorisms and philosophies that once upon a time seemed harmless if not downright cute. Habits which you may have prided yourself on accepting in the name of compromise, because good relationships require compromise. And of course you have a good relationship. Why else would you be getting married! Mouse's brain was asizzle. All these thoughts.

She stopped in the middle of the sidewalk, dizzy and hot. She thought that since she had cheerfully filmed in one hundred twenty-degree African heat, that no piddling warm autumn afternoon could touch her. The sun baked her scalp. Her sweat tickled it. The strap of her bag cut into her shoulder. Before her eyes, the well-scrubbed buildings, the trimmed palms, the expanse of white sidewalk broke up into a jostling bunch of angry gold dots. Suddenly she heard a strange chirping sound. The sound of, what was it? A macaw? Something from the jungle canopy, only robotic. CHI-RUP. CHI-RUP. CHI-RUP. She thought she was having a recurrence of malaria, or perhaps, an awful thought, a new jungle disease was popping up after having gestated for the past fifteen years. CHI-RUP. CHI-RUP. CHI-RUP. She was going mad. She felt faint. She had never felt faint in her life, but in the same way they always said you just know when you met Mr. Right, she just knew that she was going to collapse if she didn't sit down. She knew she would keel over, cracking her head on the sidewalk, and no one would ever know. Rigor mortis would set in before anyone walked by. The chirping bird robot would pick at her remains. Of course, Mouse was not going mad. She was probably not even going to faint. The chirrups issued from the bleeding-heart-liberal Beverly Hills stoplights. They were supposed to be for the blind. A seeing, hearing, able-bodied member of the middle class could hardly afford to live in L.A., period; what blind person could afford to live in Beverly Hills? The mysteries of life multiplied like mold in a bag of cheap hamburger buns during a heat wave.

What was happening to Mouse was simple. She was having a realization. It was: she could not get married.

Mouse thought, if she could only sit down. Sit down and think. Where was she? Near the Academy. They had a library, didn't they? She would go in, cool off, have a bit of a think. Or no, not think. Escape.

Like the movies it had a tendency to honor, the Academy of Motion Picture Arts and Sciences was housed in a solid but unimaginative building of toffee-colored concrete, dark-tinted glass. Getting into the fourth-floor library made getting into the Pentagon look like going to a neighbor's garage sale. Just inside, there was a squinty-eyed guard with a gun who made Mouse sign in, then directed her to the elevators. On the fourth floor, past a set of bulletproof glass doors, she had to sign in again. What company was she with? *Self*, she wrote. What was she there to research? How to (A) Get out of the wedding; and (B) Get back to Nairobi without ruining or ending anyone's life, including my own, she thought.

Trends in American Documentary, she wrote. She noticed that everyone else who had signed in above her was also with *Self*. Odd, she thought. Not at all, Mimi could have told her.

No one ever came to the Academy Library in an official capacity. Desperate people came here, people twitching with ambition. They hunkered over books on breaking into acting, directing, writing, even casting. Or else a biography of someone who had, against mega odds, broken into acting, directing, writing, and casting. People who actually worked in the movies had no need for libraries. The more successful you were in Hollywood, the less you had any need for books of any kind. It was true when Mouse came here so many years ago with Ivan. It was true now.

She got a few magazines on independent filmmaking from the librarian, who looked as if he was part of an experiment to see how long a human being could go without sunlight. His skin was the color of an almost-cooked onion. He was narrow-chested, his weak-looking arms splattered with brown moles. He wore a rag of a T-shirt, a limp thing silk-screened with a faded MR. SUCCESS across his narrow chest. Mouse guessed it was a souvenir from a student film he'd worked on years ago, when he was brimming with dreams.

His ear was being talked off by a man in a white dress shirt and lint-ridden black slacks. A Xerox repairman, a Mormon missionary, a waiter. A respectable middle-class man, whom the film industry had turned into a zealot, with a light-gray face, pink-rimmed eyes.

"–says they can give me fifteen hundred dollars. Fifteen hundred, I say. Okay. Okay. Not great. Humiliating, really, but okay. A producer, director, creative-what-have-you makes up to something like a hundred thousand *per episode*, but I say okay. Fifteen hundred. It's something. So then they say Business Affairs has gotta call. I'm thinking that's it, that's the brushoff, Business Affairs is never going to call, but then they do. A miracle, I think how I'll spend the fifteen hundred. I'll send it to the Feds, is what I do. I make shit wages, but I owe 'em anyway. I feel good about this. Success is not getting to my head. I'll pay the Feds. They call, Business Affairs does, and they say, 'Oh.' They say, 'Oh no, oh no.' They say, we have a special thing in television, an if-come clause. Why it's called this pornographic thing, who knows. But what it boils down to is, they get a free option. They've given it a name though, see. You hear the words free option and you think, 'I'm not gonna get screwed again!' But they say if-come clause, ohhh, very businesslike, and you think, 'Huh, well, I guess that's how things work.' But not me! I've broken my ass on this thing for three years. I took out another mortgage on my house to finish this sucker. I borrowed money from my *parents*. I'm forty-eight years old, Marvin. Forty-eight years old and they're telling me they don't have any money for an option. Warner Fucking Brothers doesn't have any money?"

"It's Martin," said the librarian.

From the back room another librarian appeared with Mouse's magazines, "You interested in filmmaking, are you?" she asked.

Mouse suddenly had an eerie feeling that this woman had been working here when she came here with Ivan during the Watergate summer. This woman was over six feet tall, her long spine as straight as a railway through Kansas. One of those steely matriarchs with no time or patience for osteoporosis or arthritis, whom all men loathe and fear and all women aspire to be when it no longer matters what men think. How could you forget a woman like that?

"I make documentaries," said Mouse.

"Would I know your work?" The Steely Matriarch read the slip Mouse had filled out to get the books. "Mouse FitzHenry?"

Mouse told her briefly about the disease films, about the films on the Moroccan rock climbers, about *The New Stanley*.

"Fascinating," she said.

No, thought Mouse, taking the magazines along with a book called *Africa Goes Hollywood*, it's not her. It's this place. The sad silence, the same air circulated round and round, desperation hugging the room like a cozy on a teapot.

The librarian reminded her of something Ivan had said. It was a fresh memory, not something she'd run through her head eight thousand times. She'd thought she'd manage to cull from her unconscious every glance, every touch, every thought worth remembering. Once in a while there was something new.

They had come to the Academy Library one afternoon after class to look at the script for *Sunset Boulevard*, which was housed in Special Collections. They had just seen the movie, and the idea that they could also actually read and touch and smell the screenplay was startling and thrilling. It was behind-the-scenes. It was almost like having been on the set with William Holden and Gloria Swanson. This, of course, was still during the time when words like *plot point* and *hook* were exotic movie terminology, when a screenplay was as esoteric as a Best Boy, a gaffer, an aspect ratio, before every housewife, convict, and valet parking attendant south of the forty-fifth parallel and west of Plymouth Rock had an idea for a script, before cottage industries had sprung around teaching screenplay writing and story structure, before five-year-olds knew what a screenwriter was and wanted to be one when they grew up.

It was before Africa, Mouse thought, as she sat down across from a gorgeous blond, a man with chiseled everything, curly eyelashes, a beckoning space between his teeth, breathing heavily over a book on acting.

It was before Tony. It was before Mimi got her hands on Ivan. It was in another life.

She flipped through pages of a magazine, glancing idly at headlines. The usual articles on national funding, state funding, local funding, the lack of funding. Old news. Same all over the world.

That day with Ivan he'd said that everyone who worked at the Academy Library looked like they had something major wrong with them. *Sunset Boulevard* arched open on the table between them. Mouse was wearing her yellow polyester flares, an orange gingham crop top that Shirley had made. Mimi had a blue one just like it. Ivan was sunburned from too many hours spent body surfing over the weekend. His forearm was smooth and hot against hers. He leaned into her shoulder and said, out of the side of his mouth, "That guy there's about two hundred pounds overweight. That chick there looks like a stutterer. That one there is shy, man, so shy, go up to her and say BOO!, see what she does." His stubby fingers crawled up her side like a hyperactive tarantula.

"Then we should work here," she giggled, pushing his fingers away.

"That's the part I forgot to say," said Ivan. "Everyone here? All these losers? They *all* want to make documentary films."

Articles on Third World women and the documentary film. An update on the Toronto Experimental Documentary Film Festival. None of it was very interesting. It was like reading about listening to someone play Mozart. What was fun was the actual listening. What was worthwhile was playing, or trying to play, Mozart yourself.

In the back of the magazine, under a section entitled Notices, between want ads, advertisements for conferences and workshops, calls for films and tapes, listings of funding sources and publications, was a small, odd paragraph at the bottom of the page. There was no reason her eyes should have happened on it. There was nothing remarkable about it.

It said: Kudos to award winner I. Esparza on completion of his nine-part series on death and dying in Spanish Harlem EL FUNERAL.

Her stomach squeezed up her throat. She stared at the paragraph as though it was capable of giving up more information if she just waited. That was the strategy she had taken with Ivan before, following Shirl's motherly advice, Ivan would come back if Mouse just waited. For, even though Shirl was appalled by everything early seventies, she had not escaped the influence of that popular hippie poem (vanilla paper, burnt edges, artfully shellacked onto a piece of driftwood, sold at record stores and poster-cum-headshops) that found its way onto the bedroom wall of every teen in the free world. The wisdom it offered was wishful thinking: If you have a bird and you let it go free, and it doesn't come back to you, it wasn't meant to be. If it does come back, it's beautiful.

So there was Shirl, advising Mouse to sit tight, play hard to get, wait him out...

There was Mouse, pretending to the world like she didn't care, *saying* it's over...

There was Ivan, calling the house, disguising his voice, asking for Mimi...

There was Shirl telling Mouse not to panic, he only wanted an excuse to call, in the hopes that she, Mouse, might answer the phone...

There was Ivan coming over, no one's home, wanting – Shirl was right about one thing – to talk about Mouse, wondering what in the hell was going on. Why was she so cool? What had gone wrong?

But these things he couldn't bring himself to ask. He was eighteen, half shy, half tough. He came over and used the pool when Shirl and Mouse weren't home, thinking maybe this time he'd get up his courage to ask Mimi about her. But it was the end of summer, and he was eighteen, with those heavy-lidded eyes, those hormones rocketing around under the honey-colored skin...

There was Mimi, nineteen, working at a bead shop. All day long she dusted beads in plastic boxes when she wasn't making a sale for eighty-seven cents to a bra-less girl in an Indian print blouse. Mimi thought it was over, whatever "it" was Mouse and Ivan had. A friendship, to her eyes. A platonic friendship.

Mouse was mum. Ivan came over when no one was home. Mimi was working at a bead shop, living at home. It was summer. All those songs, wistful songs of sex and despair. On the radio at the bead shop. On the radio Mimi played incessantly as she weeded the lawn, as she sunbathed, as she waited for someone, anyone to come and rescue her from being nineteen living at home in the Valley.

Mimi bought a new yellow velour bikini, the sides held together with gold rings, in anticipation of Ivan's next visit. Mouse, when he called and she answered the phone, pretended not to recognize his voice. Shirl said be patient. Mimi got an IUD from the student health service at Cal State Northridge, where she went to school during the year.

Mouse macraméed wall hangings.

Ivan married Mimi.

It was going to happen: Mouse was going to cry. Right there, in the Academy of Motion Picture Arts and Sciences Library. She would sooner welcome dysentery. Her bowels would listen to her commands, whereas her tears wouldn't. She wished she could cry like other women, like Mimi, who could sniffle and weep, sob and blubber, without losing control.

She swallowed. The first wave hit the beach of her cheeks and rolled down her face, over her chin, down her neck. "Sir, if you're done with this, another gentleman is interested in seeing it...: It was the Steely Matriarch, tugging politely at a book under the elbow of the chiseled, gap-toothed actor sitting across from Mouse.

The poor clod can't even read in peace, thought Mouse. She sniffed. Slurp slurp up her small nose. Ivan, oh Ivan.

The Steely Matriarch looked down at her. She had the tiniest blue eyes Mouse had ever seen. "Are you all right?"

"Ye-ye-ye-haa-haa-haa-haa-haa" lurched out of Mouse's throat.

"Now now now," said the Steely Matriarch.

"I'm all-I'm all-I'm all," she hiccupped. "Ri-ri-right."

"Don't," said the actor, his voice crushed with emotion, "please."

The inside of the library looked underwater to Mouse. She didn't see the tears standing in his emerald-green-thanks-to-contacts eyes. She didn't see his chiseled chin fall to his chest. He bit his tongue. "Ah-huh," his chest heaved, "ah-huh-huh-huh-huh."

"Sniffle-sniffle-oh-ho-ho" came from behind her. "Sniffle-sniffle-oh-ho-ho." It was the forty-eight-year-old Xerox repair-man with the if-come clause. His head was cradled in his arm, his bald spot showing slightly under thinning gauzy hair. His shoulders shook. "My wife said, 'Honey, it doesn't matter, you don't want to be a whore anyway.' But I do want to be a whore! To be a whore would be a promotion. Right now it's rape. They can't part with fifteen hundred dollars? Those people spend fifteen hundred on dinner and a movie."

The library filled with sighs and quiet sobs. You know how it is in a sad movie. All around you, in the dark, sniffle-sniff, the soft rustle of frayed Kleenex. These people were watching a movie, too. It was the movie inside their own heads. It was the movie of their lives. And unlike the average three-hanky weepy, where the lives of the heroines and heroes are changed (usually ruined) forever, in these movies, the movies in the heads of the desperate, nothing happened. Ever. They pushed their rocks uphill, they went to meetings, they sent out their scripts, their eight-by-tens, their reels. They did that, and they went to the Academy Library.

And nothing ever happened. They died making the same wage they did at the bead shop. Even Mr. Success dabbed at his eyes with his knuckles. Their lives made a Beckett play look action-packed.

This would have gone on who knows how long. The Steely Matriarch, whose eyes were quite dry, glared around the room in disbelief. To her, the snuffs and coughs were nothing more than disruptive noise in the library.

Suddenly Mouse felt herself being lifted out of her chair by her armpit. The Steely Matriarch steered her through the library and out the bulletproof door.

"Are you going to be all right?" the Matriarch asked.

"Ye-ye-ye-I'm fi-fine. I'm fine," said Mouse, inhaling deeply.

"You're sure? Have a drink of water."

Mouse obediently bent to the drinking fountain.

"I have an idea for a documentary you might be interested in. A history of the Academy Library. People don't know, for example, that we have a large collection of pamphlets, clippings. We have an extensive collection of cocktail napkins on which Mr. Zinnemann made his notes for *High Noon* ...."

9.

TONY THOUGHT HE'D FOUND HIS SPIRITUAL HOME. HE
had grown up in Malaysia, in Ghana, Kenya, and India. His father,
now retired, had been a middle-level officer in the British Foreign
Service. But nowhere had Tony felt so at home as in Mimi's
almost-on-the-Westside duplex in Los Angeles, California.

He loved the pace of the city, the light, the latitude, the way
everyone was always off somewhere, driving to the next meeting, the next meal, leaning into the future in their shiny cars. The
streets were so clean, compared to the streets of Kuala Lumpur,
of Accra and Nairobi and Bombay. He was shocked at how Third
World his expectations had become.

He was taken with L.A.'s fiddling-while-Rome-burned
ambience, the populace cheerfully asphyxiating itself, building
million-dollar homes that perennially slid to the valleys below.
He admired Hollywood.

Tony confessed these impressions of the city to Mimi one
day when he dropped her off at Talent and Artists. The morning
was clear, the air damp with a million sprinklers watering a
thousand lawns. *Coo-roo-roo-roo* went the mourning doves, hidden in the trees. *Coo-roo-roo-roo*, you heard them but never saw
them.

"Spiritual L.A.," Mimi muttered, "that's like plastic silverware and business ethics. The land of drive-meet-eat.
Spiritual – ha."

Tony had certainly been consumed with driving, meeting,

and eating since he'd gotten *Love Among the Gorillas* going with Ralph and V. J. Parchman several weeks before.

Usually, Tony would drop Mimi at Talent and Artists by nine, then, if he was meeting Ralph for an early lunch, he would drive to Santa Monica to Ralph's office. Because he had missed the traffic, he would inevitably arrive twenty minutes early (had he waited ten minutes longer, he would inevitably be thirty minutes late). Then they would go for lunch, Vietnamese on Venice, soul food on San Vicente, or moussaka on Montana. This regimen served to put some much-needed meat on Tony's bones, and taught him how to confidently drive seventy miles an hour on the freeway while tailgating the car ahead of him.

Today, they ate Japanese and practiced what Ralph called their dog and pony show. After lunch they were having their long-awaited, much-rescheduled meeting with V.J. Parchman.

Even though Ralph had briefly pitched *Love Among the Gorillas* to V.J.'s assistant, who had pitched it even more briefly to V.J., he and Tony should assume that V.J. will have forgotten the idea by the time they meet with him. Yes, he would have read the script before the meeting – by which Ralph meant his assistant would have sent it out to the reader, who would have read twenty pages of it, to produce three or four pages' worth of notes, which V.J.'s assistant would then condense into a single page for V.J. to skim. Even so, V.J. would no doubt need to have his memory refreshed. What Ralph and Tony needed to choose was the single best word to convey the spirit of the work. Once they got in V.J.'s office, they had approximately five seconds in which to capture V.J.'s attention and heart.

Tony thought perhaps the word should be "love." "Love, or, if we're afforded the chance to slip in another, 'love, Africa.'"

"He already knows it's Africa," said Ralph. "We can't waste time with something he already knows. I'm telling you, these people have attention spans shorter than a sneeze. Better, 'love and BO.'"

"I suppose that does capture the exotic backdrop. But I should think BO is a bit vulgar. This is a tender love story."

"Box Office is God," said Ralph, "vulgar or not. 'Love, BO,' and if his eyes haven't already glazed over, 'Redford.'"

"Love, BO, and Redford," said Tony. It did have an incantatory quality.

"No 'and,' no 'and'! Too wordy. 'Love, BO, Redford.' He'll be bored – if you bore 'em you've hung yourself."

V.J. Parchman's office was on the lot in Burbank. Ralph and Tony needed a pass at the gate to get in. Tony felt privileged and official, conducting business with the guard. He imagined a time when they would be on a first-name basis with him, when he would see the car and wave them on through. "Mr. Holladay! Mr. Cheatham! How are the rushes?" Tony made a mental note to have Mouse get him a new pair of sunglasses.

They drove Ralph's car rather than Mimi's. It was two years younger and one model up from the bottom of the line. Ralph parked far away from V.J.'s office, on the off chance V.J. or his assistant should see them. If they saw Ralph and Tony arrive in an econo-box it would reduce their chances of getting a deal.

V.J.'s assistant was a regal young black woman with a diamond stud in her nose, a beaded Maasai necklace encircling her elegant throat. Tony thought she might be Kenyan. She was, in fact, from Jamaica.

"Close enough!" said V.J., emerging from his office. "Tony, good man, is it really you? *Jambo, habari.*" He pumped Tony's hand warmly. "Don't get to use my Swahili much, but Emily here is learning. Come in."

Tony was alarmed to see that Vince had not changed. Wasn't he supposed to be unrecognizable: a smooth Hollywood producer reeking of money and opportunity? Instead he looked like a Peace Corps volunteer fresh from a good night's sleep and a shower. He wore pressed khaki shorts and a polo shirt. His thinning, graying brown hair curled over his collar, the earpiece of his horn-rimmed glasses held together with first-aid tape.

Still, there was a whiff of opulence; the shorts and shirt looked expensive. He wore cologne and a gold watch. Tony thought – no, must be my imagination – that Vince had picked up a Kenyan accent. He thought Vince was from Pasadena.

His office resembled a small ethnographic museum. Maasai spears and shields were displayed in a case on one wall. Carved masks hung on the opposite wall, illuminated by some kind of fancy lighting. Shiny ebony animal carvings occupied a long shelf beneath the masks. The coffee table was a piece of thick glass laid over a three-legged drum made from part of a hollowed-out coconut palm. His in-box was a small, brightly woven basket, the type sold by girls along the lip of the Great Rift, marked "in" in Swahili; the out-box was similar.

"Dear God, you certainly have become quite the collector," said Tony.

Tony and Ralph sat on the *faux*-cheetah skin loveseat. V.J. lit up a meerschaum pipe, his acne-scarred cheeks hollow with the effort of getting the pipe to draw. He leaned back in his chair and kicked his feet up on his desk. Tony was further alarmed to see he was wearing tennis shoes.

"So. *Love Among the Gorillas.*" He fixed Tony and Ralph with an executioner's stare.

Tony was nervous. This was it! He was overcome with the feeling that this was, as he'd long suspected, the center of the galaxy. This, the Industry. The Business. This, the last place on earth where a talentless sod with no appreciable skills could still make a fortune by legal means. It was a place roiling with absurd miracles, and here he was: at the center of it.

"BO," said Tony.

"BO?" said Vince, brows furrowed.

"What we mean –" Ralph cut in.

"Oh dear, not really!" said Vince, leaping to his feet. "It's not BO, it's Christ, I just had Allyn Meyer in here." He strode over to the end table next to Tony's elbow, peered down at a Plexiglas box in which a perfect orb of flaky white rock was preserved.

Vince sniffed until Tony was sure he would hyperventilate. "You sure you smell something, old chap?"

"No, I was – "

"It's supposed to be air-bloody-tight," said V. J. "I wouldn't have it displayed if… Allyn must think I'm a bloody barbarian." He strode back to his desk and called Emily in.

"Smell that," he commanded her. She leaned over, holding her Maasai necklace down so it wouldn't crash against her nose.

"What?" she asked.

"It smells, can't you smell it? Take it back to that, wherever you had it made, tell them I can't have my office smelling like an outhouse. It's got to be airtight."

Emily's beautiful pink lip curled as she picked up the box carefully with both hands and strutted out. "This is what you get, trying to make shit art."

"And vice versa, old girl, vice versa," said Vince. "Christ, it's such a lovely piece of dung, round as a bleeding tennis ball rolled into perfection by two terrific dung beetles at Olduvai, on the exact spot where old Zinjanthropus was dug up. Tony, old boy, you've been to Olduvai. That Leakey, such a good chap. Had a meeting with him."

Tony was mute. He smiled and pulled at the end of his nose.

"So. *Love Among the Gorillas*. Absolutely." Vince's cheeks chuffed in and out as he pulled on his pipe. He resumed his position behind his desk.

"We see it as a sexier *Out of Africa*," said Ralph.

"I want to bloody make this movie," said Vince. "Tell me how you envision it."

Tony glanced over at Ralph, who beamed at V. J. as though this was a perfectly normal conversation. "Pretty much, I'd say, how I'd written it," said Tony.

"How you'd written it," repeated Vince, mystified.

"The script," said Tony.

"The script!" said Vince. "I *creamed* over this script." He patted a screenplay in a light-blue cover sitting among the nest of papers on his desk. Tony was sure he'd ordered green covers. "I can't believe that turd isn't an absolute *rock* by now," he said to himself. "I knew I should have just picked up some rubble, but *everyone* collects rocks."

"We're going for something original, but something everyone will recognize immediately," said Ralph. "We want something serious, but also something light and playful, something profound and also, in parts, kind of dumb, you know, for the target audience."

"Exactly what we're looking for," said Vince. "But before we run it past Allyn and the rest of the VPs I'd like to make two changes."

"Certainly," said Tony. He dug in his leather case for a note pad and pen.

"First I want to use your real names. We're looking for a true-life story set in Africa. We want *Born Free*, we want *Out of Africa*. We want to be able to say, 'This is a true story' before the opening credits. To do that, we have to use your names. That's easy though, right?"

"– as a cheerleader on prom night," said Ralph.

"I don't know," said Tony. He'd never shown Mouse the screenplay, figuring he was saving himself no small bit of grief. She'd get bent out of shape when she recognized herself in the tough and lusty Kitty. Now, though, if he was going to get a deal – and from the looks of things he was – she would certainly find out about it. She would want to read the script. He could not imagine her reaction if she saw her own name in it. "Let me discuss it with Mouse."

"I'm sure it'll be no problem," said Ralph, "just a courtesy. We want to do things right."

"What was your other suggestion?" asked Tony.

"That, boys, I will leave up to you. I believe in letting the artist do his job. Even though this script is perfect as it is, let's see if we can make it more perfect."

"Indeed," said Tony. "And how, exactly, are we to make it more perfect?"

"I need…" Vince pursed his lips and waved his pipe in front of his face as though trying to beat the right words from the air, "…differences. Get it more there. Just don't get too creative on me. We want to get this thing made, remember."

THERE WAS AN agent at Talent and Artists, Thaddeus Herman, who heard Mimi ask Solly if he had any suggestions as to how she might get Mouse and Tony a screening. In response, Solly said, "Lemme get back to you. Get me Rocky Martini."

Thaddeus looked about fifteen and had degrees from Harvard in business and philosophy. He was one of the best agents at Talent and Artists. He'd recently gotten one of his worst writers six figures for a rewrite which required changing the main character's name from Bruiser to Crusher.

Mimi could not figure out why Thaddeus was so hot on documentary. Probably in order to look like an intellectual instead of a bottom feeder, which is what agents really were. Alyssia said he also wrote sonnets, which he read once a week at Casa Chez Moi on Fairfax with a bunch of other successful industry people (as opposed to the people Mimi knew). You could only imagine what that was like. "A View from Above-the-Line." "Ode to Gross Participation."

But as powerful as Thaddeus was, able to get his clients lots of money to do nothing, he was not able to get the LAFI to host a screening for Mouse and Tony. They turned him down flat. He apparently had no friends there, which was the lie he'd told Mimi, but had just assumed he'd radio in on his headset, drop his own powerful name, and show up the night of the screening. But, as Mouse had already told Mimi, the LAFI was booked eight months in advance. The LAFI had done an ethnographic film festival two years before. The LAFI had never heard of Mouse FitzHenry and Tony Cheatham, nor had they heard of Thaddeus Herman.

"We're going with the Venice Documentary Consortium instead," he told Mimi. "Very new. Very cutting edge. I got the ball rolling. All you need to do is follow up." He snuck a manila file onto the edge of her desk. Inside there was nothing but a scrap of paper with a name, E. Bomarito, and a phone number.

E. Bomarito had never heard of Thaddeus Herman either.

"Wasn't he the guy had the multimedia show on self-mutilation?"

"I'm calling from the Talent and Artists agency," said Mimi. "We're cosponsoring a series of African films by Mouse Fitz-Henry and Tony Cheatham. Thaddeus is an agent, and I'm his – an associate. Mouse and Tony just got back from Kenya."

"Did talk to a Herman few weeks ago. Lemme – sure, 's got a fourpart thing on sewage-treatment plants in the Midwest. I told him anytime. Just let us know few days ahead so's we can make sure we got enough folding chairs. Should tell you, Tuesdays tend not to be the greatest. Church upstairs gets kinda rowdy."

"There's a church upstairs?"

"Chapel of the Divine Psychics. They got a workshop Tuesday nights, Schmoozing with the Dead. The Dead can really get down."

"You don't mean –"

"– the deceased, not the Grateful Dead. Sounds like I'm talking the Grateful Dead, doesn't it?"

DURING THE FIRST week in December, almost five months before the wedding, Mouse and Mimi met one lunch hour at the Consortium "offices" to take a look. Even though Thaddeus insisted it was the cutting edge of documentary in Los Angeles, Mimi was leery. The administrative offices of the Venice Documentary Consortium operated out of E. Bomarito's studio apartment. To be more specific, they operated out of the gray rumpled sheets of his Murphy bed. Who could tell if this was avant-garde or pathetic?

Mouse was more concerned with the screening facilities than with where E. Bomarito kept his file folders. The Venice Documentary Consortium and the Chapel of the Divine Psychics were located in the old Venice Beach Fire Department. The Consortium was in the basement. There was no sign, just crumbling steps leading downstairs from a side entrance. Over the doorway, in purple felt pen, someone had written: we show anything with sprocket holes. Inside, it smelled like disinfectant and rancid butter flavoring. Shadows of God knows what scurried around the baseboards. Someone had built a projection booth out of knotty plywood and stuck a small screen on the concrete wall opposite. Smack in the middle of the room was a hole in the ceiling the size of a small child's wading pool, through which ran a brass pole. The hole had been covered with silver tape and black construction paper. Mouse stood next to the pole, hands on her narrow hips, looking back and forth between the projection booth and the screen.

E. Bomarito had soft kinky black hair and a black handle-bar mustache from which hung the leftovers of a breakfast that included something gooey and beige. A wedge of furry potbelly, featured between the bottom of his limp, tie-dyed T-shirt and the tops of his jeans, was his only other notable feature. He slouched against the doorjamb while they looked around, cleaning an ear with one of his car keys. "No box office, per se, we just stick a coffee can here by the door."

"This pole," said Mouse, bunging it with the heel of one hand, "can't we get rid of it?"

"The pole?" said F. Bomarito, "What do you mean?"

"How do you project with this thing here?"

"She didn't tell you?" He gave Mimi a chastising glance. "This used to be a fire station."

"I told her," said Mimi. "Couldn't you set up a little card table? I mean, for the box office?"

"This pole is right in line with the lens."

"Can't people just sort of schooch around it? Move their chairs?"

"Mimi," Mouse said, "I don't care where people sit, the pole is right in line with the lens."

Beggars can't be choosers, Mimi was about to say. Just screen your stupid movies and get on with it. She had a fifty-minute drive back to the office in midday traffic. When she got there, she had to do her homework for How to Write a Block-buster, while pretending to be doing her regular drudge work. The homework was to write the copy for the dust jacket of her projected blockbuster on love and betrayal in the business. The class had not actually begun writing yet. First they created the publicity campaign for their projected books, then they wrote what they considered were ideal glowing reviews, then they did the dust-jacket cover copy, then a plot outline, then character sketches, then the book. They were to think of it like eating an artichoke, Ralph had said.

"We had Werner Herzog here last year," said E. Bomarito. "He *liked* the pole."

"I like it, too," Mimi said. "We could have a brie wheel. Come on, Mouse it'll be a scene. I'll invite everyone I know, all our clients, and we'll get press releases out to the African community. Thaddeus knows people at the *Times*, we can get one of the Arts writers to come."

Mimi conned Mouse into believing that this was *the* place to premiere her films. Much better than the old-fogy and obvious LAFI. Sure, the Venice Documentary Consortium rede-fined the word funky, and sure, E. Bomarito was the type of dandruffy intellectual and lost soul who gave documentary a bad name, but she should consider it like a trendy Lower East Side alternative-art space.

Secretly, Mimi knew it would be humiliating. She could only imagine the kind of deadbeats and never-weres who would show up, if anyone showed at all. But she promised she would do PR, she said she would see if she could scam an ad in the *Times*, round up the little card table for the box office, prod the dim and revolting E. Bomarito to do whatever it was he usually did to promote his screenings. All this she promised. She promised it out of guilt. She promised it because she was not going to invite anyone to this whose opinion she respected, i.e., anyone she knew. Could you see Nita Katz, with her perfect hard-boiled-egg complexion, her bony white shoulders and red corkscrew curls stuck watching a documentary on elephantiasis from behind a pole in a smelly basement with the six or seven loneliest losers in L.A.? Mimi couldn't.

Mimi said she would invite her.

Mouse knew Mimi wouldn't.

THE NIGHT OF the screening, Mimi caught Mouse talking to herself in the bathroom mirror. Her nose was an inch away from her worried image, her dry brown hands anchored against the side of the sink. "Okay, Frances. You can do this," she exhaled.

"What are you so nervous about?" Mimi said. "It'll be great. Can I get in here to do my mascara?" She pulled her make-up bag out of the bottom drawer.

Mouse dropped the lid of the toilet and sat down, chin in hand. She wore a stretched-out black cotton sweater and black leggings, castoffs from Mimi. The leggings fell in folds around her ankles, the sweater was like a dress. Mouse resolved every morning to go out and buy herself some new clothes, but frankly she was terrified. Of the stores, the salesgirls, the selection, the prices. She had not scrutinized her looks in sixteen years, and had come to the conclusion that compared to every other woman in Los Angeles, she was a withered hag. Mimi's wrong-headed solution was a perm. Now Mouse's dark thick hair sprung straight up, a soufflé of curls. All efforts to comb it flat failed.

"You look sort of like the Bride of Frankenstein, except without the white streak. Your hair and everything," said Mimi. She hung from the waist, scrunching her own blond curls.

"Great."

"I meant it as a compliment," she said. "You look really hip instead of like a Crosby, Stills and Nash groupie."

Mouse glowered. The Pink Fiend advised her: You're just nervous about the screening. Mimi means well. After all who set up this thing for you in the first place? You're just jealous because she looks so terrific and you look like a piece of dried fruit with hair.

Mouse said nothing. Sniffy Voyeur appeared at the doorway, his big black nostrils working the smells in the bathroom. He hobbled over to Mouse and laid his pointy nose on the toilet seat between her legs. She scratched his head, worrying again that they hadn't been able to afford to get a new print of *The New Stanley* struck before the screening.

"Did Tony tell you about their meeting with V. J. Parchman?" Mimi asked.

"You mean Vince Parchman? He was supposed to be in Kenya teaching tribal mothers how to give basic medical care to their kids. He took the children to the movies – some for the first time – and told them they could make that magic, plus be richer than the richest tribesman. He got them to spend what little money they had on a screenwriting class. Some of the parents thought he was teaching a literacy class and sold cattle to pay for it."

"Not that you would've gotten any info out of Tony anyway. Ralph won't even tell me what they're doing. He's gotten really superstitious. I think it was all those years blabbing everyone's ear off about *Girls on Gaza*, then having nothing happen. It's bad luck to talk about what you have in the works."

"I'm just glad Tony is seeing about work," Mouse said. "He really likes his leisure."

"That's how I am: a sensualist who likes relaxing."

Mouse rolled her eyes at Sniffy. His old brown eyes were milky with cataracts. His breath smelled like canned tuna. In her entire life Mouse could count the times on one hand when she had ever seen Mimi relax. "How old is ol' Sniffy Voyeur? He must be, God, what, six – "

" – fifteen," said Mimi. "Ivan and I got him three weeks after we were married."

"Then he's sixteen," said Mouse.

"He's fifteen," said Mimi.

"Anyway, he's old. Aren't you, old guy?" She rubbed the top of his head with her knuckles. He drooled happily.

"He's not old," said Mimi. "He's just, he's a mature dog."

"Fifteen is old for a dog," said Mouse.

"Not that old."

"What about his tumor?"

"It's not a tumor," cried Mimi. "God, you're so gloom and doom. It could be a tumor but it's probably like some hormonal thing. Get off Sniffy's case. Come here, Sniffer, come here!" Mimi slapped her thigh.

Sniffy dropped his head onto Mouse's knee and wagged his body, gazing up at her through his cataracts. Whatever was wrong with him, he was always starving, even after he'd just eaten. Once Mouse had left a peppermint in the pocket of one of her T-shirts. Sniffy had chewed through her suitcase, clawed through all her things just to get to it. The vet said his brain was telling him he was always starving, even though he wasn't. Just like the American consumer, Mouse thought.

"Sniff! Come!" He reluctantly left Mouse for Mimi. "This stupid dog. He's just like me, always falling for people who don't like him."

"I like him."

"You said he had a tumor. Don't listen to her, Sniffy."

10.

IN VENICE, THE NIGHT WAS HEAVY WITH THE SWEET, briny smell of salt air and sewage. There was a life-size crèche on the weedy lawn next to the Venice Documentary Consortium. The three wise men huddled in adoration over a manger brimming with scraps of 35mm film. Taped over the closed snout of one of the plaster donkeys was a hand-lettered sign: AFRICAN MOVIS, then an arrow pointing to an open door leading downstairs.

When Mimi and Mouse got there, E. Bomarito was standing at the bottom of the stairs with a roll of mimeographed programs he'd typed up himself on an old manual typewriter, the kind with leaping *e*'s and clotted *o*'s.

"Got that card table you wanted. Abbey Rents. Twenty-seven fifty."

He fished the receipt from a greasy pouch he wore around his neck, "How ya like my nativity scene?"

"About the best you could say is that it redefines Christmas," said Mouse, snapping out the legs of the card table.

Shirl and Auntie Barb were the first to arrive, They staked out two seats at the end of the back row. Shirl was agitated. She kept dragging off her turban to scratch her head. Her hair had grown out. It was salt-and-pepper, half an inch long, the prickly texture of Astroturf. Mouse opened a bottle of Chablis with a multipurpose implement on her Swiss Army Knife and brought Shirl and Auntie Barb each a glass dotted with floating crumbs of cork.

"Mousie Mouse, when is this thing going to start!" Shirl cried. She took the wine eagerly with shaking, spotted hands.

"We met with that corrupt L.A. lawyer person today," said Auntie Barb accusingly, as though Mouse had suggested him. She wet her lips daintily with the wine.

The corrupt L.A. lawyer in question was Mr. Edmonton, the attorney who was bringing the suit, on Shirl's behalf, against Gateau on Melrose and the manufacturer of the ceiling fan. He had been eating at Gateau at the time of the accident; when Shirl came to at the hospital and asked for her purse she found his card, raised black ink on thick creamy stock, tucked into one of the side pockets. A note in his own hand said, "Give me a call when you feel better!"

Called him she had and, in her opinion, he had been insufferably rude. He wanted her business and now he had slighted her. He was a partner at a big downtown law firm, the kind with pastel-colored walls and matching art. He ushered her and Auntie Barb in, inquired after Shirl's health, produced two cups of instant coffee that burned the inside of Shirl's mouth, then passed her on to a surly paralegal with the fattest knees she had ever seen.

"Only God should see knees like that. She was all decked out in a leather mini. Mutton dressed as lamb."

The fat-kneed paralegal grilled Shirl mercilessly for an hour and a half. She wanted to know about every head injury Shirl had ever had in her entire life! She wanted to know what happened the evening of the accident.

Shirl had tried to explain. "Part of the reason I'm suing is 'cause I don't know what happened. I can't *remember*. Here I was all ready to scoop up a white chocolate dumpling with strawberry sauce, then BOOM!, I'm in a strange bed with tubes coming outta my nose, a strange man at the end of my bed pinching my toes and asking me if I feel."

Now, she told the paralegal, she had to write down everything. She'd start a new découpage project, then forget how many coats of shellac she'd put on. She'd go find a piece of paper to make a note to herself, but by the time she found one she'd have forgotten why she needed it in the first place. She had headaches. She wanted to eat glazed doughnuts. The only thing that kept her from going insane was helping her daughter plan her wedding.

"Don't say that, Mom, please," said Mouse. After the meeting with Nita Katz and her horrible moment at the Academy Library, Mouse had been trying to think of a way to postpone the wedding.

"It's true," said Auntie Barb.

"What about your découpage?" said Mouse.

She surreptitiously glanced over at the door. People were arriving. Mimi's friends from her book group were here. Tony had finally turned up with Ralph. Three strangers wandered in. She felt relieved. It would be a real screening after all. Not just a tedious event to which family came because they had to, and friends came so you'd owe them one when they needed bodies at some art opening or baby shower. The strangers were glum, edgy, dressed in black. Mouse couldn't care less. Maybe they read the free listing in the *L.A. Weekly*. Maybe they were actual members of the Venice Documentary Consortium. Mouse had sort of assumed there had been only one member, the odoriferous E. Bomarito.

"Oh, honey, I'm keeping you from your party," sighed Shirl.

"No. Go on. I'm listening."

"Your eyeballs are drifting all over the place," said Auntie Barb. "Everyone here does that. They pretend they're listening but all the while they're looking around for somebody more interesting. In Oregon people look you in the eye."

"The instant I told that girl with the knees that you were getting married I could see the jealousy sprout up in her eyes. Then she said, 'You said earlier that it was white chocolate dumplings in strawberry sauce. Which was it? Strawberry or raspberry?!'" Shirl burst into loud tears.

"Oh Mom, it's all right." Mouse patted her shoulder. "She was just trying to do her job."

"I want to sue the bejesus out of those cocksuckers."

"Mom."

"She doesn't know what she says anymore," said Auntie Barb. "If this had happened in Oregon, the lawyers would be more courteous. It's the constant sun here that makes them sadistic. In Portland, it's only seventy-five cents to park downtown for two hours. You should see the city in autumn."

"Great, Auntie Barb."

"Don't be facetious. That's the other thing the sun does, makes people facetious. In Oregon people are courteous and kind."

Mimi manned the "box office." Poor Mouse, she thought, stuck in the quicksand of Shirl's complaints about Mr. Edmonton. Mimi supposed she should go and rescue her, but she had already heard the entire story over the phone. Anyway, if Mouse couldn't extricate herself from Shirl and enjoy her fifteen minutes of fame, that was her problem.

"Hi guys!" Mimi waved Sather and Darryl on through. Ralph was parking the car.

Sather, eyes bulging and haggard, was talking about some recent grueling job that made working in a sweatshop sound like getting paid to do nothing.

"– it's Thursday, and I'm *still* there –"

"– he went in on Monday morning –" said Darryl. "This is the Bataan Death Edit."

"– I go in Monday morning. I asked the supervisor, is it going to go late tonight? And the supervisor goes *oohwahaha*! He's got a laugh like that, *oohwahaha*! You've obviously never been on this show before –"

"– which brings up the question, does the film industry make people deranged or are the deranged naturally attracted to the film industry?"

"By Thursday, by *Thursday*, I've been in the same room with the same six guys, and we've been eating nothing but takeout deli, and no one's had a decent shit for days – sorry, Mimi – and I'm rolling through trying to find the right take of this car up and by, but there are about seventeen takes, and they all sound alike, and I have to keep rolling through – "

" – he has to keep rolling through because he keeps falling asleep over the reels!"

" – and the supervisor is standing in the middle of the room – the guy is really demented, I'm telling you – yelling, 'Thank God for the Union, boys! We've just gone into Quadruple Platinum Overtime! We're making more than the fucking star!'"

" – but who ever has time to spend it?" asked Darryl.

" – who ever has time to go to the bank!" said Mimi.

"I made twelve thousand dollars in four days," said Sather, "then I left the check in my coat pocket, which I left on a seat in a movie theater in Westwood."

"The glamorous and sexy film business," said Darryl, gargling his wine for emphasis.

"Tony and Ralph think it's glamorous and sexy," said Mimi as Ralph stumbled in. She bumped him with her hip. "They just had their big meeting with V. J. Parchman."

"How'd it go today?" asked Sather.

"Let's just say I'm not overwhelmed with depression."

"This calls for a celebration, then."

"I'll tell you how it went," said Mimi. "V. J. had his phone calls held, then broke down and took one of them; he took notes, but also doodled. His eyes glazed over, but only twice. He loved the script, but doesn't have the money to option something right now, even though his deal's with a multibillion-dollar conglomerate. Am I close?"

This was how all those meetings went. V. J. probably had a hundred of them a month, ninety-nine of them went nowhere. Like a sighting of Big Foot, no one ever knew anyone who actually had the one-out-of-a-hundred meeting that went Somewhere, so there is no way of knowing what *that* meeting was like. Once,

in a frenzy of frustration, Ralph showed Mimi his collected date-
books. He had been to six hundred seventeen meetings that
went nowhere in the last ten years. She couldn't figure out
whether that made him a saint or a fool. Never face the facts.
Who said that? Some famous actress.

"You are such a smart aleck," said Ralph, pulling Mimi to
him and giving her a fierce bite on the earlobe.

"I'm psychic," said Mimi.

"It was actually better than we expected," said Ralph,
"which is to say it was only a moderate waste of time and we were
not overtly humiliated."

"Yippee, plan your Oscar speech."

E. Bomarito left his post at the door and began herding
people toward the folding chairs.

"How you doing, girls?" asked Mimi, stopping by to see
if Shirl and Auntie Barb needed anything. "Can you see all right?"
She glanced up, waved to Carole, who had just staggered in,
a load of new scripts weighing down her beatup leather purse.

"Are you waving at Ivan?" asked Shirl. She craned her head
around painfully.

"Ivan? Esparza?"

"I invited him."

"My Ivan? You invited my Ivan?"

"Phone number's right in the book," said Auntie Barb.
"You never think to look in the book anymore. Even in Portland
no one's listed."

"Why didn't you tell me you were going to invite him? I have
his number. You didn't need to go and look it up. I have it."

Mimi did not like this kind of surprise. For one thing she
would have worn something that made her stomach look flatter,
not what she had on, a big shirt belted at the waist. She hadn't
seen Ivan in maybe six years. He had always complimented her
on her flat stomach. She also wasn't keen on his presuming she
had anything to do with this really, when you got down to it, very
depressing screening. Ivan had had stuff at the LAFI, at big

places in New York and Chicago. He had won an Oscar, even if it was just for documentary. Then there was the Mouse situation. She would think Mimi invited him to steal her thunder.

Mimi stood up from where she knelt beside Shirl's folding chair. She would tell Mouse it was Shirl. Shirl had invited him. They would share a moment of sisterly closeness and hope. They would remember how, before the accident, Shirl loved a practical joke. They would say, see, she's okay! She's still at it! Creating havoc for her own amusement. Inviting Ivan Esparza to the screening!

E. Bomarito strode to the front of the room. The show was beginning. There was no time to talk to Mouse, also no sign of Ivan. It occurred to Mimi that maybe the joke was on her, maybe Shirl was just teasing. Maybe Shirl didn't know what she was saying, as Auntie Barb suggested. Mimi decided it was a wait-and-see situation. She found a seat in the back.

"In this age of meaningless and tawdry Hollywood product, the Venice Documentary Consortium is a nonprofit organization dedicated to the preservation and practice of documentary film in all its forms," intoned E. Bomarito, stroking his mustache.

Ralph and Tony sat next to each other at the end of the first row. Listening to E. Bomarito, Tony realized, not for the first time, that he was simply not a documentary filmmaker. He had made documentaries, yes, but he had always known he was destined for greater things, for making movies with "bulk" that people would stand in line to buy overpriced tickets to see. He just did not have the Calling, like Mouse and this E. Bomarito. In a past life, he wasn't a member of a religious sect whose main occupation was building monuments to God that no one would ever see, the building of which killed off the believers in the process.

His twinge of remorse was easily cured by thoughts of his new career in feature films. Ralph was pessimistic, but it seemed more of a habit than anything else. He grumbled and griped, but hadn't he spent two and a half hours after the meeting with

V.J. thinking of ways to make their perfect script more perfect? Also, if Ralph thought it was so bloody futile, then why was he heartened when, moments ago, V. J. Parchman blew in?

Of course they'd invited V. J., and of course he'd said he would come, but both Tony and Ralph had assumed it was merely good manners on both sides. They had both assumed that V. J. had better things to do than drive across town in rush-hour traffic to sit in a dank and dirty basement watching 16mm documentaries on obscure African subjects. But no! Here he was, in multipocketed khaki safari pants and vest, yelping that he wouldn't miss it for the world.

"My Africa!" he said, crooking his arm around Tony's shoulder, inhaling deeply, like a coffee baron enjoying the olfactory beauty of his Ngong Hills plantation. "Tony, old boy, you did invite Michael Brass tonight, didn't you?"

"Michael Brass?"

"You *have* been in the bush for ages. Michael Brass! He's got four of the five top shows on the telly. Rumor is he makes one-point-five, one-point-seven-five per week just in residuals."

"That's million," said Ralph.

"He's head of a brilliant environmental group, Stars Against Ivory. It's a quite powerful organization, really a much more together group than the Rain Forest people. Anyone can get into that – it's the bloody McDonald's of political causes. SAI is quite exclusive. They don't take just any bleeding-heart liberal. I thought certainly he'd pop by."

"I invited Michael," lied Mimi, bless her heart. She'd overheard the conversation and slid up to V. J., proffering a little plastic glass of wine, leaning into his homely face as though he were just the man she'd been waiting for. "Michael works with us at Talent and Artists. I'm Mimi FitzHenry." She slid her warm hand into his. "He said he'd try to make it, though I think we're just going to do something private with him."

"Something private?"

"A private *screening*. "Mimi laughed. "By the way, I really liked *Fatal Red Kill*."

V. J. looked confused.

"Your last movie?"

"Oh, oh! *Lethal Red Death*, yes."

"That's what I meant. Let's find you a seat."

"Something on the end, in case Michael should make it. I do need to have a word with him. I've put together a petition banning the use of pianos with ivory keys in cocktail lounges 'round town."

Mimi led him off.

"This is a good sign," said Ralph, wiping his wide pale forehead with the back of his hand. He was sweating with excitement. "Not that we should get our hopes up. Nothing plus nothing is nothing, always remember. God, Mimi is brilliant. Isn't she brilliant? If I weren't married…

Tony silently cursed himself for wishing Mouse was just a shade less of a liability. She was so…adamant. It was an unattractive quality. A bit *too* much character, at least for this part of the world. He made her over in his mind while E. Bomarito droned on, but kept getting sidetracked from imagining her smiling complacently in a nice expensive tight sweater and miniskirt by, what he imagined, would be her unbridled fury at his poaching their African experiences for a screenplay. He dreaded her anger, then was irritated by it. She had no sense of *humor*. He folded his arms. She masked this by being witty and funny. He was angry. He should be home working on the script instead of sitting here watching these quaint documentaries that he'd already seen hundreds of times.

"…we are thrilled to be showing these films." E. Bomarito continued. He had nervous tics that were a curse to his career as a public speaker. It was a kind of blink-blink-sniff two-step.

He unrolled the tight tube of mimeographed programs he'd been beating against his sweaty palm. *Blink-blink-sniff*. "Whadda we have here? *Allah on the Rocks*. *The New Stanley*. *The*

Lepers of Miesso. All really terrific and unbelievable portraits of life by Mouse FitzGerald and her husband – "

" – not husband – " said Mouse, too quick, too loud.

" – Tony Chetham." Cartoon-sized drops of sweat sprang out on E. Bomarito's furry temples. He pronounced Cheatham Che-tham.

"It's Cheatham!" yelled Ralph.

"It's FitzHenry!" yelled Mimi, encouraged.

"Sorry! Sorry! I thought you were both – I thought you were related to Mitchell Chethem. We had him here last year. He does experimental stuff, mostly underwater portraits of squids mating. Anyway," *blink-blink-sniff*, "they're just back from Ethiopia."

"*Kenya*," yelled a few folks in the back. Mouse rolled her lips inside her mouth. A bad habit resulting in chapped lips and smeared lipstick. She had to stop.

E. Bomarito ended by promising that Mouse would entertain questions afterward, then trotted to the back of the room and snapped off the lights, plunging everyone into stuffy blackness. A few people giggled. The blackness was bisected by a shaft of light. Mouse turned to see the frizzy head of E. Bomarito through the long wide window in the projection booth. He was also, apparently, the projectionist.

From the projection booth came the cymbal-like crash of a tower of metal takeup reels falling over. What was E. doing in there? He'd obviously not bothered to thread the machine in advance. The audience, numbering about twenty-five, had given up nervous laughter in favor of aimless checkout-line chat. Someone sitting behind Mouse wondered aloud if anyone had heard how video display terminals caused cataracts and miscarriages. Mouse wished she was sitting next to Tony, who was on the other side of the room. She caught a glimpse of V. J. Parchman, also on the other side of the room, and pretended she didn't see him.

E. Bomarito had a very cavalier approach to focus: the first image was a blurry ten-foot-tall red-and-blue box moving toward the camera, accompanied by the sound of squeaking rusted wheels. It was difficult to tell whether it was a man or a refrigerator with arms.

Mimi felt panic brewing in her throat. She glanced over at Mouse and was surprised to find her serene with expectation. Because she'd lived in Africa, she had adapted to inefficiency. She had adapted to the electricity going out for days at a time because some rebel group somewhere had cut the power lines. She was used to planning elaborate shoots only to be told at the last possible minute that the trip was off because the Land Rover was dangerously low on oil and there was no oil to be had anywhere until week after next. She was amused by Los Angeles, where waitresses apologized, "I'm making a fresh pot of decaf, it'll be a few minutes." Once she had waited seven months for a care package of decaf and coffee filters from Shirl.

Though her shoulders were relaxed, she sat on the edge of her chair, her fingers laced over one sharp kneecap. She was not nervous but a little anxious, and not because the all-important first image – the image they had gone to jail for – was hopelessly out of focus but anxious with the wonder of seeing her work big and with an audience. She had seen most of her documentaries small and by herself, or with Tony. She had seen them on video monitors. During the editing, which she had done on an ancient upright Moviola, the screen was no bigger than her hand. Her breathing was shallow. She was prepared to be as exhilarated and frightened as were her subjects when they saw themselves on film for the first time. Most of them had never seen still pictures of themselves, much less motion pictures. Stanley, star of *The New Stanley*, the blurry ten-foot red-and-blue refrigerator box, had never seen himself in a mirror, only in the reflection of a lake in northwest Kenya, where he had been a young man and a warrior, or in the plate glass windows of Nairobi, where he was a cripple and a pickpocket.

Stanley drifted in and out of focus. His body appeared as

it did because it was all torso, no legs. He got around apelike, via skateboard and calloused knuckles.

E. Bomarito, who was talking to someone in the obviously un-soundproof projection booth, finally settled on an image that was readable but soft.

Stanley rolled down the sidewalk toward the camera, passing the entrance to The New Stanley, the tourist hotel in front of which he plied his trade, stealing the diaries and travel journals of Western tourists. Even though Stanley was an ugly man, the whites of his eyes curdled yellow, one of his nostrils torn off in a fight, he had about him the charming air of a popular dictator.

Dented skateboard wheels squeaking, he rolled down the sidewalk forested with legs. Tourist legs. Legs in creased khaki safari pants, bare tanned calves extending beneath lightweight knee-length skirts, some calves young and waxed, some erupting with wormy blue varicose veins. Hanging beside the hip of one skinny young woman in mustard cotton culottes was a large colorful woven handbag, not unlike Mouse's signature camel-scented basket. The leather straps of the bag ascended out of the top of the frame, presumably hooking over the girl's shoulder. Stanley rolled a few feet beyond her, then, without much of a double take, rolled back, reached his muscular arm up and in, retrieving a small book from the purse. It was covered in dainty Victorian flowers, splotched with black ink, the result of knocking around the bottom of the bag with uncapped pens.

This shot had gotten Mouse and Tony in trouble. A policeman stationed by the hotel entrance to guard the tourists from just such a thing hauled Stanley off his skateboard by his grubby shirt collar and arrested Mouse and Tony for aiding and abetting. It took three weeks for the American Embassy to work its magic, convincing the Nairobi Police Superintendent that since Stanley was only lifting a diary, it could hardly be considered a crime. Mouse and Tony were released on the condition they deliver up the negative of the illegal shot. They did, after making a dupe.

The uneventful jail stay–toilet a stinking hole in the middle of the floor, diet of mushy *posho* and water, athletic rats that leaped up on the bottom bunk to nibble the lips of sleeping prisoners–Mouse refused to waste energy discussing. That did not prevent Tony from making it one of the centerpieces of *Love Among the Gorillas*.

Mouse had gotten used to the fireman's pole, and so had forgotten about it until the film started. As soon as Stanley came into focus, however, she knew she had been right. She cursed herself for allowing herself to be convinced the pole was no big deal just to avoid Mimi's accusation that she took things too seriously. The pole was not New York arty. The pole was a problem. It cast a four-inch-wide shadow that bisected the screen, which meant most of the time it bisected Stanley's marvelous, ugly face. Between the focus problem and the pole and the raucous frame of mind people had been cast into by E. Bomarito's error-filled intro, no one was able to settle down and watch. You could feel people squirming in their seats, crossing one leg, then the other. You could feel people waiting for an opportunity to laugh.

"Focus, already!" one of the strangers in black finally shouted. "Jesus Christ."

After transforming Stanley into a sort of moving abstract expressionist painting for a few seconds, E. Bomarito got it right, only to have Tony–yes, Tony! Mouse would surely never forgive him–bellow, "Pole, already!" sending the house into fits. Tony laughed at their laughter. It just popped out, but he knew it wouldn't hurt to distance himself from this stuff. He turned around to see V. J. Parchman's reaction, but his chair was empty. He had already left.

Mouse stared straight ahead, not at Tony, hunkered down in his chair like any eighth grader disrupting assembly, chuckling silently into his shirt collar. Ralph, sitting next to him, had buried his face in his hands. His shoulders jerked with laughter.

Mouse stood up without a word and went to the ladies' room. When freak accidents run in your family you tend to ask "what if" a lot. What if Fitzy hadn't decided to walk that day? What if he'd driven? Mimi didn't know how many times she'd asked that.

What if he hadn't seen the gold knot earring glinting on the hot asphalt?

What if he hadn't bent to pick it up?

What if the truck driver hadn't resorted to hundred-mile-an-hour tape but had taken his rig in and gotten the safety chain fixed?

What if Shirl had stayed on Program instead of pigging out at Gateau on Melrose?

What if Mimi hadn't lived at home the sweltering summer of Ivan and Mouse?

What if Mimi and Ivan hadn't mistaken good sex and fear of the future for love?

What if the LAFI had sprung for a screening after all?

What if Mouse had chosen to sit and stew instead of retiring to the ladies'?

What if the ladies' had been in a normal place instead of through the projection booth?

What if Shirl hadn't called Ivan?

Then Mouse would have never run into him in the projection booth, talking shop with E. Bomarito, who happened to be a good friend and fellow charter member of the Venice Documentary Consortium.

11.

IVAN SLOUCHED AGAINST THE WALL BESIDE THE PRO-
jector, one arm locked across his ribs, a skinny shelf on which to
rest the opposite elbow, moodily fingering his lips, watching *The
New Stanley* through the low wide window.

Mouse recognized him instantly. The blue light from the
screen illuminated his face. Still the high, rounded cheekbones.
Still the flat nose, the high-cut nostrils. He had a ponytail. A
ponytail made a man look like either a Milanese fashion designer
or someone who survived by selling plasma. Ivan had sold
plasma to help fund *Total Immersion*, for which he won the Oscar.
There was also a rumor he'd sold one kidney to a Newport Beach
couple desperate to save their dying child. He charged just enough
to cover post-production, prints, and advertising.

Mouse thought the ponytail suited him. Unfortunately, in
sixteen years his honey-colored hair had surrendered to the
usual flat brown fate of blonds. His honey-colored skin had gone
sallow from living on almost nothing but the wilted, congealing
stuff served at cheap All You Can Eat salad bars. He had lost more
weight than Mouse had imagined anyone so ripe and stocky
ever could. Somewhere along the way he'd gained a small gold
earring. What she couldn't see from her quick heart-in-her-
throat glance was the maniacal glint that now lit up his eyes.

Long before Mouse saw Ivan's name in the magazine at the
library she'd been preparing herself for just such a moment.
Even when she still presumed he'd fallen off the face of the

documentary-filmmaking earth, lost in the uncharted universe of middle-level white-collar executives or well-paid waiters waiting for a break, she knew she had not seen the last of him. Still, she was shocked. Her mouth flooded with saliva. Her legs shook so hard they were barely able to carry her into the ladies'.

The ladies' was painted lavender. A defaced decal from a radical feminist health clinic was stuck to the toilet paper dispenser. Mouse sat down on the toilet, teeth chattering. *Our Father, which art in heaven, hallowed be thy name.* She vaguely remembered being angry at Tony before he dropped from her mind like an anchor tossed into the sea.

Ivan! Ivan! Ivan! *Thy kingdom come, thy will be done, on earth as it is in Heaven.* The moment she'd dreamed about, the moment she'd dreaded. *Give us this day our daily bread, and forgive us our trespasses, as we forgive those who trespass against us.* Her first miserable years alone in Tunisia, working at the Corsican disco, before Kenya and Tony she'd prayed she'd see him. She concocted fantastic scenarios to put herself to sleep, willing him to wind up in Tunis. Against all reason she swore she'd glimpsed him a number of times rounding a corner near her *pension.* Years later she thought she saw him padding barefoot through the Nyali Beach Hotel in Mombasa, complaining to a gaggle of German tourists, of which he was a part, about the bathtub temperature of the lazy Indian Ocean. He appeared on the platform of train stations in tiny dusty towns, sped past her on red-rutted forest roads. They had unfinished business. She knew she'd see him again, when she least expected it. She pulled a wad of toilet tissue from the dispenser, dropped it between her legs into the toilet and flushed. *And lead us not into temptation, but deliver us from evil, for thine is the kingdom and the power and the glory.*

Unfinished business. The last time Mouse had seen Ivan was before she left for her semester abroad, the fall of 1973. It was late August, suffocating heat. Ivan and Mimi stood in the driveway on Cantaloupe Avenue, leaning against the door of Ivan's Camaro.

Mouse had gone to the doctor to get a typhoid vaccination for her trip. The minute her red Volkswagen puttered out of the driveway, Mimi called Ivan at a sporting goods store on Hollywood Boulevard where he worked. Mouse left at eleven o'clock. Ivan took an early lunch. Shirl was teaching a découpage class at the Sherman Oaks Recreation Center.

Ivan and Mimi snuck into the pool cabana. The roof was green corrugated plastic, casting an aquatic light on their bodies, striped with fierce tan lines. Mimi was grateful for her guilt, for the splinters driven into her shoulders, the result of being ground into the unfinished wooden bench by an overeager Ivan. There was a sign on the cabana wall, we don't swim in your toilet, so please don't pee in our pool.

Mimi read it over and over again past half-closed eyes over Ivan's thick brown shoulder. She and Mouse had thought it was such a riot growing up. It wasn't such a riot now. It made her angry at Mouse for not getting Ivan into the pool cabana herself.

For a month Ivan came to the house when Mouse was gone, so that if she came back while he was still there, everyone could pretend he had come to see her. On that last day though, for some reason, no one pretended. It was the heat, the weariness caused by the eternally clear California sky, the fact that Mouse was leaving anyway. Ivan and Mimi stood in the driveway, crooning to each other that they were bad, so bad, what were they ever going to do? when Mouse rounded the corner, some appropriate Linda Ronstadt song about love and betrayal blaring from her tinny radio. Ivan had his hands on Mimi's hips. *Putt-putt-putt* Mouse's car into the driveway.

"Hi," she said through the open window. She turned off the engine. Linda's wailing voice died. Her arm was hot and swollen.

"Hi," said Mimi.

"Hi," said Ivan. He didn't drop his hands from Mimi's wide hips, and there was no talk of his being there to see anyone but her. Mouse went into the house, pretending she didn't see. That night, with a pair of tweezers and a needle she intentionally forgot to sterilize, Mouse dug the splinters from Mimi's shoulders.

Six days later Shirl took Mouse to the airport.

Nine months later Mouse phoned from Tunis to say she wasn't coming home.

Mouse lurched to the sink. She cranked on the rusty faucet. First there was no water, then the pipes coughed and hawked out a brown stream that ricocheted off the drain and up the side of the basin, drenching the bottom of her sweater. "Shit," she moaned.

"You all right in there?" E. Bomarito bellowed through the door.

"Yes!" Mouse called gaily. She wrung out the bottom of the sweater, tried to pat it back into shape. She plucked at the curls of her hopeless permanent, pinched her overly tan cheeks for color.

When she emerged she saw through the low wide window of the booth that her favorite part of the film was up, an interview with Stanley in his neighborhood off River Road. He was doing his daily pull-ups on an exposed pipe in a half-finished building, alongside Clint Eastwood, a silver-furred vervet monkey whom Stanley treated like a son. Stanley counted aloud in Swahili. *Moja. Mbili. Tatu.* Clint Eastwood dangled by one arm, swatted at Stanley's heaving sweaty torso.

"Do the people in your village know where you get your knowledge of the *mzungu*, the white man?" Mouse asks him from somewhere offscreen.

"They know. I read to my people from the books."

"Do they know you steal the books?"

"They know the books are not offered to me. They know also that the *mzungu* does not miss his book."

"You don't think someone is upset when he finds out his journal is missing?"

"I see this many times. The *mzungu* looks in his bag. The

book is not there. The *mzungu* claps his hand to his forehead, like so. 'At least I still have my wallet!' he says. 'Thank God!' Many many times I see this. So long as the *mzungu* still has his wallet he does not miss the book of his life."

The scene elicited an appreciative smile from Ivan. "This is phenomenal, Mouse. Really very very good stuff." He shook his head without turning to look at her.

"I debated. I put it in and took it out." She noticed she said "I," not we.

"No, you were right. Sometimes a scene deserves to live, irrespective of its place in the piece. There are, of course, two schools of thought. One says if a scene is too good it should be cut. I say good scenes, really memorable ones, are so rare they should be used. Someday I will do a compilation film of all my best scenes with only title cards in between saying what film they're from."

"Cool," said E. Bomarito.

"If only Harris thought so. Harris is my distributor," he said to Mouse.

"Well, nice seeing you," said Mouse abruptly.

She stumbled out of the booth and back to her chair, where she perched for less than a minute before tripping to her feet, out of her seat, out of the room.

Mimi had seen Ivan's face through the window in the booth. She had heard E. Bomarito call out, "You all right in there?" She saw Mouse return to her seat, then leave.

Outside, Mouse stood shivering on the lawn by the crèche, kicking at a tuft of grass with the toe of her tennis shoe, smoking a cigarette. Even though it was nearly Christmas, which meant it should have been about eighty-seven degrees, it was drizzling and cold. The air smelled gloomy and stale.

"Somewhere I read that clouds have the same PH as battery acid," said Mimi, staring up at the dirty cotton sky.

"That's impossible."

"No, I read it in the *New Yorker*. It's called acid fog."

"Clouds do not have the same PH as battery acid."

"Not *all* clouds. Only the clouds in L.A."

"You said clouds."

"The clouds in L.A., I meant."

"Ivan's here –" Mouse started.

"I know. Shirl called him. I think this whole thing, the operation and everything, has made her half a bubble off plumb. Isn't that great? It's construction worker lingo. I heard it from the guy at work putting in the new false ceiling."

"I go to the bathroom and there he is. In the projection booth."

"Was that him? He looks like everyone else with that dumb ponytail."

Mouse swore one of Mimi's great satisfactions in life was dismissing everything that she considered interesting or important as beneath talking about, much less thinking about. She couldn't help remembering the afternoon of her discovery at the Academy Library. She had hurried back to the apartment to find Mimi doing yoga on the living room floor.

"Why didn't you tell me Ivan was doing documentary! He's won an Oscar, for Godsakes."

"That was a jillion years ago." Mimi exhaled deeply. "Sit on my ankles, would you?"

Now, although Mouse was bursting to say, "Thanks for telling me!" she was loath to give Mimi yet another juicy opportunity to shrug and drawl, "I meant to. Guess I forgot." Instead she took a marking pen out of her purse and added the missing *e* to the AFRICAN MOVIS sign.

"Shirl got his number from the phone book," Mimi continued. "I told her she could have called me. She told him you were back, you know, that you were having this little screening. He's probably hanging out in the booth because it'd be too like weird and painful. Seeing me – us – and everything. He really went off the deep end after we split. Half a bubble off plumb. You never really knew him –"

"I knew him –"

"You knew him, you knew him, but you didn't know him. He sold one of his kidneys to finance a *movie*."

"He did not."

"He did."

"The woman most full of it," said Ivan, appearing suddenly at the top of the basement stairs. He dug in the chest pocket of his T-shirt for a joint, which he lit nonchalantly.

"I can't believe you still *smoke*," said Mimi. "Mouse, can you believe he still smokes? How do you get anything *done*?"

Mouse just stared, jaw slack in disbelief, thick brows furrowed. It was hard to believe. The sisters FitzHenry and Ivan Esparza together again. He offered the roach to her. She shook her head.

"I'll have some," said Mimi before he replugged the roach between his lips, "How do you like Mouse's movies? Aren't they great? *The New Stanley* is my favorite, then *Allah on the Rocks*. They're showing that next."

"I'm afraid it'll have to be another time. Got a sound mix."

"When did you see *Allah*?" Mouse asked Mimi.

"A sound mix at this hour? Don't tell me. You've broken into a sound studio and are holding the guard hostage."

"When did you see *Allah on the Rocks*?"

"I haven't. I mean, I saw some clips. Tony showed me. Ivan, did you meet Tony? Tony is Mouse's fiancé. He's tall and English, like somebody out of *The Avengers*."

"He is not like somebody out of *The Avengers*," Mouse said hotly.

She looked down at her toes, embarrassed. "He's not my fiancé –"

"He is too –"

"Yes, yes, he's my, my – I'm getting married, but I don't think of him like that. I mean, we're partners. We make, we used to make films together. We made those films together." She waved her hand almost dismissively in the direction of the basement.

"When are you getting married?" Ivan asked. He batted the smoke away from his broad inscrutable face. "I am very interested in weddings," he said.

"You and every single woman in this city between fifteen and eighty," said Mimi. "Except me. Once was enough for me."

Ivan ignored the remark, choosing instead to ask Mouse where she was living and if he could have her phone number.

He reached over, ground out the roach on a cheek of one of the plaster wise men, then replaced it in his pocket.

12.

"SIX MONTHS LATER, SILVERMAN WAS IN CHARGE OF business affairs; three years later he found himself running the studio." Ralph read aloud from an article he'd clipped from the newspaper.

"*He found himself* running the studio? Gimme a break. They talk like the guy's a sleepwalker just woke up. I want to know, those three years, what *happened*. That's what every successful schmuck keeps a secret. They bore you till your teeth rot about their coke problem, but try to get them to talk about those three years. What, was he just sitting in business affairs jacking off, then one day the memo comes saying 'congratulations, you're now one of the most powerful people in Hollywood'?"

Wednesday night, How to Write a Blockbuster. Ralph and Mimi walked through Valley College to class. Ralph waved the article in front of his face like an irate anarchist.

In anticipation of Christmas vacation, which began next week, most of the night classes had been canceled. The halls echoed in semidesertion. As they passed a row of snack machines, Mimi glanced over to make sure they had her favorite oatmeal cookies.

"Guess how old he is?" said Ralph.

"Forty," said Mimi. She wasn't really listening. She wanted to tell him she hadn't had a chance to do her homework, in order to avoid the humiliation of confessing it in front of the whole class.

"Forty," he scoffed.

"Twelve."

"C'mon, c'mon."

"I don't know. Younger than us."

"Twenty-nine. Twenty-fucking-nine. I want some statistics, I want a *graph*. I want to see exactly how much your chances of making it decrease as your age increases. How old do I look to you?" He tipped his baseball cap off his head, smoothed his thin, dust-colored hair, ran a finger over each fair eyebrow.

"Twenty-nine, sweet cheeks." Mimi slid her hand in the back pocket of his jeans.

"Really? I really look twenty-nine?"

She wanted to say, You look three days old. "At the most."

Sometimes she felt as though being with Ralph she had all the disadvantages of wifehood but none of the advantages. Not that she really wanted to break up with him. Despite his ravings, he was better than nothing. She just wished he'd get a divorce. Not that she wanted to marry him. Anyway, she knew the divorce issue was a financial one. Although, when she was feeling insecure and bad about herself, she wondered. Last week, for example, she called his almost ex-wife, Elaine the Pain, to tell her that Bibliothèques had been rescheduled, and Ralph answered the phone. He said he was fixing her oven. As far as Mimi knew, Ralph was about as handy around the house as a debutante. Not that he shouldn't still be friendly with Elaine. They had been married ten years, after all. She sometimes wished she could be friends with Ivan, if only to make Ralph as jealous as Elaine made her.

"Ralph, I didn't get a chance to do my dust-jacket copy. You know, with the screening and, it's not easy to work with house guests around. I wish they'd get their own place. Maybe if your thing with V. J. happens."

In fact, Mimi liked having Mouse and Tony around the apartment. She didn't mind the strange hairs curling around the shower drain, clean glasses put away in the wrong cupboard, crumbs on the coffee table from someone eating toast in front of the tube. It was nice at night: the TV on but no one watching. Somewhere in a back room, the tinny noise of a radio left on. Shoes left, toe to heel, under the dining room table. People dropped by, an unheard-of thing before Mouse and Tony arrived. Lisa stopped in one day on her way home from work. Carole was at the kitchen table writing a screenplay synopsis on her portable typewriter. They smoked some ancient pot Mimi found in a baggie in the junk drawer and passed around one of those jillion-ounce plastic bottles of Pepsi, their knees propped against the edge of the table.

The kitchen sink was clogged. They watched and laughed while Tony, who looked to be above such things, attacked it with the Drano, reading instructions aloud in his *Masterpiece Theater* voice. Mimi made everyone grilled cheese sandwiches, then, still hungry, they sent out for a pizza. They talked for a long time about the greenhouse effect instead of the film business. It was the pot. It made them nostalgic for being aware of something beside their own nonexistent film careers, their nonexistent marriages and children.

"No one'll drop the Bomb," said Lisa. "Even the Arabs are too smart for that. It's pollution."

"The world will die of thirst, there'll be no water to drink, there'll be no air to breathe," said Carole.

"– our brains will he crushed under the weight of worldwide cultural mediocrity," said Tony. "If water boils out of drain, immediately add another cup of COLD water."

Mimi's attitude was, if you can't have a family, you might as well have it like college.

How to Write a Blockbuster was in its fifth week. There were eleven students, evenly divided between the young and entrepreneurial and the old and entrepreneurial. Most of them were there because they believed there was more money to be made in writing a blockbuster and selling it to television than in writing an original screenplay. One eighteen-year-old prodigy of modern life was taking the class because it was cheaper than buying screenplay software. Mimi was there because she believed in self-improvement; also, she wanted to write a block-buster so she could quit her job at Talent and Artists and take acting classes. After she'd brushed up on the Method and perhaps had some of her facial lines removed, she would get back in touch with Bob Hope.

Mimi thought she was the only one with real writing potential in the bunch, as evidenced by the fact she was so slow. Her opposite, Peg, a Brillo Pad-permed ex-nun and self-described workshop junky, turned in reams of pages each week, all featuring legions of throbbing members and twitching nipples. They had not officially started writing yet, but Peg was already on page three hundred. Ralph used to save Peg's pages to read to Mimi in bed, providing them with many a postcoital hoot. He said that Peg was also Mimi's opposite in that Peg wrote about torrid sex but never had any, and Mimi had torrid sex but never wrote about it. Torrid, Mimi thought, is in the eye of the beholder.

They met in a room that had no desks, only bright-orange plastic chairs and merciless bars of cold fluorescent light. The class before How to Write a Blockbuster was an introductory course in convenience-store management for Asians. Various exhortations were always left on the blackboard. Correct change is a must! Arrange your shelves so ladies supplies are easy to find!

Before class, with a careless swipe of a chalky eraser, Ralph would replace these exhortations with his own: Writing a blockbuster is not about writing, it is about panning for gold! or What is your book about? Your book is about a car payment! The class that met there the next morning probably read these and found How to Write a Blockbuster as pitiful as Mimi and her classmates found Introduction to Convenience-Store Man-agement. The thought of this was too depressing. Instead, Mimi pondered the oatmeal cookie she would eat at the break.

Tonight Ralph wanted to discuss how to effectively reduce your book to a blurb in *TV Guide*. Remember, he said, if you can't do it, how was some *TV Guide* lackey who probably never read the press kit which was put together by someone who never saw the movie which was produced by people who never read the book supposed to do it?

"Before we get rolling, any questions?" He bounced back and forth across the front of the room, tossing a stub of chalk in the air, cocky in his turquoise St. Bart's T-shirt, black jeans, and trademark Dodgers cap, every inch a man of confidence and success. The guy who's got "things happening" all over Town, who's feted by this producer, that director, so many agents he's lost count, who teaches for the fun of it!

Only Mimi knew the truth. How to Write a Blockbuster was a car payment.

Peg was curious about jacket photos. A mortician from Tarzana wondered what kind of hotels they put you up in on your publicity tour. Ralph chastised them. He said he didn't like these questions. They were putting the cart before the horse, when what they needed to concentrate on was how they would create a lively and enticing blurb. Ralph also didn't like these questions because he didn't know the answers.

At the break, Mimi bolted for the snack machine before anyone else had time to leave their seat. She gobbled down the Frisbee-sized cookie, which tasted vaguely like a disk of solidified sawdust, then rooted around the bottom of her purse for loose change for some M&Ms. On her way to her favorite restroom in the next complex of buildings, she expressed them straight from the bag into her throat, bypassing her taste buds.

As long as she got rid of it all before she went home, she never gained a pound. That was the important thing. She knew she did this for a reason but could never figure out what it was. She read articles about eating disorders, but they only confused her. She was high-strung, also a little depressed. That was the most she could say. In the meantime, while she tried to figure it out, she didn't want to get fat. Getting fat would only make it worse.

Chocolate and doughy things slid back up easily, so no one could ever tell, no broken blood vessels around her eyes, no croaky voice from a raw throat. She got rid only of bad food. She could keep down cucumber slices and yogurt with the best of them. It was just a thing she did to make herself feel better. She considered it sort of a hobby, like Shirl's découpage. The whole process, from eating bad food to losing it, cured her anxious moods. It gave her a sense of mission. Drive-meet-eat-purge.

After she disposed of the cookie and M&Ms, eyes smarting, stomach burning, she slapped on some Extra Fuchsia lipstick, then blotted her eyes. She rinsed out her mouth and ate a mint, then reapplied some more lipstick. Sometimes Ralph liked to follow her to this far outpost for a quickie. Mimi thought he was probably living out some high school fantasy.

He waited for her outside, glancing through the homework. He rolled it into a tube and thrust it in his back pocket. "Why do you always use this restroom?" He sidled up close, unbuttoning her shirt.

"I like the privacy, sweet cheeks."

"Me, too. Sweet boobs." He kissed her neck, sneakily tugged down one of the cups of her bra. Both cups were stretched out as a result of this weekly ritual. Mimi made a point of wearing the same bra to class so he didn't ruin every last one she owned. He had no idea how much a decent bra cost.

Mimi supposed she liked this rather dangerous behavior. She doubted Mouse did this. Although, as Ralph bombed her neck with wet, explosive kisses, she felt as though he wasn't caressing her breast so much as twirling a combination lock, an anxious safecracker in training.

She sighed. She should have finished her dust-jacket copy.

IVAN CALLED MOUSE on Saturday, just after two. It was clear, bright, and hot. One of those days when the girls were growing up and Shirl made them feel guilty for staying inside. One of those days you could see the ocean from the mountains, and vice versa.

Downstairs Mimi's Armenian neighbor sang "Jingle Bell Rock" along with the radio while sweeping her tiny terrace. Mouse watched a tape E. Bomarito had lent her, a documentary he'd worked on that had won a number of awards. Sniffy Voyeur lay by the Christmas tree watching her with his Egyptian eyes, beating his tail, big as a plume of pampas grass, on the wood floor, crooning for someone to come over and pet him. Mouse lay on the uncomfortable green wicker settee taking desultory bites out of a mushy red apple: a textbook case of post-premiere depression.

She had been anxious to get a screening, anxious to get It out there. You get a decent screening, it means you're real. It means all those years away were good for something. It means you're not just a girl who dabbles, not just a girl getting married. So now she had gotten It out there. She had gotten It out there and It stunk! She didn't need a review to tell her – not that her screening had been reviewed. She arrived at this conclusion on her own.

She thought of the time and money and effort sunk into *The New Stanley*. Had anyone ever seen such a string of visual clichés? Had anyone ever seen such camera work, newscast banal interspersed with the most obvious arty shit? Had anyone ever heard such a murky sound track? It was too long, but at the same time underdeveloped, just one more "sensitive" film about an interesting weirdo. No better than the second-rate tape she was watching now, about the blind proprietor of a tattoo parlor in East Los Angeles.

"*The New Stanley* didn't hold up very well, did it?" she asked Tony. He sat on the ottoman fiddling with the remote. He tapped the sound up, then he tapped it down. She didn't care. Awards or no, E. Bomarito's doc was a bore.

Tony was waiting to go to Disneyland. He was wearing new clothes, cowboy boots and a dark shirt that brought out his freckles, his strawberry-blond hair curling dramatically over his collar. His top button was buttoned like you saw on men in fashion advertisements.

She knew she should feel grateful Tony was marrying someone like her. Instead, she felt like she had gotten herself a cute prison warden. She knew she should discuss postponing the wedding with him but couldn't bring herself to do it. She hated her perm. She had stopped painting her fungus-infected nails. She had to find a job. She had to find a way back to Nairobi.

"You're far too critical," said Tony. "I think *Stanley* is quite a nice film. It has so many memories attached. Mind if I fast-forward?" He was waiting for Mimi and Carole. They were going to Disneyland with Carole's grandparents, who visited every Christmas from Connecticut. Their mission was not family togetherness but the opportunity to call back to their friends on Christmas day and say, "Earl! Ruth! It's eighty degrees out here! We're wearing shorts!"

Mouse loathed Disneyland. Even when she and Mimi were eight and nine she was suspicious of it. All those grown-ups pushing and shoving to prove they're still kids at heart, The only thing she had liked was the Submarine Ride, which she would go on only with Fitzy.

"Just because people *seemed* to get a charge out of it doesn't mean it was any good," she said. "You know that. Anyway, it was a sympathetic audience. They were obligated to like it."

"Can't you just accept the fact that people enjoyed it and leave it at that?" Tony watched the sped-up doc, palpating his cheeks with his fingertips, feeling for whiteheads, which he squeezed between his first and second fingers, one of his less attractive habits.

"If we could remix the sound," said Mouse.

"It's done, poppet. Put it behind you, for God's sake."

The phone rang. Mouse answered, thinking it might be Shirl, checking in for her usual after-the-event debriefing. It was Ivan.

"Ivan wants to meet for a drink later," she said to Tony, going back to the couch. It had been one of those brusk "uh-huh, uh-huh, sure, sure, okay, okay, bye" conversations. She kept it that way, professional, on the chance her voice would wobble out high and girlish.

"Hope you took a rain check. Love to chat with him," said Tony, tossing the remote onto the rattan coffee table and standing.

"I think he just meant me," she said.

"Eow! Bloody Christ! Askin' me fiancée out behind me back. What's this bugger of a world comin' to?"

"You don't care if I go?"

"Do as you like."

"She's as trustworthy as Sniffy Voyeur," said Mimi, tossing a handful of tampons into her purse. "Isn't she, Sniff-Sniff-Sniff?" Sniffy dragged himself up and ambled over for a scratch on the head. "Just be sure to take enough money to pay for both of you. Ivan's very big on inviting people places, then conveniently forgetting his credit cards. Not that he has any to forget. He's a thirty-four-year-old man and he's never had a checking account."

IVAN HAD SUGGESTED an old place on Hollywood Boulevard, prized for its layers of grime and smoke-stained walls, three bus rides away from the apartment. Even though it was December, the restaurant was humid and stuffy. The ceiling fans whirled uselessly overhead. The faces of waiters streaming past in their limp red jackets shone with sweat. At the last minute Mouse had decided to wash her jeans but had to grab them from the dryer while they were still damp so she wouldn't miss the bus. She stood just inside the door, waiting for Ivan, her waistband jungle wet and warm. She tried not to be nervous. She tried to summon up some clenched-jaw calm. She tried to pretend Ivan was a Nairobi BBC bureaucrat from whom she was trying to scam some equipment.

Ivan arrived late, wearing a yellow-and-purple-striped surfer's T-shirt Mouse recognized from sixteen years ago. Like Mouse, he wore clothes until they disintegrated and blew away. Mouse remembered that shirt, down to the holes in the armpits, from when they watched Watergate together. When he reached up to give her a brotherly clap on the shoulder, she glimpsed a tuft of dirty-blond hair peeking through a yawning seam.

Ivan was a regular at this place. He was buddies with the maître d', who until that moment had ignored Mouse, glancing at her from time to time making sure she wasn't some flotsam in off the street.

It seemed that they were having dinner, not just drinks. Menus slid into their hands, silverware was plunked down by a surly busboy. Even though Mouse was nauseated – a dinner with Ivan, love of her life! – she spread open the menu eagerly.

"What do you recommend?" She felt like a twelve-year-old pretending she was a grown-up on a date.

"The chicken salad is their specialty," said Ivan.

The waiters responded only to the kind of wave favored by marooned motorists hailing passing traffic on a foggy night. The chicken salad turned out to be an ice cream scoop full of mayonnaise studded with greenish meat, slapped on a wilted leaf of iceberg lettuce stained by a decorative circle of beets. Every bite yielded a few hidden bones, fish-hook-sharp. Ivan had steak.

"This is really strange," said Ivan, addressing the silverware, straightening first his knife, then his fork, then his fork, then his knife, then picking up both.

"How so?" How so. Her throat pounded. This was hardly the Ivan she remembered, brooding and noncommittal as a spy. The chicken salad was suspiciously greasy. She told Ivan it was delicious.

"Being together after all this time. I'm really sorry, Mouse. You know what I'm talking about?"

She surreptitiously plucked a piece of cartilage off her

tongue and laid it on the edge of her plate. She wanted to say, "You spineless creep, you broke my heart. Are all men as stupid as you, falling for someone like Mimi?" Instead she said, "We were all so young."

"I was a stupid prick."

"I wouldn't say *that*!"

"No, I was an incredible jerk. I handled it poorly."

"It's understandable. My sister is, was, really attractive to men and you were just – "

"You're too easy on me. You were always too easy on me. It was my downfall."

IIis *downfall*? She shifted uncomfortably in her damp jeans. She was beginning to wonder if maybe all this was a prelude to a confession that he had undergone some kind of religious transformation. "The thing I never understood," she said, "in that era it was sex, right? Marriage was, well, no one got married. Not like it is now. For a long time I thought Mimi was pregnant. I was never actually sure why you did it. Got married."

"Why are you getting married? Can I have some steak sauce?" he bellowed at a passing waiter.

A flat loud *ha* rolled out of her mouth. "It's every girl's dream."

"I'm serious," he said.

"It's complicated."

"That I don't believe. It's like how people say having children is complicated. Raising children is complicated, having them is embarrassingly simple. My guinea pigs do it all the time. Getting married is easy. It's staying married that's hard."

"Why did you marry my sister?"

"To keep from murdering her."

"Seriously."

"Seriously. I wanted to get her out of my system. That salad looks really bad. Did I tell you to order it?"

He reached across the table, scooped up a forkful. "The least I can do is have food poisoning, too. Maybe it would help for you to know that I used to think of you a lot, when Mimi and I..." He cast his blue eyes down at his plate.

They split a piece of carrot cake. Ivan switched from beer to vodka and soda. Mouse did too, even though her head was pounding, her stomach queasy from the heat and the conversation. The waiter glowered at the thought of having to add more drinks to the tab. Ivan told her horror stories about the making of *El Funeral*. She countered with all her nightmares from Africa. They commiserated about the lack of funding, the lack of appreciation of the documentary, they argued about *cinema verité* versus direct cinema. Ivan said he liked *The New Stanley*.

"Well, as they say, it's not the cure for cancer."

"It was great. I would tell you. You don't gain anything by people bullshitting you. Bullshitting is easy, the truth is hard. Saying you don't like something is impossible. I would tell you. It was fantastic."

"That's what Tony says, but I think he –"

"– Tony, Tony –"

"My – the guy I'm marrying."

"Yes! Tony! What about this Tony? What about this marriage? You're being very cagey about this. Aren't we friends?"

"What do you want to know?"

She expected anything but what he said. She expected him to say, "Do you really love the guy?" She expected him to say, "Could you love me?" She did! She could! It was all so confusing. She blamed the vodka, cold enough to torture a sensitive tooth. She was on her fourth. Tony could drink a half dozen and still win a game of chess. Waves crashed behind her eyes. The lower part of her face felt as though it was suffering from an overdose of novocaine. She thought about Mimi and Tony and Carole and Carole's grandparents twisting down the Matterhorn, and the table, still littered with dirty plates which the bus boy refused to clear, swayed beneath her.

"I would like you to co-produce my next piece," said Ivan. "The funding is already in place. I got a development grant from the California Committee for the Humanities. The CPB is going to kick in some, too." He told her the amount, six times the cost of *The New Stanley*.

"I'd like that very much," she said slowly, hoping to sound businesslike.

"Don't be stupid, Mouse. Don't agree before you know what I'm asking. You'll have to give it serious thought. I don't want you to get into it if you don't absolutely believe in it. Working with me is not fun."

"You got the funding, I believe in it," she said.

"I want to do your wedding."

"My wedding?" Her brain would not accept the words, the same way the change machine at the Laundromat spit back a crinkled dollar bill. He wants to do my wedding? Plan it? Perform the ceremony?

"We will call it *Wedding March*."

WHEN IVAN BROUGHT Mouse home she was relieved to see the apartment was dark. Her head was whirling; she bit her lips and couldn't feel them. They had slurped down their drinks in a sort of the-night's-still-young abandon that abruptly ended when Ivan got her to say she'd give serious thought to his proposition instead of "when do we start?" She was still drunk.

Of course, Ivan was right. There were things she needed to do. She needed, first and foremost, to talk to Tony, although she was certain he'd jump at the opportunity to be working again. She needed to sort things out, make lists, mull and stew, plot and plan. All the things she should have been doing for her wedding she would do for the movie about her wedding.

At the moment, however, she needed to clear her head. The tight hat of a promised hangover sat on her brow. In a stupor she made a cup of instant coffee, then poured it down the drain. Really what she needed was some air. She snapped on Sniffy Voyeur's leash and dragged him down the stairs. This was not a particularly safe thing to do at ten o'clock in Mimi's neighborhood, but deranged men with concealed weapons were not high on the list of Mouse's fears. High on the list of Mouse's fears was getting married for no reason. Love was not a reason. Money, certainly in this case, was not a reason. A movie: now that was a reason.

Outside, a warm wind blew the lids off overstuffed garbage cans, sending crumbled balls of wrapping paper scudding down the street. Three duplexes down, a front door stood open, offering a glimpse of people Christmas partying, the women sweating in velvet, the men in red and green plaid jackets. They spoke a foreign language.

As they walked, Sniffy Voyeur alternately straining at the leash, then stopping to mark every palm tree, lamppost, and rosebush in his path, Mouse envisioned the months ahead as they would appear on a ragged black and white work print flickering on the screen of a Moviola. Seeing it this way, her once dreaded future seemed bearable. She could tolerate – she even almost looked forward to – the upcoming weeks of trying on dresses, veils, and shoes, deciding on the cake, the flowers, the food, the formal wear for Tony, the dress for Mimi, the china, the silver, the glass. What about a priest? What about rings? What about her make-up? What about transportation? What about her period? When was that? When was the reception? Where the honeymoon? How to budget it? Why go through with it?

Now she had the why. The wedding was now a Subject, not just a profound waste of money and an opportunity for family and friends to have an emotional binge at her expense. She laughed up into the hazy night, orange with the light from the sodium vapor street lamps. She conjured up the Escher-like image of Ivan filming the video cameraman videotaping the ceremony.

Sniffy Voyeur may have been old and smelly, but he was not insensitive. He could tell by the way Mouse held his leash, by the way her sandals slapped on the sidewalk, that she was feeling good, which made him feel good. He trotted along the parking strip, snuffling out scents of interest: hardened turds, food wrappers, ossified oranges that had dropped from front yard trees months before. He picked up what appeared to be a short, thick, mottled chunk of branch and pranced with it down the block.

Ivan's proposal solved all of Mouse's problems. Her problem of the wedding and her problem of what to do next. If she didn't get funding for something soon she'd have to get a job. She could not imagine what she'd do here. Be an overworked secretary like Mimi? A suicidal sound editor like Lisa? Waitress? She made a mental note to ask Ivan about producers' fees.

Two blocks over, the apartment buildings and duplexes gave way to tiny coffee-colored stucco bungalows, bars on the windows, solar heating panels propped on tile roofs. Houses, growing up, Mouse and Mimi had been taught to look down on, whose weedy cyclone fences enclosed front lawns littered with cheap toys and car parts. White-trash houses, Shirl called them, now owned by people who drove foreign sports cars from which they were able to turn on their backyard Jacuzzis using their car phones.

Another front door was open. Inside, Mouse saw that the bungalow had been radically redecorated. It looked oppressively cozy and Victorian. The gleaming blond wood floors were covered with floral-patterned rugs, dust ruffles hung cutely from sofas and chairs, baby-blue lamps were topped with shirred lampshades, the walls were abused by wallpaper busy with lavender roses.

Mouse was reminded of a double bill she had once seen with Ivan. Halfway through the first movie there was a scene where the hero approached a dusty single-engine prop plane marooned in the desert. He pried open the door and, miraculously, found himself in a sleek upscale topless nightclub. The audience accepted this, feeding from their tubs of popcorn for the next several minutes before realizing that during the most perfectly matched reel change in the history of cinema, the projectionist had put up a reel from the next movie.

On the front porch of the bungalow, four women sat on dining room chairs, drinking spiced wine and stringing popcorn from a large red bowl, yammering amiably. Through the open door behind them, Mouse could see more women carefully laying tinsel on the branches of a tall Christmas tree. Over-orchestrated Christmas carols blared from a high-powered stereo and the motherly scent of baking sugar cookies filled the air.

Sniffy, branch still clamped in his narrow jaw, raised his head, sucking up the smell, wet nose twitching, cheeks chuffing.

"Look at the doggie woggie," said one of the popcorn stringers in a high, Sniffy Voyeur-pleasing voice. His bushy tail swept back and forth across Mouse's knees.

"I love dogs. Look at the sweet lovin wuffin. Look at the sweet face. What kind is he?"

"Collie-shepherd, I think."

"Who does your eyes?" one of the women asked, then laughed.

"Dogs are so great. They're so loyal."

"They don't care if you're in a bad mood or can only fit into your fat clothes."

"What I like is how they're always glad to see you. Always. It doesn't matter if you've just been out getting a video. You come back and it's like they haven't seen you for a thousand years."

"They don't hold you morally responsible for looking your age."

"You're like *the one*, for a dog."

Sniffy wagged his hind end and whimpered, pulling at the lead.

"What's his name?"

"Tony," said Mouse.

"Hi Tony, hi sweetie-weetie, doggie lovin wuffin puplet. Oh look at the doggie. Oh look at the sweet boy."

"He's pretty wonderful," said Mouse, patting his head.

"Let him go, let him come say hi. He won't run away, will he? What's that he's got there? A stick? Is that your stick?"

Sniffy moaned with delight. As Mouse leaned down to un-snap his leash, she got a closer look at his "stick," and saw it wasn't a branch at all but a dead squirrel, stiff with rigor mortis. Sniffy had plucked him up by his board-straight tail, belly down. The mottled dull brown Mouse had mistaken for bark was the squirrel's back.

She enjoyed these middle-aged ladies lavishing so much love on dumb Sniffy Voyeur, so it surprised her when she ignored the squirrel and let Sniffy go. Sniffy, once freed, galloped toward the popcorn bowl. The women became giggling sorority sisters, yelping, "The popcorn! The popcorn!" Sniffy dropped the squirrel just as one of the women bent down to scoop the bowl up in her arms. She saw the stick was a squirrel. She saw the soft squirrel belly, the tight little claws pulled up to its chest. They all saw it. They rocketed to their feet, the popcorn spilling, kernels bouncing around their feet like hail. Sniffy vacuumed them up with his tongue. "Ugh, God! Get that disgusting dog out of here!"

"SO WHAT'D YOU do with the squirrel?" asked Mimi.

They shared the bathroom mirror, washing their faces before bed. Mouse, who usually scrubbed her cheeks with whatever mushy bar was in the soap dish and the corner of a towel, watched intently while Mimi dabbed her face with a pink gelatinous goo flecked with bits of yellow and blue.

"Picked it up and threw it in some bushes. That looks like protoplasm," said Mouse, referring to Mimi's goo.

"You *touched* it? What if it had rabies?"

"It didn't have rabies."

"Try some," she said, handing Mouse the jar. "It's special cleanser for women who are young enough to have zits but old enough to have wrinkles."

The cleanser was as skittish as Jell-O. Mouse finally captured a dime-sized blob. "How much does something like this cost?"

"Fifty bucks," said Mimi. She rinsed and patted her face

dry, then dabbed her neck expertly with moisturizer. "It's a fortune, I know, but beauty is the same as health in my book. It's not something to skimp on. Anyway, I think it's great, about those women. Even though people say feminism is dead, a bunch of great women like that, doing the holidays without dates. I really respect women like that. Making their own lives. That's why I go to so much trouble every year to make my fruitcake, you know? I mean, I could just ignore Christmas because I don't have a family, but I still have a *life*, right? Here, use some of this. You don't want your neck to get old."

"Maybe they were lesbians," said Mouse. She bared her neck at the mirror and applied the cream in upward strokes, imitating Mimi.

"What does *that* mean?"

"They looked like they were really enjoying themselves, not trying to make the best of it."

"They probably thought *you* were a lesbian, picking up a dead squirrel."

"That restaurant Ivan and I went to was not very good." In the same way Mimi had never asked Mouse about Africa, Mouse knew she would never ask about dinner with Ivan.

"You should have come with us to Disneyland. We *danced*. Can you believe it? They have the worst bands there, they all play the same six pop songs over and over. Tony is really good. You'd think he'd look dopey, being so tall. I got hit on by this fourteen-year-old. A *fourteen-year-old*. I mean, I know I look *young*, but – not like that!"

Mouse, hypnotized by the sight of Mimi's wide mouth in the bathroom mirror, opening and closing, opening and closing, yak, yak, yak, yak, yak, yak, yak, had abandoned her broad upward strokes for tight small circles.

13

ON THE THURSDAY BEFORE CHRISTMAS, TONY AND RALPH crawled up the diamond lane. They were headed across town to meet with V. J. Parchman, who had read the new draft of *Love Among the Gorillas* and wanted to talk to them immediately. He used that word, *immediately*.

Immediately could only be good. A producer didn't summon a pair of writers to his office *immediately* if the news was bad, Tony reasoned. Despite Ralph's admonition that in this business yes meant maybe and maybe meant no, he was heartened. It put him in the Christmas spirit. It was four days after Mouse's traitorous dinner with Ivan; the morning after her unsuccessful attempt to bamboozle him into participating in a silly documentary about – good God, how could she even entertain such an idea – their wedding.

Freeway traffic limped along at thirty-five miles an hour. At this time of day, at this time of year, the drive would take at least an hour. People who had rushed out on their lunch hour to pick up a last-minute present wrapped it in the passenger seat with one hand. The usual rock tunes throbbing from car stereos were interspersed with an occasional Christmas carol sung by the latest rock icon.

Ralph cheerfully tailgated the car ahead of them: this would give them plenty of time to chant for a good meeting. They should repeat to themselves, over and over, *deal, deal, deal, deal.* Ralph said he always chanted in the car. He said that once when he went to the movies in Westwood he'd chanted for forty-five minutes to find a parking place, and there it was, smack in front of the theater, money in the meter. Chanting for a deal was an old Buddhist trick, said Ralph.

Tony stared out the window. The man in the car next to them was brushing his teeth with an electric toothbrush. Tony was not against old Buddhist techniques, even those that sounded revisionist, but he could not keep his mind on it. He was furious with Mouse.

The night before she'd asked to be taken out to dinner. A date, you know, she said, we never have *dates* anymore, as though she'd ever had any interest in them before. She got dressed up. A mint-green silk shirt she'd just purchased, quite becoming, long silver earrings, and lipstick.

Tony should have known something was up. Whenever she wanted anything she put on lipstick.

There's some wedding business I'd like to discuss, she said. Wedding business! He thought she'd meant *wedding* business. Invitations. Rings. The whole lot of endearing details brides give themselves over to.

So out they went, to a place in Beverly Hills that served Mexican food.

She insisted they order margaritas, asked how he liked bloody Disneyland. Like the dumb unsuspecting sod he was, he thought she was really interested, instead of just biding her time, waiting for him to get a little high before she dropped the bomb. The margaritas came in a fishbowl, chunks of salt clinging to the rim.

Tony admitted he liked the fairy tale rides, Alice in Wonderland, Snow White. Rides favored by toddlers and senior citizens. How did he like the Matterhorn? she wondered. He didn't go on it. Someone had to hold the stuffed animals, the hubcap-size suckers Carole's grandparents had bought for the grandchildren back home.

"Ralph had a hilarious anecdote about an editor friend of

his. Really a talented chap, apparently, editor to the stars, rock stars, and such. He had a gig in Tokyo, editing a music video. He was there for forty hours, thirty of them spent stuck in front of a small screen in a dark room. You know how it is."

"Uh-huh." She lit a cigarette, blew smoke out of the side of her mouth, her eyes on his. She was certainly a whiz at feigning interest.

"At the end he had about ten hours to spare, had seen none of Tokyo – he'd wanted to have a walk about some of the rock gardens or temples, something unique to Japan. The Japanese felt quite badly for him so they took him to Disneyland."

"Oh no."

"It gets better. The chap had worked at Disneyland when he was at university. Four years cleaning It's a Small World."

"Oh *no*," said Mouse, then, after a moment: "I had an interesting dinner with Ivan Esparza the other night."

"'Interesting,' the nebulous, multipurpose American adjective."

She began on a rather laborious description of the antisocial waiters and the evil green chicken salad. Tony tried to keep his mind on what she was saying, but he was struggling with the rewrite of *Love Among the Gorillas*. After debating with Ralph over several meals and through one preseason Lakers basketball game as to the exact way in which one made an almost perfect script more perfect, they agreed that what V.J. probably meant was the entire piece needed to be "pushed," making it more dramatic.

They rewrote it thus: The Tony character is shot by the gang of elephant poachers, rather than roughed up with the butt of a rifle; the Mouse character does not simply administer first aid but cuts the bullet out with a knife; the movies they are each working on are not foreign-produced documentaries but multi-million-dollar American feature films; the Mouse character marries the Uncle Nigel character instead of just dating him; the Uncle Nigel character has raised the Tony character from infancy instead of just getting him the occasional job with the BBC. Tony justified these changes by saying they were in keeping with the spirit of the truth. But the final scene, the wedding in the mountains among the gorillas, still troubled him.

More margaritas appeared with their meal. Mouse was expounding, for some reason, about Ivan's impressive credentials as filmmaker and fundraiser. She wasn't eating. She needed to eat. She was too thin. He liked a woman with something to hang on to. She leaned toward him, her face glazed with that earnest, furrowed look he'd begun to find so unappealing.

In the end, he thought, perhaps his character should die, and the Mouse character, upon finding him dead, offs herself. Ralph was absolutely against this. He said anything but a happy ending would kill the project immediately. Perhaps the Tony character could only appear to be dead – what was Mouse saying? A bell went off somewhere in Tony's head, like an alarm clock infiltrating an early-morning dream.

" – anyway, I told him I needed to talk to you. I felt, I mean, we are the ones getting married and Ivan, well, you know how I feel about Ivan and his work, but I wouldn't want his involvement to change any – "

"My God, did you sleep with him? Is that what you're saying!"

The couple at the next table looked up with raised eyebrows from their basket of chips. Oh goodie, a scene.

"He wants to do a documentary on our wedding. I can't believe, what's wrong with you? I can't believe you thought – "

" – our wedding? *Our* wedding?" Tony felt his face go hot with the cursed blush of the strawberry blond. He swore at himself for jumping to conclusions. He cringed, remembering how he had behaved over all that bloody business with Mouse and Uncle Ni. He remembered all his silly, baseless accusations, all those humid sleepless hours extracting tearful promises from Mouse, forcing her to swear on everything in the known world worth swearing upon that Uncle Ni had meant nothing, and that, furthermore, it was now over.

Still, she'd refused to marry him. In his mind, that had meant only one thing. Tony, ashamed of himself but unable to stop, followed her when she went out with friends, read her journal when she wasn't home, sniffed her blouses for a telltale whiff of Uncle Ni's medicinal-smelling aftershave, tortured himself with images of Mouse and Uncle Ni together in the dark womb of the editing room, struck up meaningless flirtations with the bored wives of diplomats as a way of doing to Mouse what he was sure she was doing to him. Finally, he took the job with the French production bound for Rwanda, not because he wanted the work but because one night Mouse caught him inspecting the sheets in the dirty clothes basket for signs of sex – how he was to distinguish his stains from another man's remained a mystery, even to himself – and said if he didn't take the job, she would leave him. He was angry, now, sitting in this blasted overpriced Beverly Hills restaurant, that she had elicited this stupid, humiliating behavior once again.

"I was tempted to tell him yes, but knew we had to talk."

"I should hope so. I'm only the bloody groom."

"Ivan's already got the funding. He has that series of films on social institutions. There was an article in a magazine I read that quoted someone at the NEA saying, 'I would give Ivan Esparza money to do anything.' It would be a sort of 'the making of' kind of thing. His work is respected all over the country. It would be done respectfully."

"Respectfully my arse."

"Tony, we have nothing in the works. If we don't get something going soon we're going to have to find jobs. Ivan said I could co-produce, which would mean – "

" – now, now, isn't that cozy. You and Ivan co-producing a documentary on our wedding. But that's the way you like it, isn't it? A little on-location shooting, a little fucking?"

"What about you and Ralph? Ever since we got here, there you are, two Hollywood guys-about-town lunching and meeting and I don't know what, watching football, you used to *hate* sports – "

"–I see what this is. I've neglected you so now you've decided to find a way to get back at me. You're jealous because I can pop into Los Angeles–"

"–*pop* into Los Angeles? What is this *pop* into business? You get more British every day. You weren't this British in Nairobi. I feel like I'm living with Churchill."

"What are you talking about?"

"What am I talking about? What are you talking about?"

"You want to let some manic depressive–"

"–you've been talking to Mimi, I see–"

"–may I finish?"

"Finish! Finish!"

"I won't finish until you calm down. People are staring."

"I'm sorry." She pushed her plate away and folded her hands on the edge of the table. "Tell me your objections."

His objections! She was the one, wasn't she? There in her green silk with her glorious heaving chest and pale eyes, those dark curls, which, at that moment, he wanted to grab, shaking her until she wept. His objections, indeed! He loved her, couldn't she see that? He didn't want a travesty made of the most important moment in their lives! Anyway, what about *Love Among the Gorillas*? V.J. thought he and Mouse were *already* married, in a private, intensely romantic ceremony in the Rwandan mountains among the gorillas. He couldn't let it be known that not only were they not married but that this fact was going to be brought to everyone's attention by the production of a silly and dull documentary about their wedding. He reached across the table and took her hands in his.

"I'm just thinking of us, poppet. We wouldn't have any control. You know documentary. Anything you say can be held against you. What if we had a row, like this? We never fight, generally, but say we do because, good God, we're sleeping on your sister's floor and your mother's had this beastly accident and we're trying to plan a wedding. We're suffering under terrible stress, y'know? We have a fight, and Ivan films it. We become the typical engaged couple arguing over something ridiculous, don't you see? It's quite belittling."

"Yes," she said.

What, of course, she saw was that if she didn't have Tony's participation she wouldn't be able to do the movie. She squeezed his hands. "I'm sorry I brought it up." She'd just have to think of something else.

WHEN TONY AND Ralph arrived at V.J.'s office, V.J. was sitting on the edge of Emily's desk trying to get through to Michael Brass. Emily was apparently out. A stack of mail towered on the edge of her desk. The phone rang and rang.

"–I know! I know! Mr. Brass is in meetings all day, I'm just trying to–yes, yes–I heard at the last Save the Elephants meeting that Stars Against Ivory was having a fundraiser and I was just trying to confirm–yes, I'll hold." V.J. hooked the receiver under his chin, rolling his eyes. "Michael Brass may be the most powerful bloke in the business, but his secretary is as dumb as a bleeding hippo. Go on in, I'll–yes!" he shrieked into the phone, "Is there or is there not a fundraiser? This is not just some piddling Hollywood matter, luv, the elephants are at stake–yes, I'll hold."

As Tony sank into V.J.'s *faux*-cheetah skin loveseat, he once again felt nervous. He feared that this was the end, that somehow the deal would fall through. He was also afraid that it would happen. If it happened, he would have to tell Mouse. He stood up and paced restlessly around the room, stopping to examine a silver-framed photograph behind V.J.'s desk. It featured V.J. and two mates dressed as Maasai at what appeared to be a Halloween party. Tony was impressed by their costumes. They all wore striped togalike *shukas*, black wigs, plaited with braids, stained with red clay, and dozens of beaded necklaces and earrings. Of course, they did not possess the long, looping earlobes of true Maasai, although Tony had noticed when they came in that V.J. had several beaded pierced earrings in one ear.

"You know, I haven't yet mentioned this to Mouse," said Tony. "Even though I went ahead and put in our real names."

"Nothing's happened, why should you mention it?" said Ralph.

"No, but suppose it does –"

" – look, why make your life miserable? Once, I had an idea. Okay, it wasn't my idea, it was an idea I had with someone else. Actually, it was this other person's idea. We were going to collaborate on it, then this person decided to give up the business and go to law school. So I pitched this idea around. I felt guilty, it was not my idea, and I told this person, I admitted to him that I had pitched his idea around. It was the end of the friendship. Nothing ever happened, not a development deal, nothing, and I lost a friend over it. So sit tight, we're still in the courting stages here, we haven't even kissed yet, we haven't even *held hands*, we're still eyeing each other across the bar."

"*Jambo*," said V.J. at the door. He strode in, a script – Tony presumed it was *Love Among the Gorillas* – under his arm. Just as he hurled himself into his large leather chair, the phone rang. V.J. slung the receiver up to his ear. "V.J. Parchman's office – he's not here, please ring him later."

V.J. tipped back in his chair, leveled a scrutinizing gaze at Tony and Ralph. He picked up a rubber band from his desk and stretched it between a thumb and forefinger. "So, *Love Among Gorillas*."

Tony cleared his throat. "'The' Gorillas."

Beep-beep, beep-beep, beep-beep. The discreet though insistent electronic ring of the telephone. "V.J. Parchman's office – he's not in right now." V.J. hung up, readjusted his scrutinizing gaze. "*Love Among Gorillas*. I *love* this script, I do –"

"It's 'the' gorillas," said Tony, ignoring Ralph's disapproving glare. "*Love Among Gorillas* sounds as though it's a love story between gorillas."

"Three words do much better than four," said V.J.

"I like it," said Ralph, "it's ironic, like humans are just a bunch of gorillas anyway."

"That's exactly the point I was trying to make," said V. J.

Beep-beep, beep-beep, beep-beep. "Excuse me, that blasted Emily, how long can it take to get a root canal?" He jammed the receiver against his ear. "V. J. Parchman's office – Michael!" V. J.'s sallow face lit up with an expression of rapture, an apostle gaining an unexpected audience with the Lord. "Michael Michael Michael! You'll never guess who I have in my office – " V. J. winked at Tony. He nervously twirled a hank of dull brown hair behind his ear.

Tony and Ralph could not help exchanging confused glances.

Tony pinched the end of his nose, then tucked his hands under his thighs. Mouse had once tenderly advised him that this was not a particularly becoming habit. He tried to remember if he had ever met a Michael Brass. Someone in Bibliothèques? A friend of Sather and Darryl's?

" – Tony Cheatharn, old friend from Nairobi, personally involved with the Kenyan Wildlife Federation's crackdown on poaching – lovely, yes – let me put you on the speaker."

V. J. pressed a bar at the bottom of his phone console, releasing a booming disembodied voice. "Tony Cheatham, do I know you?"

"He and Ralph Holladay, you remember Ralph, had that *Girls on Gaza* project – "

"The Script That Wouldn't Die? Sure, I remember."

Ralph smiled to hide his wince.

" – they've got this terrific project *Love Among Gorillas*. At any rate, don't want to bore you with that now. We heard SAI was having a fundraiser after the first of the year – "

"Ten thousand dollars a head. You got ten thousand dollars, I'll see you there. How'd the operation go, Tony? Was on a fact-finding mission myself a couple of months ago with ... "
He proceeded to name three or four of the most famous movie

stars in the world. "We thought the situation looked terrible, just terrible."

"Yes, quite," said Tony helplessly.

"Considering the magnitude of the problem, some good was done," said Ralph. He shrugged at Tony. Make it up.

"We were able to confiscate a ton, several tons of ivory," Tony tried. "We also captured a few of the more vicious poachers in the–"

"–Tony was shot during one of the raids," V.J. contributed, waving the script in the air as though to acknowledge he'd read the new draft and approved of this addition.

"–Jesus Christ," said Brass. "Tony, tell you what, you got five thousand dollars you come on by, my guest."

"Michael, the man just got back from *Kenya*. He's been *shot*. Maybe he could give a speech, a little update on how the battle is going, a view from the trenches."

"Sure. Why not?" With that, Brass hung up.

V.J. replaced the receiver, looking as satisfied as Hannibal the day he crossed the Alps. He took off his greasy-lensed glasses, huffed them against his chest. "We did it, old chaps."

Tony found himself nodding his head. "Right-o." This must be how people are converted to bizarre religions, he thought.

Ralph said, "So. The script."

V.J. steered his glasses onto his face, pulled his lank hair back into a tight ponytail. On the corner of his desk sat a hand-woven basket full of red and green jelly beans. He tossed a few into his mouth, "You guys know I love this script."

"–we think the ending needs to be stronger," Tony said. "Right now it ends with the wedding on the mountain. We were thinking we should go more *Romeo and Juliet*. Take out the wedding, the Tony character dies, then the Mouse character finds him and kills herself."

"The wedding is the most powerful scene in the script. It's the Happily Ever After part. Besides, this is a true-life story.

Although I do see your point, something is missing. The script is perfect, but lacking, isn't it?"

"That's just a *thought*," said Ralph. "It's not engraved in paper."

"What we have here is just a nice love story, isn't it?"

"I was under the impression that's what attracted you to it," said Tony, "the sort of classical feel –"

"What are your thoughts?" Ralph asked V.J.

V.J. tipped back in his chair, held his hands together against his lips, pondering. Minutes passed. Tony could hear a woman talking on the phone through the other side of the wall. "Good, what's good?" he thought he heard her say. He tried to think back to V.J.'s filmic writing seminar. Was V.J., then Vince, as loony then as he was now? Mouse would say that teaching semi-illiterate tribesmen how to translate the stuff of their lives into a screenplay said it all. He could just imagine the "told you so" look on her cute little face. So V.J. was crazy. Visionaries often were. Mouse's old boyfriend Ivan was crazy, also stupid. He made documentaries. At least V.J. did things like *Lethal Red Attraction* or whatever the bloody hell it was. Tony rubbed the sides of his temples. He was having trouble following his own train of thought.

"Let me just toss this out. Feel free to disagree. What about heightening the elephant-poaching angle?"

"You want more about the documentaries they're working on?" said Tony in disbelief. That could only slow things down. "Wouldn't that be a bit boring?"

"My point exactly. Movies about movies are boring. They never do well. So let's make Tony and Mouse part of the wildlife team battling the poachers."

"Interesting," said Ralph.

"I thought you wanted a true-life story."

"We do," said V.J. "Though certainly you must agree that we can be a bit flexible in our interpretation of it. When you get down to it, what's the difference between making a movie about the struggle against poaching and joining the struggle itself?"

"There's a considerable –"

" – let's not split hairs. What about, Tony and Mouse are working undercover! That could be it. Working undercover – or no, no, no! This is it! I got it!" He dug his hand into the basket, stuffed a fistful of jelly beans into his mouth. The sound of candy and dental work clashing filled the otherwise silent room.

Tony and Ralph waited politely.

"Tony is working with the wildlife department and Mouse is working with some other group undercover, only he thinks she's an ivory smuggler. That could work very nicely –"

" – yeah!" said Ralph, leaping to his feet, "and what it is, she shoots him. Accidentally. Or here! Wait!" Ralph helped himself to the jelly beans, a few bouncing to the floor. "She's in with this group of poachers and she's scared shitless because maybe they *suspect* she's undercover, and so, to prove she's on their side, she shoots Tony, she wings him, then sneaks into his camp later and cuts the bullet –"

" – good, good, good," said V. J. "Woman wounds Man, then heals him –"

"I know how *that* is," said Ralph. "We should be writing this down. Tony, write this down."

"Terrific," said Tony, "smashing. One minor suggestion. Since it's no longer a true story, I would prefer not using our real names."

"What are you – ?" V. J. sputtered, then turned to Ralph. "What is – how is this not a true story?"

Tony looked at him blankly. "How is this not a true story? It's not a true story because it never happened."

"Howz about we say not 'this is a true story' before the title credit, but '*based* on a true story'?" suggested Ralph.

"I'll have to run that by my people," said V. J.

"You still have to run the bleeding *script* by your people," said Tony. "Can't you run it all by at the same time?"

"Did I mention Redford?" said V. J.

"He's interested?" asked Ralph.

"First, we need to make *Love Among Gorillas* as perfect as we can," said V.J. He reached for more jelly beans, scrabbled around the bottom of the empty basket.

"Maybe we should change the title to *Love Among Elephants*," said Ralph.

"Brilliant," said V.J. He wagged the basket in the air over his desk. "Tony, old chap, could you? There's a big bag of jellies in Emily's closet out there. Dreadful for you, but 'tis the season."

Tony rose slowly. He could not believe this. Had he, by broaching a perfectly reasonable objection, been reduced to the role of hostess? He took the basket stiffly from V.J.'s hand. He walked slowly out to Emily's office. He felt their eyes on his back.

The closet was out of V.J.'s line of vision. Tony leaned his forehead against the closet door. He stared down at the toes of his cowboy boots, listening to the roaring tale of evil ivory smugglers, noble elephants, automatic weapons, laundered money, and juicy sex being effortlessly spun in V.J.'s office.

He could leave right now. He could catch a bus back to the apartment. He could come clean to Mouse. They could find something to produce together. He could put *Love Among the Gorillas* at the bottom of his suitcase. Better, he could burn it.

As he set the basket on the edge of Emily's cluttered desk, his eye happened on a check sitting on top of her in-box. It was made out to V.J. Parchman for ninety-seven thousand dollars, written on the account of a production company Ralph had mentioned once in passing. It was dated the week before, no clue as to what it might be for, just a check, tossed there as though it was any niggling piece of paperwork. Under the check was a copy of the latest *Variety*. The lead story was about a twenty-two-year-old film school graduate who had just sold his second script for several million.

Tony filled the basket with jelly beans and returned to V.J.'s office.

As Ralph would remind him later, at a dead stop in the

diamond lane, this was probably not going to happen anyway. It was rush hour. Pairs of red taillights marched into the dusk.

"If it's not going to happen," shouted Tony, "why are we doing it! Why are we wasting our time!"

"Same reason people don't want their brain-dead loved one taken off life support! Same reason my father had four bypass operations! The reason we open our mail and brush our teeth! The reason we get up in the morning!"

"There's hope, in other words," said Tony, "you're saying there's hope."

"To the extent that there's no hope, there's hope, is what I'm saying. You ever read *The Plague*?"

"Yes."

"Read *The Plague*, you'll see what I'm saying."

14

MOUSE THOUGHT THE ACCIDENT HAD CHANGED SHIRL, just as Dr. Klingston predicted. Her evidence was their driving over the hill to the Valley six-thirty Christmas morning to open presents with Shirl and Auntie Barb.

Shirl demanded that Mimi, Mouse, and Tony come over in bathrobes and pajamas. Any attempt to dissuade her produced a fit of rage or sulking. Mouse and Mimi pleaded. Couldn't we have Christmas at the apartment, then shower and dress and...? Couldn't we at least dress? We'll bring over our presents and we can open everything together....

Shirl, backed by Auntie Barb, who accused Mimi and Mouse of willfully making Shirl's already tough life hell, insisted they go straight from bed to bucket seat without stopping to comb their hair or rinse the sour night taste from their mouths. She wanted them no later than six-thirty, the better to duplicate the inhumane hour Mouse and Mimi used to awaken her and Fitzy, then just her, on the innocent and greedy mornings of Christmas past.

"She's always been a Christmas Nazi," said Mimi as they jounced over Laurel Canyon. "I don't see anything different this year. It's always one thing or another. She was always after Ivan to dress up like Santa. You can imagine Ivan as Santa." No way was she, Mimi, going to drive anywhere in her highly un-reliable Datsun in a *bathrobe*. She wouldn't even take the gar-bage out in her Ugly Pants, the brown Stretch Levi's for Gals Shirl had saddled her with *last* Christmas. This morning, after her run and a Merry Christmas wakeup call to Ralph, she put on paint-speckled gray sweats and a T-shirt. She put on makeup – only enough to look normal, not beautiful – and brushed her teeth. She still had a warrant for her arrest out on account of all her parking tickets, and was not about to get pulled over by a cute cop, then hauled off to jail in a patrol car, Clearasil dotting her face, her rotting coffee-stained robe flapping open as she was marched up the courthouse steps. Shirl would just have to be unhappy. She, Mimi, would just have to suffer being accused of ruining Shirl's day. She would be anyway. After all, it was Christmas.

There was no traffic, save a few hyperoutfitted, tortured bicyclists with stringy overworked flanks pumping up the hill. The air was tinged with the smell of ponderosa pine, the sky white with dry desert cold. Later, it would be as warm as any late spring day.

Unlike Mimi, Mouse liked Christmas. It was the one day a year when she didn't feel compelled to think up ways to raise money for her documentaries. It was a true holiday. She dangled her arm out the window, hand patting the breeze. The day she bought her new green silk blouse she also splurged on a lavish purple terrycloth bathrobe with a hood.

Tony wore a brown-and-gold silk dressing gown his mother had sent him from Hong Kong. He sat wedged in the backseat, his knees thrust under his chin, next to two shopping bags full of packages whose elaborate bows were getting flatter and flatter by the minute. The temperature between Mouse and Tony made the chilly morning seem Saharan by comparison.

"This is the kind of Christmas we'd try to sneak in a swim. We'd take off our black patent-leather shoes and our anklets – remember those anklets with the little lace trim? We'd stand on the first step in the shallow end of the lagoon, remember?" asked Mouse.

"We'd yell inside to Shirl and Fitzy, 'It's really warm,'" said Mimi.

"'I'll bet it is.' Fitzy would say, 'I'll bet it is.' Then we'd say, 'No, *really*. It's *really*, really *warm*.' We'd yell, 'Would you be mad if we accidentally fell in?'"

"We never yelled it," said Mimi. "I just did it. One time I pretended you pushed me."

"We never did it," said Mouse, "we only *threatened*."

"I did it," said Mimi. "It was the year we had the twin dresses."

"We always had twin dresses," said Mouse.

"Yeah, with lots of lace. I looked like the Incredible Hulk, and Mouse was all cute and girly."

"I was never girly," said Mouse, pleased to be thought so.

"Sounds like I missed a smashing time," said Tony.

"It *was* a smashing time," said Mouse. "You don't have to be sarcastic."

"I wasn't being sarcastic."

Even in Africa, Christmas had always reminded Mouse of Fitzy. Every year the memory seemed more pleasant and less tinged with pain, which in turn made Mouse sad that he had been dead so long.

When Mouse was small, it was tradition to go to work with Fitzy on Christmas afternoon. He was owner and sole proprietor of Fitzy's, a bar on then tawdry Ventura Boulevard. It was egg-yolk yellow on the outside, with no windows and had a gaudy green neon sign screaming FITZY'S, a blinking shamrock dotting the *i*. Mimi never went with Fitzy to work, Christmas afternoon or any other time. Mimi said Fitzy's looked like a place you'd go if you wanted to get knifed.

Fitzy's had catered to salesmen who sold vacuum cleaner attachments or World Book Encyclopedias out of their cars and to unhappy husbands, Irish five generations back, who'd stop in on their way home to their over-air conditioned tract houses in Van Nuys. The Valley was still the sticks, then, in 1962, hot, dull, and dusty. People living in houses that had since been demolished to make way for a minimall raised chickens in their backyards and sold pomegranates and avocados from their own trees to local markets.

Shirl had been ashamed of Fitzy's. So had Mimi. In grade school all Mimi's friends' fathers were businessmen who conducted mysterious, inexplicable "business" all day long in dress-up clothes. Fitzy wore no-iron golf shirts and was proud of the fact he cleaned the Gents' and the Ladies' with his own angry-pink dishpan hands. He hired losers who often robbed him.

The family always seemed to have money in the summer, during hot spells, around St. Patrick's Day, and at Christmas. In February they were always poor, a fallout from Fitzy's best customers' New Year's resolutions. His business was seasonal, Mouse insisted when her mother and sister complained, a word she used before she was quite sure what it meant.

Fitzy's opened at four o'clock on Christmas. Mouse would sit under the bar on the brass footrail, reading the old Atlas he kept in the drawer of his desk under the phone books and drinking Shirley Temples with two cherries.

One Christmas, one of the sad vacuum-cleaner-attachment salesmen, a regular who'd had a turkey carving-related argument with his wife and needed a drink, asked her what she was doing down there.

"Hiding from Mommy and Mimi," she said. The salesmen said he was hiding from Mommy, too. He gave her a tiny candy cane from his pocket, sticky with fine blue lint.

Fitzy roared with laughter and slapped his stomach. Mouse recognized what he called his hail-fellow-well-met laugh. It was a special laugh for the bar. At home he was quiet and read history books with yellow pages and tiny print.

"'This poor child! She's the different one, she is. Her sister and mother – you know how most women are – why say something in ten words when you can use a hundred?"

"When you can use a thousand!" said Mouse.

"When you can use a million!" said Fitzy.

"When you can use a katrillion-willion!" said Mouse.

"She exaggerates, just like her old man." Fitzy laughed until he nearly choked.

"I never ever 'zaggerate," said Mouse.

"Poor child." Fitzy shook his head.

Now, as Mimi pulled into Shirl's driveway, Mouse worried, as she did from time to time, that this fond memory was a myth, something she'd unknowingly invented on a date, at a cocktail party, in the bush, chattering idly to pass a long equatorial night, a careless half-truth fused with a harmless embellishment to create the last clear memory of her father.

Inside, a fire was roaring. It was traditional to have a fire on Christmas regardless of the weather. Mistletoe shriveling from the past week of heat was taped to the center of every doorway. Silver garlands festooned the mantle crowded with angels, elves and Santas fashioned from every conceivable material: pine cones, pantyhose, knitting yarn, magazines folded a clever way taught only in Girl Scouts, then spray-painted gold. Displayed on either end table was Shirl's collection of music boxes and snowstorms-in-a-ball. Tiny blinking lights were strung around the ceiling. Cards hung from two wide red satin ribbons flanking either side of the dining room. There was a crocheted Santa toilet paper cover in the bathroom, snowball guest soap, and candy-cane hand towels.

There were stockings for each of them. The sisters had their own red felt ones, with "Mimi" and "Mouse" written on them in green glitter, most of which had been rubbed off. Shirl had made a green felt stocking for Tony, his name sparkling in red. A plate of cheese danish sat on the coffee table along with a five-pound box of mixed chocolates someone had sent and a ceramic Santa teapot and four matching ceramic Santa mugs. Lorne Greene crooned "Merry Christmas Neighbor" on the stereo. Lorne Greene had been Fitzy's most famous customer.

"You're supposed to be in your jam-jams!" Shirl wailed as Mimi kissed Shirl on the cheek. Shirl's hair had grown back board-straight. It clung to her head like a bathing cap.

"This is what I sleep in," said Mimi. "I couldn't afford a robe."

"You should have told me, I'd have picked up one for you. Tony, dear, you can just put those anywhere under the tree. It's so nice to have a man to play Santa again! Do you recognize that on the hi-fi?"

"Lorne Greene?" said Mouse, reaching for a danish.

"It's Lorne Greene, your father's most famous customer. You know he gave that album to your father. It's even autographed. Mouse, honey, use a napkin. Oh, I forgot the napkins. Barb! Barb!"

Auntie Barb appeared in the kitchen doorway in a navy blue velour bathrobe holding an empty glass coffeepot, a frown embedded in her long dull face. "You're late," she said.

"Barb, dear, would you get us some napkins."

"The breakfast napkins or the dinner napkins?"

"The ones with the holly on them. Remember, we bought them at –"

"We put them back. The breakfast napkins should be fine."

"It's a holiday, we should use the dinner ones."

" – maybe just some paper towels," said Mouse, her cheek bulging with pastry.

"Paper *towels*," yowled Shirl. "I can't believe a girl getting married would even consider paper *towels* on *Christmas*. Tony, you look so elegant, just like, who was that, Mimi, honey, in *The Thin Man*?"

"William Powell," said Mouse, wiping her fingers on the sleeves of her purple terrycloth robe, the important issue of the napkins mysteriously and suddenly forgotten. She settled back in the couch, pulled up the hood of her robe, tucked each hand inside the other wide sleeve.

"My fiancée, the druid," said Tony, trying for a shared smile. While the robe fit Mouse, the hood had been designed for some-one with a head the size of a prizewinning watermelon. She tipped her head back so she could glare at him from under the front of it, which fell down over her eyes and rested on the bridge of her nose. She found it irritating how he resorted to witticisms when things were not going well between them.

"No, Robert Young," said Mimi. "Shirl, pass the chocolates, but just let me eat one."

"Nothing like a nice little diabetic shock before breakfast is my motto," said Tony. "Toss me one, Mouse, no nuts."

"No, it was someone else. Barb! Who was it in *The Thin Man*?"

"Mom, it was William Powell," said Mouse.

"It was not William Powell," said Mimi.

"Well, it wasn't Robert Young."

"It wasn't Robert Young, but it *wasn't* William Powell."

"Barb! Come in so we can open our gifts. Tony, will you do the honors? Find one for each of us, then we go around in a circle, beginning with Mouse. She opens hers, then Mimi, then me, then you, then Barb. Barb! Where the hell is she?" Shirl half rose in her chair, turned, and addressed the kitchen.

"She's outside, Mrs. FitzHenry."

Through the sliding glass door they watched Auntie Barb by the lagoon retrieving cookies from where they were cooling on squares of paper towels laid out on the diving board, a red and green metal tin clutched in her long veiny hand. She bent stiffly from the waist, plucked up each cookie between two fingers and placed it in the tin. The expression on her face suggested someone who had nailed a large spider with a wad of Kleenex and was depositing it in the toilet. She brought in the cookies and placed them on a stack of magazines next to the danish and the chocolates. "These are made with hazelnuts from Oregon. Even though California fashions itself as the cuisine capital of the West you can't get a decent hazelnut here if your life depended on it."

"Tony's going to pass out the gifts now, Barb."

"Shall I pour some tea?"

"Let's just open the presents," said Mimi. "You made us come over here in our pajamas already – "

"– you didn't have to come in your jam-jams, I just thought it'd be fun, with Mouse home for the first time in so long –"

"– you're not wearing your pajamas, anyway," said Mouse.

"I spent all my money on presents. I couldn't afford any." Mimi ate another chocolate.

"Tony must want some tea," said Auntie Barb. "If he's playing Santa."

"I'm quite fine," said Tony, poised on all fours by the Christmas tree, his robe tucked in the bend of his knee, exposing his skinny calves, hairless from where they rubbed against the inside of his pants. Mouse stared at them and thought of filet of sole. She turned away, stared into the fire, snapping as it sucked up the stray eucalyptus bud, filling the room with a hot medicinal smell.

Outside, the sun twinkled on the aluminum frames of the patio furniture. Shirl put on a new record, "A Colonel Sanders Merry Christmas," then decided while she was up she might as well put on a pot of coffee, and Auntie Barb said, no you sit, I'll do it, and Shirl said, you never grind the beans fine enough, *I'll* do it, and while the coffee was brewing, the fire burned down, and Mouse was sent out to the garage to retrieve a few more pieces of wood.

Across the street a bare-chested pair of twins, hair shiny blond-green from chlorine, wearing baggy hot pink shorts still wrinkled from the box, were strapping surfboards on the top of their car. They were one year old when Mouse left. Teething then, surfing now. Sixteen years had passed and she was still being sent out for firewood for the traditional and useless Christmas fire.

Christmas lists were also traditional, as was ignoring them. Mouse had asked for a lightweight jacket, cowboy boots, underwear, a book she had seen at the Academy Library on documentary great Richard Leacock. Shirl and Mimi had chided her, "We want to get you *fun* things!" The fun things included a set of mugs (Mimi); *The Bride's Friend*, "filled with tips, trends, advice and checklists" (Shirl); three cans of salmon in a shiny apple-green box stamped *Made in Oregon* (Auntie Barb); a pair of matronly, gold clip-on earrings for her pierced ears (Tony).

Mimi and Mouse also got twin electric screwdrivers from Shirl. Tony got a book from Mouse called *On Moral Filmmaking*. Shirl got a gift certificate from Mimi for her hairdresser for when Shirl's hair was long enough to be dressed again. Mouse gave everyone calendars. Auntie Barb gave everyone the salmon.

Shirl insisted they save for last a door-sized present leaning against the wall behind the tree, but she was anxious for them to get to it. Mouse opened her presents slowly, like an old lady, Mimi said, which got her a Look from Auntie Barb. Shirl eventually grabbed the electric screwdriver from Mouse's lap and finished opening it herself, ripping off the paper and flinging it into the fire. "You're a snail, not a mouse, Mousie Mouse."

"Ask her about her date with Ivan," said Mimi. Mimi was finished opening her presents, disappointed, in spite of herself, that there was nothing of interest. Her mouth ached from smiling with delight. She had eaten half the box of chocolates, and a nauseating sugar headache was upon her.

"Date with *who*?" said Shirl.

"It wasn't a date," said Mouse, tearing the paper from her last present, this one from Mimi. "All right!" She turned the box over and read it, puzzled. "What is – 'Ultrasonic Hair Removal System'?"

"It does it with radio waves. I got it out of a catalogue."

"Great," said Mouse. "I need... something like this."

"Not really," said Shirl.

"Well, it's not something I'd ask for, but that's what Christmas –"

"– you didn't *really* go out with Ivan, did you? Tony, did you know about this?" Shirl stood, bright red threads of capillaries standing out on her flushed cheeks. She went to the tree and dragged out the big present leaning against the wall. Tony leaped to his feet to help her.

"Tony, you're such a good man. He's such a good man, Mousie Mouse! That Ivan! What did you do on your date? This is too much for me. Tony, how could you let her? Take that ridiculous hood off, Mousie."

"Mom, it was only dinner," said Mouse, spreading her shaking hands in a "be reasonable" gesture.

"Dinner! You don't go out to dinner with a man at night when you're engaged to be married!"

"It was a business dinner," said Mouse. "Purely business."

"What business?" asked Mimi. "Ivan and business are two words that have never appeared together in the same sentence in the history of the English language."

Out of habit Mouse looked at Tony for support. He was flipping through *On Moral Filmmaking*, pretending to read.

"Business," Mouse hedged, "documentary business." She tried to summon up the confident expression used to persuade potential funders that the documentary they were considering investing in was not only a worthy venture but also a worthy tax write-off.

"He was interested in making a movie with Mouse," said Tony with disdain. "A documentary on our *wedding* –"

"–you mean videotaping it?" asked Shirl.

"No," said Tony, "a documentary. Like *The New Stanley*."

"What do you mean? Mouse, what does he mean?"

"Weddings have been *done*," said Mimi. "Solly has about six jillion clients with wedding scripts. I think Ivan just wants to get back at me through you. I don't know if you realize this, but he was really devastated when we broke up."

"I know," said Mouse, gripping her elbows inside the sleeves of her robe. Mouse knew no such thing. Mouse knew only that she was fed up with Mimi's boring, self-aggrandizing proclamations. *It's Christmas*, The Pink Fiend warned. *Don't be a difficult, unforgiving, uncharitable pain in the ass.*

"Oh no no no no no," said Shirl, wagging her head back and forth. "A girl's wedding is the most precious day of her life."

"Don't worry, Mom!" said Mouse. "It'll be okay. I'm not going to do anything stupid."

"You went to Africa," said Auntie Barb.

"Yeah," said Mimi, "you could have gone to Boring and lived with Auntie Barb, right, Auntie Barb?"

Shirl's face went slack with confusion. "What is everyone talking about?"

"Your daughter and I discussed it and decided it was simply too exploitative, Mrs. FitzHenry. A wedding – our wedding – is something special, not merely someone's idea – in this case Ivan's idea, and don't get me wrong, I think he's a tremendously talented chap – of good material."

Mouse loaded a glance with what she hoped was profound displeasure and shot it at Tony. How dare he cast himself in the reassuring role of man-in-charge.

"Maybe we can get him to videotape it?" asked Shirl, blotting her eyes with her bathrobe tie.

"Maybe we can get him to videotape it," said Tony.

"Open your present, then," said Shirl. She pulled herself off the couch with the aid of Mouse's shoulder and, stumbling over Mimi's feet, shuffled over to help Tony rip off the wrapping paper.

"It's a massage table, right?" said Mimi.

"It's a surfboard," said Mouse.

"I tried I don't know how hard to talk her out of it," said Auntie Barb. "She wouldn't hear of it. She's still got some of that good Oregon stubborn in her, even though she's spent all these years among wishy-washy Californians."

It was, in fact, a giant replica of a check, the kind lottery winners are frequently photographed holding, découpaged on a piece of plywood. In loopy cursive handwriting it was made out to the order of "The Newlyweds to Be" in the amount of one hundred thousand dollars.

Furrowed looks flew around the room while Shirl beamed,

hands clasped over her bosom. "I made it myself," she said. "It's a check."

"Quite," said Tony. "Good Christ."

"I told her it was too extravagant," said Auntie Barb. "I'm going to put the ham in."

"It's not for–don't you mean one *thousand* dollars?" asked Mimi, dumbfounded. Either (a) Shirl's brain had healed in a way that left her utterly deranged, or (b) she was really giving Mouse and Tony a hundred thousand dollars, in which case Mimi, who owed the feds thousands of dollars in back taxes, who had credit card debts totalling more than a year's salary *before* taxes, who would never be able to afford a house, or even to live in a decent apartment without a roommate, would have to slit her wrists.

"It's part of the settlement from that restaurant. Three hundred and fifty thousand dollars out of court. Mr. Edmonton settled last week. Such a nice man, Mr. Edmonton. We haven't got the check in hand just yet, but it's coming. I'm saving another hundred for your wedding, Mimi. I probably won't actually have it until after New Year's, Mr. Edmonton said. I knew it was coming, but I wanted it to be a surprise. Aren't you surprised?"

"We can't … it's really too generous," said Tony, still per- plexed, glancing frantically at Mouse for clues.

"You should invest it, Mom," said Mouse. "You shouldn't waste it on us."

"I have investments! CDs and IRAs and T-bills and God I don't know what. I'm set for life, what with selling Fitzy's to that Abde."

"We really can't, Mom. It's too…"

"Why won't you let me do this for you if it makes me happy!" Shirl's eyes were awash in tears. "I did the calligraphy myself."

"We love it, Mom." Mouse stood to give her a kiss and a hug. She tried to make them feel genuine. They *were* genuine. The giant check was clever. She refrained from thinking any- thing about the actual money. Just as Sniffy Voyeur would never eat a dog biscuit in public, preferring to spirit it to the farthest, darkest corner of the house to consume it in private, she would take this new development and ponder the implications when she was alone.

Shirl squirmed out of Mouse's hug. "Enough of that, where's my Instamatic? Mimi, take a picture of Mouse and Tony. You take such good pictures. If you don't make it in Hollywood, you could always be a professional photographer, right sweetie? Then just Mouse and me. Then The Sisters by the tree. Where's that camera? I thought I brought it out – Barb! Barb! Where's the camera?"

"It's here, Mom." Mimi retrieved it from the mantle, where it had been obscured in the mob of sweatsock elves and wine bottle angels. She welcomed the excuse to do something. She found Mouse and Tony in the viewfinder, grinning uncomfortably in their clashing purple and brown-and-gold robes, poised before the tree, groaning with decorations, the check displayed cutely lopsided on account of their differences in height.

She tilted the camera up just a hair, so that Mouse disappeared, so that Tony's chin was resting on the bottom of the frame, so that the angel on the top of the tree was featured, along with the seam where wall met ceiling.

"Smile," said Mimi, "you're millionaires."

15

CHRISTMAS WAS OVER. DRIVE-SHOP-EAT-EAT-EAT, drive-shop-eat-eat-eat returned to the less fattening and stress inducing drive-meet-eat. The hot weather had ended. Every morning the sky was thick with clammy drizzle.

Sometimes it rained for two or three days in a row. It was winter. People were relieved. Mimi did not even complain when she had to use some of the money from the Christmas presents she'd returned to get a new set of windshield wipers. In August her old ones had disintegrated and blown away.

It was a little over four months until the wedding.

Mimi did her best to be kind and mature. She did her best not to think, If only someone had given *me* a hundred thousand dollars. *One* hundred thousand dollars! She did her best not to wonder how she could extort some of it. One *hundred* thousand dollars! She told herself it wasn't like real money anyway, since Shirl had stipulated Mouse could use it only for the wedding. One hundred *thousand* dollars. She told herself that she would have fun, now that the sky was the limit, helping Mouse plan. She told herself that there was money waiting for her, too, when she remarried. Unless, of course, something *else* happened, which was always possible in a world where your father is mowed down by a two-ton converter gear and your mother is conked on the head by a plummeting ceiling fan. It sent her into fits of despair realizing it was more likely that a freak accident would kill her mother, leaving her rich, than that she would find a husband. And suddenly, she very much wanted a husband. She would be thirty-seven in May, too old to be sassy and independent unless you were a celebrity.

On New Year's Eve Mimi wanted to go to a huge party and get obliterated or else stay home in her bathrobe and eat a box of cookies by herself. Instead, it was the worst of both worlds: a small dinner party. Mouse and Tony, Mimi and Ralph, Carole and her new boyfriend, a playwright with a mobile dog-grooming service. He wore a T-shirt, revealing claw marks at various stages of healing, some infected. His name was Glen. He was twenty-four.

Mouse, the genius behind the bad idea, made an African dish involving green curries and an odious-looking root. It had taken six hours to prepare, not including the hours spent bumper-to-bumpering all over town just to find the ingredients. The final result had proved inedible.

They had also rented a video, suggested by Glen, that had proved unwatchable, one that was theoretically bad enough to be good. It should have elicited condescending groans, ironic comments, elitist howls. Instead, it made you feel like you were wasting your life, not something you want to be reminded of on New Year's Eve.

Ralph was sullen and preoccupied, more grumpy than usual. When they all went outside at midnight to bang pots and pans in front of the building with the Armenian neighbors, Ralph disappeared. Mimi, who had come back in to purge the pizza they had eaten in lieu of the African dish, found him in Carole's bedroom, crouching by the nightstand, talking on the phone to Elaine.

"Elaine, God! When's it due?" she heard him say. He saw Mimi out of the corner of his eye, standing in the doorway. He clamped the receiver to his chest. "Taxes," he said, his face ashen.

Mimi told herself she didn't care, even when she heard him lie to Elaine that he was home stripping wallpaper. She even went so far as to tell *him* she didn't care, that of course he and Elaine should be friends, and it was New Year's Eve, etc., etc., until they got into bed and he began touching her with that distracted look on his round face and something snapped inside her. She yelled and cried and accused him of leading her on, making her fat, and in general ruining her life.

Ralph was stunned. His pale eyebrows anchored themselves to the top of his forehead and didn't drift back to their normal place until she had sobbed into her pillow for nearly an hour, staining the pillowcase with mascaraed hieroglyphics. He patted her between her big bony shoulder blades and thought about *Love Among Elephants*.

Earlier in the evening, while Mouse and Mimi were in the kitchen cooking, and Glen and Carole had gone to track down the video, Tony and Ralph talked about the new draft. When Mouse or Mimi came in to offer another beer or to change the CD, by mutual, unspoken agreement, they changed the subject to sports or fell silent. Ralph had his own superstitious reasons for refusing to discuss his projects, and Tony had not yet gotten around to telling Mouse. It seemed less important that he tell her, now that the storyline had taken a *Raiders of the Lost Ark* sort of turn, and he kept putting it off and putting it off until finally he came to the conclusion that she didn't need to know at all.

Besides, Mouse had been annoyingly uncommunicative since Christmas. Conversing with her was like trying to make eye contact with someone from behind a drawn shade. He attributed it to the affair he believed she was having with Ivan. She reconfirmed his suspicions tonight.

Before Glen and Ralph arrived, while he was in the kitchen helping the girls with the hors d'oeuvres, he complained that they really should be going out to celebrate the new year. This was, after all, Los Angeles, not Nairobi. There were things to *do* here. What things, he wasn't exactly sure. There had to be a party they could crash, a club they could close in the wee hours of the morning. If he was honest with himself, however, he would have to admit that if Los Angeles was as exciting as its reputation held, the excitement had eluded him. Life here was weighted with the vague feeling that if anything was happening, it was happening wherever one *wasn't*. Maybe that accounted for all the driving, he reasoned. Eleven million people scurrying around, trying to find the elusive exciting event that would make them feel at the center of something big. The only time he had felt that way was during meetings with V.J., at which, so far as he could tell, absolutely nothing had happened, except a lot of work for him and Ralph. And people said Africa was impenetrable.

Of course, Mouse told him, there was nothing exciting to miss. "This city is like one of those mysterious men. You know, you always say, 'He's just quiet and seems boring, but still waters run deep–'"

" – but the reason the waters are so still is because there's like no wind, no currents–" said Mimi.

" – no fish, no *plankton*–" said Mouse.

"Sometimes a bore is just a bore."

"Most times."

"All right," said Tony, "your point is made." He opened a can of clams for the dip and overshot the bowl, dumping half the can on the floor, where Sniffy was waiting to slurp them up.

"Tony," said Mouse.

"All right!" he said, hurling the can into the sink and stomping out of the kitchen. Where did she come off criticizing him like that? Where did she come off expounding about men. He knew she was talking about him, not Los Angeles. He, Tony, was reliable, a known entity, boring. Ivan was surly, exotic, and a better filmmaker. He threw himself on the couch and turned on the box, refusing to budge. He turned on professional wrestling. The next time he bit Mouse's earlobe he resolved to draw blood.

Beyond that, Tony was not quite sure what else to do about Mouse and Ivan. At the risk of humiliating himself again, he would dearly love to catch Mouse out, but he could not afford to split up with her. V.J. Parchman needed, for some reason, to believe they were married. Even though it didn't seem to matter if the rest of the story was true, this part needed to be. Tony presumed it was so that when he and Mouse went on Johnny Carson after *Love Among Elephants* was a huge smash, they wouldn't destroy the credibility of the rest of the film by saying, "That part about the wedding on the mountain? We fudged a bit on that part. Actually, we just *live together*." Perhaps after the script was approved by V. J.'s people, and he and Ralph had gotten their money, he could admit that they were only engaged. Or maybe by then they actually would be married, so then it would be all right to split up. Of course, he didn't want to split up. He loved her. He loved her, and she was making up for all those lost years with that blasted Hispanic pseudointellectual Academy Award winner.

Instead, Tony adopted what his father called the Queen Victoria tack: do nothing and wait and ninety-nine percent of your problems will solve themselves. He spent his free time, which was considerable, working on the script with Ralph. They wrote and drank and played golf. They watched old videos of last year's Lakers games up at the house in the Hollywood Hills, which Darryl and Sather and Ralph shared.

This was fine by Mouse. She needed time alone to plot and plan. She knew it would come to this. Since Ivan suggested it, she knew. It was on her mind that New Year's Eve, while the African dish flopped, while Glen lectured them about different brands of flea dip, while the excruciating video sent everyone into a morose reexamination of the past year, while Tony bent to give her a stiff peck at midnight. It was as if she was driving an amusement-park car, the kind on tracks you pretend to be steering yourself, all the while knowing if you let go of the wheel the car will still take you to the same place. In this case, the car was headed for a place she should be ashamed to go, but wasn't. Somehow, *Wedding March* was going to get made.

Mouse had known it would be necessary to try to give back the money to Shirl. There was nothing calculated in this. She honestly wanted Shirl to take it back. If Shirl took it back Mouse and Tony would have a thousand-dollar wedding. A thousand-dollar wedding did not deserve a documentary. It was any wedding. Ivan could easily find another. If Shirl took the money back, Mouse would be saved from thinking, A modern wedding whose budget is one hundred thousand dollars *begs* to be filmed.

Mouse thought that maybe in private Shirl would see the error of her extravagance. Maybe without Auntie Barb glowering and Mimi gushing, "I'm *so* happy for you, too bad money can't buy taste," and a sherry-sodden Tony whispering, "*Enjoy* it, poppet. Cut loose," Mouse could talk some sense into her.

Instead, she made Shirl cry in the stationery department of Robinson's, at the Sherman Oaks Galleria, where Shirl always bought her Christmas cards for next year, on sale half-price. It was the day after Christmas.

"Why won't you let me do this for you? For twenty years you don't come home, now I want to give you a wonderful wedding and you won't take it. My youngest won't take a gift from her own mother," she said to anyone interested, over the dull slapping of plastic boxes of cards being unearthed from a pile by exhausted shoppers, glanced at, then chucked back. "These are nice. See, you can put your own photo in. I could put in one of the wedding."

"At least let me put half of it into…into…" Mouse racked her brain for the initials of all those modern-day financial instruments advertised on the sides of buses, "…some kind of a bank thing, a trust account or something. If we have any kids, you know, for college."

"You're not planning on having children?" asked Shirl, wild-eyed. "Don't tell me you're not planning on having children. I can't take it. I'm still sick." She dropped the box back on the pile, bent her head to her chest with both hands.

Mouse noticed the loose crêpey skin of her neck bunched up like a thin fallen sock. "Of course we are," she lied. "But Mom, no wedding costs a hundred thousand dollars, even in Los Angeles."

"You are a monster," said Shirl. "How about this: Wishing You All Good Things Now and Throughout the Coming Year. "

Mouse surrendered herself to her fate.

Mouse was dripping when she arrived at Nita Katz's Beverly Hills office. The bad weather had forced her to drag her poncho from the bottom of her suitcase. Feeling distinctly unfashionable in its green plastic folds, she made a mental note to get a new one.

Since she had been there last Nita had gotten a secretary: a leathery-faced woman with cottony blond hair and deep-set light-gray eyes crookedly outlined in black pencil sat at a desk in the small waiting room. She was busy tying tiny gold bows on hundreds of tiny white silk boxes. The silk boxes had been packed in the lids of larger boxes, scattered around the room, on the floor and on the loveseat, balanced on its round arms. "You're too early," the secretary said. Her voice reminded Mouse of Mimi's coffee grinder. "Britty said you wouldn't be here until three."

"I'm here to see Nita," said Mouse.

"You're not the messenger. I thought you were the messenger."

The secretary made Mouse step into the hallway to remove her poncho. She was afraid a stray drop would land on one of the two-by-two-inch-square tops of one of the hundreds of white silk boxes, leaving a tiny permanent stain, infuriating Britty, the bride, whose wedding would then not be perfect. The secretary could not bear the responsibility of that. In the hallway Mouse hauled the poncho over her head. She smoothed her wet hair, forgetting about the perm, then hung upside down from the waist, trying to unsmooth it.

Mouse was suddenly very interested in the boxes, their gold bows, what was inside. It was the film, uncoiling in her mind. It was like a woman who doesn't know she is pregnant taking a sudden and mysterious interest in booties.

Mouse sometimes liked to draw, but only from photographs.

She enjoyed standup comedians on television, but only when the jokes were retold by Tony. He never told them as well, but somehow she found them funnier. She liked nature documentaries far better than nature. She liked life diluted by interpretation.

She asked the secretary what the boxes were for.

Was that traditional, then, party favors for the guests?

What was in the boxes?

Were the truffles light chocolate or dark?

What was the significance of hand-dipped?

What was inside the chocolates?

Was it real champagne or a champagne cream?

When were they flown from Switzerland?

Did they need to be flown in a special refrigerated plane?

Did every guest get one?

How much did they cost?

Could I try one?

"Get yourself invited to the wedding," said the secretary, suspicious. They got crackpots every once in a while, people looking for the mediums next door. This could be one.

Nita did not immediately recognize Mouse. Remembering last time, Mouse had worn something casual, her black leggings and a black cotton sweater. Mimi had told her that no one ever needed to dress up in L.A. Style was the thing. You needed your own. Mouse decided that this was her style.

Nita's own style had changed. The linty sweater and ballet shoes had been replaced by a blue empire-waisted dress, spattered with tiny yellow flowers. Something about Nita's face had also changed. Strips of yellow and green bruises sat atop her cheekbones. Something with her nose, thought Mouse, whose tilt now afforded a good view of the deep maroon insides of her nostrils. She wore flat white shoes and white stockings. A thirty-seven-year-old girl out of a children's story, Mouse thought. She was mystified.

"I'm Mimi's sister," said Mouse.

"Mimi?" said Nita blankly.

"We met several months ago about my wedding. I just got back from Africa?"

"Right. The wedding on the beach."

She caught Mouse staring at her nose, tapped the end of it lightly with her knuckle. "Business was booming, so I splurged. An early fortieth-birthday present."

A forty-year-old girl in a children's story.

"We've changed our minds about the wedding," said Mouse, once again snuggled in the mooshy mauve sofa, the manhole-sized white saucer balanced on her knee, the heat from the bowl of cappuccino warming her chin.

Nita closed the door from her desk with the same kind of gadget Shirl used to open the garage door from her car. They both watched, transfixed, while the door inched shut over the thick white carpet. Mouse explained more than she needed to: about the accident, about Mr. Edmonton, about the out-of-court insurance settlement. She felt it was important to lay this groundwork so that Nita would understand immediately that she was serious. So that Nita would not require proof, in the form of a phone call to Mimi, or to Tony, or even to Shirl.

Occasionally Nita touched a finger to either side of her nose and sniffed daintily. She took two phone calls, one from someone she was meeting for lunch.

"...they settled out of court for about three hundred fifty thousand, a hundred she's given to me for the wedding. It's sort of outgrown the beach, the wedding. I was thinking, I have no ideas actually. I'd love to have a formal big-city wedding. Whatever is typical is what I want."

"So what can *I* do for you?" asked Nita. She ran a silver letter opener idly under her nails, now shorter, now painted pearly pink. Mouse could see the toe of her white flat tapping impatiently under her desk.

Mouse was thrown. Perhaps Nita ran into hundred-thousand-dollar wedding budgets all the time. Perhaps a hundred-thousand-dollar wedding financed her secretary, her office door opener, her new nose. Perhaps she was already booked, or had a two-hundred-thousand-dollar wedding coming in. This could not be true. In Pakistan the average annual income was one hundred and twenty-seven dollars. Mouse felt like a scuba diver diving at night without a flashlight.

"I'd like you to do it. The wedding."

"I'm sorry about your mother's accident. I am. And I'm flattered you're so anxious to work together, but, as I think I mentioned, I do work on commission, and an extra hundred dollars from–"

"–*hundred thousand.*"

"Hundred thousand?"

"Yes."

"Dollars?"

"From the insurance settlement."

"That's considerably different."

"I thought it was. But I've been in Africa."

"Have you talked to anyone else about this?"

"No," said Mouse, after a long second. "Not yet."

Nita became very quiet. Not a continuation of the quiet she was before. Not the polite quiet of someone forced to listen but actually trying to figure out how to squeeze in a trip to the dry cleaners. She was predator quiet. She was strolling through the forest and came upon something big and delicious without expecting it and now did not want to scare it off. Mouse knew this quiet from Africa. She didn't mind it. Nita would be in the movie, too.

"There's something else we need to talk about," said Mouse.

"None of this is going for the honeymoon, is it? Honeymoon expenses, the sky's the limit. Brides come in here, say they have X-amount to spend on their wedding, not realizing they can blow half of it on a honeymoon."

"We're looking into the possibility of a documentary. A 'the making of' kind of thing."

"A documentary?"

"Like for a dramatic film, a feature, sometimes they'll make a documentary on the making of a film."

Nita laughed. "Like the way, in the ladies' john, always at department stores. There are two opposing mirrors, you can see the reflection of you looking at your reflection looking at your reflection looking at – not that I don't think it's a good idea."

"Have you heard of Ivan Esparza?"

"Your fiancé –"

"– no, no, that's Tony. If anyone is known for documentary, Ivan is. He did a doc on baptism, *Total Immersion*, that won an Oscar. He would like to film this, my wedding. Rites of passage are his specialties. It's all just in the talk stages right now. Nothing is firmed up."

Nita dabbed the end of her nose thoughtfully. "I would be in it, then? I'm a very private person."

"You don't have to do anything you don't want to do. Of course not."

"– I'm just so private. Could we at least wait until the swelling goes down? I'm also getting a new rug in the waiting room."

"Nothing's firmed up yet."

"Thank you. You're being honest. We have to be honest with each other if this is going to work. If I suggest rubrum lilies for your bouquet and you have your heart set on orchids, you have to tell me. I assume you'll want a sit-down dinner. I also have in mind the perfect person to do the cake. A local artist whose *métier* is food art. None of this is going toward funding the documentary is it? The money. Movies aren't cheap, you know. Of course you know."

"No, the funding is already in place." To say those words! The funding is already in place. Mouse had never said those words in her entire life. Before it was always, "I have some grants out" (along with sixty thousand other people all applying for the same five hundred dollars) or "It's funded primarily by private individuals" (the major private individual being herself).

"The funding is not a problem." Those words she had never said. The funding had always been a problem.

Nita bowed her head in thought, resting her puffy lips against her hands, held together as though in prayer. Could Mouse give her one minute, just one minute to take care of a few things? Then they would begin. She would be Mouse's from that moment until the honeymoon. She already had ideas.

The Bel Air Hotel, for example. Rent the whole place for a weekend for the wedding party and out-of-town guests. The string section of the L.A. Philharmonic for the reception. The designer who used to do the gowns for *Dynasty* for the dress. These were all just ideas. This was presuming Mouse did not want to do a theme wedding. Theme weddings could be fun. A Victorian-Christmas wedding with snow and reindeer. A South Seas Island wedding with a Fijian Feast. These were all just off the top of her head. She would, of course, do whatever Mouse wanted.

"You'll have the wedding of your dreams," said Nita.

Mouse nodded. She blew on her cappuccino, sending tufts of foam scudding to the other side of the bowl. Outside, the gray sky spit.

Nita went out.

Britty, the bride, had come to pick up her favors. There was a major problem. A major, major problem. Britty's voice quaked with emotion. "What about the fucking doilies! Blind Irishwomen tatted those doilies!"

The secretary's voice was too low for Mouse to hear. Mouse hefted the saucer from her knees onto the coffee table and went out, curious.

Britty was short and stocky, a feature she tried to mitigate with elegantly manicured hands and purple eye shadow. A stack of gold bracelets ascended up her thick arm.

The doilies sat accusingly in a small pile on the secretary's desk. They were supposed to go under the chocolates, They were the size of a quarter, the same champagne shade as the tiny silk boxes, the same champagne shade as the piece of paper under which the pile had been accidentally hidden. Everything was ruined, moaned Britty. These favors were her mother's idea. Her mother would accuse her, now, of trying to sabotage the one thing Britty had allowed her to do for the wedding.

"There are four of us," said Mouse. "Can't we just take out the chocolates and –"

"Oh God! It'll take *forever*. The truffles'll look all, all *finger-printy*." Tears dribbled out of Britty's purple-mascaraed eyes.

The phone rang. The secretary jumped. "Nita Katz Creative Moments! ... who?" She covered the receiver with a wrinkled brown hand, "Are you Mouse FitzHenry?"

Only Mimi knew she was seeing Nita this afternoon.

"Yes."

The secretary thrust the receiver at her impatiently.

"If we are going to do this film you should not be there."

"Ivan, what –"

" – Her reaction to you will be tainted. You have never met, remember? We need her selling you on what a wedding coordinator can do for you –"

" – wait, wait, wait. What are you *doing*? How'd you get this number?"

" – it is her reacting to you and you reacting to her. For the first time. I don't want to direct two old friends *acting* like they are meeting for the first time. Get out of there now. Come over."

"I don't know where you are," Mouse stalled. She did not want to go over there now. She was afraid to go over there ever. Ivan's apartment. Ivan's bed.

"Four-twelve Eastwind, apartment B2. You know where Eliot lives? Bomarito?"

"Not him."

"In the basement, past the laundry room."

IVAN'S APARTMENT WAS next to the laundry room, once a storage room. Even Mouse, no stranger to squalor, was appalled. She stood in the hallway, sweat breaking out on her temples, rapping on Ivan's unfinished plywood door. The noise of the washing machines echoed off the dingy walls. You'd think, you win an Oscar. You'd think, you get kudos in a major magazine for finishing a film. You get that, and this is all you get. Before Ivan opened his door Mouse had a final fantasy that he actually lived in a subterranean penthouse.

He came to the door without his pants, only a T-shirt, Jockey shorts. He was on the phone, the receiver pinned to his shoulder with his jaw. His face shone with sweat. The dishwater-blond hair at the base of his scalp, too short to fit in the ponytail, was wet.

" – the lights will be set up before anyone arrives – two camera operators in addition to – yes, five-thirty – talk to you then."

"Catching you at a bad time?" she said.

"It's a sauna in here." He pointed to the dusty hot-water pipes which lined the ceiling. "I got dressed for you."

"I'm honored."

"Come in. Another project." He nodded at the telephone. "Something very easy I'm getting paid a lot of money to do."

"I'm jealous." She looked around the apartment. There were no windows, save a barred, cutting board-sized slot near the ceiling, which afforded a nice view of ankles promenading on the Venice Beach Boardwalk. The window was wide open, but did nothing for the heat. If you pulled over the single chair, a wobbly folding chair with ripped upholstery, and stood on tiptoe, you could see past the ankles, to the blue-gray slat of the Pacific.

There was a hot plate, convenient storage for several abandoned pans of aging soup. There was a bed, less than a twin. A pallet, fit for the writhings and midnight thoughts of a monk or a madman. No love happened on this bed, Mouse thought, surprised at her relief. Somehow the size of Ivan's bed was supposed to protect her from … then she flashed on the times with Tony in the Land Rover, in tents, on random uncomfortable floors. If one person could fit on that bed, two could too. Two people could fit anywhere. "I like your place," she said.

Posters from Ivan's movies were stuck to the walls with silver tape. The rest was a nest of books and newspapers: books towering armpit high against the walls, books stacked to form a sort of nightstand. Newspapers as an area rug. Dust coated everything.

A black and white guinea pig ran on a wheel in its cage atop the small refrigerator. Fresh wood chips lined the bottom of his cage, making the apartment smell like a hot, dingy pet shop.

"Does he have a name?" asked Mouse, putting her finger between the bars. He scuttled over and bit it. She blotted the pearl of blood with her tongue.

"Dostoyevsky," he said. Ivan unhooked the bottle from the holder on the side of the cage and filled it with bottled water from the refrigerator.

"Dostoyevsky's too good for tap water, huh?" Mouse said over the roar of a spin cycle next door.

"If that stuff will kill us, just imagine the effects on some-one his size," said Ivan. "Please, sit down." He pulled out the folding chair and wiped the seat off with his palm.

She sat. On the card table were books on weddings. The history of. In America. *Emily Post's Guide To*. The modern. The budget. Bridal magazines Mouse thought no one but Shirl bought. It was slightly hilarious. There was a letter on crisp white parchment, the names of the board of trustees of somewhere marching down the left-hand margin. "Dear Mr. Esparza: It is with great pleasure..." She picked up the letter. "May I?"

"It's our money for post-production. Without that we would be forced to post on videotape, something I am loath to do. I loathe videotape. I need to edit on a Moviola, to feel the film in my hands. It's erotic, the feel of film, the smell of film. To me, videotape is one more sign of the end of Western Civilization."

"Is that what you told them?" Mouse laughed nervously. "No wonder I never get grants. I always go for the 'why the world needs this film' angle."

"The world needs nothing," said Ivan. He was standing

behind her. She heard the crunch of denim sliding on, then a zip. "Except *Wedding March*, of course."

"Of course!" said Mouse. She was afraid she agreed a little too quickly.

"Is it safe to say we're in pre-production?"

"There are some things we need to talk about."

"That's why we're meeting. There is a nice place on the Boardwalk that has a salad bar. Can I take you to a late lunch?"

"Oh, no, I've already –"

"Then come with me. We can at least do the production schedule. We need to think about crew members, assistants. I have someone very good – Eliot, E., you know E. – he can roll sound, assistant edit, do anything. Documentary is a religion for him."

"I know how that is."

"I know you do." Ivan smiled, held open the door. His teeth were very straight and hard looking, like bathroom tile.

THE SALAD BAR was all-you-can-eat and didn't look particularly good. Ivan went back four times. Mouse drank enough coffee to make her thighs shake.

There was the issue of Tony. It was very difficult to do a ninety-minute movie about a wedding without a groom. As he ate, Mouse noticed Ivan had a tattoo on his wrist. She had thought it was a bracelet but saw it was a ring of film frames, green and blue.

"You get that in prison?" she asked, pointing to his thick wrist with the end of her teaspoon.

"You have been talking to your neurotic sister."

"You did get it in prison?"

"I have never even had a parking ticket."

"You don't have a car."

"I guess that's enough to make someone seem psychotic in this city." He speared a radish.

"I talked to Tony," she blurted out.

"So did I," said Ivan, "When I called for you."

"Oh God. What did he – what did he say? When?"

"He told me about the insurance settlement. Otherwise you would have planned the wedding yourself. He was proud. He is into it, which is good. The wedding. I like that he is English. It will give the piece a slightly different feel. A little class. A little storybook feel. An opportunity for social irony."

"Irony," said Mouse. Tony reserved, Tony polite, had not said word one to Ivan. She could just hear him, "Oh hallo, sport. No, Mouse is out and about seeing to wedding matters." A chilly edge to his voice, nothing more. He saved his tantrums and threats for her.

"I had an idea. I think the movie might be better from the bride's point of view, from my point of view." She rolled her lips inside her mouth, waiting.

"Tony is balking, isn't he?" Ivan pushed away his plate, lit a cigarette, exhaled adroitly through his high-cut nostrils, passed it over to her and lit one for himself.

"No," said Mouse. "Did he say something?"

"No. It seems natural he would. A man captured on film getting the harness slipped on."

"Ivan, he's the one who wants to get married. It was his idea. In Africa. I can't tell you how many times he – Anyway, don't put it on me, the scheming woman. I hate that."

"This is good," said Ivan. "I like this."

"Don't work me. I know what you're doing."

"Have I ever said how much I miss our old talks? You were the best friend I ever had."

"Ivan." She didn't want him to say anything more.

He leaned back in his chair, dug in his pockets for money to pay the bill. He counted nickels and pennies. He didn't have enough for both the tip and her coffee. Even though he ate there nearly every day, he was happy to stiff the waitress.

16

MIMI HAD PASSES TO A CAST AND CREW SCREENING OF a lesser movie by one of Talent and Artists' lesser clients. She could always tell how lesser a movie was by how many times the passes got passed on. If she had passed them on to the guy in the mail room, the movie was beneath "lesser," probably low enough to qualify as career-ruining. She had only two passes and invited Mouse. Her sister. They didn't do enough together, she thought. They hadn't been to a movie since Mouse had been home. Mimi overapologized to Tony. That was quite all right, he said, not to worry. He was going to take in a Lakers game with Ralph.

Mouse looked forward to the screening the way she looked forward to getting some much-needed dental work out of the way. She and Mimi needed to have a talk. Now that she was entering into a partnership of sorts with Ivan, it was important that she and Mimi clear the air.

This would be as easy as picking up a ball of mercury with tweezers while blindfolded. For one thing, so much time had elapsed since the summer of Ivan that Mouse sometimes thought she only imagined Mimi had seduced him right out from under her nose. After all, nothing had ever actually *happened* with Ivan. No dates, no kisses, no promises. And since Mouse had never actually had him, how could Mimi "steal" him? There was no tangible evidence that Mimi had done anything wrong. Still, Mouse had loved Ivan and Mimi knew it. Mimi knew it, and she did what she did anyway. *You're so dramatic! Dramatic, paranoid, and self-pitying. You're just jealous because Mimi had boyfriends when you never did*, said The Pink Fiend. *Don't be difficult. Be nice. Mimi loves you so much. She would never hurt you intentionally.* Mouse could not eat for two days before the screening.

The movie was at an eighteen-plex in Universal City. Mouse had never been to a –plex of any kind; when she left for Africa they still showed one movie per movie house. It was nicer than she expected. The walls were fairly solid, so only wordless love scenes were accompanied by the rattle of submachine guns from the theater next door. There were purple velvet seats – made especially in France, said Mimi. Cappuccino was sold at the snack bar. The theater sat atop a steep hill, secluded from neighboring Universal Studios by artful landscaping.

Mouse hoped that she and Mimi would go for a cup of coffee after the film. She would apologize at long last for not coming to Mimi and Ivan's wedding. She would apologize for not answering Mimi's letters. But she would not apologize for being angry.

The movie was a political thriller, featuring the usual cast of look-alike bureaucrats in dark suits having too many cryptic conversations in the backs of limousines. There were many scenes of the same men outwitting complex alarm systems, sneaking into computer rooms at the Pentagon and, in pitch darkness, planting high-tech explosives and wiretaps. There were the usual evil-incarnate assassins anxious to double-cross either side for a few dollars more.

Mimi and Mouse shared a bucket of popcorn and a large Diet Coke. They slouched in their seats, their legs slung over the backs of the seats in front of them. They kept leaning onto each other's shoulder and whispering.

"What's he doing *now*?"

"Is that the same guy?"

"Who's he calling?"

Mouse was chummy, sisterly, unhappily anticipating the unpleasant and unsisterly scene that would follow.

Near the end, when the plot was uncovered and leaked to the *New York Times* and the explosive, which Mouse had lost track of due to a sudden flurry of love scenes featuring full-frontal male nudity, was dismantled, Mimi asked loudly, "What bomb?"

For the rest of the movie, people stage-whispered to one another: "What president?" "What top-secret papers?" After the final confusing image faded, before the credits rolled, there was a moment of black during which, Mouse supposed, they were to reflect on the import of what they'd just seen. Mimi yelled out, "What director?" The audience roared.

The response put Mimi in a generous mood. Didn't it prove her timing was good, just as Bob Hope had said? She decided then to look into taking another acting class, but only after she finished her blockbuster, which she promised herself she would begin on Saturday. She strutted out of the theater scrunching her blond mop, waving to people she knew from the office. She was proud to be seen with Mouse. A lot of the people from the office knew her sister had lived in Africa. That was impressive. To some people.

At ten o'clock at night the freeway was a parking lot, a sea of red brake lights, people cursing over their bone-rattling car stereo systems. There must have been construction or an accident.

Mimi's good mood deteriorated the second they hit the diamond lane. The car ahead of them had no passengers. The diamond lane was supposed to be for cars with two or more people. No one in this town had any morals, Mimi thought angrily.

"I bet this jerk parks in handicapped parking places," she said. "I bet he doesn't recycle."

"Want to get a drink or something, a cup of coffee?" asked Mouse. She glanced over at her sister's unremarkable profile. She felt bad for Mimi, suddenly. That contrived hair, all that expensive makeup. Mouse wished Mimi suspected something.

She would be crushed when Mouse accused her of being a narcissistic, undermining, manipulative man-chaser.

"I can't drink coffee anymore at night, keeps me up. You shouldn't drink so much either. It gives you cysts. I just want to get home. Look at this traffic. I hate this city."

"Cysts?"

"In your boobs."

"I'm going to do that film with Ivan," said Mouse.

"You are?" Mimi's voice was slow and kind. Too kind, thought Mouse, like an adult addressing a child who says he wants to be president.

Mimi coaxed the car out of gear, tipped her toe off the gas. They rolled forward a few inches. The brake lights on the sports car ahead of them lit up like the slanted eyes of an exotic cat. "I think that's great. I mean, Ivan's a madman, but I guess you have to be to do documentaries. Not that you're mad. You're sort of more eccentric is what it is. If you need any help on it. I'm more into features, but if there's anything."

"I'd love you to help."

"Just don't do anything like sleep with him. I know how it gets working on a film. It's the Love Boat without the boat." Her toe tipped on the gas. They rolled forward.

Mouse chewed the inside of her mouth. To her knowledge Mimi had never worked on a film, she had worked only in an office. "That was my exact plan, Mimi. Sleep with him, then co-produce a movie about my wedding to Tony."

"I'm just saying…"

"I think we have to talk. I want to discuss this. About Ivan, I mean."

"I've just been so busy. With Shirl and my blockbuster and my job and Ralph and everything. Ivan is great with women, I have to say that for him. He makes a big thing of asking what *you* want. But I guess guys that look like that have to be sensitive to the woman. It's their only choice. Ralph's the same way."

"Ivan's not bad-looking," said Mouse, trying to check the

indignant tone in her voice. "You thought he looked like James Dean."

"Did I ever tell you about this? It was right before we broke up. Really the last straw. This was to finance some movie, his first one, I think. Every Sunday he read the car want ads, looking for cars being sold by women. He'd go and check it out. He'd schmooz with them, pretend he was really interested. The women would let him look under the hood. He'd steal some part of the distributor or fiddle with some wires, then hop in. Guess what? It wouldn't start! The women would be embarrassed. They'd say, it started this morning. He'd say, look, I'll take it off your hands for x-amount, usually half as much. They'd say okay. They were always glad to have this nice guy take their turkey car off their hands. He'd have one of his lowlife friends from a gas station come and tow it, then he'd turn around, put the wire back in the engine, and sell it for twice as much as he paid for it. He has the soul of a felon, I'm telling you."

"How did you know this?"

"We had fights. It came out."

"I'm sorry I never came home for your wedding, I–"

"No biggie. I got so drunk I didn't know who was there and who wasn't. You'll see. You have two glasses of champagne on an empty stomach, you're so plowed it doesn't matter."

Mouse stared out at the night. This conversation was like a package clearly addressed to Atlanta that had mysteriously wound up in Yugoslavia.

After several miles the traffic loosened up. There was no construction, no accident. They were quiet for a long time.

"Maybe you'll help me with one of the shoots," said Mouse.

"What shoots?"

"On the wedding documentary. On *Wedding March* – that's the title."

"I'd love to. I can't stand this place. I can't live here anymore. I know everyone says that. I need something to take my mind off it. Working on a production would be good."

"I was thinking, for the first shoot? An underwear thing. It'd be fun. We could go to one of those ritzy places on Ventura Boulevard."

"No one shops for lingerie on Ventura Boulevard. We're talking White Trash 2000. There are some good places in Beverly Hills."

"I was thinking, two sisters shopping for bridal underwear. Something like that."

"I know just the place."

"What we're going to do – although I haven't cleared this with Ivan – is shoot my stuff first. Maybe a meeting with Nita. Finding a dress. Deciding on china and silver patterns."

"Girl stuff."

"Girl stuff. Meanwhile, well, I'm just going to tell you. Tony isn't crazy about this. You were there, you heard him Christmas morning. He doesn't understand it. I don't think I presented it very well. Meanwhile, I'm going to talk to him a little more. It's a 'the making of' kind of thing, nothing exploitative, it's *serious*."

"Exploring a social ritual or something – "

" – exactly. See, you know what I mean. Why doesn't Tony?"

"You know men. They have a way of being dense."

"We are lucky, in fact, to be asked to participate at all." Mouse told her the rest of her plan. How she would then show Tony all they had shot, all the footage of her picking out her bridal underwear and her dress and her china. She would prove how harmless it was, and how flattering, really. She would talk him into it. If, after all this, he still said no, she would reimburse Ivan for the film stock they had already used with money from the wedding budget, apologizing that Tony had backed out at the last minute. This was not uncommon. All documentary film-makers knew this.

"Even I know that," said Mimi.

"Maybe even you could talk to him," said Mouse. "But not yet. You can't say anything to Shirl or Tony. You've got to swear."

"I swear. You know I do. I won't say a word. It'll be fun.

Where do you want to go for coffee? There's a cute place that has great gelato down on Beverly."

Mimi wasn't so bad. Maybe The Pink Fiend was right. Maybe Mouse was too critical. Maybe Mouse was blaming Mimi for things for which she, Mouse, was responsible. Maybe she had driven Ivan away. Anyway, Mimi couldn't help it if she was so sexy and fun that men were naturally attracted to her. Mouse relaxed, glad that she and Mimi had at last been able to talk. Sort of.

THE NEXT DAY Mimi caromed up the narrow, coiling roads of the Hollywood Hills on her way to the Big House. The Big House was her name for the house Ralph shared with Darryl and Sather. She scrunched her hair, steering with one hand, fumbled in her purse for a newly swiped tube of her trademark Extra Fuchsia, twisted the rearview mirror so she could see to apply it, nearly taking out a row of mailboxes. The Big House was irritatingly out of the way from everywhere.

Even though it was Saturday, her writing day, she had to see Ralph. She had tried to write. Earlier, she had shooed every one out of the apartment, then put on the Talking Heads and boogied around the living room dusting, then cleaned out the kitchen junk drawer, all in preparation for sitting down and doing her character sketches for her blockbuster on love and betrayal in the business. Finally, around two, she rounded up a yellow legal pad, a can of soda, and a Family Pak of sugarless gum, and sat down on the green wicker settee. But she had too much on her mind to work. She doodled a line of hearts down the margin. If she saw Ralph that afternoon, she could always write that evening.

She had not heard from him since class on Wednesday. This wasn't like him. They had had a standing Saturday night date for the past year. She supposed she could give him a call, but she couldn't just say, "Hi, when are you picking me up?" She knew PMS was making her oversensitive, but she imagined he'd cooled off since her temper tantrum on New Year's Eve.

She could always call him with a question about her block-buster, but she had used that one so many times it had turned into a private joke. "Hey, I'll show you my plot points if you show me yours." What about all this ridiculous documentary stuff with Mouse? Making a documentary on your own wedding! Who'd ever heard of such a lame thing? Even though Mimi already said she'd help – and God knew Mouse needed her help, since she was the one member of the family in the business – it wouldn't hurt to get Ralph's take on it.

The problem with calling was that Sathcr and Darryl and Ralph had a cheap telephone that didn't ring. They knew some-one was calling only when the answering machine clicked on. They nevcr picked up. Later, when they got around to replaying their messages, they never wrote them down unless it was a job offer. The fifth time Mimi got the machine she decided to drive up there. She wasn't getting any writing done anyway.

To see them, you had to drive clear to the top of the city, wasting gas and time, neither of which Mimi had. Beyond broke until she got her next paycheck, she was reduced to charging gas at an overpriced Brentwood gas station, the only place within a thirty-mile radius that accepted what few credit cards she had that weren't maxed out. She jounced over potholes with her jaw set.

The Big House was only big in comparison to the grad student-sized apartments most of Mimi's friends were forced to rent. It was, in fact, probably no bigger than the house on Cantaloupe Avenue. It was a long, chocolate-colored ranch style supported on the downhill side by spindly stilts that looked fit only for a pup tent. They rented it from a Saudi banker.

Darryl and Sather were planted in front of the TV in their Salvation Army chairs. They were watching a videotape of an old Lakers game on their three-thousand-dollar television. Mimi never understood this. They videotaped every Lakers game and watched it from beginning to end, even though they already knew the outcome. A snarl of refuse grew on the floor; empty beer bottles, crumpled chip bags, a plastic tub of curdling blue-cheese dip. The room reeked of male, Saturday afternoon indolence.

"You guys need to open a window."

"The Meem Machine," said Darryl. He was shirtless, and desultorily plucked at his dense black tufts of chest hair. He idly rolled two empty beer cans back and forth on the carpet with his bare, hairy feet. "Those schmucks, they've never had a dominating Center." He belched. "And poor Leo A. What is he? A Center? A Forward? A Forward? A Center? I ask you." Sather wore baggy cream linen trousers, black shirt, and bolo fastened with a scorpion frozen in a chunk of Plexiglas. He watched the game from behind a veil of smoke, dangling a cigarette over an ashtray he held on his palm in front of his face.

"Just in the neighborhood?" he said to Mimi, his gaze glued to the tube.

"It's Saturday and I was just driving around."

"Ah," said Sather. "You don't get enough driving in during the week?"

"Jesus," said Darryl, "*this* schmuck. How he ever got off the bench is one of the world's great mysteries." He fast-forwarded through the next quarter. Silently they watched the players zip up and down the court, men with the energy of hummingbirds.

"Ralph around?"

Darryl nodded over his shoulder toward the kitchen. Mimi could hear snorts of laughter punctuated by feeble bursts of typing.

Tony and Ralph were spread out on the Formica kitchen table, working on *Love Among Elephants*. The mess around their ankles was the same genus as that growing on the living room floor: the wrappers of pseudofood invented to alleviate boredom, not hunger. Tony sat slouched in front of the typewriter, his long fingers covered with the Day-Glo orange dust of bargain basement cheese puffs. He foraged around the bottom of the bag for the last crumbs before balling up the bag and tossing it at Ralph.

"She needs to suck the bullet out of the wound, to keep with the carnivore theme–" Ralph paced, flicking a pencil against the brim of his baseball cap. Ralph dearly wanted a laptop computer but could not even afford an electric typewriter. During the week he input whatever they'd written over the weekend into the computer at work.

"–you can't *suck* the bullet out for God's sake. You're thinking of a snakebite. You'd need to have lips like a bloody industrial vacuum cleaner to suck a bullet–"

"–depending on which blond-of-the-month they cast, it might not be a problem. It might be on her résumé, for–"

"–shush–" cautioned Tony as Mimi entered the room.

"Tony!" cried Mimi. "Everywhere I turn there you are. Hope I'm not interrupting." She slid into one of the rickety kitchen chairs.

Tony sat up, nonchalantly crossed his wrists over the sheet of paper in the typewriter. He grinned at her.

"God, don't worry, I'm not looking," she said. "You'd think you guys had the recipe for the atom bomb there."

"We do," said Tony. "Ralph didn't tell you?"

"You should have called," said Ralph. "We have to get this to V.J.–"

"I was just in the neighborhood. I needed some advice on something."

"Buy high, sell low," said Tony.

"Get the abortion," said Ralph.

"Ralph! You are so paranoid! People stealing your script ideas, girlfriends not using birth control."

"It's quite a shock," said Tony, "a FitzHenry woman asking someone's advice."

"Thanks, Tony." Mimi reached over and pinched his cheek. "I'll tell Mouse you said that."

"Now I'm done for. Excuse me," said Tony, standing. "I'll

just pop in and see what's on the box." He wandered into the living room.

"Be thinking about the scene with the models," said Ralph. "We gotta fix that talk thing."

"He's so polite," said Mimi. "Maybe it's just the accent. You know how that is? A person with a Brooklyn accent sounds rude even if they're being polite." She sighed and scrunched her hair.

"What's up?"

She tiptoed to the sliding glass door that lead to the deck. "Can we talk outside?"

A deck cantilevered out over a steep hill forested with dusty, green prickly pear bearing sharp, finger-length spines. Ralph leaned against the rail with his arms crossed, a "get on with it" expression on his face. Why couldn't he be Tony, she thought, meaning why couldn't he be my soulmate in the way that Tony was Mouse's. She hooked her foot over the bottom rung of the rail and stared out at the hazy grid of stucco and mirrored glass glinting in the late-afternoon sun.

Since she was sworn to secrecy, she started with "I have a friend who's getting married…" but the further she got into it, the more distracted Ralph became. He systematically gnawed every nail on one hand, spitting the bitten strips over the side. To get him to stop, Mimi found herself admitting it was Mouse. She recounted the events of the night before. She told him how Mouse was ganging up with Ivan behind Tony's back, and wondered what she, Mimi, should do. She wanted to be moral and ethical and still be a supportive sister. "I mean, I think some things are sacred, you know? Some things should just belong to time. Like videotaping births, I'm against that. I believe that experience should just be experience. I'm worried that Mouse thinks her wedding isn't valid unless she turns it into media." This was the first time this had occurred to Mimi. She liked the way it sounded. Philosophical. And people said Californians were shallow.

"So what's the problem?" he said flatly. "She's a documentary filmmaker, why shouldn't she make documentaries?"

"What's wrong with you? Ever since New Year's ... "

"I know, I know. This script, it just consumes you – "

" – I know, that's how it is with my blockbuster."

"I have a lot on my mind. The class and, and this, and – "

"Listen, you can't tell Tony about this. Swear? It's supposed to be a secret. If Mouse finds out she'll *kill* me. She has no sense of humor about this kind of stuff. Promise?" She sidled up to him, fitting her hips against his. "Promise?"

"What are you talking about?"

"About that dumb wedding documentary thing." She lifted up her sweatshirt, flashing a breast. "Want to see my narrative through-line sweet cheeks?"

"I'm supposed to be working."

"Want to see my plot point? Want to check my story development?" She took his cap off and put it on her own head. Over his shoulder, something caught her attention snagged on the prickly pear. Something lacy and light blue, a twisted pair of women's panties. She had a pair just like them. "Is that – What is that?"

Ralph turned out of her arms and looked over the rail. "Just a dustrag or something."

Suddenly she was not in the mood. She asked him if he had any more of those good cheese puffs left.

17

THE NIGHT BEFORE THE SHOOT, MOUSE WAS FLUNG FROM her dreams by things she never considered – things she should have thought of earlier but tucked away to mull over when she was alone then forgot about. She cursed herself.

She tried to read her watch in the light of the streetlamp. It was either twelve-twenty or four o'clock. She rolled away from Tony, tucked her hand under her pillow, stared at a cloud of fur hugging the baseboard, illuminated by the streetlamp outside. The pillow was so thin she could feel the pulse in her head beating in her palm.

Tony gritted his teeth in his sleep. The sound was like a boat tied to a dock by old ropes, creaking with the tide. He had been gritting his teeth more than usual lately. A sign, she thought, that he's unhappy with her but pretending not to be.

Mouse knew the difference between normal pre-shoot jitters and panicking over the major things she forgot to consider. She knew the normal fear of logistics. Will the lights work? Will the camera jam? Will the Nagra hold sync? Will the owner of Sins, the store in which they will be shooting, withdraw permission at the last minute? Normal documentary fears.

Among the things she forgot to consider: She never stopped to think, for example, that she would be the subject. She would be the one on-camera, the one manipulated, the one whose psyche would be spared or laid bare, the one Ivan – who, from all reports, was demented and untrustworthy – would subtly provoke to get at the "true" meaning of what it was to get married in the modern age. She could hardly stand to be a bride in front of a few friends and her family; now she was going to be a bride in front of the whole world? Except, as Mimi liked to point out, no one ever paid any attention to documentaries. Mouse never imagined she'd find any comfort in this. She never imagined she'd get married. She never imagined she'd make a movie about her own wedding with her own first true love and ex-brother-in-law. Freak accidents ran in her family, not complicated scenarios.

Another consideration: Throughout all this she had never managed to watch the videotapes Ivan had given her of *Total Immersion* and his recent *El Funeral*. She rationalized that there hadn't been time. In truth, she was afraid the films' subjects had been adroitly flayed alive by Ivan's subtle choice of images, juxtapositions, sounds. She did not trust him. Why was she doing this? She was like Sniffy Voyeur, chewing his own rear raw to rid himself of fleas.

Ridiculous doubts of the night. She hurled herself over onto her other shoulder. Sniffy, toenails clicking on the wood floor, came and hovered over her, bathing her in warm dog-biscuit breath. She tried to push him away but he was as intransigent as Gandhi. She felt a drop of drool on her ear.

IN THE MORNING, Mimi skipped her usual jog around the neighborhood. Instead, she made potato salad and turkey sandwiches.

"*What* are you doing?" Mouse said through clenched teeth, Mimi stood over the sink peeling warm potatoes. The kitchen stank of starch. She bustled around, a girl in a high wind.

"Feeding the crew. Ivan loves my potato salad." Then, loudly, "I just thought I'd make some potato salad!"

"He's in the shower," said Mouse. "It's not that kind of a movie."

"You have to eat," said Mimi. "When I worked on that thing with Bob Hope they had the most dynamite catering. They had bottled water before anyone drank bottled water. You don't have the budget for that, so –"

"–We've actually got a lot of funding for this. The California Arts Council –"

"– low budget, though. You're used to *no* budget so it just *seems* like a lot."

Carole stumbled out in her robe and socks, raccoon mascara eyes, purplish hair snarled at the crown like it had been combed with an eggbeater. She poured herself a cup of coffee, expertly tipped the sugar bowl into her cup, plunked down at the kitchen table in front of the half dozen scripts she had to read over the weekend. "Thought you guys'd be out shooting already."

"Oh, great." Mouse knew this would happen. Mimi and her mouth.

"I had to tell her. She'd think it was weird if I was making potato salad Saturday morning."

"You don't think Tony will? This is great."

"He's a *guy*," said Mimi.

"Don't worry, I won't tell," said Carole.

"'Morning, ladies." Tony was going golfing with Auntie Barb. He was wearing madras slacks and yellow socks. He sat at the kitchen table and put on his shoes. "What's on today's agenda?"

"Shopping," said Mouse. "Bride business, nothing you'd be interested in."

"We're going *lingerie* shopping," giggled Mimi. She turned from the sink, potato peeler still in hand, and struck a cover girl pose, arching her foot, plumping her hair. Mouse noticed she wore athletic shoes and sweatsocks. She looked like she was dressed for something more rigorous than trying on garter belts.

"Then we thought we'd go for a hike or something," said Mouse. She stood behind Tony, massaged his shoulders. She tried to conjure up a facial expression that would say to Mimi, "Look at how you're dressed! He'll know something's up, even if he's a *guy*. Just go along with this!" Of course, no facial expression can say this.

"A hike?" said Mimi. "When?"

"Now that sounds my speed. Perhaps when I'm back from golf."

"We can't believe you're playing golf with the Wicked Witch of the Northwest," said Mimi.

"She's not so bad, bit crusty perhaps. Got a nice swing." He stood, smoothed down the legs of his pants. "I like those – what are they – everything's connected." He ran his forefingers along one of Mouse's sides, then kissed her on the temple. "Get one of those."

"Merry Widows," said Carole.

Mouse stared at the chair legs. Inability to make eye contact is the universal sign of lying, she thought. Look at him! She couldn't. She radiated guilt like heat from an electric blanket on high.

SINS WAS IN Brentwood. Like most shops in Los Angeles, no one would miss it should it go out of business or collapse in an earthquake. Mouse marveled at this. Laundromats closed their doors. Hardware stores, gas stations, shoe repair shops disappeared, even in the short time she had been back. What stayed were places that sold only belts, or fancy wine and cheese. Mouse despaired that this was beginning to seem normal.

Ivan and Eliot were already there when Mouse and Mimi arrived. Ivan twirled his thin ponytail with his forefinger as he wandered from one end of the store to the other. Eliot crouched in a corner, hands buried in a black changing bag. He was loading the camera magazine with film. "Here we are in the trenches," he said gaily when he saw Mouse walk in.

"Hmm," said Mouse. She still held the pole against him.

Sins was long and narrow. A basketball player could stand in the middle and touch both walls. There was deep, white wool carpeting, a white marble counter, gold fixtures. White silk robes and satin slippers awaited each customer in her dressing room. Mouse could count the few gowns and teddies on display on delicate gold hangers. Everything else was secreted away. Champagne and paper-thin imported cookies stood on a small marble table, waiting to satisfy appetites whipped up by shimmying, tugging, snapping, unsnapping, and choosing.

Sins was the most promising of the four locations Ivan and Mouse had scouted. It was chosen, by mutual consent, because of its name, outrageous prices, operating room coziness, and, according to Mimi, because it stocked all the hot designer underwear. Movie stars shopped there, as well as middle-class brides spending beyond their means. Personally, Mouse didn't care where they shot: she could get a bra and a pair of panties at Sears. What did concern her was that Dani Lynx, the overly effusive owner of Sins, was charging them a hefty hourly rate to shoot on her premises. Mouse had never paid for a location in her life. Ivan said in Los Angeles everyone pays for everything.

"Isn't this great?" said Mimi, inhaling deeply. She felt like a confirmed city-dweller who'd escaped to the country for the day. She pulled out the camera she brought for production stills. These giants of documentary filmmaking hadn't even *thought* of that. "I love film. What's that saying in that Truffaut film? 'I'd give up a man for a movie but I'd never give up a movie for a man.' That's pretty much how I feel."

"What's *that*?" Mouse asked, horrified by the sight of Mimi's camera.

"Production stills," said Mimi. "Say cheeseburger."

"We don't need production stills," said Mouse. "This isn't the yearbook." She could just imagine a packet of photos accidentally left by Mimi for Tony to find.

"Stills are useful in marketing," said Ivan.

"I know," said Mouse. "I know, it's just–"

"You're nervous," said Mimi. "It's okay. All brides are nervous. You should have seen how–"

"–I am not nervous."

Ivan introduced Dani, an aging blond with a fierce dark mustache waxed to an inch of a serious dermatological condition. Mouse was beginning to recognize a man-made nose: Dani's was small and elegant, but her nostrils were mismatched. One was perfectly round, the other oval.

"So this is it?" asked Dani. She watched while Eliot heaved the camera onto his shoulder.

"Checking focus," said Eliot. He peered through the viewfinder.

There were no lights, only a small fill mounted on top of the camera, powered by a battery belt worn ammunition-belt style around Eliot's wide middle. People like Dani were always disappointed with the jerry-built quality of documentary film production. They expected the glamour of gigantic semitrucks rumbling outside, director's chairs, tables groaning with food for an army-size crew.

Mouse drifted over to a rack displaying an unidentifiable item in black lace that looked as though it'd be tight on a flagpole.

"That's our French stretch-lace body stocking, honey. Nylon mesh, with a nice cotton-lined open panel. Madonna has one in every color. You will probably want one in white. Brides always want white."

"An open panel?" Mouse imagined experts discussing politics on television.

"It means it's crotchless," said Mimi. "She lived in Africa for sixteen years," she added by way of explanation.

"Oh!" said Dani, alarmed.

"I knew what it meant," said Mouse.

"They have a lot of crotchless French-lace body stockings in Nairobi, huh?" Mimi winked at Dani.

"You didn't know?" said Mouse. "The Kikuyu invented them."

"All right, ladies," said Ivan. "I would like to explain how I work. I will not interfere, except to ask a few questions of the bride. You are to forget that I am here. It will be awkward at first.

Don't let that bother you. You will get used to it. Anyone can get used to anything."

He knelt down on one knee on the white carpet, slid the thick raggedy strap of the Nagra on his shoulder, clipped the headphones onto his ears, fiddled with a few knobs on the recorder, checking levels. Mouse, Mimi, and Dani were wired with small cordless mikes clipped inside their shirts.

Mouse had worked with cordless mikes only once before. People forgot they were wearing them. The camera could be off, but the sound was still rolling. The subject of the movie she'd worked on had been a beer drinker with a bladder the size of a pistachio. They had hundreds of feet of audiotape of him in the WC.

Sins was meat-locker cold. The air conditioning purred even in January. Mouse watched Ivan with the tape recorder, struck with a kind of vertigo.

Ivan. All the times she'd imagined him doing this or something like it. Statistics could be compiled. Over the last sixteen years, X number of hours spent sleeping, X eating, X spent imagining making a movie with Ivan. They'd done their small 8mm movies together. She had never expected to see him again. Now here it was, something big. Or bigger. A form of dream come true. There should be satisfaction. She had imagined this with Ivan, but had done it with Tony. She watched while Ivan knelt down, flipped on the recorder, checked the levels. It was simple, as ordinary as the stroke of a shoulder before a kiss. The Nagra weighed forty pounds. Lifting it required care. Backs were thrown out, shoulders dislocated. Ivan slipped on the strap, stood up. Mouse had watched Tony do this a million times. Tony, in baggy khaki shorts, the machinery working inside his knobby freckled knees, as he stood. Where was Tony? What had happened to Stanley? Who was living in their concrete house in Nairobi? She rolled her lips inside her mouth and bit them, hard. She could not afford a bout of nostalgia.

"I want something plain, thirty-two C, beige," she said.

"Buff," said Dani. "Are you sure you don't want white? It's been my experience that a bride likes to be white inside and out."

"Buff," said Mouse.

"She's practical," said Mimi.

"Let's go," said Ivan. He was too cool to say action. Eliot eased around on the heels of his flip-flops. He filmed a few feet of Ivan, the hoop box taped to the strap of the Nagra. The hoop box flashed a red dot of light and laid down a melodic "hoop" on the sound track. It was the electronic equivalent of a slate.

Dani disappeared in the back, falling twice off her sling-back pumps into the deep carpet. Even though she was not impressed by the production, she was nervous, acting like a saleswoman playing a saleswoman.

"That's not all you're going to get, is it?" said Mimi, a hysterical edge to her voice. "What about a body brief? You've got to have something sexy, you know, for your wedding night."

"We've lived together for four years," said Mouse.

"It's your *wedding* night," said Mimi.

"Do you wish you hadn't lived together?" asked Ivan.

"No, why would I wish that?"

Ivan was silent. The camera whirred. She thought she saw Eliot smirk beneath his mustache.

Dani returned with a dozen buff bras. She lined them up, a row of satiny beige sea anemones marching down the gleaming counter two by two. Mouse held one up by the straps. She was surprised to find she wasn't embarrassed; she had no problem pretending this was not underwear. It bothered her that Ivan also seemed to have no problem pretending this was not underwear. He stood with his arms crossed, the headphones down around his neck.

"This one's good," she said. She reached inside her purse for her wallet.

"You've *got* to try it on," said Mimi. "I can't believe you're not going to try it on."

"Maybe you'd like to go with more décolletage. This one has a little padding, a front closure."

"I don't need any padding."

"What about a Merry Widow? Tony, the groom, wants –"

"Has your fiancé asked you to get something special?" asked Ivan.

"I have a saucy little Merry Widow in point d'esprit stretch lace with detachable garters. I think it'll suit you, honey."

Mouse tried not to roll her eyes

"Why are you rolling your eyes?"

"Ivan, this is *ridiculous*.

"Shopping for things for your wedding or –"

"– it comes in aubergine, champagne, and ebony –"

"– the questions! I thought we talked about this. Just let the camera roll, for God's sake."

"The camera is rolling. As co-producer you should be concerned that we're wasting film."

"Listen," said Eliot, "if ya don't mind me putting in my two cents. We're tryin to establish your character through your reactions to the intimate apparel, okay? They're like visual correlatives for the way you think of marriage. It also says a lot about the virgin/whore duality in contemporary relationships."

"What?"

"That's what I was going to suggest," said Mimi, smiling at Eliot. She waved a hanger with a few strands of red and black lace floating from its arms. "Come on, Mouse. It's your *wedding*. Be daring. I'll try on one, too. Ivan loved the one I had for our wedding. Remember, you –"

"CUT!" said Mouse.

"Tulip-shaped cups, also slightly padded. Did I tell you it came in ecru, too?" said Dani.

"Don't cut it," said Ivan.

"I think it might be confusing for the audience to have Mimi addressing you offscreen," said Mouse.

"I used to be married to that one," said Mimi, flapping her

hand at Ivan. "It was the mistake of my life, but we did go to the Virgin Islands Club Med for our honeymoon."

"Does your sister's failed marriage make you nervous?" asked Ivan, calmly pressing on.

"If you want to go with a body brief instead, I do have something with a little underwire support and a high-cut bottom. It's a nice floral stretch lace that goes under anything. Some women prefer a body brief if they're going to go with thigh-high stockings."

"You can see why I divorced him," said Mimi. "I'd like the tulip Merry Widow. In red."

Mouse knew if Ivan had his way the camera would follow them right into the dressing room. This was out of the question. This documentary was about a wedding, not the tyranny of lingerie. Mouse and Mimi both agreed that there was nothing to be gained by showing Mouse hobbling around nude and knock-kneed, boobs flapping mightily, trying to tug the body brief up over her hips without ripping it. Sound was one thing. Mouse and Mimi would be happy to remove their tiny cordless mikes from their shirts and reclip them on a lacy strap. But the camera, no.

Ivan was left standing in the hallway, the camera trained on the closed dressing room door, listening. Dani stood behind him, wringing her hands.

Although she would never admit it, Mouse had never understood lingerie. Naturally, The Pink Fiend had accused her of being a freak. Women were supposed to love lingerie, even though it cost a small fortune, made you feel self-conscious, was generally uncomfortable, and never looked as alluring on you as it did on an airbrushed model, which, in turn, made you more self-conscious and, ultimately, miserable. At least this is what Mouse had deduced. Most of the time she never wore underwear. When she did, she went in for standard white cotton. She wore bras you could buy in a box at the drugstore.

Mouse stood in front of the mirror, modeling a black stretch-lace body brief, her hands on her hips. In the center was a diamond-shaped sheer mesh insert. The cups were also sheer, adroitly trimmed with more black lace to hide the main attractions. The legs were cut high, setting off the hollow sides of Mouse's thin haunches, still tan from a stint of nude sunbathing in Malindi. She fussed with her hair, ran her hands down her stomach and over her hips. Yes, it cost a fortune, but, Mouse thought, I have a fortune. She jutted out her hip experimentally. "This is ridiculous," she said.

"Do you need another color or size?" asked Dani though the door.

"What is ridiculous?" asked Ivan.

"She looks incredible," said Mimi. She stood behind Mouse in her red Merry Widow, staring at Mouse.

"Really?" said Mouse.

"You have just the bod for this kind of stuff. I'm thin, but wide." She turned sideways and sucked in her stomach. "I'm just too feminine for this time in history. I should have been born when Renoir was around. Plus, I have all these moles. I used to think they were freckles."

"Does it offend your feminist sensibility?" asked Ivan. "Do you feel as though you are a turkey dressed for Thanksgiving? A calf fatted for the slaughter?"

"All of those," said Mouse, rolling her eyes at Mimi.

"I told you he was nuts," Mimi whispered.

"Speak up, girls. Even though you're miked you need to speak up," said Ivan.

"She said you were nuts," said Mouse.

Mimi pinched her arm. Silence from the other side of the door. Mimi and Mouse giggled into their hands.

They tried on everything the obsequious Dani brought them. Bustiers and fluted tap pants and lace camibras, silk gowns and satin teddies. They wore their little slippers and asked for a tray of champagne and cookies.

Mouse tried on the saucy little aubergine spandex Merry

Widow with string bikini and stretch stockings. "I look like a whore," said Mouse, not unhappily.

"Of course you look like a whore. That's the whole point. I wish I looked like a whore. I look like one of those saloon girls from the Wild West. All I need is a hat with a big feather in it."

Mouse wondered how she ever got the impression these things were uncomfortable. Everything was soft and stretchy and smelled rich. She looked at her stained and faded jeans abandoned on the chintz-covered Hepplewhite chair in the corner and thought they should be picked up with a large set of tongs and taken immediately out to the dumpster in the alley. Suddenly she felt foolish. The concept of lingerie was against everything she believed in, yet here she was enjoying herself.

On impulse she threw open the dressing room door. "Why not?" she thought, momentarily forgetting that showing Tony footage of her traipsing around in a saucy aubergine Merry Widow and string bikini in front of Ivan's camera was not likely to win him over to the cause.

Mimi clamped her arms over herself. "What are you *doing*?" she shrieked.

"What the well-dressed bride is wearing this year," said Mouse. She glided up and down the short hallway that led from the dressing rooms, elbow crooked, palm up, hips swinging. "Here we have Mouse FitzHenry modeling a delightful Merry Widow by..." She lifted up her arm to look at the label.

"Giuseppe of Firenze," said Dani Lynx. "It looks fabulous."

"Giuseppe of Firenze. Notice the delicate panel of French lace and the delicate underwire..."

"Hubba-hubba." Eliot chewed on his mustache, training the camera on Mouse as though he was covering an event of world significance.

"Well," Mouse said, stopping before Ivan. "Whaddya think?"

"CUT," he said.

"What are you doing? I thought you wanted to film in the dressing room –"

"– I ask the questions," he said. "You do not address me. I am not here."

"I thought I was the co-producer."

"When you are on-camera, you are the subject."

Mimi lurched into the hallway, determined not to be left out. She had changed back into the red Merry Widow and was struggling with the zipper. "Don't you want to get both of us? Two sisters? Just make sure, I need to be filmed from the side –"

"– go back," said Ivan.

"Forget it," said Mouse. "The show's over."

"No, I like this. Perhaps, though, you should see if Mrs. Lynx has that same thing in white. We want to emphasize the totemic quality of the white."

"Brides want to be white, inside and out," said Mimi. "I know how that is."

"Just give me two bras, thirty-two C," said Mouse crossly. "In beige."

AFTER THEY FINISHED at Sins, Mimi drove Ivan and Eliot home, bumper-to-bumper down Lincoln Boulevard to Venice. This was less fun than she imagined. She hadn't realized she'd also be roped into chauffeuring these two clowns around. How can they live in L.A. and not have a car? She glanced in the rearview mirror right into the big glass eye of the camera. Eliot and Ivan were squeezed into the backseat, filming what Ivan called "the all-important woman talk," in which presumably much would be revealed. Ivan shot while Eliot operated the Nagra from his fat lap.

"You'll regret that you didn't buy anything," said Mimi. "You only get married once for the first time."

"I bought something."

"Two bras, big deal. In *beige*."

Mouse looked out the window.

"You can do all that weird Africa stuff and you're afraid to spring for some decent underwear."

"I am not," said Mouse hotly. Mimi was right, she was. What was wrong with her? She just could not bring herself to buy those things. Hundreds and hundreds of dollars. The yearly per capita income of Mali for a peignoir set? The monthly salary of a Tanzanian schoolteacher for a teddy? It was frivolous. It was self-indulgent. It was not serious. It was something Mimi would do. And if Mimi would do it, Mouse would not. She was depressed.

Mimi sang along with the radio. "Sir or ma'am would you read my book..." She had a good voice, she thought. Not much of a range, but a clear strong alto. If anybody saw this stupid film maybe they'd hear her singing and cast her in a musical – "'cause I want to try and take the back right turn, take the back right turn!"

"It's 'paperback writer,'" said Mouse.

"No, listen." Mimi turned it up.

"It's 'cause I want to be a paperback writer," said Mouse.

"I played this album every day of my life, I should know what it is."

Ivan laughed in the backseat. "I used to think 'life in the fast lane' was 'pipe in the Vaseline.'"

"Pipe in the Vaseline," sang Eliot in a booming bass. "I like it."

"You always have to be right, don't you?" said Mimi.

"I am right," said Mouse.

"You bought those two stupid bras," sniffed Mimi, snapping off the radio.

Mouse reached over and snapped it back on.

Unaccountably, the traffic suddenly eased up. They caught all the lights. Mouse rolled down her window, laid her head on her arms. The thick salty air blew her hair off her face. Her eyes watered. She pretended she was a dog with no problems. On the radio, another Beatles' song, one of the instrumentals from the psychedelic period tolerated by every one, liked by no one.

Suddenly, up ahead, a flurry of brake lights. A light-yellow Buick two cars up braked too late. The driver began to veer left onto the median, just as the car ahead of Mimi's Datsun clipped the Buick's rear bumper, sending it first sideways, then up, up, straight into the air, over onto its roof.

It did not look like a crash. It looked choreographed, a trained dolphin swooping into the air before falling over on its back. No horns honked. No brakes shrieked. No one screamed. There was only the homely sound of crunching sheet metal, like a trash can falling over.

To avoid the pileup, Mimi swung into the right lane without looking. Miraculously, it was clear. They sped past the Buick. The passenger window had been crushed to the size of a toaster. Wedged in the window was a rear end in khakis. The trunk had sprung open, dirty laundry was scattered on the street. The license plate was Canadian: Friendly Manitoba. Mouse knew, somehow, that the Manitobans were dead. No rear that big fits in a window that small without the fatal squeezing of some serious bones and organs.

They drove in stunned silence to a convenience-store parking lot, where Mouse called 911 on a pay phone.

Nine-one-one was more interested in knowing whether Mouse was a witness. She said she was. She described the front end rising into the air, the glint of the sun on its shiny bumper, the khaki-clothed rear end pinched in the window, the laundry scattering, Friendly Manitoba.

But did she see what *happened*? they asked, irritated. Did she get license numbers? What happened to the car that hit the Buick? Whose fault was it? The insurance company will need witnesses. Mouse didn't know.

She hung up and bought some cigarettes. She imagined the phone call, luring some farm wife in from her kitchen garden, a bunch of muddy onions dangling from her hand, only to hear the horrible news. She will get all the gruesome facts and none of the important ones. She will never know: Did they realize they were dying? Did they suffer? What were their final, confused thoughts?

She will drop the onions and toss together a funeral. It will be in Manitoba; a local minister will officiate, not some hip, oversympathizing L.A. priest who'll get the names wrong. There will be no carnation-pink hearses, no gravediggers who look like realtors sporting gold-shovel tie tacks. The final resting place will be restful, not an overcrowded cemetery with a view of the San Diego Freeway. The farm wife will make it as nice as she can, and inasmuch as these occasions can ever be nice, this one will be. Still, now and then she'll curse herself: last year we should have gone to Europe.

Mouse went back to the car.

While she was on the phone, Mimi had broken out the potato salad. Ivan and Eliot ate greedily from a Tupperware tub with tablespoons, complimenting Mimi on the salad and her quick reflexes.

"We are used to movie sound," said Ivan, licking mayonnaise from the corner of his mouth. "It's bigger than life. That's why this seemed so surreal. We are so inundated with images that reality has begun to feel unfamiliar."

"I just think when your number's up, your number's up," said Mimi. "It's like a giant Baskin-Robbins in the sky. Number seventy-two! If you're number seventy-two, that's that. How else do you explain the one person who survives a plane wreck?"

"I want to go back," said Mouse.

"By now the fuzz'll be there," said Eliot. "It'll be gridlock city. We should have gotten some shots of it while we were there."

"Are you all right?" said Ivan, leaning over the seat. He squeezed her shoulder, his eyes filled with concern.

"I want to be white inside and out," said Mouse.

"She wants to take her bras back," said Mimi. "This is exactly what I did. She wants the whole nine yards."

"I want the saucy aubergine spandex Merry Widow," she said. "I want the French what-is-it lace thing and the demicup underwire lace bra and the string bikini and the body brief and the champagne satin slippers and the red and black silk-lace teddy. I want it all and I want it in white."

"All right!" said Eliot, "Pipe in that Vaseline."

18

IN FEBRUARY, THREE MONTHS BEFORE THE WEDDING, Tony began to find Mouse's lists all over the apartment. On a steno pad left on the bathroom sink he found: *colors? rings? limo?* One morning, while folding up the futon, he spied a dusty scrap of yellow paper wreathed in dog hair underneath: *ask Tony – priest that married Shirl and Fitzy? Little Chapel of the Valley or Dorothy Chandler Pavilion?*

He thought it was cute. He told her, whatever she wants he wants.

There was no more talk about what project they would do next. Mouse surprised him one night wearing some phenomenal purple lace contraption the likes of which he'd only enjoyed before in the magazines he hid at the bottom of his suitcase. They made love after everyone else had gone to sleep, under the doleful eye of Sniffy Voyeur. He supposed she was finally happy. He knew he was.

Mouse wanted everything. Everything Nita could think of sounded good to Mouse. Personally designed invitations on hand-pressed paper, engraved in 22-carat gold ink. A horse-drawn carriage to take her and Tony to the reception at the Bel Air Hotel. Champagne imported from the Loire Valley. A wedding-morning breakfast buffet at Shirl's. A day-after send-off barbecue at Malibu, complete with volleyball match, including printed T-shirts for each team (brides vs. grooms). Gold keychains for the ushers. Gold bracelets for the bridesmaids. The church lit entirely by candles flown in from Vatican City. The Pink Fiend, who had badgered Mouse for as long as she could remember, tacitly approved.

Mouse lay on Nita's mooshy mauve sofa poring through piles of two-ton bridal magazines. There were two things Mouse did not want: (1) a theme, (2) a band at the reception whose rendition of "Brown Sugar" was so lousy they might as well play the CD.

All right, said Nita, no theme, but what image did Mouse want to convey? Would she like the wedding to have a country feel? A tropical feel? An African feel?

Move over Chuck and Di, said Mouse, is the feeling she wished to convey. Money was no object.

Mouse was only mildly surprised at her change of heart. For every action there was an opposite and equal reaction. This was a law of human behavior as well as physics. She remembered once waiting nine hours at an airstrip in a small Sudanese village to catch a plane to an even smaller Sudanese village. She and Tony read aloud from a book they had found in their hotel. It was the story of a Uruguayan soccer team whose plane crashed in the Andes. They were flying home from Peru. They were stranded in the Andes for months. Those who lived cannibalized those who died. In the end, three were rescued. When they returned to Uruguay, one committed suicide, one joined a religious order, one threw himself into a life of complete excess. Mouse and Tony decided if the same thing had happened to them, Tony would probably be the one to hurl himself back into life, cashing in on the world's blatant pleasures. Mouse, they figured, would either become a monk or work herself to death trying to get funding for a ten-part series on survivors. Well, well, well.

This was Mimi's attitude. Well, well, well. The chickens come home to roost. She was relieved. At first. Relieved and smug. Mouse losing sleep over whether to go with a chapel-length or cathedral train proved to Mimi that she was right all along: all brides want an extravagant, fairy-tale wedding and Mouse, Ms. Free Spirit-World Traveler, was no different from all brides. Was no different from her, Mimi.

Mouse began to jog with Mimi around the neighborhood each morning. Mimi welcomed the company. At first. Mimi could hardly keep up with her. Not because Mouse was in better shape but because Mimi could not stop talking, warning Mouse of impending prenuptial pitfalls. Do not, *do not*, get a facial on the day of the wedding. Eat something before, you won't eat a bite at the reception. Put Vaseline on your teeth. Mouse panted lightly beside her. "Uh-huh," she said. "Uh-huh." Mimi knew she wasn't listening, merely indulging her.

"Isn't she cute, the little bride," said Mimi, one night when Mouse was curled up next to Tony on the couch, badgering him to at least give her an idea about the sort of china pattern he would like. A nice floral Wedgwood lined with 24-carat gold? Or maybe some plain old white bone Limoges. Money was no object.

"It's an object to those of us who have to put out for the fucking place settings," Mimi yelled from the kitchen, where she was making oatmeal cookies, forking the batter into her mouth with her first two fingers.

Mouse lay on Nita's mooshy mauve sofa reading the résumé of a woodwind quartet for the pre-ceremony musical entertainment while Nita made phone calls. Lining up bands to audition for the reception. Arranging interviews with prospective florists and caterers. Finding the best wedding photographer, portrait photographer, and videographer.

Booking a famous at-home hair stylist and makeup artist who would come to Shirl's the day of the ceremony to work her magic on Mouse, Shirl, Bea Cheatham (Tony's mother, coming from Hong Kong with Noel Cheatham, his father), Mimi (Maid of Honor), Carole and Lisa (bridesmaids), and Gabrielle (Mouse's best friend, also a bridesmaid, coming from Nairobi with her Belgian husband, Wim). Mouse would also have a facial, a pedicure, a manicure, and a Shiatsu body massage. It was not easy finding a manicurist to tackle Mouse's green under-the-nail fungal disease, but eventually one was found.

Money was no object. After the usual bureaucratic delay, Shirl received her settlement, doled out Mr. Edmonton's thirty-five-percent fee and deposited the rest in a checking account on which Mouse and Tony were joint cosigners. On the advice of Shirl's accountant, the proper percentage was set aside for taxes. Mouse and Tony bought an inexpensive Toyota. Remembering Ralph's warning that no one wanted to make a movie with someone who drove an econo-box, Tony insisted upon the next up from the bottom of the line, anticipating all the production meetings he would be driving to once *Love Among Elephants* was finally a "go" movie.

The money dwindled. Still, it was more than what all but a fraction of the world made in a year. Some of it was used to foot travel expenses for Gabrielle and Wim. Mouse also commissioned Gabrielle to track down Stanley, buy him a top-of-the-line electric wheelchair, a suit coat, and an airplane ticket. Stanley had often said he wouldn't mind seeing the States; Tony said he wouldn't mind having a few more souls sitting on his side of the church. If Stanley was not at his usual post outside The New Stanley hotel, perhaps he could be found at his village, three days into the bush. *Pas de problème*, Gabrielle wired Mouse after receiving the instructions. Because it was her best friend's wedding, Gabrielle, earnest and duty-bound as a doctor taking the Hippocratic Oath, swore to do everything humanly possible to get Stanley across two continents and one ocean to witness the happy occasion.

There were moments when Mouse thought she should be shot for spending so much on what amounted to a fifteen-minute ceremony. Instead, everyone indulged her. She was, after all, the bride.

Shirl wanted to accompany Mouse to her meetings with Nita, but Mouse said she wanted Shirl to be surprised. What Mouse was waiting for was the right moment to break the news about *Wedding March*. Then Shirl, now Mouse's best friend and confidante, would be more than welcome.

Mouse insisted that Shirl use some of the settlement money for whatever remodeling she wanted to do. Although everyone coming from out of town could be put up at the Bel Air, Shirl and Auntie Barb wanted to host the wedding-morning breakfast buffet at the house on Cantaloupe Avenue. Shirl wanted to paint. She wanted new carpet installed. She wanted the lagoon drained and the bottom repainted. Mouse pored over swatches with her at the kitchen table, a box of doughnuts between them. Shirl was off glazed and onto cake, an improvement, in everyone's eyes. Her hair had grown back. She took Mouse with her to the salon when she had it dyed and, pointing to her daughter's espresso-colored curls (the perm had grown out nicely), said, "I want that."

Auntie Barb hovered, eavesdropping, in the background, her mouth a disapproving line embedded in her big wrinkled face. In Oregon, people were prudent. In Oregon, a girl knew how to make her wedding day special without spending an arm and a leg.

Since Auntie Barb had been in Los Angeles taking care of Shirl, she had subscribed to the *Oregonian*, from which she cut out articles on Oregon brides who wove their own headpieces from woodland flowers, on the potluck reception then enjoying a renaissance in the great Northwest. She left them and other pieces on the kitchen table in the morning for her sister next to her orange juice and anticonvulsant medication. Shirl thanked her, then passed them on to Mouse with a roll of her eyes.

One afternoon Shirl took out her wedding album to show Mouse. They were sitting outside at a patio table by the lagoon eating macaroons. A Santa Ana had swept in at the end of February. Dry palms rustled overhead. Auntie Barb practiced her much-admired golf swing on the patch of dichondra by the side of the house.

"Dermot and Shirley" was engraved on the cover of the

292 | KAREN KARBO

album in gold. Shirl ran a chubby finger over their names. Mouse expected her to cry. Instead she said, "Can you believe I married a man named *Dermot*? How could anyone do that to a child?"

The pictures were large and few. The requisite tender portrait of the bride, in which Shirl looked as though she was ready to burst out laughing. Fitzy and Shirl trooping down the aisle. The kiss at the alter. Cutting the cake. Throwing the garter. They were dark-haired and trim, dazed as a pair of rabbits caught in the headlights of an oncoming car. Mouse saw her chin and eyes in Fitzy, Mimi's wide mouth in Shirl.

"Mom, remember I told you that Ivan wanted to make a documentary film about the wedding?"

"Ivan" – Shirl shook her head – "what a confused boy."

"What do you mean? He won an Oscar."

"You used to be confused like that. Lorraine – down to the craft shop. You know, with that skin problem? Teaches gold-leafing? Her daughter is forty-one and hasn't had sex in eight years. She's just *green* that my Mousie Mouse has found somebody."

"We're doing it," said Mouse. "Making the movie." She explained the situation. They were shooting her portion first, in order to prove to Tony that this, too, was Oscar-winning material. If after they showed the footage to Tony he still objected, the project would be scrapped.

"It makes it even more special, Mom. Have any of your friends at the craft shop had a movie about their kids' weddings shown on TV?"

Shirl considered this. "She hasn't had a *date* since the hostage crisis, Lorraine's daughter."

Out of the corner of her eye Mouse saw Auntie Barb dashing her golf club to the ground. She stomped over, fists on her hips, the tendons in her scrawny neck taut. "I cannot bear this a minute longer. Shirl, open your eyes. She's taking advantage of your good nature, can't you see? You already said you were against this *movie* idea and she's gone ahead and done it anyway. You are footing the bill, and here she is waltzing around like the world was made for her own pleasure. You wouldn't see a girl in Oregon getting involved in some foul *movie* nonsense. In Oregon, children respect their parents –"

"– Barb, for crying out loud! If I want to be taken advantage of that's my own damned business."

"You think us Oregonians don't know what's what." Tears filled Auntie Barb's eyes.

"You Oregonians don't know when to shut up, is what I think," said Shirl, slamming the wedding album closed and ramming it back in its box.

Mouse shared the mauve sofa with Shirl. Together, they pored through the portfolios of prospective florists, read aloud to one another menus from prospective caterers. Shirl had become a fixture in Nita's office, along with Ivan and Eliot. Nita listened to all of Shirl's thoughts and suggestions carefully, her chin resting on interlaced fingers, dabbing her still-running new nose.

Eliot, it turned out, was a master cappuccino-maker and made them all cappuccinos in the industrial-sized white china cups. He made a special mocha variety for Shirl, to satisfy her sweet tooth. Ivan told Shirl, in his soft, coaxing voice, that the camera loved her. They decided, unanimously, that the wording on the invitations would read:

> *Mrs. Shirley FitzHenry*
> *requests the pleasure of your company*
> *at the marriage of her daughter*
> *Frances Anne FitzHenry*
> *to*
> *Anthony Noel Cheatham*

Shirl sobbed noisily with joy. Ivan gently reminded her not to look at the camera. She said she just wanted to make sure he was getting it all.

Money was no object. Tony was, though. He was The Groom. The reason for the wedding, but otherwise besides the point.

Heeding Nita's advice, Mouse tried to include him. When she asked him whether he thought her attendants should carry frilled rosettes or a modified crescent bouquet, he picked up the TV remote, "just to check on the ball game."

Somewhere along the way, Mouse had lost track of him. She didn't know what ball game he was talking about. She didn't know what he did all day. His big job was to get the marriage license, also put together his guest list. Instead, he bought a skateboard that said *dog cheese!* across it in bold hot-pink letters. Mouse didn't know what this meant.

Tony slouched on the couch at night, the board across his lap, making minute adjustments on the wheels. He borrowed a set of tiny screwdrivers from the ten-year-old Armenian boy downstairs, his adviser on all matters relating to the sport.

The guest list worried Tony. The only person he knew in Los Angeles, besides all of Mimi's friends, was V. J. Parchman, and he certainly could not invite him. V. J. thought Tony and Mouse were married years ago in an intimate Rwandan mountain wedding, in the fog, among the gorillas. Tony wondered what would happen to the project if he admitted that the wedding scene was pure fancy, the only lie in an otherwise true story. Nothing, perhaps. Then again, it could be the card that toppled the house, one more small problem, not insurmountable in and of itself, that made *Love Among Elephants* more trouble than it was worth. Tony decided he would think about it later, then promptly put it out of his mind.

The next day, trying to airwalk off the Armenian boy's launch ramp, Tony fell and broke his nose.

Mouse was furious because she was so frightened. She was very good at imagining the sudden death of someone she loved. She ran red lights in the new Toyota, racing to the emergency ward for an X-ray. Dusky circles bloomed beneath Tony's eyes. His nostrils were plugged with Kleenex.

"You could have cracked your head open. You could have broken your stupid neck."

"You're so cute when you're hysterical," said Tony.

"I just don't want to be a widow before I'm a bride."

"Bit of an impossibility, that."

"Do me a favor and don't be calm and witty, all right? You scared the living shit out of me."

MOUSE TOLD IVAN that Tony would be unavailable for at least a month. They were hunkered over the production schedule at a Mexican restaurant on the Boardwalk near his apartment. She thought Ivan was getting suspicious. He had twice asked her when Tony could give them some of his time. He just wanted to *talk* to Tony, no camera, maybe they could do some audio.

First she'd said Tony had a two-week stint sound-editing on a TV show, then that he was busy finishing up a draft of his script with Ralph. The first excuse was an outright lie, the second a presumption. After it became apparent that Tony and his nose would survive, she allowed herself to appreciate her fiancé's good timing. She was grateful for a truthful excuse.

"It's painful for Tony to talk," she said. "They had to put him under and go in and readjust things. It's not your average broken nose."

Ivan stared at her over his taquitos with his insinuating blue gaze. He had cut his hair. He now wore it combed straight off his forehead. He had put on weight, thanks to all the meals paid for by the production. He looked more like the Ivan whom Mouse remembered. She was no longer nervous around him, although there were moments when he pinched her waist, rested his chin on her shoulder to deliver a quiet aside, when she wondered what she was doing marrying Tony.

"Anyway," said Ivan, "I would like to meet with him before next month. After that I have another project beginning. Time will be tight."

"What project?" Mouse suddenly felt left out. He was doing a project without her?

"An environmental thing. They are paying me a lot to do

nothing. Which reminds me, I have some bad news and some bad news."

Mouse laughed. "I'm good at bad news. What's up?"

"The footage we shot at Sins is unusable. Six thousand feet, out of focus. I don't think it was Eliot. Some problem with the lens. He's having it looked at."

"I suppose we had to pay for the processing and printing?"

"That's the other problem. Some of our funding has fallen through."

"Some? How much, some?"

"Sixty thousand. It is not the end of the world. I have several other places I can go. In the meantime, I'd like to borrow half of it from your wedding account to buy a few more cases of film."

"Absolutely not," she said without thinking.

Ivan chuckled lazily. He reached across the table and grabbed her hand. He rolled out her fingers and stroked each pearly-pink nail with his thick thumb. "If you had been this tough before, I never would have married your stupid sister."

"What about, about the sixty thousand?" she said. Maybe she should think about this. She could borrow the money from the account without saying anything, then replace it ... no, she knew that story. Sinking your own money into a documentary was like lending money to a compulsive gambler in Reno.

"Something will come up," he sighed.

"Donating your other kidney?"

His gaze roamed the room, finally settling on the pack of cigarettes they were sharing. "Where did you hear that?"

"Is it true?"

"I am excessive, but not that excessive."

"Where will you get the money?"

"There are a few private individuals in town interested in nurturing my vision."

"Women?"

"Of course, women. You could be one of them." He smiled broadly and asked for the check, which he paid.

Mouse was not sure she even liked Ivan anymore. He was a politico. There were reasons beneath his reasons. He reminded her of one of those sexy, inscrutable drug kingpins in a B-movie featuring money laundering and international intrigue. At the same time she realized that liking him seemed to have nothing to do with the nature of their unfinished business.

19

WHEN BIBLIOTHÈQUES MET AT THE BIG HOUSE, ANYONE with an aversion to sitting on L.A.'s filthiest square of shag had to bring his own chair. Even though Sather's cat had been eaten by a coyote six months before, fleas still bivouacked in the carpet, waiting for a warm body to happen past so they could hop aboard. In addition, there were the usual stains and the snappy odor of old cat piss. The chairs were set up in a circle. A bag of sour cream 'n' onion potato chips yawned open on the floor: the hors d'œuvres. Every time the meeting was held at the Big House, Mimi felt like she was camping out.

Mimi had tried repeatedly to get Mouse and Tony to come along, but they thought it sounded too much like school. They weren't sure they understood the point of it. Mimi tried to explain that you got more out of a text if you discussed it with other people. Mouse said, "I don't read texts, I read books." The closer the wedding got, the snottier Mouse became. Mimi knew for a fact that Mouse read nothing but magazines.

This month the book was Ralph's pick. *The Razor's Edge*, by Somerset Maugham.

"The difference between us and the Larry character," said Ralph, "is that at least he could find God without needing a couple million bucks. At least he could be spiritual, he had that kernel of satisfaction. I'm a producer-director, but I've never produced, I've never directed, I will never be able to do the thing I love unless someone gives me a lot of money. Larry, at least, could do the thing he loved." He took a slug from his beer, stared moodily at the toes of his tennis shoes.

"How do you know you love it if you've never done it?" asked Lisa. She had broken out her pleated linen shorts, a sign that spring had arrived. An ashtray balanced on one sleek knee, brown from a recent trip to the Cayman Islands. She flipped her straight red hair over her shoulder, inhaling deeply on her Gauloise.

"I went to *film* school, Lisa. In case you'd forgotten."

"Whoopee," said Lisa.

No one had read much of the book because of the weather. This was the stock excuse. There was an unspoken understanding among the Bibliothèques that reading was done only under optimum meteorological conditions, preferably when there was nothing else better to do.

It was the time of year when for two or three blessed weeks it did not seem insane to live here. The days were warm and smogless, the nights cool, tinged with the smell of jasmine. Vast islands of peach, pink, and lavender snapdragons bloomed on the front lawns of the mansions up and down Sunset, nurtured by the hands of a thousand dutiful Mexican gardeners. High school and college students in convertibles slathered on suntan lotion at stoplights, already working on a spring-break tan. Music blared from open windows. The Dodgers were in training.

There were also the spring movie releases, so everyone was going to screenings. Luke, who was a runner at Warner Brothers, reported that no one was even reading coverage, it had been so nice.

"Then why *am* I doing this?" asked Carole. She sat next to Lisa, a script open on her lap. Carole could talk and read a script at the same time.

"Rent," said Sather. "The entire world boils down to the quest for rent."

Mimi hadn't read the book either. It had nothing to do with the weather. She sat next to Ralph, munching potato chips daintily from a cupped hand, jiggling her foot. She wore her turquoise knit mini, his favorite, and a pair of black strappy sandals. She had just had her legs waxed. She felt good.

She had not read the book because self-improvement suddenly seemed a waste of time. She had decided to get married. Helping Mouse plan her wedding made her realize it was time to give up her options and tie the knot. She would marry Ralph, get pregnant ASAP, and kiss off Solly and his teeny, torturous steno chair. They would find a starter home, maybe in Thousand Oaks or Agoura, and she would go back to school to get her teaching credential. She'd always loved kids and could do wonders with construction paper. If that didn't work out, she could always go back to being a drudge and an aspiring actress. She could always call Bob Hope.

Mimi and Ralph had never talked about how they felt about each other. She loved him, she was now sure. It was the deep, abiding love necessary for marriage. She knew, because the idea of shopping for a dishwasher with him was more palatable than the idea of having sex, which hadn't been the way she had felt about Ivan.

To this day she still wasn't sure what had gotten into her. All she remembered was that she wanted an excuse to throw a big party and was sick of all the complicated scheduling involved in sleeping together. He lived at home and she lived at home and the pool cabana had long since lost its charm. In retrospect, it sounded as though it was convenience she had been after, and maybe it was. She'd felt the same way recently when she bought an exercise bike and set it up in her bedroom because she was tired of schlepping to the gym.

Sometimes she could not believe she was that shallow, even at nineteen and hoped she had stolen the boy Mouse loved for some complex Freudian reason. The shrink Mimi saw for a while after the divorce suggested it was not Ivan that Mimi had wanted but the bond between him and Mouse. She wanted to relate to a man in a way that had nothing to do with sex. Why would I want to do that? she'd thought. "Sure, that sounds good," she'd said.

"Let's talk about your need to agree with everything I say," said the shrink.

Therapy made Mimi feel like a failure. The shrink always thought she was guiding Mimi into uncovering her true feelings, when in fact the agonized look that crossed Mimi's face was often the result of her realization that she hadn't put enough money in the parking meter. Mimi felt like she spent the entire fifty minutes making up things just so the shrink would feel like it was working. Then, the time would be up, Mimi would write her a check for $125, hoping it wouldn't bounce, and stumble out to her car to collect the parking ticket from under her windshield wiper.

Now, at thirty-six, almost thirty-seven, Mimi saw that the reason her first marriage failed was youth, pure and simple. At nineteen, marriage was just industrial-strength going steady. Once you got sick of being roommates, provided there were no kids to complicate matters, you moved on. The fact that you had no life insurance, no health insurance, no savings or assets made no difference. You were nineteen. You had no gray hair, no cellulite, and no crow's-feet either. There were more where he came from. You never thought, I would rather be unhappy with him than alone in a garden apartment with my aging reproductive organs. You moved on.

After Mimi got tired of sleeping with Ivan, it became apparent they had nothing to talk about. He drove a beer truck and took night classes in film. She went to school and worked on campus.

The marriage was like the houseplant they got for a wedding present: some exotic thing meant to live in South America. The leaves drooped and turned brown around the edges whether she watered it or not, whether she stuck it outside on their little balcony or shoved it in the back of a closet. She cosseted it with expensive fertilizer. No improvement. She talked to it, took it into a nursery for consultation. Nothing. Finally she

stopped watering it completely. It lived on in its same old withered fashion for a few more months, then died. She assumed it
was the lack of water. A friend who knew about such things came
and looked at the wrinkled ropy stems, stuck a finger in the soil
and pronounced it dead of rot. Mimi told this to her shrink. The
shrink said, "Let's talk about your need to use complex meta-
phors to obscure difficult issues." She stopped going.

Tonight, Mimi finally felt like an adult, sitting at Bibliothèques next to her future fiancé, listening to him voice his
frustration over his career. She offered him a chip in solace. He
shook his head.

She hoped they could have a heart-to-heart after the meeting. Then they could set the date, toss out her birth-control
pills, collect their wedding money from Shirl. Ralph had never
officially divorced Elaine, because he had had no reason to. Now
he would. Maybe Mimi would use some of their wedding money
to help pay for his divorce.

"I think you're doing great, Ralph," she said. "I mean you've
got this thing happening with Tony – " She didn't like Ralph
always making himself out to be such a loser. She wondered, idly,
if he would take his baseball cap off for the wedding. She hoped so.

" – nothing's happening. What's happening? You start
thinking a meeting is something. A meeting is nothing. A meeting
is filling up some development slut's datebook. Until the check
has cleared the bank, nothing has happened. And even then, that's
just money, not something up there on the screen."

"Just money," said Carole. "I thought paying the rent made
the world go 'round."

"But you have *hope*. As long as there's hope – " continued
Mimi.

"Hope is not a directing credit," said Darryl. "Everybody
has hope. The fact your fucking heart's beating makes you a
candidate for *hope*."

"In other words, Ralph has as much chance of getting a 'go'

movie as some human vegetable kept alive by machines," said Sather.

"Provided the vegetable has slept with the right people, yes," said Darryl.

"I like it," said Sather.

"In fact, there are many well-connected vegetables with films in production right now."

"Fruits, too. Har-har-har."

"Please," said Lisa.

"I don't suppose there's any chance we can leave this philosophical debate for another time and talk about *The Razor's Edge*?" said Elaine the Pain. She had missed the last four or five meetings. Mimi had hoped maybe she'd dropped out. "I read this when I was studying at Cambridge. It has held up remarkably well." She pulled her long twig-hair over her shoulder, combed the split ends meditatively with her fingers. She was as pale and disdainful as ever. Although Mimi liked to think she was above wishing this on another woman, she was glad to see that Elaine had put on weight.

Mimi had arrived at the Big House an hour early, hoping to talk to Ralph then. Elaine was already there, sitting at the kitchen table, sipping herb tea and browsing through one of Darryl's weight-lifting magazines, her cute toothpick legs crossed neatly at the knee. She had recently left her job selling car FAX machines to corporate raiders for a job selling home-exercise equipment to corporate raiders. Elaine looked as startled to see Mimi as Mimi was to see her. Ralph was out picking up the beer and potato chips. Mimi, flustered, said she was here to scope out the house; Ralph, Sather, and Darryl had said she could use it for Mouse's wedding shower.

"That's right," said Elaine. "When is the wedding?"

Mimi told her. Elaine enthused about Tony to the point where Mimi thought *they* were having an affair. What was Elaine even *doing* here? Mimi paced through the kitchen to the deck and back, trying to look deep in thought over where to put the buffet table. She cursed herself for not acting as though she had as much right to be here as Elaine.

"It's not going to be a shower shower. I had a shower shower when I got married. A bunch of bimbos oohing and aahing about spatulas was what it was. This is going to be like a pre-wedding party brunch. It will have a theme, though. It'll be kitchen/garden or paper/barbecue. Something." Why was she rattling on? She clamped her arms across her ribs and leaned against the sink.

"I keep forgetting you were married," said Elaine.

"I know, I'm such the single girl. It was a good marriage. Not a long one, but a good one. It didn't dangle on into infinity. When it was over we knew it and got divorced."

"You were married to Ivan Esparza, weren't you? The man making the documentary on Mouse and –?"

" – I told Ralph not to blab! You want the world to know something, tell Ralph Holladay a secret."

"I haven't told a soul. Girl Scout's honor." She held up three long skinny fingers. "Ivan is pretty hot these days, according to Ralph."

"He won an Oscar. For *Total Immersion*. I don't know if you ever saw it. It was about baptism or something. He started it right after we got married – "

" – behind every great man … " said Elaine.

"I did encourage him. I knew he had a lot of talent. Even though we were the poorest people on earth, I said, 'Ivan, do what you have to do.' I like a woman like that, who appreciates a man's ambitions and doesn't rag on him. It must have been a harder situation with Ralph, since he's been at it so long without a break. Ivan won an Oscar, even if it was just documentary. Ralph's still a secretary."

"An assistant," said Elaine, "like you."

"Keddy's pretty hard on him," said Mimi. "At least I don't have to go to my boss's house and wait for the plumber to come fix the toilet."

Elaine shrugged. "I'm like you, I guess. Through thick and thin."

Why are you getting a divorce then? Mimi wanted to ask.

Darryl brought out another bag of chips and ripped them open with his teeth. Sather passed around more beer. Elaine lectured for a few long minutes on the Americanness of Larry's spiritual odyssey and its juxtaposition with Elliott Templeton's snobbishness. She was a bore, but her voice was husky. Mimi thought, all you need are toothpick legs and a husky voice and you have it made. She sucked in her stomach, waiting patiently for Elaine to shut up. She wrapped her ankles around the leg of her chair and accidentally spilled her beer.

She leaped up. "God, I'm sorry."

"You'll ruin our fine carpet," said Darryl. He tossed an old sports page over it. "Don't worry about it."

Mimi went to the kitchen in search of paper towels. There were no paper towels, also no napkins. She blotted it up with a roll of blue toilet paper while Marty and Sather argued about how many film versions there had been of *The Razor's Edge* and whether it was true that a new one was in the works, a musical starring a former Olympic diver.

"They make a movie like that and they won't touch *Girls on Gaza*," said Ralph.

"We want to hear about your new one," said Marty.

"We're still ironing out the kinks."

"Come on, you've been ironing out the kinks for months. You think we're going to rip it off? Or, wait, don't tell me, it's ART," said Darryl.

"Marty might rip it off," said Ralph. Marty had recently left his hair-washing job at the Beverly Hills salon and was now the Director of Development for one of his ex-clients, who had a deal at Fox.

"Ralph, I can almost guarantee that I would never be interested in stealing something you were involved in," said Marty.

"Let's guess," said Sather. "It came from an idea by the skateboard king ... "

" ... how is his poor nose, anyway?" asked Elaine.

"It's only made him cuter," said Carole, through a mouthful of chips.

"Give us a clue," said Darryl.

"No clues. Let's get on with the fucking book."

"It's a thriller set in Nairobi, with lots of tit," said Sather.

"Give me a break, would you? I'll let you all read it when it's done."

"It is a thriller set in Nairobi with lots of ... a sexy African thriller," said Lisa. "Are we warm?"

"I like it," said Sather. "Marty, close your ears."

"Ice," said Ralph. "Not even close."

"We're warm. The main character is the son of a British Foreign Service officer, dashing but offbeat," said Lisa.

"Look, why can't you lay off?" Ralph was red-faced, spitting with frustration. "There are other reasons I don't want to talk about it. Tony, for one, wants it kept under wraps for a while. He's my partner. I am not going to screw my partner. You think this is a big laugh. Ralph has another hopeless and stupid project—"

"—we don't think your projects are hopeless, sweet cheeks," said Mimi.

A thud of silence.

"Sweet cheeks?" said Sather. "*Sweet cheeks?*"

"Whoooooooo!" Darryl clapped his hands and stomped his feet.

Ralph's oval face went slack. He had the numb, dumb look of someone who's just spent six hours at the dentist.

Elaine stared at Mimi with an expression which changed over a few long seconds from confusion to suspicion to realization, then loathing. Finally she smiled, arching one eyebrow. "Sweet cheeks?"

"All Ralph's girls call him sweet cheeks. I mean, in his class." The blood pounded in her face. She scrunched her hair madly.

"It's like a joke. Oh … sweetie pie, honey bunch. Not all of them call him 'sweet cheeks,' some say sweetie pie and honey bunch. It's a joke."

The meeting broke up about a half hour later. While Mimi was in the bathroom discreetly tossing her beer and chips, Ralph took Elaine home. Mimi was too embarrassed to hang out until he returned.

BEFORE IT WAS a restaurant, Thai Melody was a swimming-pool showroom. In the middle of the dining room was a kidney bean-shaped pool, the sidewalls tiled with blue and orange Spanish tiles. In an attempt to disguise it, the owners of Thai Melody had installed a model of a Thai palace, white with gold filigree trim, which stood on a table sunk in the shallow end.

There were pennies at the bottom of the pool. People will throw pennies into any public body of water in the dumb hope it will help make their wish come true, Mimi thought.

Mimi had invited Tony to lunch. Her rationale was that since they were going to be brother and sister-in-law it was time they really talked, instead of just trading one-liners in the hallway as they took turns in the bathroom. Also – she hated to resort to this teenage tactic, but – Ralph might have said something to Tony about the stupid "sweet cheeks" business. Was Ralph really that angry? He couldn't be.

She ordered a Thai coffee, gnawed on an already raw cuticle.

It was eleven-thirty. The restaurant had just opened. The radio was cranked up, tuned to a station that played one tired pop song after another. The suffocating smell of a newly lit stick of incense made even the ice water taste like perfume. Watching the beautiful Thai waitresses in black skirts and white blouses setting tables, Mimi decided that in her next life she wanted to be a small Asian woman.

She stabbed the whipped cream on her Thai coffee with

her straw. She had told Mouse that morning, "I am having a nervous breakdown."

It was keeping all these secrets that had done it. It was against Mimi's nature, keeping a secret. She was open and honest.

She was worried about herself. Solly was out of town and she still felt torqued out. Usually it was the time when she felt the most relaxed, when she almost liked her job, when she felt more like an average overworked, underpaid secretary than an indentured servant. Solly was at a film festival three or four time zones away. Not only was he not in the office, whenever it was convenient for him to call in she wasn't there, either. Really not in the office, as opposed to hiding in the ladies' room.

The downside was he called her at home, at midnight, at seven in the morning, just to check in. He'd called her at one o'clock the night before to see if she would go up to his house in the Palisades and get his CD player to take it in to be repaired. Her heart hurled itself against her chest at the sound of the phone. She wanted it to be Ralph, calling to apologize.

When it wasn't Solly calling at odd hours, it was Ivan. Mimi could not believe that Mouse had not told Ivan that she did not have Tony's consent to do *Wedding March*.

Whenever Ivan called, Mimi was supposed to pretend it was someone else, without letting Ivan know. Mouse expected her to say, "Hey, how are you!" "Great, great!" "No kidding!" before passing the phone off, when Mouse would pretend it was Nita Katz or Shirl, with Tony sitting there watching TV.

This morning Mouse was out with Ivan, filming at Bullock's, where she was registering for china, crystal, and silver. Mouse, who had never entertained a day in her life. The china was English bone, over five hundred dollars a place setting. The stemware was full lead crystal, mouth-blown in Japan by Zen masters. Mouse hadn't even known what stemware was. It wasn't the most expensive stuff in the place, but the most expensive that looked best on-camera. It made Mimi sick. Not that Mouse shouldn't have everything she wanted. It was her wedding, after all.

At about nine-thirty, after Mouse had already left and Mimi was in the shower, Ivan called and left a message on the machine. Ivan always left long messages, never saying who they were for or identifying himself. When she rewound the machine it took forever and she thought, wow, this must be something exciting. Hope rose in her throat. Maybe *this* was Ralph. But no, it was just egomaniacal Ivan, hogging the tape.

"Hell-o-o ... Please pick up if you're there. You've already left. Damn. I need you to stop by Kodak and pick up ten, no, make that twenty, no, ten, ten is fine, rolls of ECN. We wanted the ninety-one, and they sent us VNF. Make sure it's the ninety-one, not the ninety-two. I repeat, do not get the ninety-two, it's too slow. We need the ninety-one. Also, we do need to begin shooting with Tony, so let's set something up soon. We can just talk when I see you."

Hell if Mimi was going to transcribe *that*. She left it, knowing Mouse would beat Tony home, because Tony would be at lunch at Thai Melody with her. All these things she had to worry about. And then this "sweet cheeks" business with Ralph.

Last Wednesday at How to Write a Blockbuster, the night after her slipup at Bibliothèques, Ralph was suddenly colder than a frostbitten corpse. He was Mr. Holladay, Adjunct Instructor, instead of her babyfaced lover inventing excuses to follow her to her car at the break, sneaking a greedy squeeze in a far-flung hallway.

When he did speak to her, it was not as teacher's pet but as teacher's pest. She was not stupid, she recognized the tone of voice. He used it with Poor Peg, the Brillo Pad-permed fifty-plus ex-nun.

Mr. Holladay criticized Mimi's homework. He read it aloud to the class as an example of what not to do. It was the dust-jacket copy for her projected blockbuster on love and betrayal in the business. He called it feeble and trite, in that soft, insult-ingly patient it's-not-too-late-to-consider-beauty-school-you-talentless-nitwit tone of voice. He also said it was over three weeks late. Why hadn't she started writing?

Only the week before, Ralph had said her story was timely and spicy. It featured famous actresses who were secret lesbians, famous shits who were closet nice guys, a team of famous Israeli producers whose training for Hollywood had been the raid on Entebbe, and, of course, the Mob. Now he accused her of pandering to middle America's view of the business.

There was no love and betrayal in the film business, he said. No one ever returned your phone call, how could they love you? Betray you?

Five other people were also writing on the same topic, including Poor Peg. To them he said, "Hollywood is like sugar. People can never get enough, even though it's empty and bad for you. And remember, writing a blockbuster is not about writing, it's about panning for gold."

Mimi's face fried with embarrassment. The tips of her ears felt as though they were blistering under her head of crunchy curls. She thought she had *never* been so humiliated in all her life. She couldn't even remember why she'd signed up for this dumb class.

At the break, Ralph announced officiously that he had to pick up a handout at the Xerox center, then scurried away before anyone could nab him. He was avoiding her, there was no denying it. Mimi bought two cookies from a vending machine and tucked the second one into her purse to eat in the car on the way home. It couldn't be the "sweet cheeks" business. It had really been so harmless. She said "love you" every day to clients of Solly's whom she'd never met. No, it couldn't be that but, she knew, it was. She had humiliated him in front of his friends and his soon-to-be-ex-wife. Cookie crumbs still moist in the corner of her wide mouth, she bought a package of Sugar Babies.

Poor Peg, who'd just lost her last quarters in the coffee machine, sympathized with her.

"I don't think he likes women," said Peg.

"He likes women all right," said Mimi. Despite herself, she loaded the sentence with innuendo, then thought, why not? He deserves it. "He's been after me since the first class. I don't know what this feeble-and-trite business is all about. Maybe because I won't sleep with him. He's married, plus he has that premature ejaculator look about him."

"Fidgety," Peg agreed.

Before returning to class, Mimi vomited in the very ladies' room where, only a few short weeks before, Ralph had boldly followed her for a brief, stolen, makeout session. Hell, she thought, eyes smarting, throat burning, if I'm going to let some stupid man make me fat. She slapped on the Extra Fuchsia and blotted her eyes. She glared at her bleary face in the mirror and tried to make herself think she didn't look so bad for thirty-six. She was thin. She still had long hair. That was more than most thirty-six-year-old women could say for themselves.

While sitting in Thai Melody, waiting for Tony, Mimi tried to muster up the self-confidence she'd felt that night in the ladies'. But it was useless. Her belief in herself was like a petulant, hard-of-hearing servant who rarely heeded her demands. So what if she had long hair? She was going to base her whole sense of self-worth on the length of her hair? She longed for the kind of confidence Mouse possessed, reliable and quiet, like a heartbeat. Having a good man wouldn't hurt, Mimi thought.

The door opened, admitting a rectangle of clean winter glare, then Tony. He gently pulled off his sunglasses with one finger, watching out for his nose. He saw Mimi and saluted, waiting politely until the hostess flew to his side to do her job. She tipped up her elegantly shaped head and dimpled. He snuck a handful of pink and green pillow mints from the glass sundae dish by the cash register, followed her to Mimi's table.

He slid into the booth, smoothed his strawberry-blond hair behind his ears. "Traffic," he said, "sorry." He pursed his freckled lips, rubbed his eyes with the butts of his hands. He was tired from smiling and nodding, the sure sign of someone who's just been released from an interminable meeting.

"How'd it go?" asked Mimi. "Or am I not supposed to ask?"

"Very well, I think. We did the last batch of changes. V.J. adores the project. He apparently had a meeting with one of the vice presidents and they're already thinking of casting ideas."

"Hmm," said Mimi, in a way she hoped was enigmatic. Bored parking attendants with an eight-hour shift to kill entertained themselves tossing around casting ideas. Without taking her eyes from Tony's, Mimi poked her tongue into the end of her straw, fishing for the last bit of whipped cream. "What's Ralph's take on it? Thai coffee's great. Want some of mine?"

"Ralph is not quite so positive. He calls it the joyride to nowhere, all these meetings. But you know, time *is* money. Isn't that the American perspective?"

"It is." Time is also filling up your appointment book so it looks like you're working. You're "developing" projects but not making any decisions over which you could be fired.

"I'll take a beer, thanks." He motioned to the waitress. "V.J. liked what we did, on the whole, but thinks there are ways we can make it even more perfect."

Without going into details, Tony enumerated the sorts of things V.J. was looking for: more plot, but not at the expense of character; more character, but not at the expense of the plot. He wanted more local color, more "sparks" between the main characters, more of an environmental slant. He wanted it cut by ten pages. He wanted all this before he sent it out to the VPs.

It was like listening to someone's medical history. And it was being told, the same story laced with hope and frustration, at a hundred tables, a thousand tables throughout the city at that very moment. Maybe that was the real cause of smog, thought Mimi. The chemical reaction between kitchen grease, ozone, and a jillion sour dreams and ruined hopes.

"Ralph is not so sanguine. This is our fifth meeting with

V. J. and he keeps forgetting the name of the project. I tell Ralph he's a busy chap. It's a mark of all he's got happening."

"How's he doing – Ralph? I've been so busy with Solly out of town and all, trying to catch up. Really trying to get into my writing, too. I told you I'm working on that blockbuster."

"The film business, isn't it? Seems like a good topic."

"It's been done to death, That's why it's perfect for a block-buster. I'm still sort of in the outline phase. Has Ralph … said anything about it lately?"

"No, actually. Sorry – "

" – I just wondered – "

" – say, you've been in this business for some time, let me get your thoughts on this." Tony leaned toward her as though he was including her in some dark secret.

"I've heard it all," she said.

"This is supposed to be a true-life story, which is what V. J. found intriguing in the first place. After all the rewrites it's virtually unrecognizable, but he still insists on calling it a true story, insists on using the names of the real people involved. Ralph says we can cheat it by saying 'freely adapted from a true story,' but it's gone so far afield now … "

Tony had startling eyes, one bluer than the other. Mimi only now realized this. Ocean eyes. Nice smell, too. Cheap shampoo, the kind that always smells better than it works, a tinge of musky sweat.

"What's truth, Tony?" She fluffed her blond bangs with the tips of her fingers, cocked her head. "I mean really. It's just one more high concept."

"That's just fashionable cynicism."

"Wait to argue until after you've gotten paid."

Tony laughed, his head dropping between his shoulders. He took his chopsticks out of their paper envelope, then folded the envelope into a little square. "I was just a bit troubled by the ethics of it. I don't want to queer the project. I'm sure it will all come right in the end, but … "

Ethics? You are so cute, she thought. The waitress glided up with Tony's beer and took their order. Mimi ordered a beer too. She could blow this meal, no problem. The ladies' room was way in the back, far from the dining room and the kitchen.

"I'm not against getting paid," said Tony. "Don't get me wrong. I don't go in for suffering for art. Mouse and I can't impose on you forever. I'd like to set us up somewhere nice before the wedding. Probably sounds a bit corny to you, but I would like to provide a nice place for her. She needs a home base. She may seem happy as a lark living out of a rucksack, sacrificing everything for her work, but … " He looked down, scratched a fleck of dried food off the rim of his plate with his thumbnail. "Well, just this morning she went out to pick out her china pattern. It's bloody touching, isn't it?"

"It just goes to show you," said Mimi.

"She's become interested in the wedding in a way I'd never imagined. It says volumes about her complexity, about her as a woman. Don't you think?"

"*Volumes*. My own *sister*. I can't believe it. It's probably no secret that – not that she didn't want to marry you, she always wanted to marry you – but a wedding is, well she's kind of cheap, I guess that's no surprise either, and practical, plus she's sort of one of those hippie chicks, under the skin. She doesn't know how to have a good time. Not like me, I know how to have a good time. In fact, that's one of my main problems." What did she just say? She had no idea She kept stabbing at the same pulverized mass of glass noodles. "Anyway," she added brightly.

"I like to think her change of heart has to do with my putting my foot down. About that ridiculous thing she had up with your ex-husband. Sometimes she just needs to be said no to. Please don't tell her I said that."

"Don't worry. I am so good at secrets. I have friends, they tell me secrets and then they assume after a while that I've told, but I haven't, so we're sitting in a restaurant and one'll say, she'll go, 'When I had my abortion,' or something, and everyone'll be so shocked, and then she'll, the friend, she'll be shocked, she'll say, 'Mimi, I thought you would have told!' I never tell."

Tony's blondish eyebrows knit together in a polite but nevertheless "what in the hell are you talking about?" way. Mimi thought, It has happened, I'm a babbling schizoid.

He laid his chopsticks beside his plate. "Say, where's the pay phone here? Mouse and I were thinking about taking in a matinee this afternoon."

Mimi nodded toward the door. The pay phone was next to a cigarette machine. She watched Tony stride away, watched him squeeze between a waitress serving bowls of white rice from an immense platter and the edge of the pool. One little bump of the waitress's bum and he'd be swimming. He looked into the pool, did a double take, saw the coins glimmering at the bottom, fished for a penny, tossed it in.

There was no reason to think he'd check the messages. He would get the machine, realize Mouse wasn't home and hang up. Mimi imagined he'd have a fleeting sweet thought of his Mouse caressing linens in some department store for Our New Home, or laying her finger thoughtfully along the cleft in her beloved chin wondering whether to go with stainless steel or silver-plated flatware.

It'd be better if she was just having an affair with Ivan. An affair people understood. An affair you could blame on hormones, on wicked Mother Nature. But no hormones urged you to make a documentary. Not even greed could you blame. Dementia fuels the documentary filmmaker. Look at Ivan, look at Mouse.

Mimi carefully devoured the peanuts from her Kung Pao chicken. If Tony did check the messages, there was no reason to think he would recognize Ivan's voice. And even if he did recognize Ivan's voice … he was leaning against the wall, looking up at the ceiling, curling the black phone cord around his finger.

The answering machine. Mimi's voice, chipper and breathless. "Hi! If you're looking for Mimi, Mouse, or Carole this is the place. We're screening our calls, so don't hang up. If we don't pick up, get a clue. No, not really, someone will get back to you ASAP. Thanks!"

The machine was something Mimi bought one day on an impulse. She thought her old machine was unreliable. This was when she first began with Ralph. She was sure he was calling but the machine wasn't recording. This new machine rang four times if there were no messages. It rang two if there were messages. If you wanted to hear the messages, after the recording and the beep, you punched in a two-digit code – hers was 22 – and the messages played themselves back to you.

From across the room Mimi saw him punch 22, then wait. It occurred to Mimi that while Tony was too well-bred to throw a fit in Thai Melody, he might stomp out, leaving her with the bill. This was a problem. Even though she had invited him, she thought he would pick up the tab.

She slid out of the booth, not sure what she was going to say to him. She reached him just as he slammed the receiver into its cradle.

He stared at the phone, his big hand resting on the receiver, knuckles white under tea-colored freckles. Mimi stared up at his shoulder blades, at the strawberry-blond hair curling over his collar. He picked the receiver up and slammed it down again, then strode out the door.

Mimi followed, wringing her hands. He stood in the middle of the sidewalk, fists on his hips, staring at the lunchtime traffic inching by. He would not look at her. He chewed on his bottom lip. Through clenched teeth he said, "Do tell me what in the bloody fuck is going on."

"I *told* her this was a stupid thing to do. You think she ever listens to me? It's been like this our whole lives! She thinks I don't know anything. I'm just Mimi the airhead. I said it was a dumb idea from the start. She is so, I don't know what you saw in her in the first place, she's *weird*, Tony."

"Just tell me."

"I thought you knew. Ralph knew. I told Ralph, I didn't want to have anything to do with it. I thought he must have told you, you guys are together so much – "

"– she's doing it. With him."

"I know how you feel. Betrayed, right? It's the behind-the-back feature that's so awful. But listen, if you ever see any of the footage, even though I'm in that scene with the lingerie, I did not want to have anything to do with it."

"There's a lingerie scene?" he asked numbly.

"No! I mean there is, but it's tiny. It's not even lingerie. It's shopping. It's like, it's no different than buying light bulbs or something."

"They're fucking, aren't they?"

"Whoa – what? No, no, Tony, Tony, it's just a *movie* – "

"– she is one dead bitch – "

"Tony! It's just a dumb movie! It's not even a movie, it's a *documentary*. Tell her you don't want to do it. You're the *groom*. How can there be a wedding without a *groom*?"

"Exactly," he said through clenched teeth.

20

MOUSE LOOKED FORWARD TO THE STARS AGAINST IVORY fundraiser, to be held Saturday night at the Malibu home of television producer Michael Brass, the friend of Vince Parchman's. She hadn't been to Malibu in twenty years.

She hadn't gone out with Tony in weeks. With the exception of the callow Vince, she expected the people there would be interesting: millionaires with consciences, environmental activists, eccentric Africanists, foreigners, actors. It would be the Los Angeles version of the embassy shindigs they used to crash in Nairobi. The evening was $10,000 a couple, but Michael Brass had invited Tony and Mouse to be his guests because they had "hands-on" knowledge of Africa. This, according to Vince, who had wangled the invitation.

"That's so exciting," Mimi said. "It'll be all those famous Cause-of-the-Minute types. I remember when I went to a fundraiser for, it was either to save spotted owls or Soviet Jews, something, at Milton Grossman's. It was a jillion dollars a plate, but I got to go because Milton was a big client of Solly's. I think he also had a thing for me."

In the past week Mimi had been, if not wonderful, then tolerable. She and Mouse had stayed up talking until one-thirty one night comparing memories of Fitzy. They had gone to the movies. *See*, The Pink Fiend advised Mouse, *she loves you. She only wants the best for you. You are too judgmental. You want everyone to be just like you. When they're not, you blame them.*

Mimi had asked Mouse twice how things were going with Tony. It was very un-Mimi-like, bringing up a subject that was not just the warm-up act for her monologues on her favorite topic, herself. How was Tony behaving now that the wedding was drawing near? she wondered. Had Mouse talked to him about *Wedding March* yet? Mimi really thought she should, before he began to suspect. Did he act as though he suspected? Mimi had had lunch with him and he seemed a little suspicious. Sometimes Mimi worried that he would pick up the phone when Ivan called. No, said Mouse, Tony was fine. Preoccupied, maybe, a tad aloof, maybe, but this she attributed to his screenplay and his broken nose. Mimi and Tony had lunch together? Really? This was the first Mouse had heard of it.

Although Mimi had been to more fundraisers (bigger fundraisers, hipper fundraisers, more exclusive fundraisers), this was still in her opinion a great opportunity for Mouse to meet some important people who might one day want to fund one of her documentaries. "The main thing is, you've got to get yourself a beaded ensemble. Michael Brass is Mr. Mega Bucks. There's a place in West Hollywood where you can rent jillion-dollar dresses by the night. You should check it out."

Mouse took her advice. She went out and picked out a royal-blue strapless silk organza evening dress designed by someone who catered to First Ladies. She also rented black lace stockings and black velvet high heels. The heels were a little big, but otherwise everything was perfect. She picked out the entire outfit herself. It came with a little black embroidered clutch and a necklace of cubic zirconia. Mouse was very proud of herself.

In the car, on the way to Malibu, she had a moment where she felt a little like they were bound for the prom. It was the fullness of the dress, the way it swished when she walked. "I feel like I should have a wrist corsage," she said.

Tony was silent. He drove with his elbow on the window ledge, his cheek propped on the butt of his hand. He'd sprung for a black, double-breasted suit, which he wore with a black shirt and his lizard-skin cowboy boots.

"You look like a cowboy gangster."

"Meaning what, exactly?"

"Meaning that's what you look like. The boots and all."

Tony tossed a glance over his shoulder, sped across three lanes, exiting at an off-ramp in Santa Monica.

"Is this some new shortcut to Malibu?" asked Mouse.

"We're picking up Ralph."

"Ralph?"

"I'm sure I told you." He was sure he hadn't. She could be secretive, so could he. He refused to be humiliated this time. All that *sturm and drang* in Nairobi. It must have been the Uncle Nigel factor or some tropical virus that set him off. Inspecting her panties, reading her diary, begging and threatening. God! He cringed just thinking about it. What a dumb sod. He dug into himself and pulled out the infamous British reserve. Mouse would not soon realize how furious he was.

Ralph did not live in Santa Monica. Mouse was confused. They stopped in front of a pink stucco apartment building with the lanai arms scrawled up the side in gold relief. Tony double-parked, unfolded himself from the driver's seat and, taking the steps two at a time, disappeared behind the black wrought-iron security gate. Mouse tipped her hips off the seat, reaching under her armpits to pull up the top of her dress. She had not noticed it in the store, but the bust was a little large and kept slipping down to reveal no small amount of cleavage and the lacy trim of her black strapless bra. She wondered, suddenly, how she would get through the evening, with Tony in the worst of his latest foul moods and a dress conspiring with gravity to embarrass her.

"Mouse, hello!" A rap on the window. A woman with waist-length ash-brown hair whom she didn't immediately recognize. The door to the backseat sprung open. The woman slid in. "I'm

Elaine, we met at Bibliothèques the night you arrived." She stuck her narrow white hand over the headrest. "Great dress."

"Right," said Mouse, doubt plain in her voice.

"Ralph's wife," said Elaine.

"Right, right," said Mouse. She rolled her lips inside her mouth. She'd obviously missed something very major. She thought Elaine was Ralph's ex-wife. She had thought Ralph was Mimi's boyfriend.

As they drove up the coast, Ralph told them about Michael Brass. He was meat and potatoes, said Ralph. This was the conventional wisdom. He was unpretentious and honest. His *yes* meant yes, his *no* meant no and his *let's have lunch* meant let's have lunch. To everyone's knowledge, he had never said let's *do* lunch in his entire upstanding life. He was considered a True Original, even though his TV shows would insult the intelligence of a ferret. He was also the richest man this side of the Rockies.

Brake lights winked on, cars slowed. The right lane was closed for several miles due to a mud slide. The line of traffic filed past a half-circle of blinding pink flares sizzling on the asphalt, illuminating a mound of earth as high as a house. The slide had apparently come unglued from the bluff during a recent rain. Mouse, nose to the window, craned her neck to see the matching house-sized craters in the side of the bluff but saw only a blank, apparently intact, *café au lait*-colored wall rising up from the road. Where had the mud come from? Did Mimi know Mouse and Tony were double-dating with Ralph and his ex-wife, who was now introducing herself as his wife? She must, thought Mouse, just as she thought there must be a vast crater up there she just couldn't see.

The dress was a mistake. Mouse saw that the instant Michael Brass opened the door. The house was on the beach, a low, rambling, wood-shingled house indigenous not to California but Massachusetts. Michael Brass was as plain as his house, narrow-shouldered and drained. He was balding and sported a wispy vandyke. He was V.I. Lenin gone Maine woodsman, in a red Ragg sweater, chinos, and a pair of calf-high rubber hunting shoes.

"Come in," he said.

Mouse blushed from the tops of her too-exposed light-brown breasts to the tips of her too-arranged dark-brown hair. She held her forearms to her sides and tried to schooch up her dress, a dumb, reflexive attempt to help her look as though she was not outfitted for the Miss America evening-gown competition.

She was desperate to trade a humiliated glance with Tony, but he had nothing to be humiliated about. He could get away with it. He was a gorgeous English cowboy-gangster. Ralph wore a dark sports coat and tie, both of which could be removed. Elaine wore a plain black chemise and black flats, fit for any occasion. Mouse stumbled over the threshold in her too-big black velvet pumps. She looked like an idiot.

"How *sweet*! Throwbacks to the Reagan era! Come in, come in. I'm Tooty Brass." Inches taller and years younger than her husband, Tooty was an outdoorsy blond with a friendly overbite. She wore a light-blue corduroy shirt-dress and penny loafers.

"I'm Ralph Holladay and this is " began Ralph.

"–we're so glad you could come! If you'll come this way someone will get you some Perrier. We have alcohol, too, if you like. I'm having this catered. I usually don't believe in catering, but I felt this time. It's such a critical issue. The ivory. We're against furs, too. You don't have any furs, do you?" she asked Mouse.

"No," cried Mouse. "This isn't even my *dress*."

"Lucky you," said Tooty, hooking one hand through Tony's arm, the other through Mouse's. Mouse felt a tear of perspiration rolling down the inside of her arm. She held her breath, sure she was dripping all over the cuff of Tooty's salt-of-the-earth shirt-dress.

The house was huge, rooms folding out into rooms, but simple to the point of homeliness, with battered, tilting white pine floors and yellowing walls that cried out for a coat of paint.

The decor ran to beatup wicker and wooden furniture, blue and white knotted throw rugs, framed eighteenth-century pen-and-ink drawings of whales and shells. A ratty Amish quilt was tossed over the back of an overstuffed sofa. Both priceless antiques, Mouse imagined.

"Nice place," she whispered to Elaine, still unsure whether she was consorting with the enemy.

"Little too ostentatiously mismatched for my taste," said Elaine.

There were a hundred people there, maybe more. The house was overheated. A fire crackled in the huge fireplace. Long tables of food stretched discreetly along the walls, one featuring every known variety of caviar, heaped into earthenware pots.

Mouse was relieved to see that a few other women were hideously overdressed. Most seemed to be the wives of wealthy scions of undoubtedly ill-gotten Third World fortunes, heavy-lidded women with lurid red lips whose gaudy jewelry was out of place here at Hyannis Port West but who couldn't care less. They chattered among themselves in their native tongues.

Those in the know had dressed down. Mouse had no idea there were so many varieties of flannel shirts available in California. Flannel shirts, chinos, moccasins. Hollywood Goes to New England. They murmured about the usual things – money, deals, day care – in tight clusters. They were sanguine, self-congratulatory. Their well-kept faces shone with piety. They were rich. They were saving the world. They wore natural fibers. They swilled Perrier. They knew enough to stash their showy evening wear when partying with the eccentric Mr. and Mrs. Brass.

There were, however, a few touching bits of L.A. flash: a girl Mouse recognized as an up-and-coming rock singer wore a black-suede fringed jacket, a diamond swinging at the end of each piece of fringe. She looked almost as uncomfortable as Mouse.

Mouse turned to point her out to Tony but was rendered speechless by the sight of a grinning pockfaced man approaching them, arms extended, dressed like a citified Kenyan in *longhi* skirt, white cotton shirt, embroidered skullcap, and brown plastic sandals. This man was white, and called Tony and Mouse by their first names.

"*Jambo! Karibu!*" he crowed.

"Is that –" whispered Mouse into Tony's shoulder.

"V. J., old sport, good to see you," said Tony, clapping him on the arm.

"V. J.," said Ralph. They shook hands as though they hadn't seen each other in a decade. Ralph introduced Elaine.

"Vince?" said Mouse.

"Va-va-va-voom. You're sure a different kettle of fish from the scrawny girl I knew in Nairobe." He planted a wine-sodden kiss on her cheek. "It's terrific you could make it. There are people you need to meet."

They were dragged from stockbrokers discussing the pitfalls of investing in movies beneath an array of copper pots in the kitchen to a congregation of Tanzanians in Kaunda suits, the light-colored, collarless, short-sleeved suits favored by Heads of State, warming themselves in front of the massive fireplace. Mouse felt like a popular car being touted by an overzealous salesman.

"Meet Tony Cheatham, an old mate from Nairobi. His wife, Mouse. We lived together in Nairobe. I was over there doing the Peace Corps thing."

"Meet Tony and Mouse, old pals from Nairobe. We were tight with the elephants."

"This is Tony Cheatham from Nairobe, old pal of mine. This man knows elephants; he saw the atrocities firsthand."

"Tony and Mouse Cheatham, from Nairobe. These two were there for the elephants. They worked with the Kenyan Wildlife Department. Mouse, you made a doc on the situation, didn't you?"

Ralph and Elaine, who had never been to Nairobe, were ignored. They stood silently beside Tony and Mouse, grins pinned between their cheeks. Mouse stood with her arms clamped to her sides, more concerned with keeping her dress up than with the bald lies issuing from the sociopathic mouth of V.J. Parchman. She loathed him then, she loathed him now. It wasn't worth the effort to point out that she and Tony were not yet married, nor were they "old friends" of his, nor were they tight with the elephants, nor did they witness any atrocities. She looked down. A gap yawned between her dress and her bra. She could see her shoes.

"'If the elephant vanished, the loss to human laughter, wonder, and tenderness would be a calamity,'" said Tony.

"Brilliant," breathed a young woman with no pores and teeth as white as the bone china Mouse had just registered for at Bullock's. She was the daughter of a studio head, chattering with a gang of heirs and heiresses to corporate millions, all in their early twenties.

"V.S. Pritchett," said Tony. "Wish I could take credit for it."

"Do," said the woman. "No one's ever heard of V.J. Parchman anyway."

V.J. looked stricken.

Mouse laughed. Tony glared down at her. That was really not on, humiliating V.J., who was their bloody ticket to success, or at least off the lumpy futon on her sister's dining room floor. And the way she watched him, her lip all but curling in distaste. He did wish V.J. would stop introducing them as husband and wife, at least in front of Mouse. He loosened his tie. Seeing that Mouse's wineglass was empty, he drained his and thrust it at her. "Dear poppet, see if you can drum us up another glass, would you?"

"Love to." She took his glass. Any excuse to get away. When she was just out of view, she set them down on a pitted-oak side table. On the table was a large arrangement of fresh flowers, flanked by a collection of weather-beaten duck decoys and a handwoven basket in which snuggled half a dozen remote-control units. Mouse picked one up. On the back, written on white paper tape, it said, Jacuzzi/Pool. The other remotes were similarly marked: TV, Children's TV, Stereo, Children's Stereo, Children's Jacuzzi, Tennis Court.

There was a commotion at the front door. Mouse turned around. Through craning necks she saw what appeared to be a gang of Africans in full tribal regalia. With them she glimpsed a television actor famous for both his looks and astounding lack of talent, and through a chink in the crowd, the lens of a 16mm camera, much like the one being used to shoot *Wedding March*. Someone was filming the arrival of the African delegation.

That someone should be her! The simple sight of that lens was a life vest thrown to a girl who only now realized she was overboard. She hauled up her dress, stepped out of her impossibly high heels. She became The Mouse, working her way across the room under arms held high in a toast, through intimate conversations, over footstools and baskets and Godawful pieces of priceless folk art. *'Scuse me, 'scuse me, 'scuse me.* She knew it wasn't the News; the News had gone to video. Maybe they needed a grip, a gaffer, a production assistant. *'Scuse me, 'scuse me.* She imagined herself holding the boom, moving the lights, fetching coffee, anything but staying glued to Tony's surly side, smiling and nodding, nodding and smiling.

Michael Brass, wedged between the Africans and the actor, was being interviewed, the mike hanging above his head from the end of the boom. He explained in patient tones the necessity for a global coalition to ban the import of ivory. He stressed the importance of the cooperation of government visionaries such as our friends here from Gabon. He advocated confiscation of illegal ivory and harsh prison terms for poachers.

The camera chirred. The spools of tape on the Nagra turned. Mouse was mesmerized. She wanted nothing more than to get in on the act. She could offer to run to the bathroom for a towel to blot the shine from the bridge of Michael Brass's pallid nose. He finished his statement. The Africans reiterated what he had just said in clipped, elegant English. The actor reiterated what the Africans said in ungrammatical English studded with ums, ers, ahs, you knows. Michael Brass drew his forefinger across his neck. Cut.

The sound man snapped off the Nagra, pulled in the boom. His back was to Mouse. He was short, a dirty blond, skin the color of caramel. Black T-shirt, faded jeans, tennis shoes. He looked approachable. He had about him that familiar tilting-at-windmills-documentary-filmmaker air.

Mouse scooted around a couple trading notes on which hot producer was behind saving the whales, which studio head was into protecting the rain forest. In the split second between Mouse opening her mouth and speaking, the sound man turned around. "Just the person I wanted to see," said Ivan, not a jot of surprise in his agate eyes.

"What are you doing here?" Mouse was sure he could hear the blood rocketing through her veins. She laughed somewhat hysterically.

"What does it look like?" He slipped an arm around her, rubbed her bare back with his warm, dry palm. She hated this proprietary air of his, also that she liked the feel of his hands on her. She frantically scanned the room for Tony, sure he was lurking about behind the Cape Cod equivalent of a potted palm, steam spewing from his ears, eyes spinning in fury.

"Good news. A network news magazine, *L.A. Today*, is interested in profiling us. We represent the new breed of independent documentary filmmakers. They want to come on the set of *Wedding March*."

"Great." Just get me out of here, she thought. She dropped her shoes on the floor, fed her feet in awkwardly. Ivan held her elbow to prevent her from losing her balance. She pulled away, falling off her heel.

"I would like to have them at the wedding shower."

"Fine, fine. Excuse me, will you excuse me? I've got to – the ladies' room – "

"I can tell them the shower is all right. You don't need to check with Tony?"

"It's fine! I said it was fine, didn't I?"

"See you in the morning, then. Ten o'clock." The next day Mouse was being fitted for her wedding dress. "Wear something dark, something to represent the empty, searching, and ultimately existential state of the single adult in our society."

"That's a lot to expect from a turtleneck," said Mouse.

He enlisted his flawless teeth in an appreciative smile. "You are funny. Also, beautiful."

At that moment, Tooty Brass scurried up with a plateful of artfully arranged delicacies from the buffet. "Ivan, I thought, well, in case you're hungry." She addressed the plate nervously. "I thought, some caviar, I know how you like the red, then here's some of that pâté. Do you like pâté? You do like pâté?

"Tooty, have you met Mouse FitzHenry?"

"Oh!" Tooty's head snapped up. Her overbite adjusted itself into the requisite warm and welcoming smile. She smoothed her blond bob, nervous as a rattler crossing a firing range in broad daylight. "Of course, Arnold's wife!"

"Tony's wife, or soon to be. Mouse and I have known each other since college," said Ivan. "We are making a film together."

"Of course!" said Tooty. "How wonderful!"

"Excuse me," said Mouse. She stumbled off in search of a bathroom. She attributed Tooty's weird jitters to the normal pressure of being a hostess, coupled with feeding the crew of a documentary. Rooms unfolded into rooms. Guest rooms with brass beds painted white to protect them from the sea air. A study lined with first editions, Winslow Homer watercolors cheaply framed, hung at nonchalant angles. Two rail-thin women with swingy shoulder-length blond hair leaned against a wall in a small hallway, their arms folded across their nubby hand-knit crewneck sweaters.

"Is this the bathroom line?" Mouse asked.

Their glances flickered over her. One of them nodded curtly.

" – this is actually three beach houses connected. They had

three neighboring houses on the Cape dismantled and shipped across country, board by board."

"I love it," said the other woman.

"The walls were painted thirteen times, then wall-papered, then they scraped it off. There's something *je ne sais quoi* about a wall that's had wallpaper scraped off. Gives it such a real feel. And the floors, have you noticed they're not even? They had them ripped up and relaid off kilter. Tooty didn't like them flat. That was too California, she said, flat and perfect. Not dilapidated enough."

"Michael and Tooty are so courageous," the other woman said, shaking her head in wonder. "So ... authentic."

"Someone said when they finished the remodeling, Michael and Tooty were in France for a few months so they flew her parents out from Boston just to hang out, give it that lived-in feel. Her mother baked and her father smoked his pipe in front of the fire. I don't think they slept here, though. Tooty didn't want it that lived-in. Leaving that old-people smell on everything."

"The mildew is a nice touch, though."

"I love the mildew."

"Excuse me," Mouse said, "are you sure there's someone in there?"

"I hope not," said the same woman, who nodded. "It's a closet. Then to her friend, "All the closets are lined with a special kind of cedar planking you can only find in Shaker farmhouses."

Meantime, V.J. and Tony had moved on to hard liquor. Ralph and Elaine drifted off to talk to a producer friend of Ralph's who claimed he knew someone who might be interested in *Girls on Gaza*.

V.J. introduced Tony to several wonderful girls. Even though they were the small, big-breasted variety Tony liked, they beamed up at him idiotically, their pretty eyes less intelligent than those of that smelly dog of Mimi's, rendering them utterly undesirable. In a far corner of his mind Tony was beginning to wonder what the devil happened to Mouse, although he was relieved he didn't have to worry about her embarrassing him in front of V. J. She had undoubtedly found some Ghanian national to chat up, or perhaps a coven of brides-to-be with whom to compare wedding notes. He smiled to himself. Enjoy your exalted prenuptial status while you can, my dear.

One of the bartenders, a fellow Brit, had slipped Tony a bottle of scotch, which Tony had adroitly hidden on a window ledge behind an antique weather vane in the shape of a schooner.

He had seen that business with Ivan. The dumb girl kept forgetting how tall he was. He had seen her, standing there coyly, those black-velvet fuck-me pumps dangling from her hand, Ivan's paws all over her, whispering in her ear. Perhaps they'd just come from a frolic on the beach, a tryst under the deck, a romp among the elephants. He threw down a slug of scotch. He was a morose, irritable drunk, and because he was, he punished himself by getting drunker, thereby more morose, more irritable.

Besides the upcoming auction and African dance demonstration, the elephants were the main attraction of the fundraiser. There were two of them, male and female, kept in a large pen on the beach. Michael Brass had purchased them from Zimbabwe, and after tonight was donating them to the San Diego Zoo. Two Latino zookeepers in safari suits kept watch over them in the moonlight. Michael Brass encouraged everyone to go out and stroke their tusks. Tony imagined Mouse had been out there stroking Ivan's tusk! A pang of self-pity and desire shot through his long bones. She didn't know how lucky she was to have him! He was tall, he was smart, he was *English*. Well, he would find himself someone willing, someone appreciative. But willing, appreciative girls bored him. Mouse was the one who interested him. He sighed, drained his glass again. He was doomed to be a cuckold. He refilled V. J.'s glass.

"Nobody drinks anymore, you notice?" said V. J. "We do because we're Kenyans. I'm a Kenyan in spirit. Do I look like a Kenyan to you? In spirit? I got this in Nairobe." He fingered the fabric of his *longhi*. "Best days of my life. People there don't worry about, for example, frequent-flyer programs. I fly all over the goddamn country, they never record it, so I have to go and rustle up the goddamn ticket and copy it and send it to some mysterious fucking PO box and then it takes them nine months to credit my account, you know what I mean?" Under the influence of the scotch, V.J. had lost his Kenyan accent.

"Hmm," said Tony.

"It's modern life. I'm not saying people should be hungry, you know I'm not saying that. But hunger is a real thing. You're worried you're not going to have enough food. It makes sense. But we have food, so all that energy gets spent worrying about not having our frequent-flyer account credited."

"Hmm," said Tony.

"The richest man and the poorest man has the same amount of worry in him. This is what I learned, from Africa and from Hollywood. The richest man, the poorest man, same amount of worry. But the rich man, his worry goes for useless, stupid things. Food is a thing, shelter is a thing, disease is a thing, clothing is a thing. Frequent-flyer programs are not a thing. It makes your soul feel like a used condom tossed out a car window, worrying about your frequent-flyer program. But what am I supposed to do, not worry? Lose all those miles?" V.J. pulled off his skullcap and mopped his forehead miserably. "Don't get me wrong. I love Hollywood."

"Speaking of which," said Tony, "I've taken the liberty of dropping the wedding scene. The Tony character and the Mouse character *don't* get married in the end."

"The wedding scene?"

"In the script."

"Great. Whatever."

Tony got the distinct impression that V.J. wasn't sure what he was talking about. He rubbed his upper lip nervously. "Thought you were sort of partial to that scene. Happy ending, all that."

"You and Ralph are the *artists*, old boy. I'm just the facilitator. You want to put in a wedding scene –"

"– I've taken it out. The one we've had from the first draft. Actually, it was never true anyway. Took a bit of poetic license. It's the only part of the whole story that was fabricated, I assure you. Mouse and I, we're actually not even married. In the new ending he finds out she's been cheating on him and leaves Africa altogether."

"Terrif. Look, here's someone from the documentary." V.J. looked past him, his philosophical ramblings a part of the distant past.

"I'll have the new draft on your desk Monday, if that's all right."

"Maybe they'll want to do an interview, two mates from Nairobe."

Tony turned to see Ivan Esparza making his way toward them through the crowd. He slid the bottle back behind the weather vane, slouched against the wall.

"Tony, good to see you, man."

Tony ignored Ivan's outstretched hand. "Ivan Esparza, V.J. Parchman."

"Where are you from?" asked Ivan, staring at V.J.'s hairy bowlegs as they shook hands.

V.J. laughed bitterly. "Pasadena."

"We're old friends from Nairobi, V.J. and I. He's producing a script of mine, provided we get a go from the studio."

"They say it's a fantastic place."

"The studio? We like it."

"Nairobi. Mouse loved it there."

"Ah. Mouse."

"How is your nose? I hope she has talked to you about shooting your sequences."

Shooting his sequences, indeed! Tony would like nothing better than to take out a row of this jerk's teeth, but the thought of it made his nose throb. Besides, the New Tony was above that sort of behavior.

"How's it going? Shooting with Mouse?"

Ivan stared at him, hands on his hips. "I was married to her sister, you know."

"Busy little bastard, aren't you?"

"I knew we should have talked about this before."

"Really. Before what?"

"I cannot get into this now," said Ivan. "They're ready to start the auction. V.J., my pleasure. One day perhaps you'll tell me more about your experiences in Africa."

"Hey, all right."

Ivan joined the cameraman at the front of the room. Michael Brass stood wringing his hands apologetically in front of a table set up by the fireplace. On display were ebony carvings, Maasai beaded jewelry and weapons, wooden masks, baskets, Someone had dragged in an ancient podium and thrust a gavel into the hand of the talentless but handsome actor who was privileged to play auctioneer.

"Tooty and I are thrilled you all could make it. We would especially like to welcome our friends from Tanzania, Gabon, Taiwan, and Zimbabwe. We thank you not on our own behalf, but on behalf of the elephants. In the last ten years more than four hundred thousand elephants have been slaughtered, most of them with the use of automatic weapons ... " Michael Brass rolled out the horrific statistics.

Tony had heard them many times before. Where was Mouse, anyway? He looked around the room at all the smooth upturned faces.

Michael Brass explained that the idea of the auction was to encourage native handicrafts in the hopes of discouraging the trade in ivory. It was a heroic, misguided notion. No three-dollar basket was going to compete with the millions of dollars Hong Kong businessmen forked over for a few tons of ivory every year. Tony pulled the bottle of scotch from behind the weather vane, topped off his glass.

" … the poacher is typically an illiterate villager living in poverty. He sells a tusk for forty dollars, which a businessman in Japan will turn around and sell for one thousand … "

After he gave Mouse the boot, would she take up with Ivan? Tony swallowed a belch. She'd be sorry when he was a top screenwriter, pulling down a few million a script. Poor elephants. They really didn't have a chance.

He felt someone's eyes on him. A few feet away, a woman admired him. She was in her fifties. About thirty years ago someone had told her she looked like Brigitte Bardot and she'd never forgotten it. She wore white stretch pants tucked into white boots, a white hand-knit curve-clinging sweater. She had big rings, teeth, and breasts, little eyes, legs, and tact. Tony toasted her with the bottle of scotch.

"Noni Bertlestein," whispered V.J. "Minimall magnate."

"Worth millions, no doubt."

"Maybe she's interested in putting money into a movie."

Tony waggled his eyebrows at her. Noni Bertlestein pursed her wrinkled, heavily lipsticked lips.

"And so," said Michael Brass, "with only a bit more ado – please bear with me – I'd like to introduce someone here tonight who's worked on the front lines, as a member of one of the Kenyan Wildlife Federation's anti-poaching patrols. Rumor is, he captured quite a few single-handedly. Tony Cheatham, are you here?"

Tony dropped his eyelids, affecting what he supposed was a languid sexy gaze. He stared at Noni Bertlestein's magnificent breasts. Why not? She had them out there like a crook selling watches on a street corner. Being a nice chap got you nowhere. He reluctantly let his gaze catch hers. She cocked her head, bit her lips.

"Tony Cheatham?" said Michael Brass.

"Tony," hissed V.J.

He took a swig from the bottle. Fuck the glass. The thing you always had to remember about women was that they were like those people who said, "Don't get me anything for Christmas," then were upset when you didn't. Women didn't want respect. They said they did. In fact, they were perfectly happy if you just ogled their –

"TONY! The man wants you!" V.J. elbowed him, panic-stricken.

Noni Bertlestein is a man? What? Suddenly V.J. plucked the bottle from his fingers, pushed him up to the front of the room. A round of polite applause. What the – had he bid for something and didn't know it? No, the auction hadn't started yet. Walking confirmed his worst suspicions. He was dead drunk. He could not tell his feet from his shoes. The sides of his head felt as though they were curling toward each other. Michael Brass put an arm around him. "So, please tell us."

"Yes, Michael, certainly." He cleared his throat. The scotch rolled back up his esophagus. Would he vomit on Tooty Brass's antique hook rug? Dear Lord. "What is it you wish to know."

"Well." Michael laughed. "Anything you think is relevant."

"Relevant. Oh dear. Bit dodgy, that. Relevant." Tony wondered if perhaps he was supposed to be answering questions about the items up for auction. He picked up a carving. "This is an elephant." Obviously. "An elephant carved … carved by Africans."

"How many are out there, Mr. Cheatham, at this very minute, would you say?" asked Tooty, her brow furrowed with concern.

"Thousands, I should say. Hundreds of thousands."

"They must be *everywhere*," cried a woman with a foreign accent.

"Yes. We had a half dozen or so in Nairobi. You can pick them up anywhere."

"You had them in your *home?* Shouldn't they be locked up or something?"

"Oh no, I shouldn't think so."

"You believe in death, then," said Michael.

"I'd say the evidence is quite conclusive." Tony laughed. That was a good one.

Mouse, who had been loitering on the fringes of the party, went outside for a smoke. Tony drunk was not one of the world's more appealing sights. A member of the Kenyan Wildlife Federation anti-poaching patrol? What had he been telling people? And why? What was apparent was that he had been trying to hoodwink some Hollywood person into thinking he was more than just a humble documentary filmmaker. Mouse was surprised to find she was intrigued, not angry. It was so un-Tony-like.

A flight of rickety steps led from the deck down to the beach. The moon hung in mid-sky, casting a column of light on the ocean. At the bottom of the steps Mouse reached under her dress and pulled off her black lace stockings, burying them in the cold sand with her toes. The elephants were enclosed in a pen, built especially for the occasion, under the watchful eye of the San Diego Zoo. Steel poles had been sunk into the beach about four inches apart, around which ran a chain-link fence, five feet high.

The elephants lumbered around in circles, desultorily flipping their skinny tails. The sand *cush-cush-cushed* beneath their huge feet. A rent-a-cop stood by the shoreline, legs spread, staring up at the moon.

Mouse wondered if the elephants felt as out of place as they looked. Not many had ever seen the ocean, she imagined. *Cush-cush-cush*, around and around they went, a couple of fat, arthritic old ladies, their hides as furrowed as parched desert beds. Their tusks cast sharp shadows on the sand.

The zookeepers listened to a Spanish radio station on a transistor radio slung over the fence. Mouse nodded hello, put her face against the steel poles. When one of the elephants unceremoniously dropped a few loaves of elephant waste, a zookeeper cleaned it up with a shovel.

Mouse remembered once, she and Tony were driving up near Ngorongoro Crater, barreling around a hairpin mountain curve in the Land Rover. They came upon an elephant and her calf standing by the side of the road, waving their ears, their trunks entwined. Jaded expatriates though they were, scoffing at anything remotely safari-related, they leaped from the Rover, cameras cocked. Before they could shoot, a man jumped from the bush, yelling "Photo op! Photo op!" and demanding a shilling a shot. These were his elephants, trained, apparently, to stand by the side of the road cutely waving their ears, trunks entwined. The man was a toothless Karamojong in Western dress with a lip plug made from a 35mm film canister and a command of American English. For ten shillings apiece, they could ride the mother for five minutes. Her name was Madonna.

The zookeepers hummed along with the radio. It was feeding time. They tossed forkfuls of grass through a special slot in the fence. The elephants fed each other, twisting their trunks around a skein of reedy grass, placing it in the other's pink mouth. Their tangy wild scent was tempered by the smell of the ocean, and one of the zookeeper's overpowering aftershave. Even so, it made her homesick for Africa.

"Trying to lose me, are you!" Tony cried behind her.

She turned to see him standing behind her, straight as a general, clenching and unclenching his fists.

"What were you telling them in there?"

"I'm afraid I can't marry you!"

The zookeepers looked up briefly from their pitchforks and sniggered.

"What's wrong with you? Let's go sit down."

"I don't love you anymore."

"Can we please sit down?"

"Are you deaf, old girl! The wedding is off!" There was the vague possibility he was shouting. He couldn't quite tell. No matter. All that mattered was The Look. Like an expectant child anticipating a brief solar eclipse, he stared at Mouse's beloved face and waited. The look of heartbreak. The look of utter devastation. Of dull-eyed, slack-jawed, ashen-faced anguish. The look that said, "You have ruined my life! I trusted you and you shat on me!" At this moment, under the beady gaze of four suspicious elephant eyes, two dutiful zookeepers, and the baleful California moon, he wanted to make her pay, to wreck her, to send her creeping back to that smarmy Ivan with news that the wedding was off. The wedding was off! The movie was off! Her life was ruined! Then he would forgive her. If she behaved herself he might marry her.

He peered closer. She had the same exasperated look on her face as she did when Air Zaire had lost their luggage.

"I don't understand –"

"–you don't understand that I've had a bloody change of heart."

"When did you decide all this? Was it in there, making eyes with that, that woman?"

"Noni Bertlestein is not a *woman*. She's a minimall magnate."

"I think we should discuss this later."

"It's quite simple. It's over." He was shaking. Between her and Ivan! "I cannot discuss this now." "I think we should discuss this later." It was a well-known but little-documented fact that language patterns were transmitted like venereal diseases. Proof, as though any was needed, they were having an affair. Shooting a movie about his own bloody wedding behind his back and having an affair. No. No, no no, no no. He promised himself he would not get into *that*.

"Fine, it's over. Can we discuss it tomorrow?"

"You don't seem to hear me!"

"They can hear you in fucking Nevada." She wasn't wrecked, she was disgusted and angry. She picked up her shoes and marched toward the house.

"Your swearing. One reason I've become disenchanted."

She said nothing. He struggled behind her; his cowboy boots in the loose sand made catching up impossible.

"You lack spontaneity. One thing you can say for Noni Bertlestein, she is spontaneous."

Mouse said nothing. Was she *ignoring* him?

"I'm moving out," he shouted after her. He stared at her brown, lightly freckled back, her strong stalk of a neck, her dark curls. God, he loved her!

"With Sather and Darryl! They've said I could move in tomorrow!"

She was ignoring him. At the bottom of the steps leading up to the house, she stopped to wipe the sand off the bottoms of her feet. He caught up with her, winded and panting.

"They've said since Ralph is moving back with Elaine. I'll move first thing in the morning."

Mouse stopped. She stared at the crinkled sole of her foot crooked up on her knee. "Ralph is moving back in with Elaine?"

"She's preggers," he said, exasperated.

A look, not *the* look, but a look akin to the one Tony had hoped for passed over Mouse's face. "Does Mimi know?"

21

THIS IS WHAT YOU GET. YOU IGNORED TONY'S SCREEN-writing. You made no secret of the fact you don't like his friends. You are not here when he comes home. You don't like to cook. You have secrets. No wonder. A man wants a helpmate, not an equal. Pretend you are an equal so he is made to feel modern, intelligent, and tolerant, but never forget that what he really wants is a maid/concubine/therapist. You are a liar. You have your own mind. You are retarded in the most basic ways of femininity. No man as good as Tony wants someone like that. In Nairobi, where the pickings were slim, he tolerated you. Now he has his choice. He has blond, fanny tucked minimall magnates willing to give him everything. No wonder.

Mouse grabbed handfuls of just-washed hair and pulled. A futile attempt to strangle The Pink Fiend, who excelled in kicking her when she was down. When she was down, she believed everything The Pink Fiend said. It was the morning after the fundraiser, Saturday. She was going through all her wedding things, stored in Mimi's closet. Her bridal lingerie, the leftover invitations, the files full of brochures on Caribbean honeymoons.

Tony had snuck out while she was in the bathroom. She had been brushing her teeth. She heard the zip of his suitcase and the front door slam. Her hands shook so much the thick worm of blue gel fell off her brush and whirled down the drain.

Mouse rustled the ecru body brief with open cotton panel from its bed of tissue paper. It bore the flowery odor of Sins. She wiped her tears on the lace trim. She tried to get a grip on herself.

This didn't mean there couldn't be a wedding. This didn't mean pulling the plug on *Wedding March*. She had been faced with more difficult production problems than this. There were ways to get around anything. Look at the business with *Marriage Under Mobutu*. The bride had backed out, and they had gotten around it. Hardship was her specialty, wasn't it?

Maybe Ivan would agree to doing the film solely from the bride's point of view; it could become the story of an engagement in trouble. Now that they were no longer actually getting married, Tony might agree to play the part of the groom. They could always say after the film was finished that the stress of making the movie had caused their separation, which would make for a good bit of publicity. It could work! She must tell Tony! She refolded the tissue paper around the body brief and slid it back into the bag. But then she realized she couldn't tell Tony. He was no longer her partner – in anything.

Mimi was still in bed, the sheets pulled up to her eyebrows, trying to recapture the oblivion of sleep. When she was depressed her capacity for sleep rivaled that of a teenage boy. Her shoulders hurt from being in bed so long. She thought the scrabbling in the closet was Sniffy Voyeur searching for forgotten candy. Outside she could hear the Armenians beating their rugs on top of the carport, where they had strung a clothesline. *Thwap-thwap-thwap.* She cracked her eyelids to find Mouse staring down at her, the picture of dread.

"Are you awake?"

She stood at the foot of Mimi's bed, fully dressed, fresh from the shower. Her damp dark hair curled around her cleft chin. Circles hung beneath her light eyes.

"What?"

"We've got to talk," Mouse croaked.

"I'm too depressed."

"Please?"

"Hand me my robe."

Mimi got depressed when she gave in to introspection,

which, she was convinced, caused only confusion and misery. You started by contemplating your own pitiful lot and moved on to fretting about pollution on Venus. To what end? She thought the compulsion to think deep and hard was like the baby toe, useless to modern man and bound to get selected out of existence any generation now. Still, she gave in, last night, over a package of pink-frosted animal cookies and a bag of Hershey's Kisses. This morning she had canker sores on the side of her tongue and complete loathing for every aspect of her life. She was almost thirty-seven years old, single, with a job that wouldn't challenge a tenth grader and a dwindling affair with a married man she loved but didn't like. She hated L.A. She hated her clothes. Her little sister was getting married. She was lonely. Sniffy Voyeur padded in, thrusting his nose under her hand.

"I don't want to tell you this." Mouse followed her down the hall to the kitchen.

"Can I have some coffee?"

"Someone's got to tell you. It would be very easy for me not to tell you."

"Tell me."

"Don't think I get any pleasure out of this. I know we've had our differences. But this is not something I relish. Someone has got to tell you."

Mimi pulled the canister of coffee beans from the freezer. If no one was dead, how bad could it be? "I think I know what you're going to say, but go on."

"Ralph brought his ex-wife or whoever she is to the fund-raiser last night."

"They're friends," said Mimi, swallowing. "Ralph and I aren't like you and Tony. We aren't like Mr. and Mrs. Monogamy. We're sort of more bohemian. We go out with other people. All that jealousy stuff you guys do is so, like bourgeois. Like Valentine's presents. You guys go in for chocolate hearts and stuff."

"According to Tony, who was drunk when he told me, Elaine is pregnant. According to Tony, Ralph is moving back in with her."

"She'd been trying to get pregnant for some time, I know." Mimi ground the coffee beans, staring through the plastic top at the brown tornado inside. She imagined a tiny Ralph whirling around in there, being pulverized to a nice drip grind. She knew it. Ralph and Elaine, she just knew it. She went to the stove, shook the rusty teakettle, checking for water. "Is this fresh?"

"Yes. Well, it's yesterday's. So you already knew?"

"That's not fresh. This isn't Africa, you know. We can afford fresh water here." She poured the water out and refilled the pot, slamming it back on the burner. "Ralph and I, it was just a sex thing with us. We're both really sexual, you know how it is, well, you probably don't–"

"–I know how it is. What do you mean, I don't know how it is?"

"Don't be so sensitive. I just meant it wasn't love or anything."

"I thought you wanted to marry him," said Mouse.

"Just because you're getting married does not mean the whole world wants to get married. I know how that is, though. When Ivan and I were engaged. You're into the wedding plans and it's all so exciting and you think naturally everyone wants to do this fun thing."

The teapot rattled with an angry, pre-boiling hiss. Mimi turned it off before it whistled and dumped the water over the grounds.

Mouse sat down at the kitchen table, lit a cigarette she didn't want. It tasted stale and metallic. She had expected a Scene, replete with wild sobbing and cruel recriminations. The kind of scene at which Mimi excelled. She felt cheated. If Mimi had found this out herself, she would have thrown a tantrum; if Shirl had told her she would have keened and wailed into Shirl's comfy lap.

"I guess since we're telling secrets …" said Mimi, settling across from Mouse with her coffee. "Where's Tony?" She scrunched her curls as if he might wander in at any minute, as though he hadn't been witness to her sleep-flattened hair for months.

"He's decided to move in with Sather and Darryl. Since Ralph is moving back with Elaine, there's more room up there. It was getting a little rough, all of us living here. He took his things up there this morning." Mouse was not about to tell Mimi that the wedding was off. She would sooner suffer some gruesome African disease than Mimi's gleeful and condescending empathy.

"He knows about the movie," said Mimi softly, compassionate as a newly minted social worker on the first day of the job.

"About *Wedding March*? Oh, I know."

"Oh, good. So you've talked about it."

"Oh, sure. Tony and I have no secrets."

"And he's talked to you about it? I'm so glad."

"I said he did. Didn't I just say he did?"

"He was so furious. We had lunch at Thai Melody and he called you, or tried to call you, and got the answering machine. He heard some message from Ivan and put two and two together, I thought he was going to have a heart attack. He's got that vein in his forehead that sticks out, you know, when he's pissed. It *throbs*. He thought you and Ivan were sleeping together. I told him no, Ivan wasn't attracted to you in that way. He kept saying, 'They're fucking' – wait, let me get the accent – "

Mouse looked at Mimi. She stared at her. At the wide, thin-lipped mouth open and closing open and closing, at the big, obviously straightened teeth, at the busy plump red tongue. Mimi took dainty sips from her coffee, licking drops from the rim, cocking her head this way and that, snuggling deeper into her chenille robe. She was *enjoying* this. Mouse suddenly imagined Mimi's headstone, there, next to Fitzy's in the cemetery overlooking the San Diego Freeway. His said, *brother, husband, father, friend. He liked to talk*. Hers would say, *sister, daughter, windup teeth. We thought she'd never shut up*.

"I didn't tell you earlier because I didn't want to get

involved in something that was none of my business. You know. But since we're having a heart-to-heart. I've missed you so much, Mousie Mouse. It's so nice to have someone to really like *talk* to."

"When did you two have lunch?"

"Last week."

"Really," said Mouse. To camouflage her revelation she flipped aimlessly through the top script on Carole's weekend reading pile. It was a prince and the pauper yarn about a bus driver who was really a sultan, entitled *Days and Days of L.A. Malaise*.

A slot machine spun in Mouse's mind. So Tony had known about the movie. He had known but kept quiet. One bunch of cherries clicked into place.

He had known but kept quiet. He chose not to confront her. Instead he broke off the wedding. Another bunch clicked into place.

He broke off the wedding, which would mean the end of the movie. Or so he presumed. So he did really love her. It was *Wedding March* he was bent on destroying. Unless, the fact she'd gone against his wishes and done the movie anyway was the last bloody straw. So he *was* telling the truth, he didn't love her. A lemon clicked into place.

"– trying to talk and you're *reading*," said Mimi. "You never read."

"I read."

"Not as much as I do. What is that, anyway?"

"*Days and Days of L.A. Malaise*. It's not bad."

"That's in production now. It's supposed to be awful."

"How can it be in production if Carole's got it? She's a reader. She recommends scripts to her boss."

"How do I know? All I know is that it's in production."

"I don't think it is. It's says First Draft on the first page here."

"Mouse, it's in production. I'm the one in the stupid film business. You can never just say, 'Right, Mimi.' "

"I don't think it's in production, is all. It's not a matter of who's right."

"It's in production! All right? It's in production and it's a piece of shit!" Mimi threw her chair back and stalked into the bathroom. When she slammed the door the windows shook.

LUDVICA, THE DRESSMAKER, lived in a stucco bungalow with barred windows on a narrow street in Silver Lake. Nita had recommended her. Nita sent all her brides to Ludvica, but Ludvica accepted only a few.

No one knew Ludvica's criteria. Perfectly nice Beverly Hills socialites nudged their Jaguars through crosstown traffic just to see her, risking neighborhoods where a car parked for any length of time became a bare wall of sheet metal crying out for graffiti. Ludvica couldn't care less. It mattered not, to Ludvica, who you were or what you drove or how much you could pay. She took one look at you and either waved you away or asked you inside. If she asked you inside, it was understood that if you frowned on her chain-smoking, her habit of talking with pins clamped between her teeth, the scratchy Chopin she played day and night, her Siamese cats, the rank odor of overripe cheese that pervaded every gloomy room, she would ask you to leave. She had been known to scrap a ten-thousand-dollar gown if she took a sudden dislike to someone. She would send the client packing in the middle of a fitting, then make doll clothes out of the gown, then give them away to a children's hospital. As a result, she was one of the most exclusive dressmakers in town.

Ludvica was four-foot-ten and stocky, ageless, with a tight black bun of irregularly wavy hair. She had large breasts transformed, with the aid of a hefty old-world undergarment, into a shelf for resting her folded hands when she was deep in thought.

Her reputation had been made sewing for stars in the forties. Vivian, Lana, Bette, Joan. In the 1960s, when the world went in for jeans and work shirts, she made doll clothes and worked as a cashier at a porno theater. Now, just like America, she was back. It was morning again for Ludvica, though kinder and gentler she was not. If anything, she was crabbier and more selective than ever.

Ludvica had called Mouse "Frances." "Frances, beautiful, regal name. Mouse, silly, primitive," she said. Ludvica didn't care what you wanted. She never asked anyone what she had in mind. At their first meeting she had asked Mouse only about the wedding. Mouse, blushing, described in detail the candlelit ceremony, the imported champagne, the sitdown dinner at the Bel-Air Hotel. Ludvica had stood in front of Mouse, rested her nicotine-stained fingers on her shoulders. She had stepped back, folded her hands on her breasts, squinting through her cigarette smoke. Ludvica smoked without removing the pins from her mouth. "Princess, alluring yet shy," she had proclaimed. "I do for you."

Today was Mouse's final fitting. She would see the dress for the first time. Until today, Ludvica had sewn on a muslin shell, which had served as the pattern. It had taken four fittings to get the muslin perfect. It had taken dozens of phone calls to find the right silk taffeta for the dress, which was eventually located in Boston. It had taken seven harrowing shopping expeditions to find the fabric for the underlining, the lining, and the slip. Ludvica insisted on driving herself. It was the only time she ever got out. She drove an old gold Cadillac. She could hardly see over the steering wheel. Three flattened orange trees struggling for life on one side of her driveway attested to the fact she had no use for rearview mirrors.

Filming with Ludvica was both more and less tricky than anticipated. At first there had been some concern that she would take one beady-eyed look at the camera and send them all on their way. On the first day, when Mouse began to explain about *Wedding March*, Ludvica waved her away impatiently saying, "I work fifty-two years in Los Angeles."

She never asked who Ivan and Eliot were or what they were

doing there. She signed a release in her elaborate European hand without a glance.

She would not, however, tolerate cordless mikes, special lighting or rearranging a stick of furniture. They could be there, but they could not disrupt her work.

Because Ludvica might ask all of them to leave at any time, and because following Mouse into Ludvica's bedroom to film her easing into the dress for the first time might be construed by Ludvica as disrupting her work, Ivan and Eliot, Mimi, Shirl and Nita, waited in the living room for Mouse to make her appearance. While waiting they talked in hushed, library whispers, the better to hear the silky rustle of the dress emanating from Ludvica's bedroom.

Shirl sat on an overstuffed upholstered ottoman, her hands tucked between her knees, an Instamatic hanging from a frayed strap around her wrist. With the aid of a map, over Auntie Barb's protestations, she had driven herself to Ludvica's. It was the first time she had been alone in a car since the accident. All the way from the Valley she had driven to see her youngest in her wedding gown. She was beaming.

Mimi stood behind Eliot, the camera resting on his shoulder. She kept asking him to let her look through the viewfinder, teased him into explaining his theories of cinematography. She wore her favorite turquoise knit mini, which she happily noticed Eliot noticing. She was not so old! It was amazing how a man's appreciation of your knees could make the difference between joy and despair. Eliot, when he was groomed, was not half bad, she thought. He had a soft, patient voice and nice fingernails. He was probably honest.

Nita leaned against the blond worktable in the middle of the dining room where Ludvica labored to produce her miracles, checking her lists of things still to be done, her red corkscrew curls caught up in a ponytail atop her head. The dining room, with industrial sewing machine, professional iron and ironing board, hundreds of spools of thread arranged by color, each thrust on its own small hook on the wall, was immaculate. The rest of the house looked as though it hadn't been touched since V-J Day. The furniture was embedded with dust, forming a uniform gritty gray veneer.

Ivan stood by the hallway, a sleek jungle cat ready to pounce. Nagra slung over his shoulder, hands on the boom, headphones clamped to his ears. He was poised and ready, waiting for sounds of approach. He heard a pinched bowled-over sigh from the bedroom. "It's, it's, it's ... " sighed Mouse.

"They're coming," he said. "Let's roll. Speed. Sound."

"We are coming," sang Ludvica. "Genius and beauty both."

Shirl leaped to her feet, kicked off her orthopedic sandals and struggled up on the ottoman, beckoning Mimi over to lend a shoulder. In her excitement she took a picture of the empty hallway, blinding everyone momentarily with the flash. Eliot steadied his expressionless black glass eye on the door. Nita turned, tearing expectantly, datebook clasped to her chest. They held their breaths, waiting for the onslaught of beauty and opulence. Ludvica did not disappoint.

Ivan asked Ludvica to describe the dress.

"On a girl with such nice dark hair, I use bright white. Not so many girls can wear the bright white. This one can. This is very classic gown. Finest bright white silk taffeta in the world, Ludvica uses. Fitted bodice, princess line. She has gentrified deep v-line in front and back. Exposed shoulders. Very nice. You have a nice shoulder you should show it, my motto.

"Bodice and sleeves overlaid with handmade French Alençon lace, which Ludvica gets straight from shop in Paris. Sleeves are puffed, off-the-shoulder, ending with a ruffle over the elbow. Over the lace Ludvica embroiders mother-of-pearl seed beads and sequins. Notice. Sequins not shiny, used only to give lace nice deep sheen. It takes Ludvica two weeks, working every day ten hours, to embroider.

"See the skirt. Fifteen yards of bright white silk taffeta it takes. There are two linings. One, an underlining of silk organza,

then a lining of pure china silk. Underneath all is crinoline petti-
coat that Ludvica also makes, requiring twenty yards crinoline.
See the hem. Dainty, scalloped border. More Alençon lace. One
hundred seventy dollars a yard, this is lace.

"If you can sew, you can build a skyscraper, my motto. Proof
is this. See? Detachable train. Twenty feet long, this train.
Notice embroidered appliqués of Alençon float up center back.
Very nice. Is built to be removed at the reception, so Frances
can dance. Ludvica makes also a taffeta bow to put there after
train has remove, to make a little bustle. With little white gloves,
mother's pearls, Frances is lovely."

"How much do you think it weighs?" asked Ivan.

"Twenty-two pounds," said Ludvica proudly, her hands
laced over her breasts. "I weigh this morning."

Mouse was stupefied, encased as she was in the eighth
wonder of the world. She never wanted to take this dress off. She
loved herself in this dress. This made the royal blue silk organza
of the night before look like something she'd wear to clean the
pool. The bridal gown so heavy, so spectacular, so unlike anything
she has ever seen or felt, all thoughts of how many Third World
families could live for how many years on the amount she will pay
for this dress were banished from her mind.

How could a dress have such power? How could a dress
render Mimi mute? How could a dress seduce the ancient gaze
of love from Ivan's normally veiled eyes? How could a dress
cause a drought in the tear ducts of her normally weepy mother?
Shirl just held her head. "Oh, oh, oh, oh, oh, oh."

With Ludvica tending the train, Mouse walked the length
of the room. The dress murmured rich, contented sounds.

Mouse could hardly believe she wasn't getting married.
Maybe she had overlooked something. Had Tony really called the
wedding off? Maybe he had been joking. Maybe the sea breeze
or the groan of an elephant had blotted out the end of the
sentence. Maybe he had said, "I don't love you any LESS THAN

THE DAY WE MET" or some other convoluted Oxbridge utterance. She would call him tonight just to make sure.

"It looks just like my dress, doesn't it, Iv?" Mimi mewed.

"Who is this girl?" Ludvica demanded. "I make only originals." Ludvica pulled at Mouse's waist, selected a pin from between her teeth, made a tiny adjustment.

"Frances's sister, Mim – er, Margaret," said Shirl.

"I had a bright-white silk taffeta dress, too," said Mimi.

"Mistake for you," said Ludvica. "Ivory for a girl so yellow."

"Tony will not believe you in that," said Nita. "And him in a black cutaway. Ooh ooh ooh. What a couple."

"Just like the plastic bride and groom on top of the cake," said Mimi.

"Thanks a lot," said Mouse.

"She was giving you a compliment, dear."

"We look like plastic dolls, that's a compliment?"

"Mom," said Mimi, in a back-me-up-on-this-one tone of voice.

"She's just being sensitive," said Shirl to Mimi.

"I am not *sensitive*. Mimi has a way, she gets in these little digs and then when I point it out I'm being sensitive."

"Sensitive is not a bad thing. You say it like it's bad. *I'm* sensitive."

Ivan surprised them by sniggering.

"Fuck you," said Mimi. "You want to get married, Mouse. Get married. This is what happens."

"Margaret FitzHenry!"

"Keep rolling," said Ivan, grinning, concentrating on keeping the boom both out of the frame and over the active part of the conversation.

"I'm sorry. It's just, I'm under stress, too. No, I'm not the one getting married, but I am the Maid of Honor. That's a thing, too."

"Of course it is, dear." Shirl stroked Mimi's snarly, sand-colored hair from her perch on the ottoman.

"Mom, stop." She batted Shirl away. "It's practically like

being the bride. Only you get lots of responsibility but none of the attention."

"I'm sure Mouse appreciates all you're doing for her. Don't you, honey?"

"Of course," said Mouse.

"You're just so sensitive," said Mimi.

"It's NBD," said Nita. "Nervous Bride Disorder. They've actually been able to document it. At a wedding consultant seminar I went to several weeks ago they had a panel on it. It's like if you can imagine a Vietnam vet with PMS. It's real common. Especially among educated women."

"Women who should know better than to get married," said Mimi, "is that who you mean?"

"I'm not getting married!" wailed Mouse, suddenly. Tears sprung from her eyes. What was she doing, standing here in a wedding dress? Tony was probably out making time with the minimall magnate at this very moment.

"She is just a nervous little bride," said Shirl. "I went through it, Mimi went through it. We all go through it."

"Tone-Tony doesn't lo-uh-uh-uh-uh ... " Mouse hiccuped, screwing her fists into her eyes.

"Mouse, honey, don't do that. It's not good for your eyes," scolded Shirl.

"I was a total basket case, except at the shower. I did have a good time at my shower," said Mimi.

" ... he doesn't, he doesn't ... "

"Shower! Glad you mentioned it." Nita slapped open her date book, fished a pencil from among her red curls. "I'm having the tables delivered that day. Will someone be at the house? Mr. Futake will also need to get in a little early. He does, I'm sure I told you this, it was a real coup to get him, he's *never* available.

" ... lov-uh-uh-uh-uh me-e-e-e ... "

"Shirl, listen to this!" yelped Mimi. "This is incredible. Mr. Futake sculpts candy out of hot corn syrup. It's an art form in Japan. They look like figurines, like jade or something, only it's candy. He's going to do a sculpture of Mouse and Tony for the centerpiece. Then he'll go around the party doing requests. You say, 'Do a cat,' he'll do a cat. You say, 'Do an angel,' he'll do an angel. He can do Mickey Mouse, Batman … "

" … there isn't going to *be* any shower! There isn't going to *be* any wedding!"

"Enough! Silly girl! Off with dress. Salty tears ruin taffeta. You want to ruin dress you wait until wedding day." Ludvica began unbuttoning the dress. "Did I mention the twenty-five cloth-covered buttons and thread loops closing up the back?"

Mouse stood still, her chest silently heaving, while Ludvica's blunt fingers fiddled at her back. Since she came home she always seemed to be stuck on the wrong side of what she wanted. It was funny, actually. She sniffed, wiped her nose on the back of her hand. She laughed.

"Poor thing's exhausted," said Nita, handing her a Kleenex from a tiny pack in her purse. "This is so typical."

"Only hormones," said Ludvica. "Not to worry."

"I was much worse than this, wasn't I, Shirl? You were in Africa, Mouse, so you didn't see me."

MOUSE WONDERED: IF the brain was such a phenomenal organ, why could it handle only one facet of a problem at a time? All those folds that allegedly held knowledge. She thought alternately of losing Tony and all that meant, calling off the wedding and all that meant, stopping production on *Wedding March* and all that meant, but she could not seem to grasp all of these things at once. And if she could not do that, how could she make a decision about what to do? Maybe, she reasoned, there was only one fold per subject, only one fold, for example, dedicated to thoughts of marriage. If this was true, her fold was overflowing. That's why she was freaking out. Love- and marriage-related problems were being relegated to the fold designated for remembering how to change the battery in the smoke alarm. Just the fact she was contemplating this did not speak well for the brain, she thought.

For the past week she had been unable to sleep. Instead, she lay on the couch, chin on her chest, watching late-night TV, remoting around the stations impatiently. Sometimes she didn't even drag out the futon. She slept like that, in her clothes, the unpleasant orange sodium-vapor streetlight shining down on her from outside. Sniffy Voyeur was distraught by the change. He stood beside the couch for hours, his long pointed head resting on her chest.

Every day she resolved to do *something*. Call the wedding off, or call Tony and beg him to come back, and every day she did nothing. The most peculiar show, to which she found herself increasingly addicted, was a bingo game in the nether regions of the dial. It came on at two and featured an unattractive shiny-faced Southern couple in evening wear pulling foam golf balls out of what appeared to be a giant popcorn popper. Each ball had a number on it. "Number seventeen B, Brandy, seventeen B."

"That's one-seven, seventeen B, Chet? One seven, seventeen B. I like that number, seventeen, Chet, don't you?"

"Yes, and B, why your name *begins* with a B, doesn't it, Brandy?"

"Yes, Chet, that's seventeen B. One-seven B for our viewers at home."

It went on like this until the morning news. They never told where or how you got a bingo card, or what to do if you won, or what you won if you won.

Sometimes Carole, who was an insomniac, sat up and watched the bingo show, too. She did most of her script reading after midnight. She sat at the kitchen table in her robe and sweatsocks, drinking oversteeped cups of Earl Grey and eating rice cakes smeared with peanut butter.

One night Mouse told Carole about her theories on the brain. Carole fingered the gold rings in her ears and listened, nodding her head slowly. She had a habit unknown in Los Angeles.

She listened to what you said, thought about what you said, then she responded. Carole felt sorry for the brain. "All that potential, and what do people use it for? Screenplays."

"What are you two still doing up?" asked Mimi. She stumbled in around one-thirty, red-cheeked and tousled. Mouse didn't ask. Since the morning Tony moved out three weeks earlier, the morning when Mouse had told Mimi about Elaine, Mimi had been moody and secretive. She had been staying late at work to use the computer to write on her blockbuster, then meeting Eliot Bomarito for a late bite. Mouse could not believe she was dating the odoriferous Eliot. What had happened to Ralph?

"Is it love?" asked Carole, rolling a sheet of paper into her typewriter.

"I don't know," said Mimi, opening the refrigerator. "He's just very very nice. He's really a good filmmaker, too. He did a great piece on this blind guy who does tattoos in East L.A."

"It's awful," said Mouse. "Remember? We watched it together."

"It's brilliant!" said Mimi, slamming the refrigerator.

"We watched it together," said Mouse, "you thought it was terrible."

"God, would it kill you to let someone else do something?" She stomped out of the room.

Mouse and Carole traded glances.

"What was that?" asked Mouse.

Carole laughed. "You should see the fights I have with my sister."

"That was not a fight. We never fight. Shirl brags about it to her friends at the craft shop. I don't know how you can stand living with her, frankly."

"She pays the rent on time, cleans up after herself. We have talks. She's not threatened by me, though."

"She's threatened by *me*?"

"Oh, sure."

The way Carole said it, with a shrug and a wave of her

beringed hand, it had to be true. This had never occurred to Mouse. Not that it made any difference. In her experience, this kind of insight was like the free bonus glass Shirl used to get with a fill-up at the gas station. The glass had nothing to do with the quality or the cost of the gas, and it ended up rolling around the backseat until it broke or was thrown out. Regardless of whether Mimi was threatened by her, she was still unbearable, and Mouse could figure no way to make her bearable. She sighed and fished a rice cake out of the bag lying open on the table.

"I meant to tell you, I read Tony's script," said Carole.

The rice cake turned to dust in Mouse's mouth. She tried to chew. "Oom rem Ony's scimmp?" Tony's script! She'd forgotten about it. Her bloodshot eyes filled with tears. It was like unexpectedly coming upon one of his shirts among her laundry.

"For Allyn, V. J. Parchman thought she'd spark to it since she's looking for an Africa project."

"How is it?"

"It's on the couch," said Carole. "No worse than anything else I read. I mean that as a compliment. At least he's hip to apostrophes. You should probably look at this first. I don't know if you know what he's done. It's 'freely adapted from a true story.'" Carole slid a sheet of paper across the table. "Don't take the bad stuff seriously. I'm supposed to be harsh. It's part of the job."

Screenplay: 119 pgs.
Story Analyst: Carole Poe
Submitted to: Allyn Meyer
Submitted by: V. J. Parchman

LOVE AMONG ELEPHANTS

by
T. N. Cheatham
and
Ralph Holladay

TYPE: Action/Thriller/Love Story
LOCALE & TIME: East Africa. The Present

SYNOPSIS:

MOUSE and TONY are two young Americans. Each one heads a
different anti-elephant-poaching unit, one organized by the
Kenyan government, the other by an international wildlife watch
group. MOUSE, who came to Nairobi to model swimsuits for
Sports Illustrated, was moved by the plight of the elephants and
never went home, is "soft, sexy, and sweet" but a whiz with an
AK-47. TONY, a former Rhodes Scholar, is "rugged, decisive, and
energetic." They meet when their two anti-poaching units
ambush one another by mistake. Mouse is accidentally shot, but
Tony nurses her back to health. They make love while a herd
of elephants, with whom Mouse has "a mystical connection" (she
was an elephant in a past life) look on with approval.

Tony's UNCLE NIGEL, a bigwig exporter of African *objets
d'art* offers Mouse a job while she is recuperating. Through her
work, she learns that he is in collusion with BOAZ, the most
ruthless poacher in the country, exporting tons of tusks to Korea.
She tells Tony, and they go to the head of the Kenyan Wildlife
Federation, MR. STANLEY. Stanley tells them Nigel has been under
suspicion for some time, but not to worry, it is all under control.
Meanwhile, Tony's unit rounds up Boaz and holds him captive in
the bush, thereby cutting off Nigel's supply of tusks. Nigel,
unaware that it is Tony's patrol who apprehended Boaz, sets his
henchmen, THOMAS and STEPHEN, out to find and kill them.
Mouse overhears this one night when Nigel thinks she has already
gone home and sets out to warn Tony.

Before Mouse can find him, she is captured by Boaz's confederates. They are going to kill her but, at a nearby game reserve
lodge, some models from *Vogue* are doing a safari spread. Mouse,
using her old *Sports Illustrated* connections, promises to get
them into the photo shoot if they will let her go. She runs into Nigel
and Mr. Stanley there, cavorting with the models. She confronts
Nigel, who realizes his awful mistake. He had no intention
of murdering his beloved nephew. Together, Nigel and Mouse set
out to find Thomas and Stephen before they can find Tony. They
catch up with the two henchmen just as they are arriving in the
village where Tony's unit is based. They arrive to find all of Tony's
men decapitated, their bodies unrecognizable. Mr. Stanley's
henchmen have been there first.

That night, Mouse and Ni console each other. They make
love. Mouse leaves their bed and goes into the bush to commune
with the elephants. She rides one nude through the mist, her
AK-47 slung over her shoulder. The elephant takes her to where

Tony is hiding out. Tony says he saw her with Uncle Nigel and is leaving for the States as soon as he can get a flight out.

PRODUCTION VALUE: Good
RECOMMENDATION: Yes_____ No_____ Maybe XXX

COMMENTS:

Idea is important, topical, potentially interesting, lends itself to a prestige, big-star vehicle. Characters are by and large believable, although it is difficult to believe Mouse would console Nigel (who is still, as far as we know, an exporter of illegal ivory) by sleeping with him. Also, although it's understandable that the world of high fashion modeling would be fascinating to a band of blood-thirsty elephant poachers, I don't believe the promise of watching a *Vogue* photo shoot would be a strong bargaining chip in this situation. Everything else about this script is predictable, confused, and sometimes downright unbelievable. The plotting is feeble at worst, shopworn at best. Despite the exotic arena it's nothing we haven't seen before. The end feels tacked on. With the exception of the abrupt resolution of the relationship between the principals, everything else is left hanging. What happens to Nigel? To Mr. Stanley?

    If a major star was interested in this it might be worth doing a page-one rewrite, if only because of the subject matter, and its "freely adapted from a true story" appeal. I know you want to write off your upcoming Kenyan honeymoon, Allyn, but if I were you, I'd PASS.

CAROLE

MOUSE READ THIS with the same luscious horror with which she'd once read a medical book on African diseases, complete with full-page color photographs of every swollen, withered, rotting piece of human anatomy imaginable; the way she'd read and reread the newspaper accounts of Fitzy's death; the way she read the coroner's report she'd found one day in a file in the bottom drawer of Shirl's desk.

    She was not angry. Being angry implied that one day she would cool down. It implied a door was still open, even if only a crack. When she got angry, the door slammed. It locked. Then the locks were changed. She had been angry like this only once before. Then she had moved to Africa.

Sometime during the script's second act, when "Mouse" is trying to escape her captors, the confederates of the evil Boaz (who, she noticed, bore a striking physical resemblance to a friend in Nairobi who taught film criticism at the University), Carole slipped off to bed.

Sometime later the police helicopter *whopp-whopp-whopped* by overhead. Sniffy slept a few feet away from her, his paw crooked around his black nose, ferreting out dream scents. She lit a cigarette, then forgot about it while it ate itself up in ash, then crumbled onto a pile of slick magazines on the coffee table.

She found some comfort in the fact that *Love Among Elephants* was dreck. Also, perversely, in the fact that underneath Tony's upstanding demeanor lay a sleazy, scheming creep. She always thought he was too good to be true; here was the physical evidence.

It was after four o'clock when she hauled out the futon. She made it up with clean sheets, taking pride in her hospital corners. She slept soundly for the first time since Tony moved out.

22

IT WAS THE BEGINNING OF MARCH WHEN TONY TOOK over Ralph's old bedroom at the back of the Big House, high up in the Hollywood Hills. It took him several weeks to realize just how high up this was.

His room had cheap dark wood paneling and hundreds of wire hangers jammed into the empty closet, whose sliding door was permanently off its track. The window over the bed was broken. At night it was cold. Tony slept in a sleeping bag and hooded sweatshirt borrowed from Sather. Because the air was also dry, he often awoke with a nosebleed. He gently tucked wads of toilet paper into his nostrils and tried to go back to sleep. The mourning doves roosting in the jacaranda by the side of the house woke him up before it was light.

When he finally pulled himself out of bed, the house was empty, Pop-Tart wrappers strewn across the kitchen counter, a half gallon of milk left on the table, the sports page missing, crumbs everywhere. Sather and Darryl were sound-editing a low-budget feature, which meant working eighty to a hundred hours a week. They left before six and got home after eleven. They thought the post-production supervisor might need someone else the last week of the schedule and promised to try to get Tony on. He tried not to count the days.

Instead, he busied himself watching videotapes of past Lakers games. He read all the magazines in the house, sitting on a kitchen chair on the deck overlooking the smog-engulfed city.

He took his skateboard out once, but the streets were far too narrow and steep. Anyway, he had lost interest. He tried to get his closet door back on track but only succeeded in pulling it off.

Mouse had kept the Toyota. Tony felt it was only fair, since her mother had paid for it. He may be a heel, but a bastard he was not.

Until he got a job and could afford a car, he was on foot or forced to take the bus. The nearest bus stop was three miles away, at the bottom of the hill, next to a little café Tony was convinced was owned by a surgeon specializing in bypass surgery. Even the pancakes glistened with fat.

One day, he hiked down to the café to nurse a cup of coffee over the want ads. Streets rambled all over the hill: dead ends, driveways, apparent wrong turns. To get down, for a short time you had to go up. Darryl had drawn him a map. Tony sat in the little café until the waitress tired of refilling his cup, then walked the three miles back up to the house. The next day his legs were so sore he could barely take a step.

The phone never rang. He tried not to feel anxious. When he ran out of Lakers videotapes he found solace in the all-sports cable station.

V. J. had had the script for over two weeks. He had assured Tony and Ralph that the executives had put it on their weekend reading lists, which meant only that it would not take them three months to get to it. There was the possibility that they'd already read it and hated it: in Hollywood, no news was no news, also bad news. He did pull-ups on a bar installed across the kitchen until his biceps burned.

He tried not to dwell on his wretched performance at the fundraiser. Standing in front of the city's rich and powerful, mouthing off about elephant carvings, when what they'd been interested in was elephant *poaching*. He consoled himself with the fact that he didn't know much about poaching anyway. Nothing that Michael Brass didn't know, in any case, so the mixup was probably for the best. He came off as an endearing (he hoped) drunk rather than an ill-informed poseur. His host came off looking like a naturalist on par with Richard Leakey. Tony tried to reassure himself that whatever he had done, he hadn't been such an ass as to cause V.J. to lose interest in the script.

Still, Tony heard nothing. Hollywood had the same sense of time as an iceberg, he told himself. Not to worry. Days passed. His biceps grew. Not a peep from anyone.

If he wanted something to eat, and it wasn't in the house, he had to wait for Darryl or Sather to come home so he could borrow a car. One day the only thing around was oatmeal. He wasn't feeling quite so low then and was sufficiently inspired to attempt the cookie recipe on the back of the box. Because the muscles in the backs of his calves forbade another three-mile walk down to the little store next to the little café at the bottom of the hill, he was forced to scrimp on butter.

He spent the rest of the afternoon pitching the suitable-for-trapshooting cookies at the sparrows that alighted on the fat spines of prickly pear that grew by the acre off the deck, trying to find a reason to ring up Mouse. He wished he'd had the foresight to leave something behind at the apartment.

Now that he'd cooled off, he was appalled at the way he'd gone off his bean. He couldn't remember exactly what he'd said, but he distinctly remembered something along the lines of "I don't love you." He wished he'd been a bit more vague. "Just don't feel ready for marriage, poppet. Me feet are getting a bit of a chill." After all, he did want to marry her, he just didn't want a bloody movie made about it. Now, even that didn't seem so bad. It was not the movie that was objectionable, he realized, but that pint-sized, bedroom-eyed Oscar-winner. It was Ivan he wanted out of the picture.

"Well, she deserved it!" he said. He tipped the tray off the rail, dumping the rest of the cookies onto the field of dusty green cactus twenty feet below. Here they were entering into holy matrimony and she had deceived him! With her old boyfriend, no less! He had a right to be furious! He tried to whip himself up into his old rage, but it wouldn't work. He cursed his fuse, which burned quickly and bright. He missed her, damn it.

He found himself waiting up for Sather and Darryl, just to have someone to talk to.

He found himself thinking about asking the waitress at the little café out for lunch.

He found himself mixing up pitchers of martinis, which he drank alone on the deck as a way to pass the long chilly spring evenings. After a few days, he dispensed with the glass. After a few more, the Vermouth and the twist went. He put the bottle of gin in the freezer before the soaps and took it out after *Oprah*.

Finally, nearly a month after his precipitous departure, he broke down. He rang Mouse to see if perhaps he'd left the shirt he was currently wearing at Mimi's. It was either that or start in with the gin before it had even been chilled.

He got the answering machine. There was a new message. It was Mouse's voice, calm and competent. Tony's heart worked as though it was servicing a marathon runner and not a man making a simple phone call.

"Hi, if you'd like to leave a message for either Mimi, Mouse, or Carole, please do so after the beep. If this is Ivan, I picked up the stuff and I'll see you there."

Tony hung up without leaving a message. He went to the kitchen, pulled the gin from the freezer, rested it against his cheek. Mouse was still seeing Ivan. She was supposed to be a heartbroken wreck. Instead, she had picked up the stuff and was meeting him there! Tony twisted the cap off the gin, put the bottle to his lips right there in the kitchen, the freezer door yawning open, numbing his eyeballs.

No, he thought, no. There was degenerate and there was degenerate. A drink before dinner was one thing, but it was two-thirty in the afternoon. He replaced the gin, pulled out the milk and drank straight from the carton.

On impulse, he strode to the phone, redialed, punched in

Mimi's message code, 22. There might be a message for him. One never knew. Not everyone knew he had moved. V.J. might have gotten confused and called him there. His parents might have called. Noni Bertlestein might have called. He would not be averse to having a drink with her. From the way her owly eyes roamed over him the night of the fundraiser, chances were she'd even come and pick him up. He took a long swig of milk.

There were no messages, save one for Mimi from someone called Eliot. Tony realized that he had half-expected, half-hoped, to hear a message for Mouse from Ivan; something lewd, opportunistic and uninspired, which would confirm Tony's worst opinions of him. Only after Tony hung up did he realize the milk was sour. A few curdled chunks lingered on the back of his tongue. He swallowed, repulsed. Mouse was still seeing Ivan.

All right, fine! This was fine! It was not only fine, it was just as well. It said volumes about her hardheartedness as a woman. She was tough, tough and mean. Fine. He was lucky he was able to get out when he did. In years to come he would look back with relief. Saved from the jaws of marriage to a sociopathic bitch. Whew.

He rang the waitress at the café. She appreciated his invitation but as a lesbian wasn't really interested. Tony hung up and dialed Ralph. Ralph was on the other line. "KeddyWebb's-officecanyouhold?" he greeted him.

Tony was suddenly disconcerted that he had hitched his wagon to a bloke who sounded as obsequious as a chambermaid when he answered his boss's telephone. He held. Suddenly he was glad *Love Among Elephants* had turned out as it had instead of as a paean to his doomed romance with *her*.

"Keddy Webb's office, can I help you?"

"It's Tony."

"Where in the hell have you been?"

"Here, of course, keeping busy–"

"You got my message about the meeting? Today, four-thirty."

"Today? It's two-thirty now. I'm without wheels."

"No one told you about the machine, did they?" Ralph explained about the cheap phone, how you knew someone called only if you checked the message machine. "I've been trying to get you for days. The executives read the script. V.J.'s got a VP willing to go to bat for us. They want a few changes but are still very very very hot on the project. I can't remember whether V.J. said two verys or three. No car. Shit. You know where that restaurant is on Beachwood, bottom of the hill? I'll swing by, pick you up, three-thirty."

"This is the news we've been waiting for, isn't it?"

"We're still on the roller coaster," said Ralph, his voice more sour than usual. "I liked the new ending a lot. I always thought the wedding was the weakest part. Didn't have the bite the rest of the script did."

"Good," said Tony. "This is marvelous."

"Three-thirty, by the restaurant."

They hung up. Tony changed his clothes, debating about replaying the messages. In the end he did it only because there might be something important for his roommates. He replayed them while he watched the end of a soccer game, pulling on his cowboy boots.

Darryl's mother had called. Lisa had called for Sather. Mohammed Akmanzaadi had called for the rent. Auntie Barb, returning his call, said she'd love to play golf, but she wasn't driving all the way to the top of the city to pick him up. There were mud slides and mass murderers up there.

There were also three messages from Mouse. They were opaque, her voice stern. The messages all said the same thing: "This is for Tony. Could you please ask him to call Mouse when he's got a chance? Thanks."

So, begging me to come back! he thought gleefully. He took mincing steps down the hill. His thighs ached, sweat rolled down his scalp and into the collar of his shirt. True, Mouse had sounded a bit more angry than lovelorn, but she could be a hardhearted bitch, so what could one expect? If she was lucky he might hear her out.

He stopped at the little store and bought a carton of cottage cheese and a package of crackers, which he ate standing waiting at the corner. It was a large intersection, where five wide streets became one, then funneled down into the city. The hills were spotted with bright patches of orange and magenta bougainvillea. He inhaled deeply. He hadn't felt this good in weeks. She had called three times. And three times, in his book, bespoke urgency. He smiled at a Basset Hound tied to the leg of the bus stop. He'd call her back when he got around to it. Three times. She must really miss him.

V.J. WAS SUBDUED. Tony was surprised to find him not in his usual neo-Peace Corps getup. Rather, he wore a simple pair of khaki chinos, plaid shirt, and loafers. The shirt still had creases in it and the cuffs were Roman-collar stiff. He sported a new pair of teal-blue contact lenses that caused him to hold his eyes open very wide when he wasn't blinking furiously.

V.J. seemed to have forgotten all about what had happened at the fundraiser. At the auction he'd purchased a few new African pieces for his office: a soapstone bowl with zebralike striping and an elephant carved in ebony, which he showed Ralph and Tony while they waited for Allyn Meyer, the executive who was very very very hot (Tony, optimist that he was, preferred to think there were three verys involved) for the script. He noticed that the ossified Olduvai turd was gone from its former place on the end table.

Tony asked if they'd made a lot on the auction. "Not that my, er, introduction was as inspiring as it might have been." He pulled on the end of his nose, forgetting it was still sensitive.

"It was a great success. Next week I've a meeting with Michael. We're going to put something together to take to the networks. A dramedy about the ivory situation. Maybe do a Mr. Ed kind of thing, only with a talking elephant."

Ralph explained to Tony who Mr. Ed was. He explained what a dramedy was. Ever since Ralph had moved back in with Elaine, he did not seem his old self. He was like a razor gone dull. Today he'd forgotten his baseball cap. His few threads of beige hair did little in the way of disguising his bald pate. Tony thought he looked fed up.

"Did you raise a lot of money?" askcd Ralph.

"Money?"

"For the elephants?"

"Sure. I don't know." V. J. leaned forward in his chair and pressed his intercom. "Lauren, if Michael Brass calls, put him through." Lauren was V. J.'s new secretary, an *au naturel* beauty fresh from Bryn Mawr.

Allyn Meyer was forty minutes late. She wore her hair pulled back in a ponytail and a minimal amount of makeup. She was old-style athletic, when that meant having thick thighs and wearing tennis socks with little balls on the back instead of being an over-aerobicized sex kitten. She possessed the rare look of someone who could have risen to her position of power only through competence. Tony was in awe.

"Allyn, can I get you some – " V. J. leaped to his feet, blinking madly, beckoning Lauren from the outer office.

"Nothing, I'm fine."

"Nothing for me," said Tony, following suit.

"Nothing," said Ralph.

"As I'm sure you've heard, I shoot straight from the hip. So let's not waste time. I like this script. I love this script. Frankly, it's terrible, but that doesn't mean it isn't good. Good scripts are all good in the same way. Bad scripts are bad in their own unique way. That's what I'm after. This unique quality a bad script has. Unique, but recognizable. In our rewrite, we want to hone that uniqueness, that badness that makes it good, but lose the badness that makes it bad, so that it will be not just good but great."

"Yes, quite," said Tony. He heard Ralph exhale wearily

beside him. V. J. paced around the room, jingling the change in his pockets. He moved the zebra-striped soapstone bowl from its place atop the credenza to the coffee table, then back again.

"What we'd like to do is play up the love story," said Allyn.

"The love story," said Tony.

"Play down the thriller angle. Lose the elephant poaching altogether. Lose the intrigue, but don't lose the tension. It's too plot-driven. We want a classic love story. Boy meets girl, boy gets girl, boy loses girl, they live happily ever after."

"Romeo and Juliet go to Kenya," said Tony.

"Yes."

"Ending with a romantic wedding high in the Rwandan mountains, in the fog, among the gorillas."

"Is that what happened?" She looked down at Tony and Ralph sitting cheek by jowl on the *faux* cheetah-skin loveseat with the accusing stare of a school principal. V. J. moved the soapstone bowl from the credenza to the edge of his desk, his eyes blinking wildly behind his lenses.

"Well – " said Tony, thrown. "Metaphorically, I guess you could say."

"This is a true story. That's part of what makes it so attractive to us. The head of production comes from documentaries. He's always looking for something rooted in fact but not crippled by it."

"What about a romantic wedding high in the hills of Beverly? Would that suffice?"

"Where?"

"We're getting married," said Tony. "We were reconciled in Rwanda, and swore our undying love there, but, with all our Africa adventures, haven't gotten around yet to tying the knot. The wedding's next month."

Ralph, who had been uncharacteristically silent, looked over at him, confused. "You are?"

"Whatever you feel comfortable with," said Allyn. "Just

keep in mind that while truth is essential, it should always serve a dramatic purpose. Truth with jiggle is what we're aiming for."

"Right-o," said Tony. He crossed his legs nonchalantly, broke open his toothy smile. He didn't know what in the hell she was talking about. He realized finally that he didn't need to.

"You won't want to show this to the head of production until we do the changes, though, right?" said Ralph.

"Exactly. We want it to be more than perfect."

"I figured," said Ralph.

"It's almost there now," said Tony. "Lose the thriller, play up the love story. Lose the plot, but don't let it go soft."

"Yes," said Allyn. "You do that ... " She went to the door, turning at the last minute to underscore the importance of her pronouncement. "You do that and you've got a thousand screens at Christmas. That's what kind of picture this is."

The instant the door shut behind her thick calves, Lauren's young voice floated over the intercom. "Vincent, it's Michael on one."

"Gotta take this, guys." V.J. plopped into his big leather chair, his hand on the receiver. A kid with his hand on the bow of his largest birthday present couldn't be full of more joy or anticipation. "Get busy on the changes, we'll talk next week." They were out of the office in less than seven minutes.

"THIS IS WORKING out quite nicely," said Tony.

They bumper-to-bumpered over Laurel Canyon, behind a low-slung red Italian sports car. The vanity plate said LUCK. Tony imagined when their deal was finally struck he would be able to afford to buy one. With cash.

"I got a kid on the way," said Ralph. "I can't keep writing for nothing."

"It's not for nothing. It's on spec, but it's not for *nothing*."

"I been doing this for too long. You don't know."

"We'll just show her the old draft. It's no work, really."

"It's psychological work, having hope."

Ralph's radio had been stolen so they drove in silence.

"I thought you and Mouse called it quits," he said.

"We did. You know how it is."

Ralph laughed. "Do I."

"In fact, I was wondering, could you be a sport and drop me at Mimi's?"

"On the corner I'll drop you."

"Haven't talked to her yet, then?"

"She hasn't been to class in two weeks. I haven't seen her. When I see her, we'll talk."

"Perhaps you should ring her up?"

"Perhaps you should stay out of it."

"Right-o."

Tony let himself in with his old key. No one was home. Sniffy stretched, his rear end high in the air, his bushy tail waving like a flag. He trotted over and stuck his nose in Tony's crotch. Tony thought it was a good omen that Sniffy was eager to see him. He had never been particularly fond of the dog, and here he was, begging for a scratch behind the ears.

The wicker settee squeaked loudly as Tony sat down. He crossed his legs and waited. The blinds were open, the room lit by streetlight. He was tempted to turn on the box, but didn't want his visit to appear cavalier.

No one came. Downstairs, he could hear the skateboard champ being chewed out by his mum over the nightly news. A tinge of overboiled cabbage wafted up through the window. On the wicker coffee table was a manila folder, Mouse's neat printing on the tab. He riffled through it: receipts from *Wedding March*, miscellaneous notes. He knew he was in bad shape when he felt nostalgic for her bookkeeping. He should never have called off the wedding. He should have made a scene in his customary foolish fashion, gotten it over with.

He tiptoed down the hall to use the bathroom, carefully dropping the seat when he was done. He prided himself on that, always remembering to replace the seat. In the medicine cabinet were the usual female creams and powders, prescriptions. He took a whiff of each thing, searching for some fond odor.

In Mimi's bedroom, tucked into the frame of the mirror hanging over her dresser, were two postcards, both from Africa, curling with age. He removed one from Mombasa, held it up in the rectangle of light shining between the thin, half-drawn curtains. After he and Mouse had finished shooting *The New Stanley*, they had taken a vacation together, and snorkeled for conches on the very beach pictured on the card. The postcard was from Mouse, reporting that she had met a wonderful guy: "Tony, cute, smart and decent." He replaced the postcard, blotting the tears brewing in his eyes.

From downstairs, he heard a shrill female voice, over and over again, "No son of mine be hooligan!"

Mouse's suitcase was open on the floor. He pawed through it, swimming in guilt, then felt justified when he found missing a certain pair of red satin panties.

He was about to return to the bathroom, to recheck the medicine cabinet for her diaphragm, when he heard the lonesome sound of water streaming against porcelain. He froze. Someone was in the apartment. He hadn't heard anyone come in. Yet someone was home, using the bathroom, directly across from Mimi's room. He looked over his shoulder slowly, praying his neck wouldn't crack, praying the door to the bathroom was closed.

It wasn't. It was wide open. There was Mouse, bathed in the dim yellow light of the tiny bathroom, perched on the loo, her jeans nesting around her ankles, the heartbreaking red satin panties stretched between her shins, Sniffy's head on her naked thigh. She reached down to the wastebasket next to the toilet and retrieved an empty paper tube. She tapped Sniffy's nose with it, then placed it between his narrow jaws. He wagged his body in mad delight. "There you go, Sniffer. Is that your favorite toy?"

Suddenly she looked up.

"Hi," said Tony softly.

"Oh God." She grimaced, leaned forward and slammed the door.

Tony scurried to the living room, threw on some light. He could still hear the sounds of Mouse slamming around the bathroom.

Tony could think only of her delicate knees, the touching patch of dark where her thighs met, the cute red satin panties! All right, he would do the wedding movie. He would forgive her for her sins, of omission and commission both. Whatever had gone on with Ivan was in the past. After all, he had had a few indiscretions himself, hadn't he? He would forgive her.

"The key?" she said flatly. She stood by the dining room table, her palm outstretched. She was wearing the green silk blouse he liked so much.

"You know that blasted phone they have up there. Doesn't ring. No one told me you'd called. So thought I'd just pop around. Just had a terrific meeting at the studio. Some executives very hot for us, Ralph and me. You have on that blouse. I love that blouse."

"You are scum. The key, please."

"You're thinking it's sexist, my feelings for you in that blouse."

"I read your script."

"You read my ... oh dear. When? How?"

"How? I'm reading at the third-grade level now. You didn't know?"

"Mouse ..." He had never seen her like this. Calmer than a professional assassin on Valium, eyes marble-hard, cheeks flaming. She hated him. He saw that clearly enough.

"Will you please allow me to explain?"

"No. Just leave. I want you to leave. Riding through the savanna nude with an AK-47? And the key, please."

"That was V.J.'s idea."

"I have a mind to call my mother's lawyer."

"It didn't begin that way – exploitative. It began as a true
account of our romance. That's the script I wrote. If you'd read it,
you'd see."

"Did you think I'd never find out?"

"I was going to tell you. I was always going to tell you.
Nothing's actually jelled yet, you know. It seemed pointless until
there was something concrete. I was going to change the names,
am going to change the names. There was some … confusion.
It's all part of the bloody game, you know. Getting a 'go' movie.
The names will be changed. I knew you'd be livid." He heard the
pleading in his voice. She stared, her gaze glued to his, silently
allowing him to indict himself. He knew this technique. It was
the way you got the goods from someone you were interviewing
on camera. Ask a simple question, never interrupt, then wait
for the victim's natural compulsion to justify and overexplain to
do the rest. Well, he was smarter than that.

"Anyway, what right do you have accusing *me*? That blasted
wedding documentary. You and Ivan carrying on behind my
back."

"That's completely different."

"How is it different? I don't see how it's different."

"In *Wedding March* truth isn't just a gimmick, for one thing."

"You know bloody well that the presence of a camera,
any camera, turns an event into a performance. Documentary's
as much a pack of half-truths as anything else. You think Ivan
isn't exploiting you? Isn't going to make the film say whatever he
damn well pleases? At least if something is freely adapted from
a true story no one suffers under any illusions. Besides, I strove
for a metaphorical truth, which is a far deeper and more honest
truth than you find in any documentary."

"A more honest truth?"

"True to the spirit of the event rather than the actual
occurrences." This sounded pretty good. If he didn't make it as
a writer-director, he could always be an executive.

"You made me a *swimsuit model*, Tony. A dimwitted, morally irresponsible, slutty swimsuit model."

"Based on how smashing you look in that black bikini."

"You think I'd sleep with a man to *console* him? In my past life I was an elephant? I cannot talk about this. It's not bad enough that you trashed my life, then you ... " She shook her head. "You disgust me."

"Can't we just put this behind us, poppet? Those things I said? On the beach? Didn't mean any of it, not a syllable. I found out about the wedding movie, I was furious. You know how I get. I wanted to, I don't know, get back at you. I behaved badly."

"You don't get it, do you? When I think of you I get *nauseous*."

"I'll do the movie, all right? I'll do *Wedding March*."

"I want to take a *shower*. When I think of you, of us, I feel polluted. I feel like those people living next to toxic-waste dumps, only it's like the dump's *inside* of me."

"And *Love Among Elephants*? It's rubbish. Come with me back up to the house and watch me burn it. I'm going to be dead honest with you, all right? I came here tonight to ask you to marry me because that's how the picture ends. The head of production comes from documentaries and is very partial to stories based in fact. It was necessary for us to live happily ever after. For the picture. I told Allyn Meyer we were getting married for the sake of the movie. But now I'm here, I see you again. I'm miserable up there, away from you. I do want to marry you, I always did, movie or no movie. And even though we had a terrific meeting today, even though Allyn Meyer is very very very hot on *Love Among Elephants*, I will burn it. I will call her tomorrow and tell her everything's off. That's how much I love you."

"Call her now."

"Pardon?"

Mouse strode across the room to the telephone, picked up the receiver, held it out to him. "Call her now."

"It's after six. She's liable to have left already."

"Leave a message."

"This isn't the kind of thing you leave a message about, poppet. There's a certain *protocol*. Anyway, I should speak with Ralph, you know, he's my partner, after all. Can't just pull the rug out from under one's partner."

"You pulled the rug out from under me."

"We pulled it out from under each other. Tit for tat. And you, old girl, are getting the better deal. I'll do *Wedding March*. Call Ivan and tell him it's back on."

"It was never off," she said.

"One of the things I adore about you is your persistence, Mouse. What were you planning on doing in the way of a groom, if I may ask?"

"I'm marrying Ivan," she said. "When you go, please leave the key."

23

THE MORNING AFTER THE NIGHT MOUSE HAD READ *Love Among Elephants*, she had called Tony. She called him again in the afternoon and again the following day. She left three messages on the answering machine. His failure to return any of her calls had given her full license to drive to Venice to see Ivan.

She hopped in the car without phoning, failing to heed one of the city's unwritten laws: *never ever* drop in. She sped down residential side streets, odd routes she'd learned from Mimi that circumvented freeways, stoplights, and signs. Routes known only to natives. Her next-up-from-the-bottom-of-the-line Toyota still seemed the height of luxury, with its plastic new-car smell, its radio with speakers in the backseat, its jet liner-like meters and dials.

Every radio station DJ seemed nostalgic that night for songs popular during the Watergate summer, the summer of Ivan, and for other love songs, too, songs about which a suspicious Shirl used to say, "My love does *what* good? Let's get *what* on? Why don't we do *what* in the road?" Songs that – when you heard *the* song, *your* song, on the car radio on the way to meet *him* – were enough to make you believe in destiny. Never mind that it played six times an hour, twenty-four hours a day.

Mouse stopped at a 7-11 for a pack of cigarettes and a Coke. It was drizzling; the air heavy with the acidic smell of wet smog. Clouds sat low on the city. She drove with the Coke clamped between her thighs. She rolled down the window and yowled at the top of her lungs into the orange night, sailing down the wide streets, rolling through intersections after a careless glance, beating out the bass line on the steering wheel.

Love was a rose, a flame, a drug, a heat wave, an opening door, a key we must turn; you can't buy it, hurry it, keep it; it can be right or wrong, weak or strong, short or long; it don't come easy, it takes a little time, it's a game of give and take; it can break your heart, tear you apart, make you happy, make you weep.

The songs were dumb but potent. They transformed her into something dangerous: a boy-crazy sixteen-year-old with the determination and birth-control savvy – if not the wisdom – of a grown woman. *Tonight's the night!* she sang. Time to settle up, she thought.

Her wedding was off. Tony – just the sound of his name caused aftershocks of fury – Tony was history. She would have a few days or weeks with Ivan, then head back to Nairobi. Perhaps she would move into his overheated subterranean basement apartment. Perhaps, now that *Wedding March* was off, they would find another project to do together. Perhaps they would even return to Africa together.

The dim basement corridor leading to Ivan's apartment was strangely quiet. Mouse, exhilarated from the drive, was unsure how to approach this. To she of the meticulous production schedules, the superannotated date books, this felt reckless, unwise.

No one was in the laundry room, which accounted for the lack of sloshing, banging, whirring. She dragged her fingers along the stucco wall, enjoying the light tearing of her fingertips. She wore lipstick, her good-luck green silk blouse.

As she passed the laundry room, Ivan's door opened a few inches. A woman's tan bony arm reached out from inside the apartment. Dangling from her hand was the immaculate cage of the coddled guinea pig, Dostoyevsky. The hand gently placed Dostoyevsky on the floor just outside the apartment. The door closed.

Mouse would later admit to every charge Shirl and Mimi ever made about her disabled feminine instincts, for she found it more curious that Dostoyevsky was transferred from his normal place of honor atop the refrigerator to the hallway than that a woman with a slim tan arm was inside Ivan's apartment. The woman, she assumed, was a friend, a neighbor, perhaps a fellow member of the Venice Documentary Consortium. She squatted in front of Dostoyevsky, who was more interested in running in his exercise wheel than biting her finger. *Eeekk-eeekk-eeekk*, the wheel squeaked as he trotted in place.

The door opened again. This time it was Ivan, shirtless, the top button of his low riding jeans undone, a cigarette between his lips. "Doss, we can hardly record with you making all this noise—Mouse! What are you doing out there?"

She stood up. Her body pounded inside her skin like a swollen ankle bandaged too tightly. She stared at Ivan's body. She had never seen his scar. She'd never thought to look for it, assuming his alleged kidney donation to the wealthy, desperate Newport Beach couple was like all of Mimi's other exaggerations and white lies. The scar was little more than a seam, slightly puckered, white against his honey skin. It began just under his sternum, swooped down around his side, ending in the small of his back. She saw the whole of it when he turned to pull on a shirt.

It was then she also saw Tooty Brass hastily pulling up the rumpled sheets of Ivan's narrow monk's pallet, wearing one of his old T-shirts. The love song Mouse was humming to herself dropped from her mind like a stone.

When Ivan invited her in, she was too thunderstruck to protest.

"Tooty, you remember Mouse FitzHenry? Mouse, Tooty Brass." Ivan ground out his cigarette on a bent beer can, hoisted his Nagra onto the kitchen table. He flipped back the cover, checked the tape. "We were just about to record some effects. I'm cutting *El Funeral* to broadcast length for PBS and thought while I was at it I would remix the sound. I have always been a little ashamed of it."

"Sure," said Mouse. To Tooty she sent a stiff nod in hello.

Tooty sat on the edge of the bed, a few feet away, clutching her clothes to her lap. Her blond bob clung to her head, smeared mascara had found a home in the lines beneath her dilated eyes. She didn't seem quite so outdoorsy in the dreary mess of Ivan's windowless apartment. Instead, she looked stringy and weathered. Nevertheless, Tooty lifted her chin, tried on the indulgent smile of a good sport. "Ivan, I really should be going."

"Tooty, you must stay. Now I have two of you. This is perfect. Please. I need you both. If you will just watch this tape, you'll see what I mean. Please." He coaxed her back down onto the edge of the monk's pallet. "Mouse, please, sit." He patted the bed next to Tooty.

He snapped on the TV, which sat on an overturned crate, slid in a tape, fast-forwarded to a scene where a Hispanic family of six was crowded around the dinner table.

Tooty and Ivan, Ivan and Tooty. It was impossible. At the same time it made perfect sense. She was rich and bored. He was arty and bad. He stood watching the videotape, his baseball player arms crossed over his chest.

Mouse watched while the family passed a bowl of gray mashed potatoes around, then a tub of margarine. The sheets beneath her were still warm. Tooty stared grimly at the video, her skinny bare legs crossed beneath the wad of clothes on her lap. Mouse couldn't help wondering how long this had been going on. Had she gotten him the gig at the fundraiser or had they met there? Did they have furtive public rendezvous? Did Mr. Mega Bucks suspect?

"Valentino's family, their first meal without him," said Ivan. The mother looked as if she'd had every fluid drained from her body; still, she went through the motions of making sure everyone had enough to eat. Her husband, who taught world history, driver's ed, and coached basketball at the local high school, complained about budget rollbacks. The youngest son wondered, what was going happen to Valentino's car. "The sound is too busy, isn't it? It sounds like a banquet, not six people in mourning."

He clicked off the video. "Now what I need you to do …" He cleared stacks of books and papers from his wobbly Formica table, then set it with dishes from the sink, where they were apparently stored in their permanently dirty state. He added a few glasses, crusty with flecks of orange juice, greasy silverware abandoned at the bottom of the dish strainer.

"Excuse me," pleaded Tooty, creeping into the phone booth-sized bathroom to get dressed.

"We must get this done before someone decides to do laundry," said Ivan. " You know how loud it gets in here. This is our window of opportunity." He patted the back of one of the folding chairs. "Come. Sit."

Stupefied, Mouse moved from the bed to the table. "How long?" She nodded toward the bathroom.

"We met at the Oscars. She has a serious interest in my documentaries," said Ivan.

"We're shutting down *Wedding March*," said Mouse. "Tony and I have broken it off."

"Oh?" Ivan adjusted the shotgun mike in its stand, set it on the edge of the table. The mike was six inches long, encased in a gray foam windscreen designed to absorb ambient noise.

Tooty emerged fully dressed, with hair brushed, makeup freshened, her humiliation left in the bathroom along with Ivan's T-shirt. She swung her fluffed-up bob, resorted to her beguiling overbite. She was a trouper. "Ivan, this is *silly*. Can't we do this later?"

"*Wedding March* is off," said Ivan.

"It's off?" said Tooty. Her face said this was a personal affront. "How can it be off? *L.A. Today* is coming to the shower. It's been all arranged. Michael had to call in quite a few favors to get it set up."

"Tooty has been very generous in supporting the project,

both in terms of cash and in-kind donations," said Ivan. "Tooty, sit right here across from Mouse."

"I'm sorry," said Mouse. "It just didn't work out."

"*What* didn't work out? Isn't the thing nearly shot? And what about the distribution deal?" said Tooty. "We've got a major distributor lined up. It's going to play in *theaters*."

"Tony and I. The relationship."

"Who's Tony?"

"Her fiancé," said Ivan, "her ex-fiancé. Now, what I need you to do is pretend you are eating, but slowly, slowly. Take time to chew, do not hurry. Remember what they are eating. Mashed potatoes, peas. Think. How does it sound when a woman in mourning eats her peas?" Then, into the mike, "This is dinner at the Escobars', the night after Valentino's death, take one."

"Ivan," said Tooty, exasperated.

He threw her a murderous glance. "Cut. Tooty, we must get this done before someone does their laundry. Dinner at the Escobars', the night after Valentino's death, take two."

Tooty and Mouse obediently chewed with nothing in their empty mouths, scraped their empty plates with their forks, picked up empty glasses, tipped them up to drink, placed their knives on the rim of the plate, swallowed.

"And cut."

"How much money have we spent on this?" said Tooty.

"Hundred, hundred-ten thousand."

"There's no chance you'll patch it up?" said Tooty.

"Sorry," said Mouse.

"This was going to be Ivan's breakout film."

"Well, I suggest this," said Ivan. "Mouse and I should get married. Dinner at the Escobars', the night after Valentino's death, take three. This time even slower." He picked up his dirty orange juice glass and pretended to drink.

Mouse and Tooty stared. The spools of tape on the Nagra recorded the appalled silence. Ivan cut an imaginary piece of meat.

Marry Ivan. *Marry* Ivan! Yes! It was perfect.

He doesn't love you, shrieked The Pink Fiend, *how can you marry a guy to make a movie? It was one thing when you were making a movie because you were getting married! Benazir Bhutto had an arranged marriage,* Mouse said to The Fiend. *He was married to your sister! You're sitting here with his mistress!* Mouse speared her invisible peas with the tines of her fork.

"You don't mean that," said Tooty. "What about us?"

"It would be good for us. You are never going to leave Michael. I wouldn't want you to. This way, any suspicions he may have about your interest in my work will be put to rest."

Mouse laughed. Six months ago she resisted marriage to a man she then loved. Now it seemed she would marry anyone. It proved that Shirl's worst admonitions about teenage sex, that once you got your feet wet you'd do it with anyone, actually applied to getting engaged. She cut an invisible wedge of butter from an invisible butter dish and laid it on her invisible mashed potatoes. If an arranged marriage was good enough for the Prime Minister of Pakistan, it was good enough for her. *It's not even a feature!* moaned The Pink Fiend.

"I would leave Michael. You know that. All you need to do is say the word."

"No. It's better this way. Mouse and I are friends, Tooty, old old friends. It's nothing like with us."

"I just – I'm sorry – I'm not very modern. I love you."

"Mouse and I are like brother and sister. We grew up together."

Mouse looked from Tooty to Ivan and back. Shirl was right. Mimi was right. Mouse was a love rube of the first order. She snuck some of her invisible peas to the invisible dog begging by the side of her chair. Yuck, peas! "What *did* happen to Valentino's car?" she asked.

"Mouse and I are *friends*, Tooty. Nothing would change between you and me."

"I wish you'd quit saying that, *honey*," said Mouse.

"Will you...live together?" Tooty's voice trembled.

"We can always say the stress of making the film broke us up," said Mouse. "Good publicity."

"After the release date is set," said Ivan.

"Read my mind," said Mouse. "We should go on *The Newly-wed Game*.

A sob escaped from Tooty's throat.

"Think of it like Benazir Bhutto and Mr. Bhutto," said Mouse.

"What are you *talking* about? Ivan, what is she talking about?" Tooty dabbed at her eyes with her fingers.

Ivan got up and went to where Tooty sat across the tiny table. She wrapped her arms around his thighs, buried her face in his groin. Ivan stroked her head. Mouse dropped a dollop of invisible mashed potatoes on her tongue and stuck it out at them. Ivan caught her. He smiled his slouching half-smile and winked. Mimi was wrong. Ivan didn't have the soul of a felon; he had the soul of Lucifer. He was recording all of this.

24

IN APRIL THE CITY SUFFERED A HEAT WAVE SO FIERCE
people thought spray deodorant had finally done in the ozone
layer. It was a hundred and four degrees at noon, at midnight,
eighty-five. The evening news opened with the latest weather
report, bumped from its normal back-of-the-bus position after
sports. Records were broken in both humidity and bad air quality. The favorite excuse of the optimistic, "at least it's a *dry* heat,"
expired on damp lips. Smog sealed sweat into people's pores, then
laid on a coat of grit for good measure. Even at the beach and
high up in the Hollywood Hills it seemed as if the earth had abandoned its orbit, leaving Los Angeles stranded under its own foul,
toast-tinted sky.

Mimi walked through the parking lot of Valley College, the
first chapter of her blockbuster in a manila folder under her
arm. Already the folder was turning to mush where she gripped
it in her sweaty hand. Her blond curls were sticky with melted
setting gel. She passed three boys on bikes peddling lazily
between parked cars, gouging the doors with keys from their
bicycle locks. She thought she should tell them to stop, threaten
to call the cops, but she was too hot and nervous to speak.

The chapter was the product of Mimi's recent great revelation, which, like most great revelations, had been inspired by
nothing and everything. It occurred at work, in the ladies' room,
the day after Mouse dropped the bomb about Ralph and Elaine,
while Mimi was purging her lunch: bacon-bleu cheeseburger,

steak fries, mocha milk shake, wedge of Kahlua cheese cake, bag of Sugar Babies.

It was not just Mouse's news about Elaine's pregnancy that had done it. Nor was it Ralph's using her "sweet cheeks" slip-up at Bibliothèques as an excuse to snub her, saving him from having to tell her they were finished. Nor was it that after Ralph had snubbed her, he hadn't had the guts to call to see why she'd missed three weeks of How to Write a Blockbuster, like a good instructor should. Nor was it that after all this he then had the nerve to phone late one night, skunk drunk at a baseball game, asking would she be up later. Could he just stop by? He missed her, he said, missed the *fun they used to have*. What fun? He complained, she listened, they screwed, roll credits.

It was not just that Alyssia, her fellow drudge, bee-stung lips, twenty years old, Yale grad, was promoted to assistant. Nor that Alyssia now had a real office with a real chair and had to answer the phones only when the secretary was away from her desk. Nor that until the new secretary was hired, Mimi would slave for both Solly and Alyssia's boss, Thaddeus Herman.

It was not that she was thirty-six going on thirty-seven and still had to rely on money from her mother to help pay her bills.

It was not that her little sister was getting married.

It was all of these things coupled with what had happened that very morning. Mimi had kitchen duty that week, which meant sprinting between her desk and the kitchen, making sure the glasses and coffee cups left on the counter all morning long by the agents and assistants were rinsed, dried, put away in their proper places. The president of Talent and Artists had a fetish for a clean kitchen, and more than one drudge had lost her job when too many cups were allowed to pile up in the sink.

All four of Solly's lines were ringing at once. Mimi tore from the kitchen to her desk, wiping her hands on her skirt.

"SollyStein'soffice ... He's out at a meeting, may I leave word?"

"SollyStein'soffice … Mom, hi, it's a madhouse here lemme call you back."

"SollyStein'soffice."

"Bob Hope calling for Solly, please."

"Solly's out at a meeting, may I leave word?"

"Please, He can reach me at home after seven."

"I'll tell him."

She hung up.

She stared at the poster over her desk. Bob Hope! Her salvation! Bob Hope! Her ace in the hole! Bob Hope had called *her office!* She had him right there on the phone, right there on the other end of the line. And she had done nothing.

After she finished disposing of her burger, fries, shake, cheesecake, and Sugar Babies, she brushed her teeth. Bob Hope right there on the line. She had done nothing. She was all show and no go. She spat into the sink, wiped her mouth with a scratchy paper towel. She had done nothing. She was almost thirty-seven years old. If she didn't do something soon, she would be an old lady, bent over some public john in a dress that looked like upholstery, ridding her shriveled self of a box of chocolate-covered cherries or some other old-lady candy. Her hair would be short and brown by then, if not gray. Miniskirts would be ancient history. She would be single, childless. She would have done nothing.

She started her blockbuster that night after work. It was all she could think to do. If she hustled she could get the first chapter done by the last night of class, the same night as Mouse and Tony's shower up at the Big House.

When she got to class Ralph was at the front of the room, deep in conversation with Lex Waldorf, their special guest for the evening. Mimi had forgotten about the long-promised special guest. Lex was a New York literary agent who specialized in blockbusters. He had a full head of graying black hair, a slim waist, a gold watch. He was easily thirty-five, if not thirty. She thought she heard Ralph pitching him *Girls on Gaza.*

Ralph introduced Lex, reeled off the mountainous sums

he was famous for wrangling out of publishers. Lex would entertain questions after the break. He sat on the sidelines in one of
the orange plastic chairs, occasionally taking a call on his portable
phone.

In the meantime, Ralph wondered, did anyone have any
new material? He sat on the edge of a graffiti-scarred table at the
front of the classroom, swinging his legs. The sweat ran down
the sides of his face, darkened the armpits of his Hawaiian shirt,
the band of his baseball cap. He took no special notice of Mimi.
She was grateful. If he had been the teeniest bit decent she
would have lost her nerve. She raised her hand.

"Well, well, well," said Ralph. "We thought you'd flaked
out on us."

"I didn't have time to make copies for the class. So I
thought I'd just read."

Ralph made a point of looking at his watch. "I presume
you don't have too much."

"Enough," she said, handing him his copy.

"We're all ears," sighed Ralph.

"It was a crystal clear blue Los Angeles day when Rolf
Hollandaise got into his gray metallic Mercedes Coupe with CD
player and two cellular phones (in case his passenger, usually
the long-legged blond fiber artist with the big bazooms, also the
most powerful talent agent in the city, Mina FitzHugh, also
needed to call someone powerful and famous) and roared mer-
rily out of the driveway of his twenty-five-thousand-square-feet
multimillion-dollar Beverly Hills estate with twelve bedrooms,
each done in a different Ralph Lauren motif, and a bowling
alley in the basement.

"Rolf was neither tall nor short, fat nor thin, blond nor brunette, handsome nor ugly, but every woman who ever met him
harbored a deep and burning lust for him the instant she laid eyes
on him. In fact, Rolf looked not so much like a talented, powerful, and famous film director, but a three-day-old baby. Even so,

he had mesmerizing aquamarine eyes that drove women with big tits mad.

"Rolf was headed that bright crisp sunny day to meet Mina for a Talk. She was the one who had asked for it, begged for it, moaned for it. The last time they made burning and fantastic love while Mina, with her smooth long legs and blond shiny hair, was handcuffed to her six-thousand-dollar antique brass bed made up with Laura Ashley no-iron two-hundred-thread-count sheets of beautiful hundred-percent cotton, and wearing an *ET* mask, she had rasped hoarsely, 'Rolf, please, we need to talk.'

"Rolf Hollandaise did not like to talk. Talking, about anything, reminded him of his dark and dirty secret, of which he was so ashamed. It reminded of his poverty, his musty one-room apartment filled with nothing but—just to think of it made his smooth yet manly complexion blush crimson red–books. Yes, books. For before Rolf skyrocketed to fame and fortune he had been the lowest of the low, an adjunct professor of English. Rolf would rather have a barium enema than a Talk. He would rather flash his mesmerizing aquamarine eyes. He would rather have a passionate and wild affair with a firm-flanked thirty-two-D-cup blond or make a sensational and magnificent box office smash. Talk was what had queered it with his wife, Ellen Hollandaise.

"When he had met Ellen she was a blond with knockers the size of cantaloupes and mute from having witnessed a burglar, who had broken into her eleven-thousand-square-feet multi-million-dollar Holmby Hills estate, accidentally drop her mother's dazzling diamond and ruby collection down the sewer gate just outside the driveway while making his escape. In other words, Ellen had been perfect. Then she let her sensational flowing blond hair return to its bleechy natural brunette, stopped her weekly silicone injections, and, through the help of five-days-a-week one-hundred-fifty-dollar-an-hour therapy, learned to speak. Now she was one of the most famous talk-show radio hosts in the city.

"Mina FitzHugh's office was in the penthouse of the most

beautiful skyscraper on Sunset Boulevard. It overlooked all of Los Angeles, all the way to the peaceful blue Pacific Ocean. Her office was decorated in peach, with black leather furnishings from Conran's, four Andy Warhols on the wall. She made her multimillion-dollar deals from a huge and magnificent leather chair behind a thirteen-thousand-dollar oak desk. Mina was not only a talented talent agent and fiber artist, she also had a monster trust fund. She would never have to work another day in her life if she didn't want to.

"'Mr. Hollandaise is here,' said Solly Seinberg humbly. Solly Seinberg was Mina's secretary and occasional love slave. He was five foot six, weighed two hundred fourteen pounds, and had brown hair and brown eyes. He sat outside her office on a tiny steno chair that did nothing to support his wide toaster butt. He was miserable from the moment he walked in at nine-thirty every morning until he left at seven o'clock every night, and would have it no other way. For Solly Seinberg adored Mina and would gladly suffer anything just to be near her and her perky bazoombas.

"'Send him in,' commanded Mina, eager with lively anticipation.

"Rolf strode in, wearing his seventeen-hundred-dollar lizard skin cowboy boots and tight Calvin Klein jeans that made it look like he packed a bucket of golf balls between his legs. She looked up at him and was lost in his mesmerizing aquamarine eyes. Could she do it? Yes, she could. Even though she was a luscious blond with a cute turned-up nose, cornflower-blue eyes, and a sensational body (39-23-35), she was made of steel. Rolf could not get away with this. Even if he was the most talented, the most powerful, the most famous director in Hollywood. Even if his latest movie, *Speculum!*, was making them both millions. For yes, Mina FitzHugh was also Rolf's agent. She could make him or break him with a sweep of her elegantly manicured hand.

"I ran into your wife,' purred Mina gruffly. 'At the Beverly Center.'

"'Grrrrr,' grumbled Rolf sexily. He came around behind Mina's chair and laid a suntanned hand upon her Evan Picone silk shirt-covered boob. 'Let's not talk about her.'

"'She's pregnant,' Mina barked angrily. 'You said you weren't sleeping together.'

"'Honey, oh baby,' added Rolf, fumbling lustily with her top button. They had had many juicy adventures right here in Mina's palatial office on the genuine Tibetan wool carpet hand-woven of high-quality five-ply yarn, and Rolf was looking forward to one today. Maybe Solly with the big doughy tush would join them.

"'Rolf,' she yelled crossly but not unsexily.

"'Yes?' Solly Seinberg poked his head in.

"'Not you. Hold my calls. Call Dustin Hoffman and cancel my lunch.'

"'Of course,' mumbled Solly humbly, slinking away.

"'Weren't you seeing Hoffman about *Girls on Gaza?*' Rolf inquired seriously. He sat down across from her. No mind-boggling and luscious sex until this talk was over, Rolf realized glumly. *Girls on Gaza* was his most precious and magnificent project, a musical about a troupe of Las Vegas dancers stuck in the Green Zone. But even though he was the most powerful, the most famous, the richest director in Hollywood, no one would touch it. It was a stinkerooni.

"'I'm not seeing anyone on your behalf until you tell me what is going on. She was buying out *Baby Guess?* when I saw her. She had just spent over a thousand dollars on crocheted hats. You said you weren't sleeping with her. You said you were getting a divorce.'

"Rolf paled handsomely. He'd thought Ellen was pregnant. He'd caught her throwing up four times last week, once in the ninety-five-dollar-an-ounce Beluga caviar at a brunch they'd given for the Reagans. Also, on their seven-thousand-dollar Arts and Crafts-style sofa, which you used to be able to pick up at any Pasadena antique shop for a song until Barbra Streisand started collecting it. 'I am getting a divorce,' he lied easily. 'We just haven't firmed up the details yet.'

"'Ellen said you were thrilled about the baby.'

"'Ellen is a lying bitch,' he breathed furiously, 'and … and a brunette.'

"How can you say that about the mother of your child? You are true sleazoid. I'm calling every executive, every producer, every director, every story editor, every secretary in this town and telling them that *Girls on Gaza* is the most overreaching, the most hopeless, the most pedantic and silly piece of crap ever written, and that you are a worthless, overrated hack. That if I were them I wouldn't let you direct traffic, much less a forty-five-million-dollar musical set in Beirut. And I'll get Solly on it too. You think just because he's an assistant he doesn't have any power, but he'll spread the word, too. He talks to more people than I do. He'll let everyone know the truth about you. That you're a beast to work with. That you go over budget. That you're a closet smart person. You'll never work in this town again ….'

The room was bursting with horrified silence. What *is* this? they wondered. Had this girl gone mad? Had she really been having an affair with Mr. Holladay? Was his wife really pregnant?

She has. She has. She is.

Mimi didn't care if Ralph never spoke to her again. She'd given up trying to be modern and liberal, at least with men. She agreed with Rolf Hollandaise: talk *was* a waste.

She had never had a better time in school, except the student-faculty softball game in sixth grade, where she struck out Mrs. Sword, who'd written on Mimi's report card under Comments that she would not be surprised if Mimi was knocked up before she got to high school.

She stared up at Ralph innocently. The table squeaked as he swung his legs. He gripped the edge beside his knees, the color gone from his knuckles.

Lex Waldorf stopped taking phone calls.

There was the usual minute of self-conscious silence,

while people battled with themselves over whether they should be the first to speak. Ralph, who usually ended up demanding, "Well, people?" to get the discussion started, said nothing.

"I would like to know, *how* is Solly Seinberg her love slave. You don't really go into that," said Poor Peg. "The *ET* mask was really a nice touch, though."

"And how you say he looks like a baby, then you say he has a manly complexion," said someone else. "Which is he, baby or man?"

"Good question," said Mimi.

"What's this fiber artist business?" asked one long-faced guy with two missing fingers and an East Coast accent. "It's a rather abstruse notion. And we never see any of her work."

"If you can use abstruse in a sentence I don't know what you're doing trying to write blockbusters," said Mimi. She heard a rich, unfamiliar laugh from the other side of the room. Lex Waldorf. Glancing nervously in his direction, she was stunned to see him give her the thumbs-up sign.

Ralph swung his legs. Up and down they went, like some demented person on a swing. His baby eyes were flat with rage. His lips bloodless and gray, like two dead fingers.

Mimi saw that the class was not about to let on. They were going to behave like a group of Vacation Bible Schoolers on an outing at the beach, ignoring the couple having intercourse on the towel next to them. They were going to pretend this was just your everyday blockbuster.

They weren't going to giggle, they weren't going to say "Yo, Rolf, I mean Ralph, hubba hubba, what a guy." And Ralph, a prick, but no dummy, figured this out.

"The writing is serviceable," he said, "but I question the execution."

I'll execute you, Mimi thought.

"I also have trouble with the section where Rolf promises Mina he would no longer sleep with his wife," he said, patting the top of the clean white pages of manuscript. "No man would actually say that. Mina might have read that into something he said, but she has no right to be angry with him for having a child with his own wife."

"He said it," Mimi said. "Mina is a literalist with a photographic memory, like my sister, who I patterned her after."

"Whom you patterned her after. Anyway, in the future, when you write about male characters, try to put yourself in a man's place. Think. If you were married to an intelligent, stable woman, and were having sex on the side with some amusing twit, would you make that kind of rash statement?"

"Mina is not an amusing twit," Mimi cried. "She's a fiber artist and talent agent."

"Just answer my question. Isn't it preposterous for a man to promise some twit he won't sleep with his own wife?"

She folded her arms, stared at the spot on the floor under his swinging tennis-shoed feet. She'd forgotten he'd also gone to law school, the sadist.

"I'd do it, make a promise like that," said a softspoken, fortyish minor actress who always seemed to get stuck playing the beautiful woman hacked up in the first ten minutes of classy slasher films. "You know, heat of passion."

"Thank you very much," said Mimi. "There was passion. At least at first." She glared at Ralph. "Plus, who's to say that Rolf isn't a big jerk? Who's to say I'm not going to have him hit by a train in the next chapter?"

"I know how that is," said the actress.

"A woman might make that kind of *faux pas*," said the Yank with eight fingers, "but I'm with Ralph. I don't think a man, even a stupid one, ever would."

"So besides having constructed a completely unbelievable scenario, you don't really know the simplest things about your characters, Mimi, do you? Any other comments?" Ralph flashed a wide, condescending smile.

"Mr. Holladay? I'm a little confused. Where does he tell Mina he wouldn't sleep with his wife? I mean, I see where Mina says that's what *he* told *her*, but where does he actually say it? Don't we need to see that?" asked a thin girl in black, who looked too young to know about any of this sleaziness first hand.

"It's here, on page – " Ralph flipped through the pages.

"He never says that," said Mimi. "In my book he never says it. Only in real life. That time we got food poisoning from the scallops at that place in Hermosa, Ralph."

A few gratifying giggles erupted behind her.

He skimmed each paragraph, pretending he was looking for what he knew wasn't there, for what he realized were his own lying words. His face turned the purple-red of what is known in blockbuster talk as his throbbing member. "I must have been thinking of something else," he muttered.

"Where'd you say it was?" asked someone else.

"Scratch everything I just said," Ralph stammered. "I was thinking of another story."

"Same story, final chapter," Mimi said, scooping up her file folder. She slung her purse over her shoulder and strode out.

She heard Ralph hurriedly announce a break, after which they would return to discuss the all-important use of the adverb, then anxious footsteps echoing behind her in the empty hall.

He was coming after her. Ralph, full of explanations. He had sounded so desperate the night he'd called from the baseball game. He probably genuinely did miss the fun they used to have.

"Mimi," he called.

She turned, in what she hoped was a dignified manner. Dignity was something she needed to do more of. "Yes?"

"Elaine wasn't really buying a thousand dollars' worth of hats, was she?"

Over Ralph's shoulder she saw the class clustered just outside the door, bombarding a patient Lex Waldorf with questions. She should be there! Didn't he stop taking his phone calls while she read her chapter? Didn't he laugh? She couldn't very well go back now. It was the chance you took when you went for the grand exit.

"No," she said. "You aren't a rich and famous director, either."

She kept walking.

25

SKILLET, SKILLET, SKILLET, SKILLET, SKILLET, SKILLET, skillet, skillet, skillet, skillet, skillet, skillet. You see how it is when a word is repeated over and over again? It becomes no more meaningful than the sounds made by an infant struggling for speech. It begins to sound silly. Imagine the word was "marriage."

Mouse had said this word to herself so much, repeated it aloud so often during interviews conducted by her brand-new fiancé, heard herself repeat it over and over again while syncing up the rushes of these interviews, that she didn't know what it was anymore.

Now the wedding, she knew what that was (candles from the Vatican, Fijian orchids, a twenty-two-pound wedding dress, a sit-down dinner at the Bel Air Hotel). She knew what *Wedding March* was (the euphoria of pre-production, the grind of production, the tedium of post, the amazement and satisfaction that the final product makes any sense at all; distribution, exhibition, awards), but marriage? Marriage, marriage, marriage, marriage, marriage, marriage, marriage? She couldn't remember why she was against it, and she had no idea why now it seemed no more odious than signing up for a summer softball league. As a result, she was looking forward to it.

It was a little less than a month before the wedding. The afternoon of the wedding shower, Mouse dropped over to see Shirl. She found her in the backyard spraying fixative on a plank of découpage lying on the perennially struggling patch of dichondra.

A pad of paper hung from a piece of black yarn around her neck, the better to help her remember things. Herb Alpert and the Tijuana Brass blared from the hi-fi. The waterfall burbled into the newly refurbished Lagoon. Despite the cruel heat, celebration hung in the air.

Mouse had told no one about the change in grooms, except Nita, who, for a moment, paled with the idea of losing her commission. They debated about whether they should send out announcements:

> *Mrs. Shirley FitzHenry*
> *requests the pleasure of your company*
> *at the marriage of her daughter*
> *Frances Anne*
> *to Ivan Jose Esparza*
> *instead of*
> *Anthony Noel Cheatham*

Nothing sounded quite right. Anyway, after doing some quick figuring, Nita didn't think there would be time to get the announcement printed and mailed out before May 11. Instead, she suggested treating the shower as an engagement party. Mouse agreed this would be the easiest way, but felt her mother deserved advance warning.

Shirl pulled down her air filter mask and stood back to admire her handiwork, humming along with the Tijuana Brass. She didn't hear Mouse, who came and stood beside her.

"What's up, Mom?"

"It's you! I thought it was Barb! Don't look, don't look. It's your present." Shirl smacked her palm over Mouse's eyes.

"I didn't see anything."

"You saw it!"

"I didn't."

She did, though. It was photograph of her and Tony, taken during the making of *The New Stanley* in Stanley's village in northwestern Kenya.

She remembered the moment it had been taken. Tony

had just told the crew about the time he left the windscreen for the shotgun mike at a hotel where they'd been staying in Dar es Salaam. The maids had found the six-inch gray-foam tube under the bed. Mystified and titillated, they turned it over to the proprietor. When Tony went back to find it, the proprietor pulled him aside and asked him where he, too, could get such a wonderful American sexual aid.

In the background of the photograph the crew members were doubled over in laughter. A group of villagers off to one side tittered shyly into their hands. Mouse and Tony were in the foreground, throwing a sideways grinning glance at each other, the proud glance of possession that says, you are really the one, aren't you.

"I thought you were Barb, coming back with the wrapping paper," said Shirl. "Go ahead and look. Isn't it nice? I have a bigger thing for you anyway. This is just a little thing. I love this picture. You two have a good time, is what it shows."

"Mom, come inside."

"Inside, why inside? What's wrong?"

"It's cooler inside. We need to talk about something."

"Are you pregnant? You're not pregnant. You should have waited a year, gotten used to married life. Your father and I made a mistake that way. I barely knew how he liked his socks folded and there I was morning sick with your sister."

"Can we go inside?"

"Tell me now!"

"Mom."

"Tell me! You're frightening me!" She stamped her foot. Tears filled her faded spaniel eyes.

"Tony and I aren't getting married."

"Aren't getting married? The wedding's off. Is that what you're saying?"

"No, the wedding's still on."

"Oh God, that beautiful dress! And all those lovely flowers." Shirl sobbed into her paint-stained hands. "Mimi so wanted to be your Maid of Honor. That kind of thing means so much to a girl like her."

"Mom, please, come sit down."

Shirl allowed herself to be led to the patio table, muttering about the invitations and the Limoges, the five-foot wedding cake, the shoes she'd had dyed special. Mouse went to the kitchen and got a glass of water. By the time she brought it back to the patio table the ice cubes had melted.

"The wedding is still on, Mom. Listen to me. The wedding is still on."

"That nice Nita had to pull all those strings just to get the church on the day you wanted."

"Mom, I'm marrying Ivan. Tony and I had a falling out. We had no business thinking about marriage in the first place. And then, you know Ivan and I have always been friends. It just seemed like, why not? There'll still be a wedding. I'll still wear the dress."

"Ivan? Ivan who?"

"Ivan, Mom. You know Ivan."

"Not that confused Mexican boy Mimi was married to?"

"Yes."

Shirl pulled a Kleenex out of the pocket of her pantsuit, dabbed at her nose, considered this for a moment.

"I liked that Tony."

"I did, too. It just didn't work out. L.A. seems to have brought out the worst in him, in us."

"So now you know the worst. That's the perfect time to marry. No surprises. The week before I married your father, come to find out he had a habit of cleaning his fingernails at the table with the salad fork. I still married him, and had you two lovely girls. That Tony's nice and tall. He's got a good jaw. You should think of your children."

"It's complicated, Mom." She didn't think she should drag his offensive screenplay into this. "If it hadn't been for your accident, we never would have gotten engaged in the first place."

"My accident? What in God's name does that have to do with it? I wake up in my hospital bed, next thing I know Mimi's there telling me she's called you in Africa and that you're getting married."

"We didn't get engaged until after we came home."

"No, no. Mimi said you were getting married. She found you in that Zaire place. She thought at first maybe you already got married. The connection wasn't so good."

"We were working on a *film* about marriage, Mom, a *film*. We weren't getting married. We were never getting married."

"Frances Anne FitzHenry, I lay right in that hospital bed and you promised me you'd wear white. You promised me you'd do it in a proper church."

"I–I did. But I thought you were dying. I'd been away all those years. Here you were in the hospital, and after what happened to Dad. I thought you *wanted* me to get married."

"That's the dumbest thing I ever heard," said Shirl. "You're a grown woman. You do whatever you want. Did I ever make a stink about you living in a foreign place? I certainly did not."

"You didn't want me to get married?"

"Of course I wanted you to get married, but that doesn't mean you should get married on account of me. Those are two different things. I want you to get married because that's a mother's job. If the truth be known, I always in my heart of hearts expected more from you than just marriage. Mimi always used to tell me that when she had her period she felt like she was doing something. You were never like that."

Mouse stared at the waterfall tumbling over the red rocks into the shallow end of the lagoon. Her father's pride and joy.

If Fitzy hadn't stopped to pick up the earring in the crosswalk, he'd be alive today. If she and Tony had gone to Mimi's book group instead of straight to the hospital …

"Is that your ring?"

"Oh," said Mouse, holding her hand up for Shirl to admire. Ivan had immediately presented her with a hefty white diamond, a single carat in a platinum setting. She swore she'd seen it before on Tooty Brass's stringy brown finger. Shirl examined it, then Mouse's thick pearly pink fingernails.

"Well, that's lovely. Nice he gives you a ring. Tony never sprung for a ring."

"He wanted to give me one, but I wouldn't take it."

"You still have that fungus under your nails?"

"I'll always have it."

"Oh, well. I like your polish."

They sat for a moment. Shirl sipped her water. She took a pencil from behind her ear and wrote on the pad slung around her neck: *get picture of Mouse and Ivan.* Mouse suddenly envied her mother's genius for adjusting to improbable circumstances. She would outlive all of them.

"Ivan is all for black and white as the colors? He's all for prime rib and baby carrots at the reception dinner?"

"Everything. He's being a prince."

"You gave me a scare, honey. I went to six different shoe places to find the right shade of taupe for my shoes."

THE DAY OF the shower, the Big House was busier than Heathrow over the holidays. The carpet cleaner. The window washer. For some undisclosed reason, the plumber. The house had a merciless western exposure, no air conditioning. After about one o'clock it was ten degrees hotter inside than out. Forget frying an egg on the sidewalk; an egg fresh from the fridge would be hardboiled by the time you cracked it on the edge of the counter.

Nevertheless, the parade of service people marched on. Rental tables and chairs were delivered. A sheet cake arrived. Phone calls from the florist, the caterers, the assistant to Mr. Futake, the corn syrup sculptor, inquiring as to the number of burners on the stove.

Tony felt like the bleeding butler, letting people in, answering the phone. He felt put upon, abused, a forgotten stick of suddenly very important humanity there at the top of the frying city, for at 12:27, between a phone call from a guest needing directions and one from the window washer asking should he bring an extension for his ladder, V. J. Parchman called with good news. Solid good news, unlike the normal spongy Hollywood variety rife with contingencies and suppositions.

Allyn Meyer wanted to buy *Love Among Elephants*.

Allyn Meyer wanted to buy his script! They'd turned in the new draft (really the original first draft with new covers) only the week before. It was the *Romeo and Juliet* in Kenya version, wherein he and Mouse exchanged vows in the Rwandan mountains in the fog, among the gorillas. Tony hadn't expected an answer this quickly.

"Get yourself a lawyer if you don't already have one," said V.J. "She's only offering Writers Guild Minimum, which is hardly enough to qualify as money, but there it is."

"This is bloody fantastic!"

"There's another thing – I suppose you should have your lawyer get with her about this – she wants you to waive your option to do the first rewrite."

"So she really went for the love story. Did she say anything? Did she like it? Obviously, she must have liked it."

"She's getting the idea off the street, is what's happening here."

"Have you rung up Ralph, yet? He'll go berserk."

"I don't think she has any intention of following through with it once I'm gone."

"Once you're – you're not headed back to Nairobi, are you?"

"Nairobi? You gotta be kidding. I'm going over to head Michael Brass's new production company. I'd love to take this project with me. We couldn't offer you anything up front, of course, but there'd be a lot on the back end, including a guarantee that we won't hire any other writers. You'll see it through to the final print."

"I've got to speak with Ralph. We've got to speak with Allyn, What is Writers Guild Minimum anyway?"

V.J. told him. It sounded like a hefty sum until he figured what it would be after he split it with Ralph, then paid taxes and a lawyer to negotiate a contract. Then it sounded like just enough to buy a next-up-from-the-bottom-of-the-line Toyota.

Tony reiterated that he needed to speak with Ralph and rang off. *Allyn Meyer wanted to buy his script.*

Ralph wasn't at the office, nor was he at home. Tony left messages at both places. He tried to call Mimi. She was at lunch. He even tried to call Darryl and Sather at the editing rooms, despite the fact he was furious with them for still allowing Mimi and Lisa to use the house for the wedding shower when the wedding no longer included him. It was positively inhumane. What was he supposed to do? Hang about like a good old sport, wish Mouse and that creep his best? Propose a toast?

"You don't have to be there," Darryl had said before they left that morning. "I'll come home, give you the car, you can take off." Then Sather called and said they had to have a reel on the dubbing stage at seven the next morning, and probably wouldn't be home until after midnight.

"You promised you'd lend me your bloody car!" Tony had shouted.

"What am I supposed to do?"

Now, now that he was a working screenwriter – *Eow! Allyn Meyer wants to buy me bloody script!* – he really had to get out of there. No working Hollywood screenwriter would be caught dead lurking about the shadows of the wedding shower for the woman he was at one time engaged to marry, but who was now marrying someone else. No working screenwriter was obligated to be a good sport.

He stood on the deck in the full rage of the sun, toasting the view with a fresh bottle of gin. "I sold a script!" he called to the smog. "I am a screenwriter!" he sang to the limp forest of prickly pear stretching down the hill beneath the deck. The strong urge to call Mouse with the news was a knife in his heart.

Lisa arrived, a little after six, struggling through the house with a deck chair from her own patio, the backs of her wet legs imprinted with the pattern of the upholstery on her bucket seats. She'd been dropped off by Carole, who was already headed back down the hill to pick up some of Mimi's potted plants.

"Potted plants!" Tony followed her out onto the deck. "What do you need potted bloody plants for? It's a wedding shower, for God's sake, not a meeting of the frigging ladies' auxiliary. I desperately need to borrow your car."

"You guys live like cavemen is why we need the plants."

"We sold our script."

"Who? You and Ralph?"

"We haven't sold it. The money isn't in the bank, but we got the call. I got the call. Anyway, Mouse and Ivan are liable to be here any minute, and I – "

" – the nervous groom," said Lisa, arranging the chair by the railing, stopping to admire the persimmon sun sinking behind sheets of smog in the western sky. "People always say it's the bride. How much are they offering for the script?"

"Don't tell me no one's told you!"

"What, is it on the front page of *Variety* or something?"

"About the blasted wedding!" Tony had already suffered a consolatory phone call from his parents, whom Mouse rang up two seconds after she'd given him the boot. He'd also received a letter from Gabrielle and Wim in Nairobi telling him how terribly sorry they were to hear about the split. He presumed if those people knew, everyone did.

"Is there a way we can pull the speakers out here?" She mopped her forehead with her arm. "Jesus, at least if there was a breeze. What were you saying about the wedding?"

Before Tony could construct a phrase which communicated the gist of the situation without rendering him ripe for pity, there was a knock on the door. At the same time, the answering machine launched into its series of chirps and clicks which announced someone was ringing in. "Good God," he moaned. He had a pounding headache from the gin, from the onslaught of service people, from the prospect of being trapped here while the loathsome Mouse and Ivan were celebrated by all of his and Mouse's friends, from the frustration – good God! He hadn't felt this pent-up since his boarding school days, passing the lingerie catalogue around the dormitory at midnight – of not being able to share his good news.

"Hang in there," said Lisa. She grabbed the phone in the kitchen. "Get the door, would you?"

"No," said Tony, "absolutely not."

After a good fifteen seconds of insistent rapping, the door opened. A foreign-sounding tenor called out: "Anybody is there?"

"This is insufferable," said Tony, striding through the house to the entryway.

At the door was a tall Japanese, almost as tall as Tony, with a swingy Beatle haircut and an underbite. He wore a ruffled evening shirt with a red bow tie, and showed no signs of suffering from the heat. "Mr. Futake," he said, pumping Tony's hand and bowing slightly. "You Tony Cheatham, groom?"

"No, but come in." Past Mr. Futake, in the driveway, Tony saw another Japanese in a tux unloading aluminum pots, tins of corn syrup, ten-pound bags of sugar, and a small brown case from the back of a four-door, charcoal-gray import still bearing its dealer tags. A car. A car that would be parked here in the drive, presumably all night. The assistant, with the girth and lightheartedness of a Sumo wrestler, plowed past Tony, immediately commandeering the kitchen. Lisa had finished on the phone. Tony saw her out on the deck struggling with a speaker the size of an icebox, a loose wire trailing dangerously between her legs.

"Mr. Futake, I'd like to have a word with you, if I may."

"I do groom." He mimed a few sculpting gestures.

"Wonderful. But I'm not, I used to be the groom, but I'm not any longer."

"Sure," said Mr. Futake amiably.

Soon, the close air of the kitchen was heavy with the smell

of melted sugar. It made Tony's teeth hurt just to inhale. Mr. Futake and his assistant peered into the vat of hot corn syrup and argued in Japanese. Tony stood behind them wringing his hands.

"Mr. Futake," he tried again. "I have a bit of a favor to ask. If you'll indulge me. You see, I used to be the groom, but there's been, we've had, anyway, the point I'm trying to make is, my ex-fiancée is marrying someone else. You can imagine how embarrassing that is for me. I've also just sold a screenplay, so it would be doubly embarrassing for me to be ... "

"Sure," said Mr. Futake, his black Beatle hair swinging as he nodded his head. He snapped open the brown case on the counter, took out a red cloth utility belt, tied it around his waist, then extracted a half dozen gleaming silver instruments that would look at home in the hand of a dentist.

" ... in any event, I won't stand on ceremony with you. What I was wondering, could I perhaps borrow your car? Just for a few hours. I'm fully insured and have an excellent driving record."

"Car? Sure."

"Splendid." Tony exhaled with relief.

Mr. Futake took a long, thin, tongue depressor-like stick from the case, dipped it in one of the vats on the stove, pulled out a golden viscous glob of hot corn syrup.

"I'll just wait till you're done there," said Tony, checking his watch. Perhaps he'd drive out to Santa Monica, see if Ralph had turned up ... or no, didn't he have that writing class tonight? Perhaps he'd drive out to Valley College.

With a few turns of the wrist, a few confident swipes of one of the more cruel-looking pieces of pseudo dental equipment, Mr. Futake sculpted a small Porsche, which he presented to Tony with a bow. "Car."

"Car. That's bloody clever of you, isn't it? Now, if I could, presuming it's all right with you, of course, if I could just have the keys to your car. The keys? To your car?"

"Key? Sure."

Mr. Futake sculpted Tony a skeleton key.

"Good Christ," said Tony, "you haven't understand a word I've said, have you?"

Mr. Futake sculpted Tony a small sad hippie hanging from a cross. "Christ," he said.

Tony thanked Mr. Futake and went to his room. What was he going to do? In the city with the most cars on the planet he could not lay his hands on one. Here he was a *screenwriter*, and never had he felt so stuck. He had broken into *Hollywood*, and he was feeling the way people did in life rafts, dying of dehydration while floating in the middle of the ocean

He stumbled over his ridiculous cowboy boots in the dark, shot-put them to the back of his closet, *thunk-thunk*, threw on a pair of threadbare gym shorts, hiking boots, and a T-shirt. He hadn't worn these clothes since Nairobi.

He would just have to walk. The café at the bottom of the hill closed at nine; after that he would read magazines in the store until it closed, then ride the bus around until midnight or so. He would keep trying to ring Ralph. It was pathetic, but there was nothing for it.

He got no farther than the front door. He opened it to find a gaggle of people with video cameras and clipboards, wearing the deeply insincere smiles of television journalists, crowded on the front porch. Coming up behind them were Mouse and Ivan followed by someone else hauling *their* equipment. One of the television journalists, a young woman with a gargantuan mouth framed in purple lipstick, rustled through the papers on her clipboard. "We're from *L.A. Today*. You must be the groom."

He slammed the door in her face. Christ! Was the *news* here? Without thinking, he galloped back through the house to his bedroom. His head boomed. Sweat flooded his eyes. He would just have to wait in his room. It was really not on, a screenwriter of his stature stuck playing the role of the jilted lover. He'd close the door, not make a peep until the party really got swinging, then climb out the window. He sat for a very long time. In his shorts, in the dark, on the edge of his bed, he sat. He heard the front door open, then slam, muffled chattering, yips of delight. Who in God's name was out there? Mouse didn't know that many people. They must all be friends of Mimi's. The broken window, which had caused him to see his breath on a number of recent cold nights, admitted not a wisp of a breeze. He dared not turn on the light for fear someone on the carpeted highway to the bathroom at the end of the hall might see it. A diamond mine could be no hotter or stuffier than this loathsome room in this loathsome house in this loathsome city, he thought. He blotted the sweat from his face with his T-shirt. This was not the life of a famous screenwriter, or even a struggling screen-writer. Even Mimi's doddering mutt had it better than this.

THE FACES OF the guests were red and wet from hiking up or down the hill from wherever they'd managed to park. The night smelled not of the late spring flowers blooming up and down the hillsides but of the inside of a gas station service bay.

Ivan refused to make the announcement. He was too distracted with the filming of *Wedding March*, with the crew of *L.A. Today* taping him filming *Wedding March*. In addition, he was reluctant to make it seem as though he had somehow snapped Mouse out from under Tony's nose. He respected Tony. He did not want to appear to be gloating.

"Are you gloating?" Mouse asked.

"Of course I am. Warner Brothers is very interested in distributing *Wedding March. American Film* wants to do a cover story on us."

"You're kidding."

"When we are finished, the Museum of Modern Art will show *Total Immersion, El Funeral,* and *Wedding March* as a trilogy."

It was decided that Nita would make the announcement. Shirl was too shy with all these young people, and Mouse had suddenly found herself embarrassed. She was sure that even in modern-day Los Angeles, where a husband is no less a status symbol than is a car phone, this would seem perverse. Mouse

FitzHenry marrying not the man whose name appeared on the invitation but her sister's ex-husband, her own ex-true love? Would they be shocked? Would they find her sociopathic? Would they want their presents back?

The presents were piled high on a table on the deck next to the railing. Kitchen/barbecue was the theme Mimi finally decided upon. As a result, among the presents, were several portable barbecues that looked like gift-wrapped space ships.

People asked, "Where's the groom?" Mouse said, "He's around here somewhere," then tried to capture Ivan's attention. But Ivan was too busy with the Nagra, too busy being the serious and original independent documentary filmmaker for the cameras of *L.A. Today*. Even though he was now the groom, he refused to give up control of his tape recorder. The forty-pound Nagra hung from its frayed strap from one shoulder, the headphones sat casually around his thick neck. He could operate the controls without looking.

It would be very simple, he said, even humorous, for Eliot to film him and Mouse making a toast while he, Ivan, recorded the sound of their glasses clinking. The *L.A. Today* people would then videotape Eliot filming Ivan recording Mouse.

After the confusion at the front door (where had Tony disappeared to, anyway?), Ivan had pulled aside the *L.A. Today* producer and briefly explained the situation, that Tony and Mouse's wedding used to be the subject of *Wedding March*, but now it was his and Mouse's wedding. Yvonne, the producer, was thrilled with this new angle, which would give their viewers an insight into Ivan's personal, as well as his professional, life.

Outside, on the deck, Nita tapped the side of her wineglass with her fork. She was wearing a pink pinafore and plastic sandals. The city stretched behind her, the blanket of lights glowed dull yellow in the heat. *Ping-ping-ping*. "Turn down the music. Will someone turn down the – thank you."

Mouse stood to one side, worrying the rim of her glass with her thumbnail.

"On behalf of my friend and client Mouse FitzHenry, I have a little announcement to make –"

" – I'm not pregnant!" Mouse blurted out.

A few people laughed.

" – who was it who said never explain, never apologize? Anyway, whoever it was, in that spirit I'd like to tell you all there's been a change in plans. This shower isn't for Mouse and Tony, it's for Mouse and Ivan. Congratulations, you two." She toasted them, then took a dainty sip.

The silence that followed was less palpable than the response of, say, two doting parents who've just discovered that their *summa cum laude* daughter is going to marry a thrice-divorced shoe salesman.

Down the hill, on the far side of the forest of prickly pear that separated the Big House from its neighbor, a group of kids were playing Marco Polo in their backyard pool.

"Marco?" shouted a young, faraway voice.

"Polo!" hollered one of Mimi's friends from Bibliothèques, his voice amplified by cupped hands.

Everyone laughed. Mouse downed her vodka and soda, took a bold bite of the wedge of warm lime hung on the edge of the glass. No one cared! Someone turned the music back up. The bartender squeezed between conversations, collecting drinks to be refreshed. Discussions continued where they left off: who'd gotten what deal at what studio; what recent undeserving screenplay had sold for what outrageous amount; who had tossed in the towel and moved to what idyllic spot to work in a bookstore or movie theater.

Mr. Futake worked from a card table set up near the presents, charming people with his cars, cats, and Batmen. No one congratulated Mouse, but no one took back a present, either. Mouse felt her worry slide away. Warner Brothers wanted to distribute *Wedding March*! *American Film* was going to do a profile! A trilogy at the Museum of Modern Art!

L.A. Today videotaped Eliot filming Ivan recording her.

Lisa struggled toward them through the crowd, a plate filled with button-sized dabs of food raised above her head.

"Lisa. Thanks for doing this," said Mouse. "You've done a beautiful job."

"So is Tony dating anyone, do you know?" asked Lisa, systematically working her way down a carrot stick with her front teeth.

"Mousie Mouse, I can't believe this! Now we'll really be sisters!" Mimi had sprung up from nowhere. For a moment Mouse wondered if she'd snorted something, so huge was her gummy wide smile, so hysterically messy was her straw-colored hair, so high and loud and cajoling was her voice. In fact, Mimi had just blown in from her last How to Write a Blockbuster.

"I take it things went well?" asked Mouse.

"Oh, God! Lex Waldorf was there. He loved my book. You should have seen Ralph's face. Did I tell you what I did? I gotta tell you. Lex is so hot, he gets people *movie* money for *books*. So, Mousie Mouse, you and Ivan! I can't believe it! Shirl already called me at work and told me after you'd talked to her this afternoon. Why didn't you tell me? Ivan the Terrible, let me give you a congratulationatory, or whatever it is, kiss." Mimi sidled up to Ivan, threw her arm around his shoulder and planted one casually on his lips. "Are we going to be on TV? Ivan's my ex-husband. Lex Waldorf wants to see the book when it's done, that's how excited he was. I think I'm going to give up acting and do writing."

"Ivan's your ex-husband?" asked Yvonne.

"It's like ancient history," said Mimi. "We were kids."

"How do you feel about your sister marrying him?"

"Really great. It's a wonderful thing. Fun, kind of like sharing clothes. You know, she was going out with Ivan first. It's true! We were all eighteen or so. They were in film class together. I don't know *how* he got interested in me. l was the older woman, I guess, mysterious or something. Anyway, now Mouse finally has her man. We will have to sit down and have a *long* talk. It's like how you put a handicap on a golfer, that's what I'll have to do with her. All his bad habits, I'll tell her."

Mimi excused herself, then threaded her way back through the crowd on the deck, through the sliding glass door and into the living room, where the bar was set up. She ordered a mineral water from a Samoan who admired her legs.

Someone put on the Stones. Mimi kicked off her black strappy sandals and danced by herself. One of the bartenders, not the Samoan, snuck out from behind the table and danced with her. The living room was dark and hot, lit only by lights of the deck. The booming bass line echoed the blood in Mimi's veins.

So Mouse was marrying Ivan. The news was unexpected but hardly a surprise, Mimi thought. This was a world where young fathers were run down by two-ton converter gears while crossing the street, where mothers were beaned by ceiling fans while innocently cheating on their diets, where average white girls of the middle class ran away to Africa. A world where the unexpected happened and the expected didn't.

Mouse was lucky she had Mimi to smooth the way, to advise her on handling Ivan. Not that Mimi had had any success. Not that Mimi was even going to have the time, what with dedicating all her time to finishing her blockbuster. She made a mental note to get Lex Waldorf's number from one of the Rolodexes at Talent and Artists. She would call him when the book was finished, then he would seduce the publishing world on her behalf.

She was through with Ralph. She was through with money problems, with eating problems, with married men. She would go back to her yoga class. She would eat more tofu. First, though, one last little purge, an easy one, the half dozen Ding Dongs she'd bought at a convenience store and wolfed down on the way to the shower.

After the song was over, the bartender reluctantly excused himself and returned to pouring margaritas. Auntie Barb, a finger jabbed in one ear, turned the stereo down so low only the hum of the speakers could be heard.

Outside, on the deck, *L.A. Today* prepared to tape a formal interview with Ivan. Yvonne arranged him in Lisa's fancy wooden deck chair, in front of one of Mimi's potted plants. The special wedding-shower photographer had arrived and was roving around blinding people with his flash.

Mouse stood by the railing, chewing her bottom lip raw. She stared down the hill at the boys paddling around the pool, seething. She wondered if their young lives were informed with as much unmitigated bullshit as hers was. She could not shake Mimi's voice from her head: *I don't know how he got interested in me. I was the older woman, I guess, mysterious or something.*

Then there was Ivan, no better than Mimi, really. Mouse listened while he mused about the nature of filmmaking and love. About how he and Mouse had found each other after all these years. About how in this time of cynicism and national apathy the force of true love was not to be underestimated. About how he believed people were made for one another. About how, if he did not believe all these things, he might feel terribly guilty for the breakup of Mouse and Tony's engagement. However, in his opinion, Love was second only to Truth in its power to make one Whole.

Mouse didn't know whether she was going to be sick or just needed to lock herself in the bathroom until the wedding was over.

Tony sat in his room. In his shorts, in the dark, on the edge of his bed, he sat. There were things he hadn't taken into consideration. For one, that climbing out the window was impossible. His bedroom was on the same side as the deck; stretching away twenty feet below it was the steep hill dense with cactus. For another, that in this wretched, stifling heat he would actually need to pee. After ascertaining that relieving himself out his bedroom window was impossible without a chair or the joints of a contortionist, he stood by the door, listening for a moment when the coast might be clear and he might make a run for it.

He made the mistake of opening the door – silently he

opened it! Just a crack he opened it! – to peer out, just as Mimi was walking by.

"Tony? Is that you?" She opened the door, switched on the blasted overhead light. "God, is it stuffy in here."

"Hallo, Mimi. How – how's the party?" He tugged self-consciously at the end of his nose, held his legs together. In view of the state of his bladder, he really didn't have time for a chat. "I'd join you, y'know but … You're not going to believe this. We sold our script, Ralph and I."

"No! Are you serious?"

"Quite."

"Does Ralph know? Ralph doesn't know. I just saw him at class. Oh God, congratulations! Let me " She reached up and wrapped her arms around his neck. "You're so nice and tall. Do you want to hear one of the truths of the world? The short girls always get the tall guys and the tall girls always the short guys. Why do you think that is?"

"Nature's way of producing only so many jockeys and basketball stars, I imagine."

"You are so funny and smart. I mean that as a compliment."

She looked in his Pacific Ocean eyes, ground her bony hips against his. There was nothing between them but his paltry gym shorts, the thin linen of her skirt. He always suspected Mimi was something of a goer. Suddenly he forgot why he even opened his door, much less had to go to the loo.

"Allyn Meyer says it's going to be a thousand screens at Christmas – the movie, I mean."

"You feel nice," said Mimi.

He closed his eyes briefly. When he opened them he saw Mouse rooted in the doorway, arms crossed. Face pale and furrowed with shock and displeasure. "Mouse," he croaked.

"No, honey, it's Mimi," purred Mimi.

"What is going on?"

"Mousie Mouse! We were just talking!" Mimi leaped from Tony's arms, scrunching her hair wildly.

The bloody hell we were, thought Tony, cursing the sudden tightness in his shorts. Biology conspired with truth to make men lousy liars. "I don't see it's any of your business anyway," he said.

"I don't believe this," said Mouse.

"Tony sold his script. We were just talking."

"You were not talking."

"So what if we bloody weren't?" said Tony. "The future Mrs. Ivan Esparza. Mimi was congratulating me."

"You always overreact," said Mimi. "Doesn't she, Tony?"

"Don't I know it."

"You were not just talking. I know what talking is. You were not just talking. You were not just congratulating him. Congratulations is a handshake."

"You take things so seriously, Mousie Mouse. It's sweet. No one in L.A. takes anything seriously."

"Don't say it's sweet. You know you don't think it's sweet."

"I do think it's sweet, Mousie Mouse."

"Don't call me Mousie Mouse, don't say it's sweet. What were you doing in here?"

"It's NBD," said Mimi confidently to Tony. "Nervous Bride Disorder. I never had it this bad, though. When Ivan and I were engaged –"

"Stop it."

" – I'm just saying I know how you feel."

"You do not know how I feel."

"You don't have to yell. She doesn't have to yell."

"I do have to yell! Stop for one second! Will you? Can you? You were in here making the moves on Tony. Just admit it."

"I was just *congratulating* him, all right? Anyway, you dumped him, so I don't see you have any right –"

"The split was mutual," said Tony.

"So you're going to start sleeping with him."

"I don't know. We don't know, do we, Tony? Things happen. I don't know how, but they do."

"You don't know? Try all that wriggling around! Batting those big brown eyes! That soft little voice you put on! It's an insult to men, is what it is, thinking they all just find you naturally irresistible."

"You're just jealous because men don't find you irresistible, because Ivan didn't find you irresistible."

''What Ivan found irresistible was you topless sunbathing in the full view of him and me and the Rosenthals next door. Let's just be honest about that much. If we can." Mouse vanished from the doorway.

Mimi stomped out after her, back down the hallway, following Mouse through the living room and out onto the deck.

"This is not my fault. You're marrying him now, anyway, so why are you making such a big deal out of this?"

"We're trying to work on our film and you're lying there in broad daylight with quarters on your nipples."

"What, was I supposed to tiptoe around and not live my life because you were kissing up to Mom and going to summer school?"

At first people thought this was a joke. Or they didn't think it was a joke, but feared if they acknowledged it was serious they might somehow be found unhip. Instead, they stood around grinning sheepishly over their wineglasses. They hoped it was just some new interactive wedding-shower party game.

Ivan, however, smelling good material, stood up abruptly in the middle of his interview. Yvonne was asking him something about subjectivity versus objectivity in documentary. Eliot took this opportunity to take a break. He put the camera down and went inside to get a piece of cake. The camera sat beside the deck chair. Ivan hoisted it inexpertly to his shoulder, asked Yvonne if one of her men could roll sound. He was not used to shooting, not used to balancing the forty-pound camera on his shoulder. He threaded his way along the railing until he reached the table loaded with presents, where Mouse and Mimi stood hurling insults. Mouse turned to Shirl, who was drawn from the kitchen, where she was chatting with the caterer, by the sound of her daughters' upraised voices, a bee seduced by the piquant odor of a family fight.

"Girls, girls, what's all the fuss?" asked Shirl.

"The instant she heard your car pull out of the driveway she threw on her bathing suit bottoms and ran out to the pool. Ivan and I would be doing storyboards on the patio table and Mimi would come out, 'Oh hi, didn't know you guys were here.'" Mouse glanced over and saw the expressionless black glass eye of the camera trained on her. "Ivan, not now."

"You could have taken your top off! I don't see what you're getting on me for. You're the one getting married. You're the one that's gone to Africa and had all this fun."

"You knew how I felt about him. You asked him to rub suntan lotion on your back while I sat there watching."

"Can I help it if I burn easily? If I need suntan lotion?"

"She always wanted to play strip poker with me and Ivan. Then she'd lose on purpose."

"Of course I lost on purpose. That's the whole point. Mom, would you tell her?"

"You knew how I felt," said Mouse. "Ivan, stop. Now."

Mouse tried to put her hand over the lens, but Ivan danced away, back toward the railing.

"How you felt? Who cares how you felt?" demanded Shirl. "You've always been the one with everything! The brains, the looks, and determination. Your father's daughter with my good luck! You've had all those wonderful experiences abroad. You've made all those movies, had two marriage proposals. I don't know what happened with you and that wonderful Tony, you threw him on the rubbish heap God knows why. If a long time ago Mimi won a boy on account of whatever few charms she has, just let her have that, would you? Maybe you should just go on back to Ethiopia or wherever the hell you were. You wound up with the boy of your dreams, now be a little charitable to those less fortunate than you. Don't you listen to her, honey." Shirl put her arm around Mimi's shoulders.

"I'm a big nothing, rub it in!" Mimi sobbed into her hands.

"Ivan, as co-producer, I'm telling you. *Turn off the camera*," said Mouse.

Ivan leaned out over the railing, angling to get the full view of Mimi's teary face. "I didn't say you were a nothing. How could I say you were a nothing? You're my oldest and boldest! You've got all these things happening with Bob Hope and this new agent person Lex-whatever-his –"

"Nothing is happening. Nothing ever happens to me. She gets to go have adventures and I have to stay home and be a stupid secretary."

"No one made you stay home, honey."

"Fitzy always used to take her to the bar. Did he ever ask me? Never."

"You didn't want to go. You were too good for it," said Mouse.

"He made you those special Shirley Temples. In the big milkshake glass. With two cherries. He never made one of those for me. Never, not once."

"He wanted to. You were always on a diet."

"Are you saying, are you saying, I'm …*fat*?" Mimi's eyes widened. Her sobs vanished like a bad case of hiccups cured by shock.

"No. You were always on a diet or something."

"But I'm not *fat*. I'm wide, but I'm not *fat*. I watch my weight. Don't I watch my weight?"

"She does watch her weight," said Shirl.

"If you could call it that," said Mouse.

"What do you mean?" said Shirl. "She's always watching what she eats."

"I hear her in the bathroom. All the time. Throwing up."

Crack! In an instant Mouse's sentence was knocked clean from her mind. A vibrating wall of silver tinsel dropped before her eyes. Her cheek pounded with bruise and blood. She thought there must have been an earthquake. She must have fallen, hitting her cheekbone on the railing. Then she heard Shirl's voice: "Mimi, put that rolling pin down!" Through the tinsel she made out Mimi, by the present table, a long, cylindrical package in her hand, tied at both ends with curly white ribbons like a giant piece of taffy.

And behind Mimi, backing up, backing up, filming it all was Ivan, Ivan behind the expressionless black glass eye. "Yes," he said. "Perfect."

Mouse, her own glass-green eye already swollen shut, reached out to cover the lens with her hand, but he twisted out of her reach.

He stumbled back against the railing, smacking the spot where one of his kidneys should have been. But the kidney was gone. His balance deserted him. Backwards he plunged over the railing, onto the forest of dusty prickly pear, twenty feet below.

26

HAD IVAN NOT WON AN OSCAR, THE STORY MIGHT NEVER have made the news. Instead, all afternoon the next day blond anchorwomen crooned a single sentence between commercials: "Academy Award-winning director dead at thirty-four," knowing everyone who heard this would try to compute the age of Steven Spielberg.

Mouse wondered, not for the first time, how people survived surviving. How they survived witnessing something like this, then went home and flossed their teeth.

Ivan lurched over the railing, his fall only partially broken by the thick ping-pong paddle arms of the prickly pear below. His head stopped, but his spinal cord kept going, crushing his brainstem, killing him before his heels hit the ground. There were no other head injuries, and only one long rip on the side of his face, that looked as though it was inflicted by an ice pick, not the flimsy spine of a cactus.

Every time Mouse closed her eyes she saw him, heard the uneventful-sounding smack of his back against the railing, saw the elaborate red and black pattern on the bottom of one running shoe, the strip of honey-colored skin as his T-shirt came un-tucked before he disappeared from view. She heard the sound he made, a mildly annoyed "hun," the kind people made when they tripped over bedroom slippers in the dark.

That night, Mimi pulled out the futon for her, wrapped some ice cubes in a washcloth for her cheek, pressed a glass of herbal ice tea into her hand. Mouse understood that The Pink Fiend was half right. Mimi did love her, as she loved Mimi, which did not mean they were above going at each other armed with cruel truths and rolling pins.

Mouse went to bed, fully expecting never to wake up. Things she took for granted were suddenly profoundly unreliable. Gravity seemed untrustworthy. At any minute her heart, bored with its lot in life, might suddenly quit beating. Sniffy Voyeur slept with his head on Tony's old pillow, snoring like an asthmatic.

But Mouse did wake up, late in the morning, the Los Angeles sky as dull as a plastic shower curtain encrusted with soap and dirt. She ate a bowl of cereal and put in a load of laundry.

Mimi dusted.

Academy Award-winning director dead at thirty-four. People thought maybe it was the guy who did *Batman*. *L.A. Today* had managed to catch the last few seconds before the uneventful-sounding smack, and the competing networks offered to pay handsomely for it: a thousand dollars a second. The film in Ivan's camera revealed no secrets, but registered the jolt, then, like the point of view of someone traveling backward on a ferris wheel, the flash of the floodlight bolted under the eaves of the roof, the blank Los Angeles night sky, the smear of lights, the downhill neighbors' pool hanging upside down and slightly out-of-focus from the top of the frame. The network was delighted to have it; they said it reflected the banality of death, the chaos of a great filmmaker's last moments. This was what the production assistant told Jana and Raoul Esparza, Ivan's parents, from whom she had to acquire the footage. Mouse cringed when she heard this. It sounded like something she might have once said, like something Ivan might have said. The network paid Jana and Raoul fifty dollars.

Jana and Raoul Esparza had no money for a funeral. They had money saved to send their youngest to a state university, but no money for the burial plot of their oldest, no money for a wake. Mouse wanted to pay for it with some of the wedding money. Jana and Raoul were moved by her gesture, and allowed her to spring for the casket.

They were surprised to hear that Ivan and Mouse were planning on marrying, but found comfort in the realization that their son had found someone who'd made him happy before God recalled him. This was how Jana talked. She was a devout Catholic and consumer affairs advocate.

Jana and Raoul were confused when they learned that Mouse was Mimi's sister. Mouse did not even mention *Wedding March*.

Mouse and Mimi met Jana at Ivan's apartment. They needed to find some appropriate clothes to bury him in. They met on the Venice Beach Boardwalk in front of Ivan's building. The landlord had already let Jana in. She stood waiting for Mouse and Mimi, the ocean breeze blowing her skirt against her still shapely old legs, Ivan's hairbrush clutched to her chest, threads of his dishwater-blond hair snaking through the bristles.

Inside, Dostoyevsky trotted in his exercise wheel. The phone company had already somehow gotten wind of what happened and the phone had been disconnected. Mimi was good about producing boxes and bags for shoes and shirts, about boxing up his reams of papers and books for Mouse, with Jana's permission, to sort through at a later time. Jana, who had never been to her son's apartment, was pleased that he almost had an ocean view. She took Dostoyevsky home to give to her youngest, still in high school.

Academy Award-winning director dead at thirty-four. They led the news with this sentence, then didn't pay it off until after a report on the unveiling of a new men's cologne created by a white collar criminal recently released from the upscale penitentiary where rich people did time. The report on Ivan's death featured clips from *El Funeral* (which the anchor mistakenly identified as images from Ivan's own funeral, which had not yet occurred), a brief comment from a very famous documentary filmmaker whom Ivan had met once briefly at a film festival in Bilbao, who said the world had lost a pure and uncompromising visionary, and the reaction of Mouse, whose "films on Africa have won wide acclaim."

Mouse admitted Ivan was once the best friend she ever had, a person she knew from long ago. Mouse was interviewed by Yvonne, the *L.A. Today* producer, and fonted as *Mouse Fitz-Henry, girlfriend of victim*. Mouse called the station to complain that Ivan was a victim only of his own stubbornness and voyeuristic nature, also that while she was his fiancée she was hardly his girlfriend. Yvonne's response was to ask Mouse if she could interview her in depth for the *L.A. Today* profile of Ivan, which would be aired early to take full advantage of the timeliness of the topic.

After the wake, held at Jana and Raoul's house in Pico Rivera, Shirl invited Mouse and Mimi back to the house on Cantaloupe Avenue. Shirl was anxious to invite Tony back to the house as well, but he made the mistake of bringing a date to the funeral, Lisa. For once Mouse and Mimi agreed with Auntie Barb, who found this in exceedingly poor taste. Lisa, who barely knew Ivan, wept inconsolably onto Tony's shoulder. Mouse and Mimi decided over a package of late-night chocolate-covered Oreo cookies that Tony looked embarrassed, as well he should.

Mouse told Mimi about Ivan and Tooty Brass. She told her about the day she discovered Tooty and Ivan together in his apartment; about how she tried to call Tooty the night of the accident so the poor woman wouldn't have to hear about it on TV; about how Tooty's housekeeper said Mrs. Brass was just outside bidding goodnight to some guests, and could Mrs. Brass call her back?, then never did; about how she didn't come to the funeral, even to stand discreetly behind the other mourners at the graveside; about how Mouse, angered, tossed her stupid one-carat diamond set in platinum into Ivan's grave. She didn't care how many documentaries she could fund with that bloody diamond. For once, Mimi was speechless.

That night Mimi and Mouse slept in their old beds. Mouse stayed on the next night and the next and the next. Since it appeared that Mouse was moving home and that Shirl had recovered, Auntie Barb, who was loath to spend the summer in evil California, left for Boring, Oregon, where she would arrive just in time to watch her rhododendrons bloom.

Mouse sat by the lagoon all day long, doing a jigsaw puzzle with Shirl. It had a thousand pieces which fitted together to depict a cluster of headlines from the *New York Times* announcing world disasters. After she finished this puzzle, she would start another one, preferably a landscape.

In the evening, Mouse wrote notes to everyone invited to the wedding, explaining. She wrote on cheap, plain bond in her own hand. She couldn't think of one good reason to leave the backyard.

Mouse had already received a few wedding presents, and these she returned. She paid Nita her commission. She was not sure what to do about the shower presents. To her knowledge, they were all still on the table on the deck, up at the Big House. When she called up there, hands shaking, willing Tony to answer the phone, she got the machine. Suddenly shy, she asked anyone there to call her back. Darryl did within the hour. He said not to worry, Lisa had taken care of everything.

On the day Mouse and Shirl would have otherwise finished the puzzle, they were drawn away by *Till Death Do Us Part: The Cinematic Genius of Ivan Esparza*, which aired locally on prime time.

There was a woman on the show named Mouse FitzHenry with dark hair, large light eyes, an odd dimpled chin, a bruised chipmunk cheek, talking with great authority about Ivan's approach to documentary, about his commitment to reshaping reality so it would conform to the truth he was dedicated to conveying, about how he died in the heroic attempt to capture and control the uncapturable and the uncontrollable.

"You have always been my smartest," said Shirl, easily impressed by multiclaused sentences.

Mouse was appalled. What was she *talking* about? She found herself hoping that Tony had been right all along, that metaphorically she was a swimsuit model, that in her past life she was an elephant, anything but this earnest person with Answers.

When asked by Yvonne how Ivan had chosen her as a collaborator, Mouse rambled about *The New Stanley*, about the films on tropical diseases, singing bats, and African killer bees, the tiny, little-known tribes whose ancestral homes were at the bottoms of narrow caves, the Berber rock climbers.

"Just little ole me, capturing the uncapturable, controlling the uncontrollable," snorted Mouse.

Shirl told her if she did not stop rolling her eyes they would become permanently stuck up there.

The next morning, while Mouse was eating a bagel and reading the comics, she received a phone call from someone at one of the studios, an assistant to one of the vice presidents, Allyn Meyer, who wanted to meet with her regarding an African project she had recently acquired, a love story set in Kenya.

Mouse demurred, saying she needed to check her schedule.

Actually, she was anxious to finish the jigsaw puzzle. She could not possibly think about leaving until it was complete. She went outside in her big purple robe to where the puzzle lay sprawling on the patio table. Just as she was about to snap the penultimate piece into place there was a healthy, but minor, earthquake; a rumbling shudder that bounced half the puzzle off the table. A few pieces disappeared forever into the pool filter.

Mouse called back Allyn's assistant and said she would love to meet Allyn anytime anywhere.

Tony would also love to meet with Allyn, but that was apparently no longer an option, now that she had purchased *Love Among Elephants*. Her People talked to his and Ralph's People, was how it now worked. Her People were the studio business affairs people; their People was a lawyer Ralph was referred to by his boss, Keddy Webb. No one but the lawyer returned Tony's calls, including V. J. Parchman, who now worked for Michael Brass, wore penny loafers and was called "Vincent." Ralph, who recently discovered he was going to be the father of twins, was more than happy to accept Writers Guild Minimum and waive the option to do the first rewrite. The day they signed the papers they celebrated, sort of, at a seedy bar called Ye Olde Rustic Pub, around the corner from the apartment he and Elaine now shared.

"We're on the map," said Ralph. "We acted smart. You should always take the money and run."

"I just wasn't quite so keen on relinquishing so much control. Who knows who'll come in now and bugger the thing up."

"I got news for you, just the fact you're in this business means you relinquish control. Listen what I just said, '*you're* in this business,' *I'm* in this business. We have sold a screenplay. It's something. This alone separates us from about a half a million other people staggering around this terrible city, their calendars filled with pitch meetings, their heads filled with ideas capable of being explained in four words. Next year, on our income tax, we can put *screenwriter*. I'm hoping to God there's at least one girl in there. They did the ultrasound today. Elaine and I razzed the technician, 'How many penises do you see in there! Don't say two, please, don't say two.' Girls are easier, that's what we hear."

"Like Mouse and Mimi, for example."

"Jesus, I forgot about them."

Ralph had to take off after one drink, some baby-related business. Tony wandered around the quiet streets of Santa Monica, writing down phone numbers of apartments for rent, enjoying the lonely smell of the damp salt air. With his share of the money he would buy some kind of used car and move out of the Big House. He did not think he could take another Lakers game. He knew he could not take the memory of Mouse pounding on the bathroom door, moments after that self-important sod had plummeted headfirst into the cactus patch, her voice frayed with horror, nearly unrecognizable: "Tony, please, Ivan's dead."

Mouse's meeting with Allyn Meyer was postponed twice, then, on a cool bright day in early May, a week before she and Tony, then Ivan, were supposed to be married, it finally took place.

When Mouse returned from the meeting, Shirl was standing on the front porch in a flutter.

"A *boy* called you!" Shirl hollered across the lawn, flapping her hands. "Some foreigner here for the wedding! He needs to be picked up at the airport. I didn't know what to do. I wrote down his flight number. Pan Am number 137 from London. He came all the way from wherever it was. Stanley was his name."

"I think we should call Tony."

"Tony! This poor man's come all the way from Africa, Mousie Mouse. You better hustle your butt down to the airport."

"It's not that." She didn't mind going to the airport. She felt terrible that Stanley had made this long trip for nothing. Gabrielle had obviously never told him the wedding had been called off. She had taken all that trouble to find him, then forgot about him. Mouse imagined Stanley on his skateboard going round and round on the carousel in baggage claim, abandoned like a lost suitcase.

No, it had nothing to do with Stanley.

"Mom, call Tony."

"I'm not your social secretary. You call him when you get back."

"Please, tell him I'm not here. Tell him you just got home. Say you don't know where I am, and you found Stanley's message on the machine. Say you didn't know what to do, and that's why you're calling him."

Shirl pursed her lips to keep from smiling.

THE RELIEF MOUSE felt when a calm woman at the Pan Am ticket counter told her Stanley's flight was just clearing customs was doubled when she reached the waiting area and saw the familiar lean back of a tall freckled man with curly strawberry-blond hair.

Tony anxiously peered over the heads of people streaming in from the International Terminal. People covered with the film of travel, wan from no sleep, bad airplane air, and noxious pear cobbler.

"Well, if it isn't Tony Cheatham!" said Mouse. *Calm down,* advised The Pink Fiend. *Hysteria does not become you.* Nervously, Mouse fingered the collar of her green silk blouse. This was absolutely ridiculous.

"What are you doing here? Your mum just rang me up, said she didn't know where you were. I can't believe no one told him the wedding – about the change of plans."

"I'm sorry you had to come all the way out here." She felt her face bloom pink with the lie.

"It's no trouble, no trouble at all." Tony tugged on the end of his nose. "Be good to see Stanley again – say, I saw you on the box the other week. Very smooth."

"Oh, that. The Revenge of the Masked Pedant," said Mouse. It was difficult to look him in the eye. She was sure her scheme, a profoundly silly one that violated every firmly held value and belief she had about such things, a scheme worthy of *How to Get a Teenage Boy and What to Do with Him Once You Get Him*, could be read clearly on her forehead.

"You all right?"

Don't tell him. Do not tell him. Do not let him think that you orchestrated this whole thing just so you could see him, just so you could circumvent that age-old female problem: how to make it look as though fate, and not a crafty woman in love, was behind a chance meeting. "I made Shirl call you," Mouse blurted out. "I was home. I made her call you and tell you I wasn't so that you'd come here. Then we could accidentally run into each other."

"You could have just rung me up, you know." To hide his

smirk he bent his head, taking a sudden interest in a hard beige bud of chewing gum mashed on the linoleum.

"That would've been too obvious," said Mouse.

"Quite. This is much more subtle. Making it look as though our meeting was an accident, then confessing you planned it. But really, you could have just popped by. Were you afraid I'd send you packing?"

"After you saw this, yes." Mouse reached into her laundry basket-sized purse and pulled out a copy of *Love Among Elephants*.

"Where in the bloody hell did you get that?"

"Allyn Meyer. She saw me on TV and we had a meeting. I'm rewriting it."

Tony's show-dog grin dropped from his face. "You're *what?*"

They were interrupted by the hum of an electric wheelchair at the far end of the hall. It was Stanley, looking raffish in a double-breasted black linen sports coat, the tip of a red handkerchief peeking from his pocket. He steered the chair between two bouncy flight attendants. They yattered with the high spirits of the hugely entertained.

"Where on earth did he get that jacket?" said Mouse. "He looks terrific."

"You're rewriting *my* script?"

"What do you think Stanley will make of Rodeo Drive?"

"But you're not ... you're not a ... a frigging screenwriter. This is absolute madness."

"What will Watts look like, to Stanley? Or the Venice Beach Boardwalk?"

"Just tell me one thing – I know this is rather rude – how much are they paying you?"

"Enough."

"Enough? Are you daft? There's no concept of enough in this city. One meeting and you're hired. Have you any idea how many meetings I've suffered through?"

"I've got an entire case of ECN left over from *Wedding March*. After I get paid I'll have enough to process and print it.

There'll be enough to pay us real salaries, Tony. Small ones, but real ones."

"The first thing you'll take out is the swimsuit models on safari, isn't it? Be honest. I can take it."

"Never. That's my favorite part."

Tony and Mouse traded grins. To Mouse, their smiles felt dangerously familiar, like those they'd once carelessly tossed to one another in a dusty African village.

"Perhaps we could call it *The New Stanley Goes Hollywood*. Or no, *The Newer Stanley*," said Tony.

"We could do a whole *Stanley in America* series," said Mouse.

"Here are my friends who got married!" said Stanley. "Tony and Mouse, may I present Janine and Tracy."

"Congratulations," said Janine or Tracy.

"Thank you," said Mouse. She reached over and squeezed Stanley's shoulder. She imagined him, suddenly, propped in a patio chair by the lagoon. The chair she saw had a bright red and pink floral cushion that would complement Stanley's rich umber skin. In the background the gurgle of the lagoon's water-fall would harmonize with the oceanic sound of the wind in the palms overhead, conveniently covering the whir of the camera. At Stanley's elbow, a touch of visual irony in the form of either a bottle of overpriced designer water or a cocktail with a parasol in it. She and Tony would interview him after a trip to Disney-land. There would be the usual battle over who would get stuck rolling sound.

"We should probably wait until he's had some sleep and a meal before we pitch our idea, don't you think?" Tony whispered to Mouse, looping his arm around her shoulder.

"I do," she whispered back.